Robert Edric was born in 1956. [ ]
Garden (1985 James Tait Black P[ ]
(1986 runner-up for the *Guard*[ ]
Eclipse, The Earth Made of G[ ]
Heaven, The Sword Cabinet, [ ]
(shortlisted for the 2001 WH Smith Literary Award) and
Peacetime (longlisted for the Booker Prize 2002). *Cradle
Song* is the first book in the Song Cycle Trilogy, the second
book, *Siren Song*, is now available from Doubleday.

Acclaim for
Cradle Song

'Deeply intelligent novel . . . it is refreshingly anchored to
recognizable realities and is infinitely the more powerful for
that. The vertiginously devious plot twists all close like a
fist around the throat of the reader.

In prose as dry as a bone left to bleach in the tropical sun,
Edric delineates a relentlessly dark world where human
motives and desires are unreadably murky, all truths are
provisional and compromised, and human complicity casts
a long shadow over our best intentions. Robert Edric makes
it impossible for the crime novel to be considered the
country cousin of serious literature any longer.'
The Times

'Skilfully written . . . both disturbing and sensitive'
Sunday Telegraph

'Edric shows he has the potential to be a formidable crime
writer' *Sunday Times*

'Edric creates an intricate plot in which every theory is
cleverly chewed over' *Mail on Sunday*

'Edric brings a brand of Spartan prose to the party that
makes the tiniest occurrence momentous' *Arena*

www.booksattransworld.co.uk

'*Cradle Song* is a superbly paced book . . . This is classic crime noir . . . Edric can also produce beautiful prose and arresting images as well as incisive social satire . . . Magnificently achieved'   Giles Foden

'Highly accomplished . . . Fans can look forward to his usual sharp realized characters operating in a tense, pressured environment'   *Independent*

'His novel is something substantial and distinctive . . . Edric has a clear, almost rain-washed style, eminently suitable for his Hull setting . . . *Cradle Song* is a strong and serious novel, soberly entertaining and well worth your while'
Literary Review

'A rewarding experience . . . This is murder at its most foul, crime at the deep end'   *Spectator*

Peacetime

'There aren't many novelists whose new book I would read without question (Banville, Marias, Proulx) but I would read a new novel by the Yorkshireman, Robert Edric, even if its blurb told me that it was about a monk calculating how many angels could dance on a pinhead . . . If other novels deserve this year's Booker Prize more than *Peacetime*, then they must be very remarkable indeed'
John de Falbe, *Spectator*

'*Peacetime* has a seriousness and a psychological edge that nine out of ten novelists would give their eye teeth to possess . . . it will be mystifying if, 50 years hence, Edric isn't taught in schools'   D. J. Taylor, *Sunday Times*

'A marvel of psychological insight and subtly observed relations . . . Why Edric has not yet been shortlisted for the Booker Prize is a mystery'   Ian Thomson, *Guardian*

'Edric is one of those immensely skilled novelists who seems fated to be discovered insultingly late in a productive career when caught in the arbitrary spotlight of Booker nomination or television adaptation. Booksellers take note: this is a writer to put into the hands of people looking for "someone new" ' Patrick Gale, *Independent*

'This is a novel of ambition and skill, at once a historical meditation, an evocation of a disintegrating society and, perhaps most strikingly, a family melodrama . . . *Peacetime* deserves the recognition that Rachel Seiffert's Booker-nominated début received in 2001'
Francis Gilbert, *New Statesman*

'A gripping read, full of meaningful conversations and bleak introspection' *Sunday Herald*

'Edric's evocation of far horizons, tumultuous seas and drifting sands is masterly . . . There are many memorable things in this novel . . . Edric has cleverly created a microcosm to represent a world still haunted by its terrible past and uncertain of its future'
Francis King, *Literary Review*

The Book of the Heathen
'The best historical fiction has something to say about the present as well as the past. Edric has demonstrated this in his previous novels and does so again, with accomplishment, in his latest work . . . Edric, prolific and critically acclaimed since his prize-winning debut in 1985, has struck an especially rich vein of form of late . . . the writing is as clear and intelligent as ever, without being showy, and achieves the vital unities of theme and story, past and present, personal and political. Europe's colonial grip may have relaxed since Victorian times, but Edric offers a characteristically subtle counterpoint to the relationship between men, and between the strong and the weak in today's global economy'
Martyn Bedford, *Good Book Guide*

'Stunning . . . evocatively brings to life the stifling humidity and constant rainfall of the Congo'   John Cooper, *The Times*

'Edric is a prolific and highly talented writer whose books give historical fiction a good name. They are distinguished not only by their formal skill and wide-ranging subject matters, but by their hairless, unshowy prose. In *The Book of the Heathen*, he uses suspense and thriller techniques to telling effect. His linguistic minimalism can also be effective – his low-key description of a hanging is quite the most harrowing I've ever read'
Sukhdev Sandhu, *Guardian*

'Many respectable judges would put Edric in the top ten of British novelists currently at work . . . as a writer, he specializes in the delicate hint and the game not given away . . . the terrritory Edric colonizes is very much his own'
D.J. Taylor, *Spectator*

'Relentless . . . an impressive and disturbing work of art'
Robert Nye, *Literary Review*

'More disturbing even than Conrad in his depiction of the heart of darkness . . . out of the pervading miasma of futility – conjured up with Edric's usual atmospheric masterfulness – loom cameos of savagery and heartlessness. Their subjects sometimes recall George Orwell's writings. So does the terse, trenchant unforgettableness with which they are conveyed . . . rendered in prose whose steadiness and transparency throw the dark turbulence of what is happening into damning relief. Admirers of Conrad will soon spot affinities between this book and *Heart of Darkness* . . . but where Conrad leaves "the horror" at the centre of his story unspecific, Edric gives his a hideously charred and screaming actuality that sears it into the memory. It will be surprising if this year sees a more disturbing or haunting novel'   Peter Kemp, *Sunday Times*

Also by Robert Edric

CRADLE SONG

Robert Edric

BLACK SWAN

CRADLE SONG
A BLACK SWAN BOOK : 0 552 77142 2

Originally published in Great Britain by Doubleday,
a division of Transworld Publishers

PRINTING HISTORY
Doubleday edition published 2003
Black Swan edition published 2004

1 3 5 7 9 10 8 6 4 2

Copyright © Robert Edric 2003

Set in 11/12pt Melior by
Falcon Oast Graphic Art Ltd.

Black Swan Books are published by Transworld Publishers,
61–63 Uxbridge Road, London W5 5SA,
a division of The Random House Group Ltd,
in Australia by Random House Australia (Pty) Ltd,
20 Alfred Street, Milsons Point, Sydney, NSW 2061, Australia,
in New Zealand by Random House New Zealand Ltd,
18 Poland Road, Glenfield, Auckland 10, New Zealand
and in South Africa by Random House (Pty) Ltd,
Endulini, 5a Jubilee Road, Parktown 2193, South Africa.

Printed and bound in Great Britain by
Cox & Wyman Ltd, Reading, Berkshire

Papers used by Transworld Publishers are natural, recyclable
products made from wood grown in sustainable forests. The
manufacturing processes conform to the environmental
regulations of the country of origin

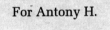
For Antony H.

1

Two years ago, in the empty warehouse directly beneath my office, three teenage girls robbed and then killed a 63-year-old man. They beat him unconscious with lengths of timber, and then continued kicking him as he lay on the ground. The girls had lured him into the building with the promise of sex; it was what the man had come looking for and what he had found. The girls told him they worked together or not at all, and he quickly agreed to the price they asked him. He was attending a business seminar at the Holiday Inn on the marina, and had come across the dock to Humber Street because one of the barmen there had told him where to start looking for what he wanted.

The man's body was found at four the following morning by one of the fruit wholesalers opening up his store.

The oldest of the girls was fifteen; another fourteen years and two months; the third only just thirteen.

The fifteen-year-old was already working as a prostitute and was known to the police. The two younger girls, while admitting to offering sex to the man, swore that it had only ever been their intention to rob him, and from the start their stories conflicted, creating the fissures into which their individual lawyers worked themselves. The older girl said she had not undressed in front of the man and that he himself had not even taken off his jacket. The youngest said she had exposed herself to him and that she had allowed him to fondle her. It was the role of the two others, she insisted tearfully, to encourage the man with lascivious comments and promises of their own. The older girl continued to insist that nothing sexual had taken place and that the attack had started as soon as the man was alone with them in the warehouse.

All this happened in the summer, before nine in the evening, and the high, empty room was dry and warm and filled with dusty light. The whole building was being slowly and intermittently renovated. It had once been a warehouse and a ship-chandler's, and a narrow lane opposite its entrance had run directly to the wharfs and waiting vessels, also long gone, on the river.

The names of the three girls were not revealed until after their conviction, but Hull was a small city and everyone knew who they were.

A picture of the murdered man was shown on the front page of the *Hull Mail*. It was an old, poor photo, and in it he looked much younger than sixty-three and was grinning broadly, wearing a dark suit and a tie pulled tight into his collar. An appeal was made for the members of his family to contact the Hull Police. Most of the other delegates at the Holiday Inn professed to know him, or something of him, and most referred to him as their 'colleague' or 'business associate', thereby conveniently distancing themselves from him. Respected, well-liked, good at what he did. Complete disbelief at what was already being suggested concerning the circumstances surrounding his death.

I forget his name, and remember only that he had no living family – parents dead, one ex-wife, also dead, no children, no brothers or sisters. Not even any of those distant cousins who might have known him when they were all children together, but whose affection, familiarity and contact had long since evaporated. He was a man completely alone in the world. The three girls could not have chosen a better target, and except for the uncontrollable rage which infected all three of them on that summer's night two years ago, they might afterwards have disappeared just as easily and as completely as they had appeared to him, and as his own salacious imagining had begun.

The *Mail* called them savages. The oldest girl boasted afterwards that she had been working as a prostitute since she was thirteen and that her services were in great demand. The police and the CPS pushed her to reveal the names and addresses of her clients, but she refused to do this, as though – like any child with a secret – she believed that in this precious confidentiality might somewhere lie her distant salvation.

The defence of the two younger girls was more straightforward. Though denying it, their lawyers worked secretly in tandem. Their argument was simple: their own clients were the gullible and impressionable friends of the older girl and they had accompanied her on the night of the murder only because she had implored them to, and because she had promised them a share of the night's proceeds. Neither of the two girls, the lawyers insisted, had any notion of what was about to happen. The prosecuting lawyer expressed his scepticism at this and was supported by the judge in his summing-up.

The 63-year-old man was left for dead, and died between four and six hours after the attack took place. Cause of Death was considered to have been a blow by a brick to his skull. The pathologist considered it likely that he was already unconscious when this occurred, and that the brick was more likely to have been dropped on him where he lay than for him to have been struck by it during his struggles. At their trial, both younger girls insisted that this final act had been performed by the fifteen-year-old.

Humber Street was sealed off for a day while the body was examined and removed, but this seemed not to concern the wholesalers and market men, who drew up on Queen Street and then moved everything to and from their stores by trolley.

I had arrived there less than a year earlier, three months after John Maxwell's retirement and my decision to continue working alone. Our old office off the West Dock Road was scheduled for demolition six days after our departure. It was what had helped John Maxwell to make up his mind. We went together to watch the building come down. It crumpled beneath the swinging lead weight as though it were made of cloth, and 120 years of existence was flattened in less than an hour. John Maxwell said, 'Good riddance,' as we finally turned away from it and brushed the dust from our shoulders.

The fifteen-year-old girl was sentenced for an in-definite period to a Young Offenders institution in Bedfordshire, where, as part of her Court Order, she was to undergo a lengthy process of psychological assessment.

The two younger girls were separated and sent to institutions in Northumbria and Hampshire. The judge was less convinced of their guilt, though by this he meant only the true extent of their intent on the night of the killing. None of the three girls had a father who still lived with them. The mother of the oldest girl had worked as a prostitute herself, and though it could never be revealed in court, this information as much as her daughter's own confession determined that the girl would be treated differently from the others, and that the crime and the outrage it provoked would have its proper focus.

I remembered all of this now for two reasons. Firstly because of the man I was about to meet and his reason for wanting to see me. And secondly because several weeks after the murder in the warehouse, I saw that a small Cellophane-wrapped bouquet of red and yellow stems had been laid close to where the man had been killed. Little remained of the rubble-strewn floor and exposed brickwork of the room in which he had died – the floor was now sheeted and the walls plaster-boarded – but sufficient of the room's stark and unwelcoming character remained to suggest to anyone with even the vaguest recollection of what had happened there, that here was a room which would for ever bear some faint but undeniable echo of that night's events.

It intrigued me to see the flowers, knowing that the murdered man's relatives had been sought but never found. My curiosity was satisfied several weeks later, and long before the girls' trial began, upon the appearance of a fresh bouquet – yellow and blue this time, but equally small and unimpressive in anything other than its mawkish intent.

Passing the warehouse door shortly after the appearance of the second bouquet, I saw a woman sitting in the open window space, looking out and smoking. I knocked on the frame and went in to her. She reacted nervously to my sudden appearance and told me immediately that she wasn't trespassing and that she was about to leave. She glanced several times at the flowers as she spoke.

'I know about the flowers,' I told her. 'I rent an office upstairs.'

She looked up at the ceiling, from which electrical cables hung into the room like coiled nooses.

'Did you know him?' I asked her.

She shook her head. She wore a short coat and her legs were bare.

'I just wanted to come and see, that's all. I thought that it might make some sense, coming here, seeing where it all happened.'

'It was your daughter,' I said, finally realizing what she was telling me.

'She's everything they say she is,' she said. 'I hardly saw her from one week to the next. I've got three others. Even the Education Welfare Officers stopped coming when she turned fourteen. Lost cause, see?' She looked directly at me for the first time. 'Her and me alike.'

'Has she told *you* what happened?'

'Everything. They've told me they can't use any of it in court. It'll be mostly lies, anyway. She's a good-looking girl, old for her years – all that kind of stuff goes hand in hand with lying.'

I didn't fully understand her, and so I said nothing.

'I doubt if anyone will bother to look too closely at *him* and his dirty part in it all,' she said. She motioned to the flowers.

'Why do you bring them?'

She considered this for a moment. 'It's as much for her sake as for his. Don't worry, I won't be coming again. What was he playing at? The youngest was just a kid. What do you think he had in mind for *her*?'

I shook my head.

Above us, a phone rang, and though it was not my own, I told her I had to go.

'Don't believe everything you hear,' she said unexpectedly, as though suddenly anxious that I might leave her having formed a bad impression of her daughter based only on what she'd just told me.

'No,' I said.

She turned back to the empty window frame and folded her arms across her chest.

It was not simply cold and comfortless grief in which she wrapped herself and mourned the loss of her fifteen-year-old daughter, but the eternal and inevitable regret felt by all parents when they discover that the last of the ties by which they imagined they would be bound to their children for ever have finally been severed. And, in truth, looking at the woman then, wondering what more, if anything, I might have said to her in parting, I imagine those bonds had frayed beyond repair long before the summer's night when that final act of severance had been so brutally and irrevocably performed.

2

All I knew of James Bishop was that five years ago his own teenage daughter had either left home or been abducted and that, following a two-month search for her, a man was arrested in connection with the disappearance of her and several other girls. A single body was subsequently found, but not that of James Bishop's daughter. At his trial, however, the man who had confessed to having had some part in the murder of the dead girl admitted that he had abducted and killed Bishop's daughter, too, along with several others, but that their bodies would never be found. As far as I remember, in the absence of any evidence other than his uncorroborated confession, the man was never charged with these other murders and the cases were left open. James Bishop's daughter's body was never found.

I had never met James Bishop before, and nor did I remember his face from the press or police appeals. If I tried hard, then perhaps the schoolgirl face of his daughter might come back to me, but it would be the innocent smiling face of every schoolgirl over which the shadow of an early, violent or mysterious death already hung. Similarly, I could not remember the name of the man who had confessed to the other murders, or how and why the murder and disposal of James Bishop's daughter was implicated in these related crimes. The name of the girl whose corpse had been recovered was also beyond my recall.

James Bishop had called me two days earlier, late at night. He said he wanted to see me urgently and then complained that he was unable to arrange anything for at least forty-eight hours. He was out of the country on business, he said, and was flying back late on Tuesday evening. He told me he would come straight to me from the airport. I told him to wait until the following morning and detected his fleeting irritation at having lost even that small measure of control over our meeting. We fixed a time, and before I hung up he asked me if I knew who he was. I told him I did, and no more. I told him I was sorry for what had happened to him and his family, but that I would prefer to talk to him face to face.

'I thank you for your courtesy,' he said. 'And your discretion.'

I had been neither courteous nor discreet, but before I could say anything more, he added, 'What I meant was, do you know who I am *now*?'

I told him I didn't understand.

'I'm sure this must sound unnecessary to you, Mr Rivers, and perhaps even insensitive, but I hope you will believe me when I say it has nothing to do with why I wish to see you.'

I asked him if he was talking about the business abroad to which he had just referred, surprised at the speed with which we had come from his murdered daughter to his work, and wondering if this switching of tracks had been deliberate, or simply something he was unable to prevent himself from doing, a light shining forward instead of back. He had already used my name twice, as though he needed this confirmation of who I was and why he was coming to see me.

'I only know what I remember from the television news and the papers,' I said.

The remark disappointed him. There was a long pause, and I imagined him rubbing his face. 'It's late,' he said.

I confirmed the time of our appointment and told him how to find me.

On Wednesday morning, I arrived at the office early. I had been too busy in the intervening time to find out much more about James Bishop's missing daughter. It was obvious to me that she had been killed soon after her abduction; and whatever Bishop wanted from me now, I hoped he understood this, too.

He came to my door and waited outside without knocking. I saw his outline through the opaque glass. As I waited for him to enter, a second, smaller figure arrived to stand beside him, a woman. My first thought was that his wife had accompanied him.

It was a bright, clear mid-November morning, and the sun shone in a block against one of my walls. The dirt of the unwashed window created a pattern of clouds high on the same wall.

Finally, Bishop knocked and called my name.

He came in, paused and looked around him. 'So,' he said loudly. He came towards me, making a small drama of pulling off his gloves and extending his hand to me.

He was in his early fifties with short, steel-grey hair. The woman who followed silently in his wake was twenty years younger.

'Alison Menzies,' he told me. 'I hope you don't mind.'

I did, but said nothing. I held out my hand to her and she glanced at Bishop before taking it.

'I'm Mr Bishop's chief legal adviser,' Alison Menzies said. 'He and I are due elsewhere in an hour's time.' She looked at her watch to emphasize the point.

Bishop, I noticed, watched her with a look of amused admiration – a look he might have saved for the first adult assertions of his own lost daughter.

19

'An hour. Right,' I said. I took off my own watch and laid it on the desk.

Alison Menzies alone caught the gesture and frowned.

'There is nothing I feel I cannot say in front of Alison,' Bishop said. 'I'd like you to understand that, Mr Rivers. I'm not one of those people who confuses his private life with his public or business life. But at the same time, I do understand the need for everyone concerned to understand the full implications of what is happening, and for those same people to be fully aware of the consequences of whatever it is they are involved in.'

'Right,' I said. Ground rules.

He finally sat opposite me and indicated for Alison Menzies to pull up a seat beside him.

'I assumed you were here in connection with your lost daughter,' I said, wanting to end these opening gambits and leaving only the slightest of pauses between the words 'your' and 'lost'.

'I am,' he said. 'Forgive me.'

'And in that connection, Ms Menzies is what—?'

'I would prefer it if a full and confidential record of everything that passes between us in this regard could be kept for future reference,' he said. 'This has lasted for so long now, and despite what you might think of me, how I might appear to you, these past five years have been unbearable, scarcely endurable. Most of what you see is an act, a face for the world.'

I doubted that, but again I let the remark pass.

Alison Menzies took a laptop from her case and settled it on her knees. She held her fingers over the keys, waiting.

'I asked Alison to make a brief record of our agreement,' Bishop said.

What he meant was that he didn't want *me* to misunderstand anything *he* told me.

'Fine,' I said. 'In which case—' I took out my mini-disc recorder and placed it on the desk between us. Its presence there clearly unsettled Bishop, but he could not bring himself to say so. 'No misunderstanding,' I said.

Alison Menzies began tapping silently on her laptop.

'Has something happened, something new?' I asked Bishop as he was momentarily distracted by the expert movement of her manicured fingers beside him.

He held a hand to his mouth and took a deep breath. I saw the faint staining on his fingernails and offered him a cigarette, which he took.

'How much do you know about my daughter's abduction and murder, Mr Rivers?'

I told him.

'And that's all?'

'A little more notice and I could have found out the names of everyone involved, had a look at the court transcripts, read all the various and relevant reports.'

'No – it was my intention that you should do none of those things. I want you to come to this work with fresh eyes.'

'Tell me what you think that work is,' I said.

He nodded at my bluntness and all it implied. 'Don't worry,' he said. 'I'm not going to take out a photograph of Nicola in her school uniform and with braces on her teeth, wave it in your face and tell you that this is my lost daughter, tell you that this is what she still looks like, tell you that she's in heaven and that God and his angels are looking after her after everything that's happened to her. None of that, Mr Rivers. I know she's dead. She was never *lost*, Mr Rivers. I know she's dead, and I know that the man who confessed to killing her did, in all probability, kill her. I might not have accepted this at the very beginning, but I accept it now.' He paused and took another deep breath. 'And what I live with now I will live with for the rest of my life. Of course I would like to know everything for certain. I would even like, one day, for somebody to discover where Nicola is buried or hidden or where she was – where she—' He stopped.

21

Beside him, Alison Menzies also fell still.

Bishop took out a handkerchief and blew his nose.

'I said "lost" ', I told him, 'because I couldn't think of any other word.'

'I know. You'd be surprised how many words there are when something like this happens, and how little they all come to mean. She's dead, Mr Rivers, and you and I need not avert our eyes from that particular understanding.'

'Tell me what you want me to do,' I told him, and even before he started speaking, Alison Menzies's fingertips were again moving silently over the keys.

James Bishop put away his handkerchief.

'The man who confessed to killing Nicola was called Martin Roper,' he said. 'I could have brought with me a folder a foot thick with all the reports and articles I've collected on him. I will, of course, make this available to you if you imagine it will be of any use to you.'

'Fresh eyes,' I said.

'When Roper was arrested he was twenty-one years old. He was a suspected paedophile whose speciality was taking photographs of young girls. The police had already been to see him on several occasions before they turned up something which connected him to the murders. To read the papers today you might imagine that the world was full of such men, but I doubt there are any more of them now than there were five years ago, fifty years for that matter.'

'Internet porn and specialist sites must have done something to stimulate demand,' I said.

'Perhaps. But how many men would it turn into monsters who were not already monsters in their own hearts? That's what they called him – a monster. But that kind of language clouds reasoning, Mr Rivers. He was a murderer, perhaps a rapist, perhaps a paedophile, perhaps a torturer. Those things might make him a monster in the eyes of the world and the tabloid press decrying him to that world, but it is only a convenient name, and it obscures considerably more than it reveals.' Everything he said continued to sound rehearsed.

'I would still appreciate seeing everything you've collected,' I said.

'Because it will tell you everything you might need to know about Roper, or because it will reveal something to you of me?'

'Both,' I said, honestly. 'I still haven't heard what it is that you want me to do for you.'

Alison Menzies stopped typing and the two of them exchanged another glance. She lifted her hands from her lap. Bishop motioned to the recorder on the desk.

'Just tell me,' I said.

'Several days ago, the day before I contacted you, I received a phone call informing me that Martin Roper was about to appeal against his original conviction on the grounds that it was unsafe.'

'Exactly how many days ago?'

'Four.'

'*Two* days before you called me.'

'There was no ulterior motive for the delay. I just didn't know what to do.'

'Presumably you called your family lawyer.'

'Of course I did. He told me to tell him everything that had been said. He's making enquiries. He told me there had been talk of an appeal for some time, but that until now nothing had been set in motion.'

As he spoke, Alison Menzies watched him with that same faint light of concern in her eyes.

'Are you in any way involved in this, Ms Menzies?' I asked her, hoping she would answer me before Bishop did.

She turned to me. 'I work in corporate law,' she said. 'It's all I know, give or take the basics.'

'I've only known Alison two years,' Bishop said.

Alison Menzies held my gaze, though whether in an attempt to convince me of her honesty, or to suggest that she was not as blindly obedient to James Bishop as he might want to believe, I was uncertain.

'All I'm doing here is keeping a record,' she said.

I said nothing.

'What does it matter?' James Bishop said.

'Who called you?' I said.

'He said he was a local reporter, a stringer for one of the nationals, connected to a local agency. He seemed to think it was big news. He told me that the appeal was set to go ahead and how did I feel about it all? Why didn't I take this opportunity to tell *my* story before all the civil liberties people and do-gooders got involved? That sort of thing.'

'And you said what to him?'

'I hung up on him.'

'Did you get his name?'

Bishop shook his head.

'And presumably there was no mention of the agency he worked for.'

'How many are there?'

'And you did nothing to try and trace the call?'

'He withheld the number.'

'Had you heard anything else recently about the appeal?'

'We hear something every few months, but it's never amounted to anything so far. Besides, Roper stands no chance. "Life", the judge said, and with a list of recommendations that will keep him in prison for at least another twenty years.' He took another cigarette.

'In all probability,' I said, 'it was a slow night at the news desk. Someone realized that five years had passed and decided to do some stirring. Ask you how you feel about the appeal, and of course you're going to respond. It blows up, sells a few papers, nothing comes of it, it disappears.'

'Until next year, and then the one after, and the one after that.'

'*That* wasn't why you came to me.'

'No.'

'But if it was connected to any of the local news agencies, I'll find out. What did the caller sound like?'

24

James Bishop shrugged.

'Any accent?'

'Something, but nothing I'd be able to identify again for certain. I'm not very good at that sort of thing. And it was on a mobile, not very good sound quality. It sounded as though he was driving.'

'Can you try and be a little more specific about exactly what he said to you? Did he say he'd heard an appeal was likely or definite? Did he know when it was or what it was based on? Or did he just want to get your reaction to the possibility of an appeal?'

'I honestly can't remember what he said. "We understand that Martin Roper's lawyers are lodging an appeal against what they consider to be his unsafe conviction. As the father of one of his alleged victims, how do you view this turn of events?"' He stopped speaking. He had remembered more than he imagined he would and this unexpected recollection had hurt him.

'And then you hung up,' I said.

'And then I hung up.'

'It should be simple enough to establish for certain whether an appeal is imminent,' I said, wondering why this had not been his first line of enquiry.

'Who'd tell us?' he said angrily. 'The police? They told us damn all worth knowing the first time around. They were damn all use to us then. Everyone knows how quickly they jumped at Roper's offer to tell them what he knew – though God knows why he felt the need to bother, not after that single murder had been proven. I told them then that I didn't want Nicola's abduction and murder to be included as part of some tidy "case-solved" package solely on the word of that man.'

'They must have had their reasons for believing he was telling them the truth,' I said. 'They wouldn't have let those other unproven killings enter the equation if they didn't think it would help to make their case against Roper.'

James Bishop shook his head at this. 'That's *exactly* what they did,' he said.

Alison Menzies attracted his attention and held up her watch to him.

'All I'm asking you to do, Mr Rivers, is to find out what's happening for me. When all this happened five years ago, my wife and I felt as though we were being held at arm's length from everything. We were numb with shock and worry and our fears for Nicola and our fears for our future without her. I won't let that happen to us again. I won't relinquish any power or control I might still possess in this matter. She was my daughter, she still is. I loved her then more than I ever loved myself, and I love her now even more. It might not seem a particularly great or noble or even a worthwhile claim to you, but I mean it. I still feel her loss every single hour of my life, and there is nothing I wouldn't do to discover the truth of what happened to her. My dilemma, you see, is that I will not accept without some qualification, some verification – call it what you will – the words – the lies – of the man who professes to have killed her. In short, if anything *is* about to happen, then I want to be aware of absolutely everything *as* it happens, and I want to know what more might now be done to reveal what Roper alone professes to know.'

'And if there's nothing new to discover?'

'I don't believe that.'

'Forgive me, but your belief or otherwise in any of this has little bearing on how the police or the CPS might now proceed. Without important new evidence, there is little chance that the circumstances surrounding your daughter's death will ever be re-investigated.'

'Which is precisely why I wish to engage your services, Mr Rivers,' he said.

'Until I'm charged with interfering with police inquiries.'

'You said yourself, the chances are they won't be

interested, that the appeal will come and go on technicalities and a wave of legal bills.'

It wasn't what I'd said, but I considered this.

And seeing that I had no other serious objections to raise, James Bishop took out his cheque book, leaned forward onto the desk and wrote out a figure for cash. It seemed a strangely outdated and emphatic gesture, but one he appreciated being able to make. He tore out the cheque with another flourish and pushed it across the desk to me, deftly pressing the Stop switch on my recorder before withdrawing his hand.

He could not disguise his relief that our first meeting was finally over.

He rose, walked to the window and looked out. The view of the busy street seemed to please him. Then he went to the mirror opposite my desk and studied himself. It was a heavy, gilt-framed mirror covering a third of the wall, blistered and pocked across its entire surface where the silvering had degraded. I had retrieved the mirror from one of the other empty rooms, where it had once been used by naval men to inspect their new uniforms full-length at their fittings, stiff and blue, buttoned and braided, and perhaps the first they had ever worn. I imagined them turning their caps a fraction of an inch one way and then the other, up and then down, as they savoured the moment and the rush of their own undisguised pride.

James Bishop examined the blemishes covering his own face.

Alison Menzies turned off her laptop, closed and secured it with its digital lock.

'I'll send you everything,' James Bishop said, looking at my reflection in the mirror.

'And I'll find out everything I need to know to begin with,' I told him.

He kept his eyes on mine. 'I have every faith in you,' he said.

Alison Menzies opened the door and stood beside it. James Bishop retrieved his coat and his gloves.

'Every faith,' he repeated, and again he held out his hand to me.

Alone, I felt like the third player in a one-act, three-handed drama, the only one working without a script, and the only one oblivious to the stage-directions long since memorized by the others. 'Involved' and 'concerned' were two of Bishop's favourite words, and he used them interchangeably, simultaneously drawing me towards him and keeping me at arm's length.

I went to the window and watched the two of them walk quickly along the street to wherever he had considered it safe enough to leave his car.

3

Tony 'Sunny' Summers owned Hull's only independent news agency. He gathered all the local news worth knowing and sold it to all the local papers, most of which had long since stopped knowing or caring what was and wasn't worth printing. And when something bigger happened locally, then he sold it to the Nationals. Recently, he'd acquired an advertising agency, and he designed and wrote advertising copy for the papers' smaller customers.

I'd known Sunny for twenty years, ever since we'd spent the night in adjoining cells following a fight in Victoria Square. We'd both been released without charge the following morning and had walked together to Hessle Road for a late breakfast, after which we'd spent the afternoon and evening, the night and the following early morning drinking ourselves back into our respective stupors, but this time managing to avoid the drunken violence. He was a trainee reporter then, anxious to leave the city and work anywhere else. He stayed three more years and then went to London with his pockets full of applications and references. It was the last I saw or heard of him for almost seven years.

The next time I saw him he was back in the city

covering a train crash for one of the Nationals, staying in the Royal Hotel, the best Hull has to offer. He got hold of me and we met for a drink.

We both still bore the scars from our introductory fight – him at the corner of his mouth, me buried in my left eyebrow where a police surgeon had put two stitches into a cut which wouldn't stop bleeding. Today, I doubt the wounds would add up to much more than an inch of faded white line.

At that meeting ten years ago, he seemed to me to be a different man entirely, contented with his life and fulfilled in his work. He told me about the promotion he was waiting for. He spoke of coming back to live in the North, and seemed genuinely excited at the prospect. True to form, at the end of an hour together, we compared our fading scars and he went off to join a group of other journalists there to file on the same rail crash.

I forgot about Sunny after that, and the next time I saw him I felt embarrassed to approach him. I got a call from the desk at the same police station where we'd been held for the night to say that he was back there and that he had asked them to contact me. I went immediately, convinced that a mistake had been made.

He was waiting for me in a room full of other people. Someone had recently been sick and the room still smelled of it. At first, I didn't recognize him, and was about to leave and find out what was happening, when a man in the far corner of the room raised his head and then his hand to me. I went to him, doing my best to hide my surprise and uncertainty.

He was unshaven and dirty, hung over and barely able to open his eyes or to speak. He told me to spare him a sermon and to get him outside. I collected his few belongings from the desk. There were no charges against him. He'd been found close by, drunk and barely conscious, and had looked to the constable who'd found him as though he might choke. He was taken inside, washed and left in a cell for the night.

Outside, he told me what had happened.

He and his wife had separated three years earlier, and their twelve-year-old daughter had gone to live with her mother. Sunny had seen her every other weekend and for longer periods during the school holidays. Six months after their separation, his wife had filed for divorce, and Sunny had promised her – more for their daughter's sake than his own – that he would comply with everything she wanted and make the whole unhappy process as painless as possible for the three of them.

Less than a month later, his wife and daughter were both killed in an accident on the M25. His wife had been driving, his daughter asleep beside her. It was almost two in the morning and there were no other vehicles involved in the accident. An eye-witness said the car had simply driven off the motorway into a concrete pillar. It was the day after his daughter's thirteenth birthday, and they had been returning from his wife's parents in Essex, where a party had been held. Sunny had not yet given his daughter the present he'd bought for her.

He had been unable to cope with the loss, and soon after he had resigned from his job, pretending to himself and to anyone else who still cared enough to listen to him that he was going to work as a freelance.

When I asked him how long he'd been back in Hull, he said a few weeks. His mother had died while he was away and he'd come back to live in the small house she'd left him on Mayfield Street. When I asked him what he was doing and why he hadn't contacted me earlier, he said nothing and merely pointed to himself in answer. I asked him if he needed another drink and he considered this and then shook his head.

He stayed with me for a month after that, eventually returning to Mayfield Street, where the first thing he did was fill a skip with everything his mother had left in the house, and then redecorate from top to bottom. He was hardly a competent painter, joiner, plumber, glazier or wallpaper-hanger, but the work served its purpose and applied the brake to his life.

Sunny's agency was above a cycle sales and repair shop on Spring Bank, flanked by a Chinese take-away and an off-licence. A narrow, gated tunnel led between these to the rear fire-escape, at the top of which the Summer International News and Advertising Agency proclaimed itself.

I rang the bell and waited for the automatic door release. I was unlikely to find Sunny himself there so early in the morning, but I knew that Yvonne would be in.

Yvonne had run a secretarial employment agency for the previous five years until her two partners – both women her own age – had persuaded her to buy into a larger, franchised organization providing the same services at inflated prices, and which had then gone into receivership, leaving Yvonne responsible for more debt than she had imagined possible. Then she had met Sunny, and between them they had worked something out. 'The wreckage clinging to the wreckage,' she used to say. Now she worked for him, and while she owned none of this new enterprise, she behaved like a partner rather than an employee, and Sunny, in his own careless way, appreciated this.

Yvonne opened the door and grinned. She balanced a cup and a saucer, a pen and a cigarette all in one hand. 'He's in,' she said, nudging me into the room behind her, and then whispering, 'Come and save me from this ocean of boredom,' as I passed her. She put down the crockery, the pen and the cigarette, embraced and kissed me on the lips. The gesture surprised me and my lips stayed pressed close beneath the pressure of her own. I held my hands a foot from her arms. Over her shoulder I saw Sunny at his desk, a phone wedged between his cheek and shoulder. In the far corner of the room sat a youth of sixteen or seventeen, watching us with his mouth open and looking back and forth between Sunny and Yvonne.

Sunny continued talking.

'Is he watching?' Yvonne whispered in my ear.

Sunny heard her. He was meant to. 'Not particularly,' he said. He shouted 'Goodbye' into the phone and let it fall into its cradle. He rose and came to where I stood, still wrapped in Yvonne, and patted my arm.

'He'll be getting jealous as hell,' Yvonne said loudly.

Sunny returned to his desk.

The youth in the corner went on watching us.

Yvonne finally relaxed her grip on me and stood back. 'You're actually quite a useless kisser,' she said.

'I know.'

She retrieved her tea and cigarette.

'Mr Summer—' the youth said.

'Yes, Bob, what is it?'

The youth deflated. 'It's David. David.'

'Meet Bob Cratchit,' Sunny said to me.

The boy looked at me suspiciously, as though I too were a part of the joke he would never understand.

'There's nobody called Bob Cratchit,' he said to me. 'He thinks it's funny. It's his idea of a joke.'

Yvonne went to him and stroked his head. He flinched.

'It *is* funny,' Sunny said. 'And it *is* a joke.'

Every surface in the room was covered with paper. Beside the youth's desk, the fax machine came to life and he returned to watch the sheet of paper as it emerged.

'He dreams of ripping out a ticker-tape and running across the office screaming that the Japs have bombed Pearl Harbor,' Sunny said. He motioned that the machine had stopped and the youth tore off the sheet and brought it to where Sunny sat.

'Good boy,' Sunny said to him.

'No sugar,' I told him, indicating the jug of coffee.

He looked at us both as though we had spoken to him in a foreign language.

'He's here on a fortnight's work-experience scheme,' Sunny said. 'Miss Lonelyhearts insisted.'

'He's my friend's neighbour's sister's son,' Yvonne said, as though this explained everything, which it often did, in Hull.

Sunny called her 'Miss Lonelyhearts' because, in addition to all her other work, Yvonne compiled the adverts for several dating agencies. Men seeking Women. Women seeking Men. Someone seeking Anyone.

'Is that why you're here?' Sunny said. 'Come to place an ad?' He looked at me intently, already beginning to guess at why I was there.

Yvonne returned to her own desk. She was five years older than either Sunny or myself, but looked five years younger than both of us. Since the collapse of her own marriage, she had lived alone, and currently had the fullest social life of anyone I knew. I'd been salsa dancing with her; I'd been on a wine-club outing, and I'd been out for meals with her. She reviewed cafés, bars and restaurants for several free-sheets and said exactly the same thing about everywhere she went. Recently, I'd imagined that she and Sunny might have been getting closer, but both of them denied this. Her affection for him, and his for her, was unmistakable.

'She's taken up fencing,' Sunny said.

'That's handy.'

'Touché,' Yvonne said, and thrust an invisible rapier at me.

Then, just as I was about to explain to Sunny why I was there, he held up a hand to silence me and said, 'No time. I'm due in court in ten minutes.' The Court Centre was a fifteen-minute walk away. He rose and picked up his coat from where it lay beside his chair. 'Come with me.' He gathered together a pad, pens and a recorder. Yvonne threw him several tapes.

Beside the youth, the fax came back to life, and he watched it intently.

I told Yvonne I'd see her soon.

'No you won't,' she said. 'You care as much for me

as he does.' She indicated Sunny, who stood patting his pockets.

Beside the fax machine, the youth became even more interested in the sheet of paper it was pushing out.

Once outside, Sunny led me down the narrow alley and out into a lane running along the rear of the buildings.

'Well?' he said as we emerged onto Spring Bank and crossed the road to a piece of wasteland upon which several benches had recently been planted. There had been plans to build a small park, but so far only the benches had materialized, used by weary shoppers during the day, and by gangs of alcoholic teenagers at night.

'James Bishop,' I said.

He thought for a moment. 'Which part of him?'

'He's concerned that the man who killed his daughter might be about to lodge a successful appeal against his conviction.'

'Martin Roper,' he said. 'Never any proof that he actually killed Bishop's daughter. He was convicted of killing a girl called Hayley Forbes, fifteen. It's *her* parents who should be concerned. This will be nothing to do with Bishop.'

'But the case on his daughter *is* still open?'

'Only insofar as it hasn't been officially closed. Roper's confession led to nothing, made no connections. It stank right from the start. It's why the police just went with the single charge. What does Bishop want from you?'

'Just to keep him informed of everything that happens, to keep him involved and—'

'Involved? How can he be *involved*? If it happens, it happens. He'll be as powerless now as he was then. He's a big noise in the local business community, that's all – Civic Society, Rotarians, that sort of big – public big.'

I waited a moment. 'His daughter was still

35

murdered. Perhaps abused before she was killed. He just wants to find out what happened to her, perhaps even where she ended up.'

'You don't sound very convinced,' he said.

'That I'll find out? Or that it's what he wants from me?'

'Both.'

'I just wanted to know what you knew about it all.'

'I don't like him,' Sunny said. 'He looks after himself. First and foremost, and without a second's hesitation. He always takes care of number one. Never forget that.'

'His daughter was still murdered,' I said.

'And he's carried that one single fact round with him like a giant, open, pitiable wound ever since.'

I considered the remark uncharacteristically malicious, but I accepted it for what it was from him and said nothing. I was still uncertain as to why he had insisted on leaving the agency before discussing Bishop.

'How do you know an appeal's likely?' he said.

'I don't. All I know so far is what Bishop's already told me. A reporter called him.'

'Any name?'

I shook my head.

'Paper? Agency?'

'That's why I came to you.'

'He didn't really tell you a great deal, did he? He just wound you up and set you going.'

'You're going to be late for court,' I said.

He shook his head. 'Part of it makes some sense,' he said absently.

'Which part?'

He hesitated before telling me. 'Three days ago, Martin Roper was transferred from Rampton back to Hull. Why? We get a lot of our work from the prison. I have a few warders I can talk to.'

'And one of them told you he was back?'

He nodded.

'Is it likely that they'd bring him back here?'

He avoided answering me. 'The red-tops could fill a week of fronts and specials with this kind of stuff.' He took out his pad and started making notes. 'What else did Bishop tell you?'

'Just that he had his own file on the trial and on the search for his daughter.'

'Nicola,' he said. 'Roper abducted her, and probably three or four others, then allegedly raped and tortured them, filmed it all, and in all probability was only one member of a paedophile ring.'

'No one else was ever convicted,' I said.

'I know. There were lots of different angles at the time.'

'Perhaps I should talk to someone who was involved,' I said.

'You can try,' he said. 'Though I doubt anyone will be too keen to hold anything back up to the light again after the fiasco it became last time.'

'What happened?'

'They went for the bird in the hand – Roper – and all the other little birdies scattered and flew away.'

'Was this common knowledge?'

'Would James Bishop have known about it, you mean? Of course he knew about it.'

'He said something about being unable to ask the only man who might know where his daughter was buried.'

'He was lying. It's something he does well.' He patted my chest. 'I take it he didn't postdate the cheque.'

'No.' I hadn't looked.

A bus passed us close to the kerb and sent up a spray which splashed an inch short of our feet.

'If Martin Roper *is* preparing for an appeal, what grounds will it be on, I wonder?'

I told him I didn't know. 'You don't even believe James Bishop received that anonymous phone call, do you?'

'I'd be happier with a recording of it. Or a name. Or

an organization. Or even a good reason for making it.'

'*You* do it all the time,' I said. 'Find a speck of dandruff and turn it into a head of hair. A butcher drops a sausage and it's "Pig Eats Baby".'

'Not with something like this. Trust me.'

'So what about the simple fact that Roper's been brought back to Hull. Surely—'

'They'll say it's all part of normal procedure. By which time, we'll have played every card we have and they'll tell us again to go away and not to say anything about it to anybody. If there *is* something there, then I can't afford to jeopardize my own chances of getting and selling whatever there is to be got and sold.'

'And meanwhile, Nicola Bishop—'

'Don't. When you can convince yourself, then you can try and convince me. Until he came to you, you'd seen her face in a crappy colour reproduction five years ago on the front of the *Mail*. You didn't know her, you didn't know him, and you didn't know what had happened to her. No one did, not for certain. So don't prod *me* with her now. *You're* the one who took his money. You're the one who had better get things straight before you start rattling old cages.' He stopped abruptly and leaned back on the bench.

'What about the court?' I said eventually.

'I can stand in the City Hotel or the Burlington and for the price of a pint I can learn everything I might have heard in the previous three hours. I sent Cratchit out for the lists earlier. Nothing. He brought them back to me as though he'd just ridden from Aix to Ghent.'

'Business must be good if you can pay him to do nothing.'

'Yvonne owes his mother a favour. I top up an allowance for him. I become part of the great public–private enterprise initiative we hear so much about. The name of the agency gets added to a list of all those other worthy business participants. One acne-riddled youth watching a fax machine.'

'So you're really just doing it for Yvonne,' I said.

He smiled. 'Believe what you like.' He turned to face me. 'Martin Roper. My recommendation would be to stay as far away from him as possible. I know this piece of informed and dependable advice will fall on deaf ears, but I'm still saying it. Some of the original trial was held with a cleared gallery. He told the court everything that had happened – everything he *said* had happened – to those girls. He took photographs, filmed them – that's what he was – a purveyor of kiddie porn as it was once quaintly known. There were sackfuls of material evidence, thousands of pictures and films. He did it. And even if he didn't do *all* of what he confessed to, then he definitely got off on confessing to it.'

'Were you in court?'

'Some of it. I got most of it afterwards from a few lawyers and court officials I know. Nothing I couldn't have picked up second- or third-hand from a dozen other places, but all of it with some substance, all of it enough to wrap a story round, and most of it unprintable enough to turn your stomach. Whatever else you want to believe, and whatever you want to believe of what James Bishop tells you, make no mistake about Roper. You're never going to see him; they won't let you anywhere near him; but just be warned.'

'Do you have anything I could look at?'

'I'll think about it. I have boxes full of the stuff we filed during the original trial. You're not going to find anything there that ten million others don't already know about. Perhaps if you read the papers more often . . .'

'What – "Pig Eats Baby"?'

'There's a whole different world out there,' he said, pointing one way and then another, as though undecided about which direction that whole other world lay.

4

James Bishop called me twice the following day. The first time to tell me that he had appreciated my seeing him and agreeing to help him. And the second time, early in the afternoon, to let me know that he would send me all the information he had amassed concerning the disappearance of his daughter and the trial of her alleged killer. Courtesy calls. Impulse. And again the same precise and stilted language, as though he was reading from a carefully worded contract that already existed between us. I remained suspicious of his true motives, of all he was not yet telling me.

I was in my office when both calls came, but I picked up neither. I called him back later and left a message telling him when I would be there so that he might courier his file to me. What concerned me even more than his motives for engaging me was the knowledge that he, too, was aware of my suspicions. Perhaps he believed there was something amid his papers that would convince me that he was nothing more than a grieving father unable to move on from the death of his daughter until he knew for certain what had happened to her. Or perhaps – as I'd suspected from the outset, and as Sunny clearly believed – he was hoping to use me to find a way to his daughter's killer.

By the time of Bishop's second call, I had already considered several approaches, any one of which might reveal to me more clearly why he was so insistent on the investigation.

I called Sunny, but no one answered.

It was almost seven. It had been a bright, dry day, but night had fallen at four.

On the floor above me, the woman who rented the open space to give her exercise and yoga lessons was holding a small class. I heard her music and her instructions through the timber and the ceiling. It was a strange feature of the way the building had been converted that a lesser sound from above would often carry further and more clearly than a much louder noise from below.

The woman had been there a month and worked mostly in the early evenings. She had introduced herself to me, but I'd forgotten her name. We passed occasionally in the corridor and on the stairs. She struck me as being wholly and happily self-obsessed. She always carried a sports bag, and usually a bottle of water, from which she drank every few minutes. Any conversation with her always turned quickly to her assessment of my own stress levels and self-neglect, which she probably considered to be a form of pernicious self-abuse.

I left my office and locked the door. I padlocked a hasp beneath the handle, but knew how cosmetic a precaution this was.

I crossed Castle Street into Prince's Dock, waited twenty minutes for a bus which never came, and resumed walking. An ambulance sped along Guildhall Road ahead of me, followed by two police cars, flashing but silent, and passing effortlessly through the sparse evening traffic.

5

The body of Hayley Forbes had been found on a disused and overgrown railway siding outside Goole. The railway had been used to deliver coal from a colliery to a spur line which fed the wagons directly to the power station at Drax. The colliery had closed in 1986, the siding finally abandoned two years after that. The pit site had remained empty and derelict and awaiting the redevelopment which never came. An ex-miner walking his dog had found the corpse.

This was quickly identified as Hayley Forbes, fifteen, who had gone missing almost seven weeks earlier. It was established that she had been dead for anything between twenty-one and twenty-eight days, and that she had been killed elsewhere and then brought to the siding. The dog had found her between a stack of disused sleepers and a mound of ballast kept there by the railway to carry out local repairs. Someone had scraped the ballast over her in an ineffective attempt to conceal her. It was suggested by one of the investigating officers that this had been done with no serious intent to hide the body. A few minutes' more work and the corpse might have been hidden for years, perhaps for ever. This led to speculation that whoever had brought the body there had been disturbed as they had disposed of it.

Cause of Death was strangulation, though it was quickly apparent that Hayley Forbes had incurred a great many other injuries on her head, torso and limbs, and that she had been subjected to a sustained and brutal sexual assault involving several assailants before she was killed. Initially, the police said as little as possible concerning these injuries and their causes, but they were unable to conceal for long the true extent and nature of what had been done to the girl.

It was their belief, a press officer later announced, that Hayley Forbes had been abducted with the purpose of being abused like this, and that her injuries had not been some coincidental part of a less determined abduction. Hayley Forbes's mother sat and wept only a few feet from the man who said all this.

A list of other missing girls of roughly the same age was compiled. Connections were sought and further searches organized. Old ground was gone over. A wave of public revulsion followed the discovery, and the police responded to this.

The discovery of Hayley Forbes's body gave everyone concerned a useful focus. It was still considered likely by many that the other missing girls were simply that – missing from home – and until evidence to suggest otherwise was uncovered, it was difficult for the searching forces to co-ordinate their efforts. With the discovery of Hayley Forbes, they said, they finally had what they needed to launch a proper and thorough investigation.

Forensic and pathology experts were able to establish that some of Hayley Forbes's injuries had been inflicted post-mortem, perhaps by assailants who did not realize she was dead. An early report described her as having been injured and killed in 'a frenzy of uncontrollable abuse and mutilation' and the phrase stuck and dogged the investigators. It was equally likely, a further report suggested, that Hayley Forbes's attackers were perfectly aware that she was already dead, and that her death did nothing to stop their assault. The mark of the ligature remained as vivid on her neck as a velvet choker.

All this was over five years ago. Neither Child-Protection nor Sexual-Offender registers were so scrupulously compiled or updated then, and nor was their use in inquiries of this sort considered so essential or so valid.

I looked at the photographs of the murdered girl – photographs endlessly repeated during the following weeks as the search for her killers intensified. And then printed again when Martin Roper was eventually caught, tried, convicted and imprisoned. It was easy afterwards to see all the necessary connections, to see how clearly and reassuringly all the facts and details of the case had meshed together and grown solid.

I learned all this from the files of clippings Sunny gave me. He and I sat together at the agency. He was unwilling to let me take the files away now that he might need them again, and I was grateful of his offer to go through them with me. He asked me to tell him if I came across anything of interest in the clippings, anything related to what little James Bishop had already revealed to me. Nicola Bishop was listed among the other missing girls, all of whom were being sought, none of whom had yet been found.

I sat at Yvonne's desk. A three-part picture frame stood on one side, revealing her flanked by the faces of her two sons as they had been as schoolboys. Both were now in their late teens, one away at university in Manchester, but this was how she preferred to see them every day.

Sunny assured me we would not be disturbed. He asked me what Bishop's own files had contained, and I told him that I wanted first to see what all the local and national papers had revealed before going on to consider any reshaping or retelling by Bishop. Sunny also had in his possession a transcript of the trial itself, and I read this as he went through the folders of his own cuttings.

It was not a long transcript. The confession of Roper had been read out in camera. He confessed to killing four girls, including both Hayley Forbes and Nicola Bishop. It was a damning, if less than confirmatory, confession, and in the face of it his appointed barrister had effectively admitted defeat. He had observed all the proprieties, of course, had displayed just the right amount of indignation at the unfair hearing he considered his client to be getting, but eventually Roper himself had publicly criticized the man and had repeated large parts of his confession to the listening court and press gallery. There was never any doubt that his conviction would be secured, only some concern over the seeming ease and hurried nature of its getting. The likelihood of any appeal five years later had not occurred to anyone involved in the trial. Justice had been demanded and that demand had been satisfied.

'Detective Chief Inspector Sullivan?' I said to Sunny. 'Is he still around?'

'Retired. He was the Senior. Roper was his last case. There was some suggestion among his junior officers that when Roper began to talk, the powers-that-be moved Sullivan up into sole charge of the case so that when he retired a year later—'

'He'd go garlanded with praise and glory.'

'And with a full and generous pension and citation. He wasn't necessarily a dishonest man, by all accounts, but he had a reputation for being set in an old mould, for twisting things to meet his own ends and for getting his own way. He was renowned for taking credit where it wasn't due. He'd made a mess of a case a year earlier – another sexual offence thing, not children – and it had left a bad taste. He had a fondness for mouthing off to the press when it suited him. He liked to make things personal. When Hayley Forbes was found, he went on the box and invited the killers to contact him personally.'

'And?'

'Nothing happened. Sullivan liked to think that it was his way of doing things that led to Roper's conviction, but you'd be hard-pressed now to find anyone else who shared that belief. He worked with a team out of Queen's Gardens. I daresay some of them are still there. He wasn't a stupid man, just—'

'Blind to his own faults?'

'His wife died suddenly and unexpectedly six months after he'd retired and they'd moved to the coast. I imagine the move was her idea.'

'What first pointed them to Roper?'

'I'm not sure. One minute they were still talking of assailants in the plural, of half a dozen or so likely suspects, and the next anyone knew was that they'd made an arrest, searched Roper's home and found everything they needed to tie him to Hayley Forbes and make their case.'

'Meaning someone told them about him.'

'"Information received." "Acting on a reliable informant."'

'And Roper confessed to having played some part in the killing of Hayley Forbes, Nicola Bishop and two others.'

'Lindsey Perry and Jennifer Wilson. Told them everything they wanted to know. Insisted he didn't want a solicitor present.'

'But presumably there was one.'

'Of course. Even Sullivan wasn't that stupid.'

'And Roper told them everything? Just like that? It all sounds a bit convenient.'

'To say the least. I haven't seen the actual statement, but, essentially, yes – he told them everything. Everything they already knew and everything they had yet to discover. It all fitted. He did it. There was a room at the rear of his studio. The girls were killed there, he said. There were almost four hundred pieces of evidence submitted at his trial. Roper, apparently, was already known for having a thing about young girls. He'd indulged himself in the past, but recently – or so the story went – the past six months – he'd been unable to control himself, gone too far.'

'Do you think he'd rehearsed what he told them before he said it?'

'Of course he had. But what difference would that make? He wasn't lying; he just wanted to make sure everything was clear and straight before he said it.'

'And when he confessed to the three girls whose bodies have never been found?'

'What can I tell you?' He continued searching through the papers.

'Psychiatric reports?'

'By the vanload, I would imagine. Not for the eyes of you or me, though – not while Roper is still in custody. It's in the transcript and court reports. The psychiatrists stood up in court and told everyone what they thought of him.'

'Is there any family still here?'

He closed his eyes in the effort of retrieval. 'His father died when Roper was still a boy. His mother was alive when he was arrested – he was still living at home with her somewhere out in East Hull. She died later. They had a caravan out at Easington, near the gas terminal. There was a fire or something. There was even some suggestion that she might have killed herself with the shame of it all. They were supposed to have been close. He was an only child.'

'The police don't seem to have taken too much convincing that what Roper was telling them was gospel,' I said. 'All the reports on the discovery of Hayley Forbes suggest more than one assailant, but Roper never even mentions, let alone implicates, anyone else.'

'Like I said, Roper already had a reputation. His name came up when they finally started compiling their lists of Likelies. When he was eight he attacked the ten-year-old daughter of a neighbour. Kids' stuff, probably, but the woman wanted him prosecuted for it.'

'What happened?'

47

'Nothing. Later, when he took up photography, he made his money taking the kind of pictures you wouldn't want developing at Boots.'

'None of which would necessarily point to him being a rapist, a sadistic torturer or a murderer,' I said. 'Presumably the girls posed willingly for him.'

He shrugged. 'He still confessed, and it's still how most convictions get made to stick. It's not like *Quincy* any more. It's not even like *The Rockford Files*.'

At midnight, Sunny fell asleep.

And by two in the morning I knew everything there was to know about how the investigation and the trial had been reported. I made a note each time Nicola Bishop was mentioned. I photocopied those reports in which Roper was alleged to have spoken of her, along with the two other missing girls, all of whom he had refused to locate for the police once they had made clear their intention of prosecuting him for the murder of Hayley Forbes alone. There were some among the investigating officers who remained sceptical regarding what Roper professed to know about those undiscovered bodies, but there were always too many others, it seemed to me, Sullivan included, hanging on Roper's every word and desperate for the case against him to be secured and closed.

At three, Sunny lifted his head from his arms and looked around him. He frequently slept at the agency. He considered me for a moment and then closed his eyes again. I shook a sheaf of paper at him to suggest I was still reading, but by then I too was only half-awake.

Later, I left the agency and left him where he lay. It was how Yvonne must have found him on countless mornings, and it would be my guess that she stood and looked at him for several minutes before quietly crossing the room and gently waking him.

6

Later that morning, approaching noon, I received all the clippings James Bishop had collected. I remained intrigued as to why he should have been so insistent on me seeing this collection, and why he had gathered it together in the first place – something he must have undertaken immediately after his daughter went missing, and while he and his wife were at the centre of the storm surrounding the deaths and disappearances of all the girls.

I signed a form to say that I had taken delivery of the two albums and that I accepted full responsibility for them while they were in my possession.

Each book was two inches thick, cloth-bound, and each was wrapped in tissue paper, beneath which the name Nicola was embossed in silver. On the first was written 'Nicola Bishop, 1984–1998', and on the second simply 'Nicola, 1998'. I felt as though I had been handed someone's album of wedding or christening photographs – something to be handled with care and reverence, and something to be endlessly remarked upon. I lay the two books on my desk and cleared the area around them. It was not difficult to believe that they were now James Bishop's most precious possessions.

I waited before opening the first of the books, the one that would finally reveal his daughter to me from her birth onwards – the whole of her short life, in fact. Someone passed by in the corridor outside. Across the road, a lorry reversed into an entrance which gave the driver only six inches clearance on either side, and he came noisily back and forth across the narrow street in his manoeuvring.

Immediately inside the album was her full name. Nicola Sarah Elizabeth Bishop. The old and the new, past and present, tradition, remembrance and continuity. These, too, were embossed in silver, and the wording beneath everything which followed was carefully and neatly written. The tissue of the binding continued inside, a protective sheet between each page of thin black card.

I turned the first few pages feeling as though I ought to be wearing soft white gloves. When I coughed, I turned away from the book.

The first picture was of the girl an hour old, less, held in her mother's arms, her sleeping face bunched tight as a fist, dark against the blanket which cocooned her. In the next, James Bishop and her mother held her between them. *The proud and happy parents*, the writing said.

The baby went home, started crawling, walked, fell, turned into a small girl.

The small girl started to grow, grew, stood, fell again and walked.

She wore a thousand outfits, surrounded herself with a thousand toys.

She spoke, she changed, she started school. She was dressed as a ballerina; she wore a riding outfit. Her birthdays arrived. Christmases came and she sat amid drifts of wrapping paper. Easter caught her with her face covered in chocolate. She held up a rabbit; she wrapped her arms around a golden labrador; she posed, grinning uncontrollably with her head inches from the nose and mouth of a pony, a rosette already pinned to its bridle.

She hugged her mother; she kissed her father; she sat at the centre of family gatherings.

She wore her first school uniform when she was no older than three or four, and every few pages afterwards, she wore another, or an identical one newly bought.

She changed even more. She was once fat and then grew thin and stayed thin.

Her hair grew, curled and shaped at first, and then fell straight and into a succession of styles as she began to assert her own identity. Towards the end of those years, the hair changed colour, dyed, blonde, blonde and brown, golden brown, dark brown, almost black, long over her eyes and then cut abruptly short.

Her face changed; she learned how to pose for the camera, always the centre of attention.

She acquired a figure to start the process of turning from a girl into a young woman. She showed off her exposed shoulders. On a beach she wore a bikini. She sat by a pool wrapped only in a towel, holding out her palm to the photographer in a half-hearted attempt to stop him from taking her picture.

She posed in a group with a dozen other girls, all of them outrageously dressed and made-up, *en route* to a Hallowe'en party.

One last Christmas shot of her sitting in her dressing-gown with her long hair tied back in a ribbon, a piece of jewellery held up to the camera.

And after that, a series of nine photographs all taken on the same occasion, a family gathering, a summer's day, men and women standing in groups with food and drink, a pool, a marquee, a smoking barbecue. And Nicola Sarah Elizabeth Bishop somewhere in each of the photographs, even if she was no longer their chief subject.

What I was seeing, I realized, were the last photographs taken of her by James Bishop while she was still alive. They might even have been photographs unseen until after her disappearance, those tiny, frayed parts of life that refused to fade or fall away completely into the past, and which drifted into those other unbelievable existences; those innocent and unthinking parts that one sought and seized like jewels because they existed so inadvertently, because without them life for those left behind might prove to be unbearable, and because they were *proof* of something, all those undeveloped photographs and answering-machine voices, even if no one was entirely certain of what.

There was nothing after the nine photographs of that summer's day. I sought the fourteen-year-old girl out in all of them. In some, she was little more than a distant blur. In some, she stood half-hidden in a group of others. In one, she looked directly at the photographer and pulled a face of disapproval.

Four months had passed since the previous picture, labelled 'Easter 1998', and showing Nicola and her mother sitting together on a beach, the girl finally as tall as the woman, slim and growing and all too clearly aware of all that was happening to her, of her new place in the world. The shadow of the photographer, presumably James Bishop, lay across their feet. Neither woman nor girl seemed particularly keen to pose for the picture, their smiles tight and thin. Her mother holds her hand at some distance from her face to shield herself from the bright sun, casting its shadow over her eyes and nose. Nicola stares directly at the photographer. The sky in the picture is blue. The sky in all of the outdoor shots is blue, and the sun is always shining.

There is an earlier picture of Nicola, aged four, standing beside a snowman a foot taller than her. She is holding a snowball as though about to throw it. Even there the sky was blue and the sun was shining.

Following the party sequence in which she is an incidental participant, the final few pages of the album remain empty until the very last leaf, which is inscribed, simply, 'Nicola, 7 August 1998', which is the date she was lost to them.

I closed the book and sat back from it. The second remained unopened beside it. I folded the tissue back around the jacket and returned it to the padded envelope in which it had arrived. It had served its purpose. It might have held ten times the number of photographs that had been put into it by James Bishop, but he had remained selective. Here was his perfect daughter as he wanted to remember her, and as he wanted others now to see her. Perhaps there were a hundred other albums, each one designed and compiled to serve its own specific and different purpose; each one designed, perhaps, to keep that precious and perfect girl alive in someone else's heart. I even imagined that every one of the people standing unsuspectingly around her at that final party might have possessed an album of their own, given to them by James Bishop as part of his own determined remembrance of her.

I was about to open the second album when the phone rang. I waited for my answering machine to click in and then listened as James Bishop asked me if I was there. I picked up the receiver. He had been about to let his impatience show and was caught momentarily off-guard by my sudden presence. He told me he'd called the previous day. I lied and said I'd only just arrived at the office. I told him his albums had arrived safely.

'I know,' he said. 'I have your receipt.'

'Perhaps you should have held on to them. They're obviously very precious to you.'

'I just wanted you to see her as we once saw her,' he said. It sounded like the first completely honest thing he'd said to me.

'I understand that,' I told him.

He was anxious to ask me what, if anything, I had discovered about Roper and his appeal, and I was just as anxious not to tell him. I still knew nothing beyond what he himself already knew.

'I haven't looked properly at the second album yet,' I told him.

There was a moment of silence.

'I hesitated before sending it,' he said. 'It might seem strange to you, perhaps even a perverse thing to do. There's nothing in there that you yourself couldn't have cut from a dozen papers. It became a kind of obsession with us. It felt to us as though they were all talking about a different girl entirely, not our daughter.'

'It's a common feeling,' I said.

I lifted the cover of the second album and saw that where there had been photographs in the first book, in this one there were only newspaper clippings, most of which I would already have seen at Sunny's the previous night.

'I've been looking elsewhere,' I said.

'I expected you would. Let me know when you've finished with the albums and I'll send someone to collect them. I'd appreciate it if you could keep them somewhere secure until then.'

'Are they your only copies?'

He hesitated a second. 'No, I have others. The photographs, I mean. I suppose you might say that the second book already exists in the public domain.'

'Whereas in the first she was still only *your* daughter.'

'Something like that. Look, if you think it will help, keep them both a little longer.'

'"Help"?' I said.

'To understand a little better how we feel about this, how we felt then, what all this did to us.'

'Of course,' I said. 'I'd appreciate that.' It was what he wanted to hear. 'I'd also like to speak to Nicola's mother,' I said.

'Of course. And she'd be happy to see you. We were talking about it last night. She wants to see an end to this as much as I do, Mr Rivers.'

'I'm sure.'

'Would you like me to arrange a time?'

I told him I'd let him know, that there were things I needed to do first. I wanted to see his wife alone. Nothing would be gained by watching the two of them together, sitting side by side, surrounded by those same photographs and listening to her repeat everything he had already carefully prepared for me.

'Have you heard anything at all?' he said.

'It's only been thirty-six hours, Mr Bishop.' It was a hand held to his chest and he stopped coming. 'It might also be useful if I could speak to someone at Nicola's school,' I said.

'I doubt if that would serve any real purpose. It's been so long.'

'I realize that, but it was a big part of her life; presumably, a number of her friends went there.'

'Some of them. Not many. The head-teacher was called Mr Watson. I'm not even sure if he's still there. I can find out for you, if you like. I paid for a bench and a tree in Nicola's memory. There's a trophy for achievement in extra-curricular activity. The Nicola Bishop Memorial Trophy. The school held a service. There's a picture in the second album . . .' He was again lost for a moment in this sudden, unexpected remembering.

'I'll be discreet,' I said. 'I'll explain the situation.' And if the need arose, I would do it without his blessing.

'I'll call them, let them know you have my authorization,' he said.

Like your wife would have had it to see me. 'I'd appreciate it.' It was increasingly clear to me that he intended relinquishing as little of his own involvement in this as possible.

Hoping to divert him, I said, 'What was the occasion of that final sequence of photographs, the party?'

'Some business affair. PR. It never hurts. We were entertaining some of our associates from the Continent. Plus, I was a mayoral candidate that year.

We had a party every summer. Bit of business, lot of socializing.'

I could imagine.

He went on. 'I won't pretend it was Nicola's or Patricia's favourite way of spending a weekend, but they both understood why it had to be done. Why do you ask? I put the pictures in because . . .' His voice faltered.

'I know why you put them in,' I said.

'If you look closely you can see the navel stud she's wearing,' he said. 'A week earlier she'd had her navel pierced without telling us. Naturally, there was an argument, and to help smooth things out I bought her the stud. She's wearing it in the film,' he repeated. 'And five days later, she went missing. There's no real connection, I just felt—'

'You don't need to explain,' I told him. It was where she lived last, where the future and all its promises and pleasures still existed.

A moment later, he hung up.

I saw little in the second album that I hadn't already seen sitting at Yvonne's desk and going through Sunny's files. Except that here the cuttings were neatly cut out and pasted into place, in order, their sources and dates meticulously recorded. And except that here Nicola remained for ever the focus of events. It was a short and awful story, and hindsight did nothing to cushion its blows or lessen the impact of its abrupt and terrible revelations.

Every report mentioned Nicola by name, and this was why they had been chosen and preserved. Often the reports said little more than that she was one of several girls still being sought by the police. Plea after plea was made. James and Patricia Bishop made several of their own.

And then, gradually, came the veiled suggestions that her disappearance might have been in some way connected to the death of Hayley Forbes.

Later still, with Roper's scarcely creditable

56

confession, the focus changed again and her death became the unverified fact it had remained ever since.

The same few photographs accompanied each report. Presumably they were the ones released for use by Bishop. In one, Nicola wore her school uniform; in another she looked older, wearing jewellery and make-up, a strapless dress. I saw immediately what purpose the different poses served. In some of the articles she was pictured alone; in others she was placed alongside pictures of the remaining missing girls. James Bishop offered a reward for information leading to her discovery or return – even then hope still flickered – and occasionally his own face appeared briefly among those of the girls.

And then the solitary, frequently used picture of Martin Roper started to appear, taken from his previous police record, and as misrepresentative of him as the pictures of Nicola Bishop as a twelve-year-old in her blazer. There was a picture of Roper in Sunny's file taken three years after his arrest, and the photographs could have been of two completely different men. Because of his confession, there could be no doubt that this was the face of a murderer, a monster.

Some of the articles restricted themselves to reports of his life and past crimes; others speculated on the whereabouts of the other missing girls – the girls he had already – 'gleefully' one paper announced – confessed to having killed and buried.

Some went even further and speculated on the ring of which he had supposedly been only a single member. These were the reports which interested me the most, but again there was little here I hadn't already encountered a dozen times over in Sunny's files.

The second album showed me a father obsessed to the point of being blinded, but that was all. Perhaps another father might not have felt the need to compile the album; but perhaps another father still might have nurtured his hatred and disgust to more destructive ends. I went back to see what, if anything, had been written about the other parents and families, but found little apart from their names and addresses and the all-too-predictable pleas and prayers they too offered up when everything and everyone else had failed them.

I looked for the clipping Bishop had mentioned concerning his daughter's memorial service at her school. In the accompanying photo, James Bishop stood with a girl called Angela Hill, a close friend of Nicola's, who had written a poem for the occasion. Patricia Bishop is conspicuous by her absence from the picture, which includes a dozen of the school's senior teachers, and thirty or so pupils all impeccably dressed in identical uniforms standing in a semi-circle around the dedicated bench and recently planted tree.

At midday I watched the few remaining traders drag in their last pallets of oranges and cabbages and congregate in a group to discuss the day's trade. A small fire had been lit nearby, and the sooty smoke from this rose barely ten feet off the ground before sinking back down in the cold and thickening air, giving the men gathering beside it the appearance of standing up to their ankles in water.

7

The man Sunny had described to me was among six others in the side-room of the Sportsman, a two-minute walk from the main entrance to the prison. Two of the men played pool and the others sat together along the back of the room and watched, commenting on each shot played. The players were poor, and just as many points were conceded in the game as earned.

Sean Wallis was one of those watching. He sat at the end of the line of men, his elbows on his knees. They all drank pints, a surfeit of drinks already collecting around the table.

It was not yet ten in the morning. The bar catered to the comings and goings of the prison shifts, and to the visitors who arrived early and were forced to wait. The smell of frying filled the small room and the men frequently called out to ask how long their food was going to be. A solitary woman, in her sixties, looking as exhausted as most of her customers, supervised the bar. When she was absent, the men helped themselves and put their money in the till, calling in to the kitchen to tell the woman what they had taken.

I sat with only three others in the small front bar, my head down in a paper, waiting for my opportunity to catch Sean Wallis alone. The three other men sat alone and apart from each other. None of them looked as though he'd had a night's sleep. One of them, a man in his early twenties and with a tattoo on his cheek, kept a tight grip on the hold-all beside him. Each time the door to the back room opened, he looked up and then just as quickly looked away again.

Before entering the bar, I'd gone to a piece of land on which second-hand cars were sold. A Portakabin stood at the centre of the site. Beside it, a youth washed one of the cars, a box of polishes and waxes at his feet. Establishing my reason for being there, I shouted to ask him what time the car lot opened. He was reluctant to answer me, but eventually he told me it depended on what time the owner arrived. He guessed at eleven. Or twelve.

In the bar I made a point of complaining to the land-lady that I'd previously been told ten. She told me the owner would be in the bar at noon. I remarked on the noise being made by the men around the pool table.

'Night shift,' she said. 'Prison.'

And having confirmed that much, Sean Wallis was easy to pick out from Sunny's description.

I watched as the woman went through to them with a plate of sandwiches. She stood with them for a few minutes and then returned to the bar.

Wallis had a shaved head, and unlike the others he had already removed his jacket, shirt and tie and sat in his uniform trousers and a clean white T-shirt. He was twenty-eight, perhaps thirty. He complained loudly when another man, rising to get to the table, spilled drink on him. Wallis skimmed this from his chest and lap and then rubbed at the stains it briefly left. The man beside him laughed at him and told him to stop worrying. He put a muscular arm around Wallis's neck and pressed a fist into his cheek. Wallis laughed at this and waited for the man to release him. The man was short, with the half-inch tips of his inch-long hair dyed vividly blond, white almost.

According to Sunny, Wallis was awaiting a

disciplinary hearing for an alleged breach of confidentiality, and he was only still working while he awaited this because the prison was short-staffed, and because his union had insisted. I'd asked Sunny if he thought Wallis would talk to me, and he said he doubted it. It was talking to Sunny and others like him that had led to the charge against Wallis in the first place. It was Sunny's belief that Wallis, guessing the likely outcome of his hearing, was already looking for work elsewhere.

The landlady came to my table and picked up my empty glass.

I followed her back to the bar.

She asked me if I was buying or selling a car.

'Buying,' I said. 'Hopefully. Probably.'

She told me what I owed her for my drink. It was the end of our conversation.

In the pool-room, an argument began between the two men at the table and Sean Wallis rose to stand between them, holding one of the men at arm's length from him, his forefinger stiff in the face of the other. The room grew briefly silent. The landlady turned to watch. And then the man Wallis was holding laughed and the tension was released. Wallis relaxed his grip and the man took a step back from him and pulled straight his jacket. He picked up one of the glasses and drained it. The other man shook his head and turned away.

Wallis remained standing. He pulled on his jacket and announced he was leaving. There were a few entreaties for him to stay, but he ignored these.

I finished my drink and left the bar ahead of him, crossing Hedon Road to stand in a bus shelter complete with a notice announcing that buses no longer stopped there. The whole of the road was being excavated prior to its widening. Rubble littered what remained of the pavement.

Wallis came out of the bar and crossed to join me.

Neither of us spoke. After a minute I pretended only

then to have seen the notice and I asked him if it meant what it said.

'Nothing's stopped here for years. Security.' He motioned towards the prison.

'You mean they might tunnel from there to the bus stop?' I said.

'Some of the stupid fuckers would come up underwater.' He motioned again, this time in the direction of Alexandra Dock behind us.

I offered him a cigarette – which he took – waiting until his hands were wrapped around my lighter before saying, 'My name's Leo Rivers and I'm a friend of Sunny's. I wanted to ask you one or two questions about Martin Roper.'

I had expected him to respond violently, but instead he drew sharply on the cigarette and moved further into the shelter, behind the advertising hoarding where he wouldn't be seen by anyone else coming out of the bar.

'Summers tell you that it was talking to him that got me in front of the tribunal in the first place, did he?'

'Talking to him for money,' I said.

'And that's the deal with you, is it? How much?'

I said I'd pay him a hundred if he told me everything I wanted to know.

'About Martin Roper?' he said.

'About Martin Roper.'

'And supposing there's nothing to tell about the dirty twisted little fucker?'

I took the five twenties from my pocket. Whatever else happened, he was going to demand the money up front. After that, I was going to pay him for however much or little he told me, and so it was pointless me pretending that the money still acted as leverage.

'Popular little fucker,' he said.

'Meaning someone else has already been asking?'

'Meaning the Governor told us not to say a fucking thing about him being there. Told us not even to confirm or deny that he *was* there.'

'Are you telling me he isn't there?'

'If he wasn't there, why would we get orders to say nothing about him? Work it out, Sherlock.'

'What do you know about his appeal?'

'Fuck all.'

'If there is going to be one, it'll be common knowledge soon enough.'

'But not soon enough for you, right?'

Across the road, the door to the bar opened and two of the other warders came out. They were two older men. They pulled on their jackets against the cold and walked together past the used-car lot towards the city centre. Wallis ducked slightly and watched them go.

'Nobody saw you,' I said.

'Who gives a fuck?'

'You, presumably.'

The two men turned a corner and were lost to sight.

'They're going to give evidence at my hearing.'

'Against you?'

'It isn't for or against. It's just what they know and what they've heard.'

'And either way it won't do you any good.'

'I'll be long gone by then, pal.' He grinned at the realization. He straightened and moved closer to me. 'Roper's a twisted little fuck. He did everything they said he did and he makes no fucking bones about it. Everybody knows he did it. He's *proud* of what he done. And no fucking appeal's going to change any of that.'

'Not even if his lawyers start shouting about an unsafe conviction on the grounds that too much concerning those three other missing girls got tied in with his single murder conviction?'

'It was a sound conviction. What's going to change that? So what if there's a bit of new hand-wringing over all that other stuff?'

'How long has he been back here?'

'Week, ten days.'

'There was nothing in any of the papers about his return.'

'Fuck the papers. You think everything gets announced to them? There's people come and go from that place you wouldn't want within a hundred miles of you, pal, let alone near your kids.'

'So presumably he's kept in isolation.'

''Course he fucking is. Probably always has been.'

'Has anyone been to see him?' It was all I really wanted to know from him, and he hesitated before answering me.

'See him?'

'His legal representatives. Visitors.'

'Word is, he hasn't had a single visitor since he was convicted. Five years, nearly six.'

'Journalists must have tried.'

'His call. He turns every Visiting Order request down. The quacks and basket-weavers have all had their shot at him, but I can't think it's done them much good.'

'He keeps himself to himself?'

He laughed. 'You make it sound as though he's got a say in the thing. Twenty-three or -four-hour lock-up, that's Roper.' He looked at his watch and scanned the road on either side of us.

I asked him if he was waiting for someone and he said he wasn't. I asked him why he'd come into the shelter if he knew no buses stopped there.

'Keep this out.' He tapped the side of his nose.

'Who else tried?' I said.

'Tried what?'

'You know what.'

'I told you—'

'You were lying,' I said. I took out another forty. It would all come from Bishop in the end.

A minute passed before he said anything. 'Some copper made an application. Big mistake. Word is that the Governor slipped up and rubber-stamped it. Roper blew a fuse and threw it out, got his lawyers or whoever on the case.'

'And that was it?'

'As far as I know. These things happen.'

'So, whoever made the application might just have been sending a message to Roper to let him know that they knew he was there?'

'There would have been easier ways.'

'Bent warders, for instance, who don't take their responsibilities too seriously?'

His expression darkened. 'Everybody in this fucking world is bent,' he said.

'If you say so. What do *you* think would happen if it became common knowledge that Roper was there?'

'How do you mean?'

'He received a dozen death threats at the time of his trial.'

'Then he'd probably get a dozen more. Who cares? Save the tax-payer a bit of money.'

'They'll do that by sacking you,' I said.

'The union rep reckoned I'd just get another warning.'

'*Another* one?'

He laughed. 'I was never cut out for the work, anyway.'

Another of the warders – the short, blond-haired man – came out of the bar, and Wallis watched him closely.

'Were you waiting for him?'

'Something like that. You've had your money's worth, now fuck off.' He continued watching the man as he walked along the road in the opposite direction to the first two. 'Bit of business,' he said.

'If you hear anything else,' I said.

'You can come looking for me and give me some more money.' He pushed me away from him, left the shelter and followed the other man.

I waited until both of them had turned into a side-street and then I crossed the road and ran to where they were. I stopped at the corner and looked quickly round to where the two men stood together at the open door of a telephone kiosk. The blond-haired man was speaking into the receiver and Wallis was standing in the half-open doorway.

I left the corner, retraced my steps to the shelter and then continued walking to a small newsagent's. From inside the shop I could see as both men re-emerged onto the main road, walked to the bar and went back inside.

8

The walk back to Humber Street cleared my head.

I called Sunny and told him what had happened. He'd made a few enquiries of his own and told me that no one he knew had yet admitted to having called James Bishop concerning Roper's return. No one had lied to him, he said. And by asking he had alerted everyone else who might have shared his own journalistic interest in the case. Yvonne wanted to speak to me. She took the phone from him.

'You saw Sean Wallis?' she said.

I told her I had, but that he'd only confirmed what I'd already been told or guessed.

'He's got a girlfriend and a new kid. Six months. Apparently, Wallis and her are in some sort of dispute over child-support payments. I don't know if it's official.'

'He didn't strike me as the doting kind. Meaning what – that she wants more from him than he's prepared to give her?'

'Meaning he's probably giving her nothing. I just thought you ought to know.'

'And you discovered all this how?'

'By using my womanly wiles, how else? Friend-of-a-friend stuff.'

'Have you heard of any sums being mentioned?'

'She'll want all she can get from him. Apparently, it's not the happiest of relationships. He turned up in the middle of the night a few days ago, drunk, threatening her and threatening to take her to court to get custody of the kid for himself.'

'He's all mouth,' I said.

'I know. Everybody knows. But it would probably be better to have some money and to know it than to be broke and know it.'

It might explain why he was prepared to jeopardize his hearing by talking to me, but I doubted it. He was a long way past caring about that.

She guessed what I was thinking. 'It might also persuade him to take an even bigger risk if the price was right,' she said.

'Meaning that someone might try to get to Roper via him?'

'It's worth bearing in mind. Sunny's shaking his head at me. I might have to kill him and take over the agency. He wants to talk to you. You owe me a drink.' She handed the phone back to Sunny.

'The girl and the kid exist,' he said. 'It's not news.'

'How many of the other warders would bend the rules to do what he does?'

'"Bend the rules"? You don't want to know. Stop worrying about Roper; he's not even in the equation. What do you think is going to happen – that Bishop's going to use you to find a way to him after all these years? It's not going to happen. Roper is just going to sit tight. Even when the appeal gets under way, there's every chance that he himself will never appear in court.' He blew out his breath. 'Look, get back to Bishop. Go and ask him to start telling you the truth instead of swamping you with all his pictures of the rosy past.'

'Supposing Bishop had tried to see Roper,' I said. 'He tried, he failed, and so he came to me.'

'He won't have been anywhere near. Bishop doesn't

take those kind of shot-in-the-dark risks. The application to see Roper was intended to do something else; it was never meant to actually succeed. Why would Bishop want to stir everything up again? To what end? Roper stays in prison for the rest of his natural anyway, and Bishop and his wife put themselves through the grinder all over again? Why?'

'He *might* still consider it worthwhile, one last chance to find out what happened to his daughter,' I said.

'Straws and clutching,' he said. 'Apart from which, I've got something a lot more useful for you.'

'A map of the hidden bodies?' I immediately regretted the remark and he understood this and let it pass.

'I've been going through the last of my files on the trial, peripheral stuff.'

But before he could explain any further, Yvonne took the phone from him. She gave me the address of the girl and her baby. Ten minutes passed before I was able to speak to Sunny again and ask him what he'd found.

9

James Bishop returned to see me later that afternoon. He'd called an hour earlier and asked if I'd finished with the albums. I'd suggested meeting somewhere more convenient, but he'd insisted on coming to the office. I asked him if Alison Menzies would be with him and he acted surprised at the remark. He seemed unconcerned by what little I told him about Wallis.

He came alone, and again he composed himself at the door before knocking and entering.

Once inside, he went first to the giant mirror and stood before it, studying himself, turning his head from side to side, like a man searching for something that he alone had not yet seen or acknowledged.

I watched him closely and did nothing to disguise my interest.

'So you know, at the very least, that he's been brought back here and that his appeal is going ahead,' he said without turning.

'And *you* knew that much before you even called me,' I said.

He closed his eyes briefly.

'Were the albums of any use?' he said. 'Tell me honestly.'

'I appreciated seeing them. I won't pretend to be

able to share your loss, not where it matters, but having seen Nicola I can see what she was to you and I can see what you lost with her death.'

'But the albums still told you more about me than about her, right?'

'What did you have to gain by pretending not to know that Roper had been brought back here?' I said.

'Nothing. I suppose I assumed it was important for you to find it out your own way. You have a reputation for being thorough, and I appreciate thoroughness. You can be thorough in this in a way I never could be.'

'There would have been cheaper and more discreet ways of finding out,' I said.

'I know.'

'Everything so far suggests that Roper's appeal will fail,' I said.

'I always understood that if an appeal was allowed to proceed, then it stood a better-than-even chance of succeeding.'

I considered this in silence.

He remained standing at the mirror, his back to me.

'I put the first of those albums together a month after Roper was convicted,' he said. 'I could feel her slipping away from us, even then. I wanted to be able to remember her, to remember her exactly as she was. Does that sound strange to you, Mr Rivers – that a father should begin to forget his own daughter? It's what I felt happening. There were so many images of her at the time of the searches and the trial, so many other people talking about her, telling me about her – my own daughter – people – so-called experts – who had never even met her, never known her, that I began to feel they were taking her away from me, that their claim on her was now somehow greater than my own. I have countless videotapes – birthdays, holidays, Christmases, outings, Nicola playing the piano, Nicola riding her pony, Nicola on a beach, Nicola in her new dress, all the usual stuff, and for months after she was lost I couldn't bring myself to watch a single frame of any of them. It was all *too* real, brought her *too* closely back to me. And so I turned instead to all those photographs and went searching for her there. They were my most valuable possessions. I made countless copies of them. It was how I wanted to see her and remember her. It was how I wanted her to *be*.' He half-turned to me, but then caught himself and turned away, his eyes again meeting mine only in the mirror. 'You've read the accounts of what Roper and the others did to those other girls, how Hayley Forbes was found, what they must all have endured before they were killed. Surely you can see how necessary, how vital some other memory, some other *idea* of Nicola was for me. She was always "Nicky" at home, but that never seemed appropriate in light of all that was discovered. We called her Nicola when she was in trouble, when we were angry with her. It was just one more way she was taken away from us.'

'Did your wife feel the same?'

'Patricia? Not exactly. Her own grieving was loud, immediate and intense. She and I have never been the same since. I won't pretend it was ever a perfect marriage beforehand, but neither of us was ever going to do anything to end it or to force the other to do something.'

'You had affairs?'

'I had affairs. None of them serious or long-lasting, but yes, I had them.'

'And your wife?'

'Two that I knew of, possibly another. Again, nothing that would cause her to throw away everything that we had together. We weren't leading those lives of quiet desperation so beloved of the poets, if that's what you're thinking.' He finally turned and came to the desk. 'Do you have anything to drink in here?' he said.

'I'm a private investigator,' I said. I pulled out the bottom drawer of the filing cabinet to reveal the bottle and glasses it contained.

'I thought perhaps dirty cups,' he said. He smiled and looked suddenly exhausted.

I poured the drinks.

'Nicola's death brought Patricia and me together in a way neither of us would have believed possible.'

'It would have been the final act of severance for most parents, strong or otherwise.'

'I know. And for a long time afterwards I think we both waited for that axe to fall. A few months after Roper was sentenced, Patricia took an overdose. I'm still not convinced that she was entirely serious in her intent, but I saw the gesture for what it truly was. She told me one night that she genuinely believed she had nothing left to live for. Neither of us could understand how, until then, we had lived such straightforward, comfortable, and, essentially, uncomplicated lives, and then how something so far beyond anyone's experience or expectation could reach in to us – to *us* – and grab us so tightly by the throats. Everything we had, everything we knew, just knocked to the ground and crushed. What good were our values, our principles, our notions of right and wrong after something like that? She wanted me to tell her why something like that had happened to us.'

I filled his empty glass and pushed it closer to his hand. He looked at it but didn't pick it up.

'And in trying to impose some reason, something to counter all those fears, you came to sound as though you were arguing against her,' I said. 'As though you – you alone – could begin to understand what had happened to your daughter.'

He nodded. 'To accept the unacceptable. To pretend to understand something which defied all reason and understanding.' He picked up the glass. 'She became pregnant again eighteen months after Nicola went missing. Which was something of a miracle in itself. Sex for us had become little more than a consoling distraction.'

'What happened?'

'She miscarried at twenty weeks. Everybody understood, of course, everybody sympathized. I imagine there were even those who thought it was for the best.'

'And that was about the time you compiled the album of Nicola's life.'

'I imagined it might be something she wanted, too.'

'And it wasn't?'

'She threw it in my face. I gave it to her at a small family gathering, I forget what. And she stared at it in disbelief and then threw it in my face. Someone else picked it up, saw what it was and gave it back to me without looking any more closely at what it contained. Patricia left the room, and even though half of those present hadn't got the faintest idea of what had just happened, they all said how sorry they were, how understandable everything was.'

'When exactly the opposite was true.'

He finally raised the glass and drank from it, running a hand across his lips.

'I lied to you three days ago because I hoped you might have begun to understand some of all this. After the trial, we felt abandoned. Everyone else packed up and moved on, leaving us stuck where we were and unable to move on. It seemed to me that there were so many loose ends, so many questions that should have been asked, but weren't.'

So many more places to look for the body of a murdered girl which were never searched.

'There's every indication that the conviction relating to Hayley Forbes will stand,' I said. I knew how cold and useless this attempt at reassurance would sound to him.

'And if I was *her* father, then I'm sure it would count for something.'

'Is that what you really want from me – to find out with a greater degree of certainty what happened to Nicola?'

He absently repeated the phrase. 'I need it more than I want it,' he said, equally absently. 'I don't want to

74

live for another thirty or forty or fifty years *not* knowing for certain what happened to her.'

'And if finding out only makes things worse?'

'It can't. Like I said, I no longer look for reason in
any of this. I know what a perverse and self-serving
thing logic can be. I just want to know. Whatever
happens, knowing cannot be worse than not knowing,
than all the imagining and guessing we've done these
past five years. Believe me, if I wasn't convinced of
that, I wouldn't be here now.

'And I won't pretend to you that I owe it to Nicola to
find out what happened to her. I'm doing this for
myself: it's a selfish act. I can't even pretend to myself
that it's what Patricia wants, not truly. She agreed to
my coming to see you, but only, I suspect, because,
like me, she once thought there might be some end in
sight to it all by now, that we might have come to
terms with what happened to us, that the wound
would at least have *begun* to heal. *Our* problem – hers
and mine – is that after Nicola was killed, nothing else
mattered. All those things that had once seemed so
important to us, they just vanished, evaporated. All
our little secrets – all our *big* secrets – all our avoid-
ances and lies, all those little omissions and
deceptions that keep any marriage or relationship
afloat, they all went. It's a difficult thing to cope with,
Mr Rivers – absolute honesty and openness. When
nothing matters – not even living or dying – then
everything loses its meaning and value.

'And then afterwards, once you finally accept that
nothing is ever going to be the same again, and that all
those old and reassuring and sustaining values have
gone for ever, you begin to impose new ones. You
begin to make trade-offs. You make bargains with
yourself. Except this time it isn't something small and
achievable. It isn't, Oh, I'll stop drinking for two
nights, but then I'll get wasted on the third; it's bigger
things, things that from the very outset you know are
beyond your control. And, usually, they all start, these

trade-offs, with the phrase "Please, God, just let Nicola be safe somewhere and I'll—", "Please, God, just let everyone have been wrong and just let her be missing from home and I'll—", "Just let a stupid mistake have been made and put her back on the doorstep one morning, crying and telling us all how stupid and unhappy she's been and I'll—"' He drained his glass and I gave him the bottle.

'And Roper?' I said.

He considered the question before answering me. 'I suppose if I'm being entirely honest, I don't care one way or another what happens to him. I want him to stay where he is, of course; I want him to rot until he starts to die, and I want him to die knowing what a wasted and pointless life he's lived. I want all that, but at the same time I do understand that there's nothing I can do about what happens to him from here onwards.'

'You're an influential man. You could press the police to make sure nothing changes. You could ask them to look again at some of those loose ends, ask some of those unasked questions.'

'My influence, as you call it, and such as it now is, extends only to those few people over whom I might be said to possess some power or control. It's money, Mr Rivers. As much as I might want to be liked or respected or admired for my noble and sterling character, my good works and charitable nature, it all comes down to money in the end. At the last count, I employed 120 people, and I doubt if there's a single one of them who, if I sacked him or her tomorrow, wouldn't turn around and tell me to my face that I got all I deserved.'

'Even those men and women with daughters of their own?'

'*Especially* those people with daughters of their own. Because they, you see, would know exactly what it was they were wishing on me. The rest would still belong to that vast majority of people who don't and can't have the faintest idea of the depth of that darkness out there, or the sharpness of the blade pressed so close to their throats. I hope you'll forgive the melodrama, Mr Rivers, but what good was all that so-called influence and power when Nicola was abducted and probably tortured and raped and humiliated before she was killed? What smallest pain did it ease or prevent then?'

I waited for him to finish because it mattered to him to say it. It was another of his rehearsed speeches, but no less painfully or unshakeably felt for that. It was all he had left to him. It was where the last vestige of his own humanity remained. And it remained, persisted, because, like the same uncertain feeling in the prostitute mother of the murdering girl I'd encountered downstairs, he did not know how to shake himself free of it, did not know how deeply it was now boring into his bones.

We sat without speaking for several minutes.

'Tell me exactly what it is you want me to do,' I said.

'You said it yourself – I want you to find out.'

'To find out what? Be precise.'

'Everything. I want to know what's happening now, and I want to know what happened then.'

'And you still refuse to believe the confession of the one man who might be able to tell you all this?'

'How can I? If he was telling the whole truth, if he didn't have some ulterior motive in making his confession, if he wasn't looking out for someone else, why didn't he say then what had happened to her and where she was buried or how he'd disposed of her body? Even if there was nothing left to find, he could still have done something for us, and for the parents of the others.'

'Forget Roper,' I said, seeing how implacable he remained. 'There's enough to go on without him. There's no doubt that an appeal will complicate matters, but it might just as easily work to our advantage in bringing more of what happened to light.'

'His so-called invisible "associates", you mean?'

'Them. And the concerns over how the original investigation was handled.'

I refilled my own glass.

'Which brings us to the second album, I suppose,' he said.

'Whatever your motives for compiling it, you gave it to me to make sure there was nothing I'd overlooked, including all the criticism immediately after Roper's trial relating to how the police had acted in securing that single conviction.'

'I compiled it because I couldn't believe they wouldn't do more once Roper was in prison.'

'Everything in his confession relating to Hayley Forbes was confirmed by the forensic evidence,' I said.

'I know. And I won't lie to you and say that I'm not 99.9 per cent convinced that exactly the same happened to Nicola.'

'And the 0.1 per cent?'

'This,' he said. 'Here, now, you, me, this.' He looked directly at me. 'It's a good place to live every now and again, that 0.1 per cent. All those sympathetic and understanding people, they all want you to believe that there's some kind of statute of limitations on how you feel about this kind of loss. Well, there isn't. It doesn't get any more bearable, and you don't get any better at coping with it. You might *appear* to, but that's all. People just assume things are better, and after a while it's easier all round not to try and disabuse them.'

'Let them go on thinking they're sharing something with you?'

He continued looking at me. 'Which is something I don't want from you, Mr Rivers.'

'And the final reason you compiled that second album', I said, 'was because for a long time you harboured ideas of somehow getting to Roper and killing him yourself.'

'I was going to find a murderer already serving life

with no hope of release and then offer to pay his family a fortune if he could get to Roper and kill him.'

'With a little torture thrown in?'

'With a lot of torture thrown in.'

'It might still be an option,' I said.

He shook his head.

'There would be plenty willing to try for you.'

'And if it had happened five years ago, it might have given me what I wanted.'

'It wouldn't have,' I said unnecessarily.

The two albums lay on the desk in front of him. He picked them up, smoothed flat their tissue covers and put them carefully into his case. I told him it would be useful for me to have some photographs of Nicola other than the stills taken close to when she had disappeared. I didn't know what use they would be, but I knew he would appreciate me asking for them. Everything else I needed, I had already drawn from Sunny's files.

He rose, momentarily surprised by how much he had drunk. He made a joke of steadying himself.

'I appreciate being able to talk like this,' he said. 'Bill me for this hour.'

'Two and a half,' I said.

'What?' He looked at his watch, and then at the gathering darkness beyond the window.

10

I was about to leave shortly afterwards, when someone else knocked at my door and then came in without waiting for my answer. I continued pulling on my coat.

He loosened his scarf and made a show of looking at every part of the room around him.

'I was looking for' – he pretended to hesitate and took a piece of paper from his pocket – 'Leo Rivers.'

'You missed him. He went an hour ago. If you want to leave your name and a number I'll get him to call you in the morning,' I said.

'That's a pity,' he said, but with no real disappointment in his voice. He took out his laminated warrant card. 'Detective Sergeant Finch,' he said.

'You could have gone through the motions of searching for it, perhaps even pretended you were brave enough to come in here without it,' I said. I took the card from him and looked at the photograph. The small birthmark on his cheek seemed more vivid on his cold flesh than in the picture.

He took it back, laid it on the desk and sat down. I did the same.

'Put it away,' I told him. 'I'll remember what you are.'

'I don't intend wasting your time, Mr Rivers,' he

said. 'And I'd appreciate it if we didn't have to go through all this. It's not exactly a coincidence that I'm here. I wasn't led here by strange voices or lights in the sky. You were seen earlier this morning. The Sportsman.'

I shook my head. 'Not me.'

'I have a timed and dated photograph of you sitting in there if it would help.'

'I was working,' I said.

'I don't doubt it. In fact, I know exactly what you were doing. First in the bar, and then afterwards in the bus shelter with wayward warder Wallis.'

'You're watching him?'

'Among others.'

'In connection with his disciplinary hearing?'

'That might come into it.'

I took off my coat.

He laid his own across his lap.

'You don't work locally,' I said. It was a prompting guess. I hadn't seen him before, but that meant nothing; his accent wasn't local.

'National Crime. You might say I'm here on a kind of temporary secondment.'

'And is that why you're here now?'

'You might say that.'

'Meaning you'll ask what you want to ask, but if it suits you afterwards—'

'I'll deny all knowledge of ever having met you.'

'Martin Roper,' I said.

'Possibly,' he said.

I took out my recorder and stood it on the desk. He looked at it for a moment and then flipped the tape out. 'I don't think so.'

'Am I going to fall down the stairs on my way out?' I said.

'First thing this morning, someone is sitting in a bar waiting to see Carl Boyd and—'

'Carl Boyd?'

'Cropped, dyed-blond hair. You saw him. He's the

man Wallis was waiting to see when you popped up. The one he took off with briefly after your own little encounter in the shelter. How much did that cost you, incidentally?'

'It cost my—'

'Your client. How much?'

'Fifty.'

'Wallis wouldn't spit on you for that. Let's call it a hundred, minimum. You should have said sixty. Who's going to start splitting twenties? Anyhow, there we are, waiting for the boy Boyd, and who should turn up but you. The watcher was a local man. He recognized you, not at first, but eventually.'

'I might just have been thirsty.'

'Of course you might. And that's why you spent almost an hour pretending to read a newspaper and all the time keeping your eye on the pool-room.'

'So what's going on between Wallis and this Boyd?'

He considered his answer before speaking, letting me know that he was giving me more than he needed to give me, that something reciprocal now existed between us. I offered him a cigarette, which he took.

'Most of the Class Cs which find their way into the prison find their way there via Boyd and one or two others.'

'Including Wallis?'

He fluttered his hand.

'So are you connected to the Drug Squad?' I said.

'I don't think they'd need a man like me to crack something like this open.'

'No,' I said.

'No one ever stops the stuff completely,' he said. 'Occasionally there's an outcry and everything gets confiscated, but not for long. Boyd works hand in glove with stewards on the ferries. It's still mostly cannabis – the low-level convicted felon's regular drug of choice – and mostly it's on a scale small enough for everyone locally to keep tabs on.'

'Are you suggesting that the forces of law and order

hereabouts might be complicit in all this? I'm shocked.'

'No, what's shocking is Boyd or Wallis thinking they're getting away with all this unobserved. The current estimate is that they're probably doubling their wages with it.'

'And soon they'll get greedier?'

'Perhaps.'

He was telling me all this because it didn't concern him. Martin Roper being in the prison was still too big a coincidence.

'So what do you think Carl Boyd is to me?' I said.

He laughed. 'I don't think you had the faintest idea who he was until I just mentioned him. Bear with me. Our man in the bar comes back, tells us what happened, shows us his pictures, and there you are.'

'And because *you* are here, in Hull, in connection with Roper and not Boyd or Wallis, someone informs you?'

'Let's just say I was intrigued to understand what possible connection there might be. Perhaps you're working on behalf of another prisoner's family and hoping to meet up with one of the warders, who knows? Why else would anyone be *there* at that time in the morning? I asked around. No one knew where to locate you. You worked with John Maxwell. He's still very highly regarded, locally. I'd hoped people might laugh when I mentioned your name.'

'John Maxwell went when—'

'We know when John Maxwell went, and why.'

We.

'And so someone eventually pointed you to me,' I said. 'Then what?'

'Please, I'm a detective. Someone said you were tight with Summers. I went to see him. He and Yvonne, of course, denied having seen you for weeks. They were very good – they didn't even exchange eye signals. You should check your messages more often – he'll have called to tell you I was coming.'

'And he will know who you are by now and have started working things out for himself – why you're here, for instance.'

'Nothing of which he will know for certain. Unless you tell him. Which, all things considered, might not be the wisest thing to do.' Backtracking. 'Unfortunately, the sallow youth in charge of the fax machine chose that moment to return with the ham and pickle sandwiches and so not a great deal more was asked or told.'

'And so here you are,' I said.

'And so here I was ten minutes ago, when who should I see leaving but local worthy James Bishop.'

'Perhaps he has yoga classes upstairs.'

'Or perhaps, having got wind of Roper's return, he was here asking you to find out what happened to his daughter for him. Roper sitting in the prison, you sitting in the bar, our man sitting beside you, James Bishop sitting in this very chair, and now me and you, sitting here and marvelling at how wonderful and ful-filling a day's detective work can occasionally be.'

'I have to respect my client confidentiality,' I said.

He laughed. 'No, you don't. It doesn't exist. It's just words to make everyone feel better about being deceit-ful. It's just something you make up because it gives everything the appearance of being cosy and discreet and which helps to get the bills paid on time.'

I rose, went to the window and looked out. His car was parked twenty yards along the road, outside the Sports and Arts Club. If he'd arrived when he said, then he would have seen James Bishop leaving. He would also have had to have known who James Bishop was to have identified him before coming up to see me.

'The white Vectra?' I said.

He gave me the registration. 'And, yes, I already knew who James Bishop was.'

'So have you been watching him, too?'

'Not really. Not *watching* watching. Just keeping an eye on him.'

'So to speak.'

'So to speak.'

'Because of Roper's appeal?'

'At the time of his daughter's disappearance, James Bishop swore publicly to get to Roper and to kill him.'

'He said a lot of things. A lot of people said a lot of things.'

'I know.'

He knew considerably more than he was telling me. He knew either because he'd been involved in the original investigation or because he was involved in another one now.

'What you're thinking', he said, screwing up his eyes as though making a difficult calculation, 'is that I've suddenly just become far more useful to you than you were ever going to be to me.'

'No – what I'm thinking is that you've just realized that *I* might now be of some use to you because of my unexpected connection to James Bishop. Why come up here otherwise?'

He considered this. 'Don't worry, no one believes in the bloody-revenge theory any more. Someone spoke with James Bishop after the first trial. I doubt he could tell us or promise us anything now he didn't tell us or promise us then.'

'Someone?'

'Someone.'

'And Roper?'

'What about him?'

'Were you invited here by the locals to see what new information *he* might be willing to reveal?'

' "Invited" might be stretching a point. Let's just say I'm part of a wider investigation. Apart from which, anything new that Roper might have to let out of the bag now, he'll be saving for his appeal where it will do him the most good.'

'The word at the time was that Sullivan was too keen to close the book on him and all he'd confessed to, that the net wasn't cast as widely or as urgently as it might have been cast.'

'I love all these mixed metaphors,' he said. 'Is it a speciality?' He knew everything there was to know about Sullivan and the original investigation. 'I know all about Sullivan. The feeling at the time was three-cheers-all-round for a job well done and a child-killer behind bars. There was a great deal of pressure, top and bottom, to get this one over and done with and tidied away.'

'Is that what *you* are telling me now?'

'They were all local girls and their killer was a local man caught by the local force with a local born and bred at their head. It was what everybody wanted to see. The first of the girls had been missing almost a year before Roper was caught. A year of that kind of publicity.'

'But you and your own masters still believed a greater opportunity was being missed?'

'We knew Roper wasn't operating alone. We were a specialist unit. Paedophilia, seven years ago? What was it? Who wanted to know? Don't confuse any of this with those current late-night Internet dabblers dipping their toes while their wives and own kids are asleep.'

'And despite what was known, everyone was still told to back off.'

'The local Chief Constable made a lot of noise. We were accused of coming in at the last minute and attempting to steal the limelight from all those hard-working local boys with Sullivan at their head.'

'And you think the appeal might finally provide you with the opportunity to do something now that you weren't able to do then?'

'We're not sure the appeal will achieve anything at all.'

'But the thought of *something* happening, of the possibility of *legitimately* going over old ground is already beginning to stir a stick through the mud?'

Neither of us spoke for several minutes. He'd told me more than he had intended to tell me. I suggested leaving and going to a nearby bar, but he said he'd rather not. He was driving to Leeds later that night.

'Was there ever any doubt in your own mind that Roper was guilty?' I asked him.

'For the death of Hayley Forbes? None whatsoever. He did it. They didn't make public half of the details of what he'd done.'

'The half you used to check against her corpse.'

'And the details they did release were more than enough to create the sense of public outrage which gave the locals all the reasons they needed for speeding things along towards the end.'

'And for Sullivan's achievement in catching him to become the PR job it was needed to be,' I said. 'Was there ever enough evidence to make any of the other cases stick?'

'Nicola Bishop, for instance? It was decided by the CPS that those charges where the bodies hadn't been retrieved and examined might take something away from the charge relating solely to Hayley Forbes. There would always be doubt by association, just as there was condemnation by association. The prosecution were angry when Roper's defence began making those same suggestions. The judge should have stopped them dead there and then and withdrawn the jury, but it was too late. It was the only defence Roper had and they knew it. They also knew that it was unlikely to save him or even to reduce his sentence for killing Hayley Forbes, but they couldn't resist using it. Strangely, Roper himself was unwilling for it to be brought up in his defence.'

'And now it might form the basis of his appeal?'

'I imagine the prosecution thought the other bodies would have turned up by now and that there would have been plenty of evidence tying them to Roper, in which case none of that uncertainty or suspicion would have mattered.'

'And if the other bodies had turned up, you would have found a way of using the discovery to open things up again in the hope of identifying and getting to Roper's mysterious accomplices.'

He laughed at the word. 'Whatever you or Summers or James Bishop might prefer to believe, there was never anything mysterious about Roper's accomplices. Roper was never their accomplice. He was a procurer, that's all. Unfortunately, at the time, our experts weren't able to establish a single conclusive connection between Roper and anyone else in the network. There's a likelihood that he sent material to over two hundred others, but the system was rigged in such a way that, although we could trace it all going out, we could never identify the recipients. Coded links were established all along the line which broke the traceable sequence of transmission and reception every time. It was six, seven years ago. All this stuff was only just beginning. It was still unregulated. Very little prior to this had alerted us to how sophisticated these networks were becoming.'

'But they still needed men like Roper to supply them.' All I had known so far was that Roper had made good use of his photographic skills and contacts to sell pornographic pictures and videos of the girls he had persuaded to pose and perform for him. The fact that he was involved with an early network sending out material to paedophiles was news to me. I knew by the way Finch spoke that he assumed I understood all this already. I did nothing to disabuse him.

'To run most of the risks, yes,' he said.

'Surely, the ring will have disbanded when Roper was arrested. They wouldn't risk going on operating, not knowing what he might reveal.'

'You'd be surprised what they believed they could go on getting away with. It was a profitable business. Some of their customers were paying upwards of three hundred pounds a month for what they were being sent.'

'Couldn't you trace them that way?'

'No law to say they have to identify themselves. Still isn't. Payment in cash or money order. No way, anyhow, of getting to bank files without a warrant relating to specific and provable charges.'

'Did Roper never suspect he was being used, or that he'd be sacrificed when the time came?'

'Suspect? He revelled in it. By all accounts, he was getting a little carried away with himself, with what he thought he could achieve, what he could provide, what a linchpin he'd become. And why not – he'd been getting away with it for long enough already, working by himself.'

'*If* he was responsible for the deaths of those other girls,' I said.

'Do you know something which says he wasn't?' He looked at me without speaking for a moment. 'Is that what you'd tell James Bishop? That someone *else* was responsible for his daughter's death, someone who's never spent a single day in prison and may never do so?'

'If it was the truth,' I said.

'There isn't anything. It's just hard to accept that Roper got away with it for so long, that's all. With or without such an inept investigation.'

'How many girls do you think Roper used?' I said.

'Ten times more than those whose names ever entered the inquiry. In the beginning he only worked with those who were happy, for whatever reason, to comply with what he wanted. Older teenagers pretending to be younger, that sort of thing.'

'And always girls?'

He clicked his lips. 'As far as we know.'

'Can I see what he was providing?'

'Not officially. I'll see what I can bring back with me from Leeds.' Which meant that he did intend using me and my connection to James Bishop to his own ends.

'Why Leeds?'

'It was as close, the first time, as the locals would let us come. It suited us. We already knew there was a ring operating in West Yorkshire, and I suppose we hoped that sooner or later we'd find a connection between this ring and the one Roper catered to.'

'How much of this can I relay to James Bishop?' I said.

'I haven't told you anything he hasn't already known for the past five years. And if he didn't know it for certain then, he'll have long since worked it out. At the time, he was as angry as we were that all the energy and attention of the inquiry was being focused solely on Roper at the expense of the others.'

'And so he might not truly believe that Roper, despite his confession, was solely responsible for his daughter's death.'

'I'd hoped you might have worked that much out for yourself by now.'

'It would have come to me before too long,' I said.

He rose to leave. He seemed suddenly tired at the prospect of the journey ahead of him.

'What I still don't understand', I said, 'is why, knowing what he knew, Roper didn't try to take all or some of the others down with him.'

He laughed again, knowing that I'd been saving the question. 'We thought at first that he'd done a deal with them – keep them out of it and they would provide the evidence that would guarantee the success of his appeal.'

'It doesn't seem likely, not after five years.'

'It's not. Except we have to remember that with the wholesale and unexpected disappearance of most of the computer-based evidence, Roper suddenly wasn't holding such a strong hand.'

'It disappeared?'

'Went missing.'

'Sullivan's team?'

'Do you want to suggest that, or shall I?'

'He could still have told you everything he knew, implicated many more,' I said.

'Which is why those of us currently involved prefer scenario B.'

'Which is?'

'That he knew he was going to go down for the murder of Hayley Forbes and that guarantees were made to him to the effect that everything else would be repackaged – all the doubts and confusion thrown up by his confession, all that public outrage at the abduction of the others, to which he also confessed, and for which he was always considered responsible, but for which he was never charged because of the absence of any hard evidence – and all of it ready for use by his lawyers at an appeal.'

'Bit of a risk, I would have thought, knowing that he might still serve life for the murder he was convicted of.'

'What other option did he have? Except perhaps Roper wasn't as mindlessly greedy, as evil or as blind as Sullivan tried to make him out to be at the time, and he put aside a little insurance.'

'Evidence to incriminate the others if his appeal failed?'

'Sullivan wanted Roper convicted hard and fast. Anything or anyone else involved was only going to dilute or cast doubts on his own achievement and glory.'

'But you remain convinced it exists, this evidence?'

'And that, on whatever basis Roper's appeal is lodged – and everyone's still looking at the undisclosed bodies, remember – surprise, surprise, this new evidence turns up, gets its first proper hearing and Roper's chances of walking from an unsafe conviction suddenly look much brighter. They drag up everything else the investigating team didn't do properly in the first place, they get a sympathetic judge . . . On a scale of one to ten of it happening like that, I wouldn't rate it any higher than a three or a four. But, like I said, it's considerably better than what he's got now.'

He went to the door and waited.

'So what happens next?' I said.

'Meaning?'

'Will you let me know if anything new does turn up?'

'Officially? Probably not.'

'And if I go on stirring that stick through the five-year-old mud ostensibly on James Bishop's behalf?'

'You *are* that stick,' he said. He opened the door and then closed it again. He came back to the desk, took out a piece of paper and wrote a number on it.

'What *are* you going to do now?' he said.

I shrugged. 'Go and see Sullivan? Go and see James Bishop's wife.' It was as much as I wanted to say. 'Go on flapping about like a little silvery fish to see what comes up out of the depths to take a bite at me like you intend.'

'Be warned. Sullivan is up to scratch on all this. Don't imagine that anything you say to him stays with him. He's a vain man; he knows what all this raking over cold ashes is likely to do to his reputation.'

'And that's worth more than all those dead and missing girls, is it?'

He considered this, perhaps waiting for me to apologize for the crass remark. 'To him it might be.'

He went after that, and I waited where I sat for several minutes wondering why he had just revealed so much to me – knowing only that I had been told for a reason, and that, as yet, I didn't have the faintest idea what that reason might be.

The muted music of the evening's exercise class came down to me from the room above. Outside, the rain had turned to sleet, and it gathered in floating balls around the streetlights.

I left, keeping step along the corridor with the dancers above me.

11

I went to the address Roper had been living at with his mother at the time of his arrest. It was the house in which he had lived all his life; it was where Sullivan had arrived at five o'clock on the morning of the tenth of October, 1998, to arrest him in full view of everyone watching.

The Preston Road Estate had seen better times, and they would be times beyond the memory of most of the people currently living there. Most of the houses had been sold off to their tenants when the opportunity to buy them first arose. A few people bought cheaply, sold early, made profits and moved out. Most – those who had not lived there so long and who did not qualify for the large discounts – committed themselves to first-time mortgages and bought at what they were told were below-market prices. But they were first-time buyers in a first-time and failing market and the properties did not hold their value. The new owners saw their debts and losses mount. Housing agencies moved in and bought up what became available. People in debt sold their homes at a loss and returned to renting. Private developers followed the agencies, and the loan-sharks followed the developers. It was called debt-servicing.

On the day I arrived I got lost and drove in circles

trying to locate Roper's old home. The directions I was given only complicated matters.

I had come because so far everything I knew about Martin Roper and about the disappearance of Nicola Bishop had either been told to me by others or I had read it in the words of others.

When I started working with John Maxwell much of what we did involved either repossession or debt-collection of sorts. When we occasionally did undertake work that was genuinely investigative, he always told me to find out as much as I could from the mouths of those involved. And then to forget nine-tenths of that and go to the places where those people lived. I thought at first that he was joking, that this approach was too simplistic, as delusive and evasive as all those self-serving spoken accounts, but I soon learned that he had a point. He called these forays his 'site visits', and said that because we weren't looking for what everyone else was looking for, we would either see something different from everyone else, or see the same things differently. Sometimes, this return to base worked; sometimes it didn't. Regardless, he insisted it needed to be done. If you listen too long to what the same few people are telling you, then after a while you hear only their voices. Sometimes, he once told me, the noise made by a gate swinging on its hinges in the darkness, or of a distant car driving quickly away, was the only sound you should be listening out for.

He taught me that nothing was ever wasted, however incidental or inconsequential it might at first appear. The important clues were never big or obvious: you were never going to be pointed towards them by people who didn't want you to see them. A thing you discovered for yourself, however small, and however quickly you might afterwards disregard it, was always something worth dis-covering. Something you were told or pointed towards was just another line in a maze.

I sat with him for seemingly endless days tracking

errant husbands and wives. 'Errant' was his word. He lived by a simple code, and regardless of how often or how forcibly he was disabused of this, it was something he always returned to at the start of each investigation. He taught me not to judge people until I properly understood them. He taught me not to judge people by their own standards. He taught me to understand those standards but never to confuse them with my own. He told me the day I started working with him that honesty was always the best policy, and I laughed at hearing this. He told me to go on laughing. He told me never to let my work become a crusade. Good and evil existed everywhere, and all too often the two were indistinguishable one from the other. When the client stopped paying, he said, we stopped investigating. Most of them, he said, didn't know what they wanted in the first place, so all we could assume in most instances was that people wanted to know for certain something they had so far only been able to guess at. Leave retribution and revenge to them, he said. Revenge was a dish best served with a big and well-documented financial demand stapled to it.

He taught me the basics – how to look, how to follow, how to unravel – and the rest I picked up by working alongside him. I was paid according to results, and some weeks it was nothing.

After eight years together, he'd retired. He went back to his own birthplace in County Durham and had lived there ever since. We still spoke occasionally. For a year or so after his departure I'd rung him for advice, and for five or six months he'd given it.

It was why I'd gone to the Preston Road Estate, why I was sitting outside the former home of a man who had confessed to the murder of four teenage girls and whom the world had christened a monster.

In the small front garden a For Sale sign and a For Rent sign had been planted, neither with much hope of success. I could see at least a dozen others in the neighbouring gardens.

I left my car and went to the door. The house had been long empty. The glass in the door had been smashed. A scorch mark rose from the letter-box. Someone had boarded over the downstairs windows. Arcane symbols had been painted beside each door-way by the power companies.

I walked back to the street. A man came towards me and stopped to watch me, doing nothing to disguise his interest.

'I was supposed to meet the letting agent,' I said, indicating the sign.

'And?'

'You don't know where their nearest office is, do you?'

'They never turn up. No point. Nobody ever rents. The council sometimes puts people in from bigger shit-holes, but that's all.'

'Not a good place to rent, then?' I said.

'There's a small office down there.' He pointed to the line of shops further along the road. 'It's not always open, just somewhere for them to advertise.' He looked at the house. 'You seriously interested?'

'I'm not sure.'

Our conversation was at an end and he walked away from me.

I went to the shops and found the letting agent's. I went in and asked the woman at the desk if anyone could show me the house.

She rifled through a mound of leaflets. She looked at the few details. There was a blank space where the self-defeating photograph should have been.

As she handed me the leaflet, the door behind her opened and a young man in a badly fitting suit came in to us.

'Can I be of any assistance?' he said immediately.

The woman, twenty years his senior, looked at him disparagingly.

'Peter Talbot,' he said, and held out his hand to me. The cuffs of his shirt were too long. His top button

96

showed above his tie. I shook his hand. Customer relations.

'This gentleman was interested in renting number thirty-seven,' the woman said.

'I'm sure something can be arranged.'

She told him the name of the road, and if he understood anything by this, then nothing showed.

'I was wondering if I could have a quick look round,' I said.

'There's a dozen others practically within sight of the place,' the woman said, convincing me that she, at least, knew something of the house's history and that she did not believe my reason for wanting to see it.

'I'm not really bothered,' I told her. 'It's only for six months. It looked much the same as all the others.'

'If the gentleman wants to see number thirty-seven, Janice, then that's what he shall see.' He said this with what he probably imagined was a flourish. He took the details from me. 'I'm free now, if you like.' He turned back to the woman. 'Do we have a key?'

'Of course we have a key,' she said slowly, as though talking to a child. She went to a filing cabinet and took out an envelope.

'What first attracted you to one of our properties?' he asked me. 'And, if you don't mind me asking, to the whole notion of renting as opposed to buying?'

'Perhaps he saw the place first,' the woman said.

'Yes, Janice, thank you.'

'Is it not a very popular property?' I said, feigning doubt.

'No different from a thousand others,' he said. 'So, rest assured, if it doesn't suit you, I can personally recommend half a dozen more.' He shook the key in my face. Before leaving, he picked up a briefcase, another brochure, a mobile phone and a pager. 'I'll be at—'

'Number thirty-seven,' the woman said.

'Half an hour tops. The place will do the work for me.'

'Don't forget to mention the southerly aspect,' she said. She smiled coldly at me as we left.

He made a big deal of holding the door and saying, 'After you.' Customer care.

'She didn't seem too keen on the place,' I said to him as we walked back to the house.

He checked his phone for the messages it did not hold. 'Third generation,' he said, holding it up for me to see. 'This time next year I'll be showing you houses on it. Janice? Ignore her.'

'I just wondered if it had a history or something.'

'History? All properties have a bit of history attached, it's what makes them unique, different from all the others.'

'I meant a history of faults or something, damp, rot, that sort of thing.'

'Every single one of the properties we prepare for letting undergoes a rigorous forty-point inspection. Forty. Anything comes up, we deal with it.'

We arrived at the address.

I looked along the line of forlorn and empty houses.

He seemed surprised by the broken glass and the burn mark on the door. 'That needs seeing to,' he said. 'I'll just . . .' He took out a pen and wrote on the brochure. 'Don't worry,' he told me. 'You decide to rent, and everything will be sorted before you move in. You have my personal guarantee on that. You have my word and you have the company guarantee.' He opened the door and motioned for me to enter ahead of him.

The house was cold and damp and smelled of its neglect. The scorch mark on the outside of the door was twice the size on the inside. The carpet, too, was burned. I made a point of looking at this.

'Kids,' he said. He wrote again on the brochure. 'No respect for nothing.'

A small table stood at the bottom of the stairs, and a neatly stacked pile of junk mail had been piled on it. A solitary brightly coloured envelope lay on the circle of burned carpet.

'Lucky the place didn't burn down,' I said.

'Always looks worse than it is, that sort of thing. They don't mean anything by it. They just get it into their heads to do something and there's no stopping them.'

'Has it been empty long?'

'Six months?' He didn't know.

Following his public and well-publicized arrest, Roper's mother had been threatened and intimidated throughout the duration of his remand and trial, but had refused to leave the house. She had died in the caravan fire over a year later.

She had stayed away from his trial, but throughout it had insisted on her son's innocence. Even in the face of his confession, she had gone on proclaiming this. It had been pointed out to her that Roper had been living with her all the time he had been procuring, filming and killing the girls, but there had never been any evidence to suggest that she had known of this, or that anything had taken place at the house itself. Roper had rented a small photographic studio at the rear of a chemist's shop on Anlaby Road, which had long since been demolished, and where a sheltered-housing complex now stood.

'The smell soon clears,' he said. 'Once you get it aired. Six months, you said. What is it, new job?'

'How did you know?' I said, encouraging him.

'I'm a good judge of human nature,' he said, as though this explained everything. 'Don't tell me – wife and kids waiting to move in once you've got somewhere sorted. How many?'

'Two,' I said.

'That would have been my guess. Don't tell me – boys, six and four.'

'Seven and four. That's incredible.'

'It's this work. You get to meet a lot of people. Usually, it's not property we're selling, it's people.'

'Right.'

I opened the door to the room looking out over the

street. A plain brown carpet covered the floor. A gas-fire stood in a hearth of artificial stone.

'Easily make this a cosy little family house,' he said.

The whole property had been sealed, taken apart and searched during the days following Roper's arrest. The front and back gardens had been dug up. Roper's mother had been prevented from going back there for a week. A camera had been lowered down the chimney. The drains had been inspected. Holes were drilled in wall cavities, and the floorboards were taken up in all the rooms. Nothing was found.

The Anlaby Road studio had been demolished less than two months earlier, along with the line of shops of which it had been a part – a fact frequently raised by the police's critics once Sullivan's original operation to catch Roper had come under scrutiny.

Roper's mother had known nothing of her son's involvement with the other men or with the under-age girls who had posed and then performed for them all.

'There's another downstairs room, dining, and then the kitchen,' the youth said. 'What line of work is it?'

'Sales,' I said, thinking as I spoke. 'Sales rep for IT installation.'

He looked puzzled.

'Between you and me,' I said, 'I work for a firm that sells and installs computer systems for other firms that haven't got the first idea what it is they're buying or what they're going to do with it once it's installed.'

'Right. IT,' he said. 'Will I have heard of it?'

'Infotech,' I said.

'Clever,' he said.

'They think so.'

He told me what computer he owned, how invaluable it was to him, how long he spent on the Internet most nights, and how many of his friends he had met as a result of this.

The kitchen was small, cramped and badly arranged.

'Everything to hand,' he said. 'Besides which, I don't

imagine you'll be spending too much time in here yourself.' He winked at me.

I went to the rear door and looked out over the garden, as neglected and as bare as the one at the front of the house.

If it occurred to him to wonder why anyone with such a high-powered job as I professed to have was looking at such a dump, then he was also sufficiently aware of his likely commission on any lease not to mention it.

He came to stand beside me. 'You're looking at a day's work, less. Bit of decking, some grass for the kids. You could even put in a few plants, bushes, that sort of thing.'

I sensed then, in those few words, that he had finally lost faith in securing my signature.

'I'd hoped there might be some sort of garage or something,' I said. 'Company car. They prefer to know it's secure at night.' There were rows of padlocked garages throughout the estate, some attached to nearby houses, but most rented privately by owners who had no use for them. Every single one, over four hundred, had been searched by Sullivan's team.

In one, over two hundred stolen televisions, four hundred video recorders and almost twice that number of car radios had been found. In another, a nineteen-year-old mother was found to be living with her two children, having been forced out of her nearby home by a violent boyfriend. When told she could not continue living there, she said she preferred it to the house. The garage was carpeted and she and her children had everything they needed there.

'Can I look upstairs?' I said.

'We rent from the top to the bottom of the range,' he said to me. 'I'm stuck here, showing these, but we have properties everywhere – you name it – Willerby, Anlaby, Cottingham. I can give one of our other branches a call if you like.'

'The fact is,' I said, lowering my voice, 'I'd be out

there like a shot, but my wife isn't too keen on coming here at all. It looks as though I might be making the move by myself, going home at weekends, that kind of thing. Naturally, the company will help with the move, but they won't be too keen when they find out she's dragging her heels.'

'And so you wanted somewhere cheap and functional?' he said.

'I'm away a lot, customers.'

'Hotels, that sort of thing?'

I went to the bottom of the stairs and looked up.

He studied the brochure. 'Bath, three bedrooms, access to a loft space, unfloored.' He read off the dimensions of each of the rooms.

I went up ahead of him.

The smallest of the bedrooms was big enough for a single bed with barely a foot of space on either side of it.

The hatch to the loft was out of reach in the landing ceiling.

The smell of damp in the bathroom was twice as strong as anywhere else in the house. The lines of white grout between the tiles around the sink, toilet and bath had long since turned brown.

The second bedroom was as empty as the rooms downstairs. The bare boards were revealed. He followed me into it, but could think of nothing to say in its favour.

I left him there and went alone into the third bedroom at the rear of the house. It was from here that the computer and printer Roper had used at home had been removed. All the equipment from the Anlaby Road studio had disappeared at the time of its demolition.

I remembered an account of a press conference at which Sullivan himself had ridiculed the suggestion that what he was doing in removing and searching the computer was either illegal or unethical. He played to public sentiment. He knew as little then about the

102

technology and its capabilities as the vast majority of those watching him and craving only the conviction of the monster in their midst.

The room still contained a bed-frame, stood on its end against one of the walls. A line of four sockets had been fitted beside it. Two more lay by the door. A cork notice board remained fixed to one wall. A triple phone socket sat beneath the plastic window-sill.

The police had expected to find much more. They had expected everything in the house to confirm for them the guilt of the man they had arrested there and who was already making his controversial confession. Hayley Forbes's body had been found at the disused railway siding twenty-eight days earlier. As part of his confession, Roper had drawn a map of the siding and had located the body on it.

'Looks like somebody used it as an office or something,' the agent said. 'You could do the same with it.'

But by then we both knew that I would not be renting the house, that no one would, that it was long beyond salvation. There had been calls for it to be destroyed, but these had been unsuccessful. It had first been rented eighteen months after Roper's trial. In the following four years it had changed hands three times, remaining empty for increasingly longer spells between tenants.

I went to the cork notice board and studied its pattern of holes, as though there might still be something to see there after all those years, as though only Roper had ever used it. Perhaps a photograph had been tucked behind the board and overlooked by one of Sullivan's men. Perhaps a book of matches advertising a cheap hotel had fallen through a gap in the floorboards.

A hundred drawing-pins were still scattered across the board. Perhaps one of them still contained Martin Roper's thumbprint. Perhaps one of them contained the fingerprint of one of the missing girls. The police had taken everything away. They had searched the roof space, drained the water tanks, taken out the light bulbs and scraped up the dust from beneath every piece of furniture in every room into evidence bags.

There was nowhere else for me to look.

Back outside, he gave me the brochure and his card. I indicated where my car was parked.

'I'll say you're thinking about it and that you'll be in touch, shall I?'

'Sure,' I said.

He held out his hand to me again. 'Pleasure meeting you.' For a moment he forgot the name I had given him, but then he remembered it and made a point of using it before we finally parted.

12

Detective Chief Inspector Richard Sullivan had retired to Kilnsea on the east coast at the neck of the Spurn peninsula in May 1999, ten months before his official retirement was due, and four months before Roper's eventual conviction for the killing of Hayley Forbes. I knew from the reports in Sunny's files that although there had already been some early unofficial criticism of the way Sullivan had handled the case, this had remained largely low-key and unpublished. It had apparently been Sullivan's own decision to bring his retirement forward upon the local Police Authority agreeing – especially in light of his recent and much publicized achievement – to award him his full pension.

The official reason for him retiring early was his wife's long illness. She had died in Kilnsea seven months later.

I drove out of the city eastwards, through Keyingham and Patrington, across the boundary of Sunk Island and the Humber in the south.

The world was flat here, all sky and the occasional steeple, and the sea only inches below the level of the drained and reclaimed land it endlessly entered and occasionally threatened. The families who lived and farmed here clung to this mud and clay like wild grass. It seemed a soulless place – a place without obvious landmarks or variety. Tractors, abandoned twenty years ago after their final, faltering day's work, still stood rusting in the corners in which they had been left.

Outside Hedon, a long avenue of severely pollarded willows rose from the flatness like clenched fists.

In one of the photographs in Sunny's files, Sullivan and his wife posed together at the gate of their retirement bungalow. 'A Rest Well Earned', the headline said. Sullivan stood with his arm around his wife's shoulders. She stands a foot shorter than him and the gesture looks both unwanted and unnatural. The bungalow was her own short-lived dream, not his.

Twenty years earlier, Sullivan had had a reputation as a violent man. The world of policing had changed around him, and he had clung to the rock and anchor of his solid, nose-to-the-ground, hard-won reputation. He had risen through the ranks and had become unassailable. In the photograph, the bungalow, its garden, garden gate and name-plate are all clearly visible.

Beyond the Long Bank Bridge, where the Spurn peninsula became visible, I slowed down. The road here was narrow, and built up along only one side. Some of the dwellings betrayed their origins as the railway carriages they had once been, the dimensions of their walls and windows still clearly discernible. Some of the houses were used only as holiday homes, closed and secured at the end of each summer until the following Easter. I estimated half the dwellings to be empty on the day I drove past them on my way to see him.

It had been perhaps seven or eight years since I had last been to Spurn. It was a popular destination for people from the city. I wondered about the closeness of Roper's mother's caravan – itself long gone – less than two miles away at Easington.

On the other side of the road lay an expanse of

ploughed land, as dark and shiny as chocolate, and broken only by the steep and narrow drains which flowed into the Humber half a mile away. The tide was out, but the mud-flats shone and reflected the sun in blinding planes.

It was an empty, abandoned place, and I imagined that many of those who came to live there after lives elsewhere soon regretted the decision and returned to their true homes. In another valedictory article on Sullivan, the bungalow was referred to as his wife's 'Dream of a Lifetime', and one long anticipated, according to her husband. Both of them must have known how close she was to dying when the article was written and they said what they said.

The road curved, and in the distance I saw the raised end of Spurn and its lighthouses and lifeboat station. The buildings along the road grew fewer and more widely spaced, and it occurred to me that I'd come too far. No car travelling along the road at this time of year would ever pass unnoticed.

I drew to the side and got out. A concrete culvert and rusted sluice gate had been built into the low bank, and I climbed onto this to look around me. In every direction, towards the sea, towards the estuary, and back into the Levels of Holderness, the land stretched seamlessly into the glare of the sky. Cattle grazed on the land beyond the bank, sunk to their knees in the winter grass and soft ground.

I returned to the car, studied the copy of the photograph I had, and looked back along the houses. Towards the far end of the road, three or four buildings from the end, and beyond which only the telegraph poles ran, stood Sullivan's bungalow.

I drove to it and stopped at the gate. The name-plate was no longer in place, but it was the same house. The small garden was already stripped and pruned for the coming winter in that exposed place: a lawn, a few roses, a path bordered by white stones gathered from the beach.

There was little chance that Sullivan had not already seen me.

I left the car, opened the gate and walked to the door. I expected to see him watching me approach, but there was no one.

The bungalow was more substantially built than those on either side of it, both of which were mostly wooden in construction. A small, curved porch framed the door, into which was set a circle of coloured glass.

I rang the bell.

I waited, hearing someone inside, a radio or television being switched off. I stood back from the glass and watched as someone came towards me.

Sullivan opened the door, looked at me and said nothing. He was slighter than I had imagined him to be. He wore black polished shoes, trousers held up by a belt fastened a notch too tight, a white shirt fastened at its cuffs, and a dark blue Police Association tie.

'Mister Sullivan?' I said.

'Would saying "Detective Chief Inspector" be giving too much away?' he said. Then, and afterwards, every time he spoke he gave the impression of having a bad taste in his mouth, as though the whole world had turned sour upon his resignation. The expression on his face seldom changed.

'Detective Chief Inspector,' I said.

'You can add "retired" if you think it gives you some advantage.'

I was unprepared for this immediate hostility. I had spent the whole of my journey considering what I was going to say to him.

It was clear to me that he already knew who I was, meaning that someone still on the force was keeping him informed – someone else, perhaps, who resented Finch's present involvement, possibly an old member of Sullivan's original team, perhaps even the watcher in the bar.

'I'm Leo Rivers,' I said.

He looked over my shoulder at my car and then slowly along the full length of the road. 'I know who you are,' he said. 'But, more importantly, you *know* I know. And because I know who you are, you can also take it that I know *why* you're here. And, to keep things simple, you knew that, too. And shall I tell you something else? While you were driving out here looking for this place, you've been looking out of your window and wondering where they might be buried. You can deny it if you want, but we both know it's the truth.'

'Is that what *you* still do?' I said.

He swallowed. 'James Bishop,' he said.

'I'm here on his behalf.'

'I know you are. But I bet he never once told you that for a year after Roper's trial in which his daughter finally disappeared for ever, he used to come all the way out here to try to see me, to harass me; to stand outside shouting in at me all the ways I'd failed him, failed the pair of them, failed them all.'

'I didn't know that,' I said. 'He was confused and angry. He felt let down.'

'He doesn't need you making excuses for him now,' he said. 'And, just for the record, I don't give a toss how he felt. He wasn't too confused or angry to attempt to bring a private action against me, was he?'

'What happened?'

'Internal inquiry. The results were presented at a closed hearing which said there was no case to answer.'

'You were protected,' I said. 'Mistakes were made that shouldn't have been made. Everything was forced into a neat and face-saving—'

'Save your breath,' he said. 'I've heard it all before. And from bigger men than you. I've even heard it from men I once respected, men whose orders I obeyed; men I'd looked up to for twenty years. And do you know what? I'll tell you. I wouldn't do a single thing differently if I had it all to do again.' He smiled.

I took a risk. 'You were the last of a dying breed,' I said. 'If anything like this came up again, men like you wouldn't be let anywhere near it.'

He remained calm. 'Oh, I don't doubt it. It's a new world now. They do things differently. But that doesn't mean I have to agree with how they do those things. Let me tell you something, Mr Rivers, something so that we understand each other properly right from the start. Martin Roper confessed to having fucked every one of those teenage girls he also confessed to having killed. Everyone of them. First he fucked them, and then others fucked them while he held the camera. He fucked them where every sweaty, spotty adolescent queuing up to fuck them was going to fuck them, but never got the chance. And he fucked them everywhere else, too. He fucked their arses and their mouths. Oh, yes. And being such a performer, being such a poor, misunderstood man, he handed them over to others to do the same. What's wrong? Didn't you come across any of this in the transcripts? Wasn't any of it written down in those words in the Files of Evidence? What was it? "Unlawful Intercourse"? "Gross Indecency"? Well, I'll tell you – "Gross" was the word. You saw nothing of what I saw, you heard nothing of what I heard. And you—' He stopped abruptly, panting slightly.

We were both still standing in the open doorway.

He looked over my shoulder again, to a man who had arrived at his gate, a neighbour. Sullivan raised his hand and the man did the same. They exchanged a shouted remark about the weather and the man continued walking to the road's end.

'Come inside,' Sullivan said.

Inside, the bungalow was as immaculate and as sterile as the garden had been. A strip of clear plastic ran along the hall carpet. Photographs of Sullivan at various ceremonies and events lined one wall. No one entering the bungalow would be in any doubt as to its occupant and the life he had once lived.

I followed him to the rear room.

A small fire burned. Photographs of his wife, his children and grandchildren lined the mantelpiece, most of the shelves and the top of the television.

'You don't know a single thing, Mr Rivers,' he said, his voice again calm, his back still to me. 'All you're here for is to take what I give you. Well, fuck that. I'm not going to answer your questions. Why should I?'

'You might be vindicated by—'

He laughed. ' "Vindicated"? I don't need vindicating. The inquiry *vindicated* me. The trial *vindicated* me. The force—'

'The force patted you on the back and pushed you firmly into touch,' I said. 'And just because nobody told you to your face what an embarrassing cock-up you'd made of the investigation, it was still what you saw in all their faces when they started talking to you about your early retirement. No one ever said it, but it's what everyone thought, what everyone knew. It's what *you* knew, and if you didn't know it then because you weren't prepared to face the truth, then you certainly know it now.'

'Roper did what they said – what *we* said – he did.'

'And that's still your fall-back position, is it? Even now, after almost six years? Build a solid case on the murder of Hayley Forbes, but don't worry too much about the others in case they somehow weaken or compromise that one case?'

He held a hand to his chest. 'I'm a copper. You think it was *my* decision what got included and what got left out? Out of my hands, all that.'

'You're lying,' I said. '*You* were always the one in charge of the investigation. You were the Senior Investigating Officer. If you'd wanted to do something about the others, then you could have done it. No one doubts that you were under pressure to make—'

'Fuck pressure. I'll tell you something else: you're right – I did hear all the knives being pulled out for me. And do you know what they did, those men I'd

111

respected, those men like me, who'd come up through the ranks, those men who knew I could be trusted to do what *they* wanted me to do and who knew I could be depended on not to drag their names through the shit when I wandered into it – they told me to undergo a course of counselling. Pressure, stress? Fucking nonsense. Told me to see a police psychiatrist. "Oh dear, what a shame. Poor old Sullivan suffering from trauma – still, entirely understandable and everything – especially in light of what his poor wife's going through – grounds for early retirement. Three fucking cheers all round."'

'They knew that if you stayed, men like James Bishop might have gone on hounding you, them, and keeping everything out in the open.'

'The courts would soon have shut him up.'

'The courts aren't always right.'

He applauded me slowly. 'So it was me and ten of *my* friends who fucked his beautiful, innocent daughter in the mouth, was it? *Me* who put her in those clothes and stuck a syringe full of crap into her arm so that she didn't know whether she was coming or going while I let those ten other men into the room?'

'Shut up,' I told him.

Even he sensed that he had said too much.

'It's only what Roper told us,' he said. 'He tells us everything and then the CPS tells us there's no corroborative evidence beyond that relating to Hayley Forbes. *They* were the ones who told us where to build our case. And then, to top it all, the Prison Service psychiatrists tell us that Roper might – just *might* – be making it all up. They can't tell us for certain *why* he might be making it all up, of course – except to tell us in their own evasive fucking language that he might be sick in the head. Sick in the head. What a joke. We'd be laughed out of court after what he'd already told us. James Bishop might have thought that he wanted the truth, but what he really wanted to hear was a version of the truth that didn't include all

112

the things I already knew and he didn't ever want to know.'

He pointed to one of the photographs on the silenced television.

'My granddaughter, son's girl. She was nine when that was taken. She's fourteen now.'

I sat without speaking for a minute.

He rose, went to the picture, picked up the frame, looked at the smiling face for a moment, set it down and came back to me.

On the television the contestants on a quiz show applauded themselves at each of the prizes they won. A stacked hi-fi stood beside it. A computer sat in a laminated cabinet, its screen and keyboard on top.

Sullivan saw me looking at all this.

'The kids use it when they come,' he said. 'Never had much use for it myself.' He watched the silent television for a moment. I wondered how often all these others came to visit him there. A low stack of game disks stood beside the computer.

He turned back to me. 'I knew John Maxwell,' he said. 'It's the only reason I opened the door to you.'

'I wouldn't have traded off that,' I said.

'Tell me honestly,' he said. 'What did James Bishop tell you about me? That I was corrupt, that I didn't give a toss about his daughter or any of those other missing girls so long as I came out of it all smelling of roses? Did he tell you that I'd grown bitter and twisted out here and that I clung to past glories, out of step and out of touch with the world?'

'He blames you for not having properly investigated and prosecuted Roper and the others for the abduction and murder of his daughter,' I said.

'But he still closes his eyes to everything else?'

'What father wouldn't?'

'What else?'

'He thinks you left too many unanswered questions and that they're the reason Roper's appeal is going ahead now. He sees Roper walking free, he sees his daughter's death remaining for ever unresolved, and he sees your handling of the case having played a large part in that. He says he was kept at arm's length from everything last time around and that he won't let that happen to him again.'

'There's usually a good reason for keeping people at arm's length from things,' he said.

'I can imagine.'

'No, you can't. Tell me their names.'

I didn't understand him. 'Whose names?'

'The names of the other girls Roper confessed to killing.'

'I can't,' I admitted.

'Well, I can tell you. Even after five years I can tell you. I can tell you their names, their ages, their heights, their eye and hair colour. I can tell you what they were wearing when last seen. I can tell you which of their school-friends spoke to them last. I can tell you which of their mothers couldn't stop crying when we spoke to them. I can tell you which of their fathers and step-fathers and mothers' boyfriends sat looking guilty as hell all the time we were with them. I can tell you which of them were believed still to be virgins. I can tell you which of them had already slept with seven men before she even met Roper. I can tell you which of them had slept with at least one of her mother's boyfriends. I can tell you which of them looked after two younger sisters every day, and which one of them worked four hours every night in a residential care home for two pounds an hour. I can tell you which of them smoked, which of them drank regularly, which of them had already started taking drugs, with or without Roper's assistance. I can tell you things about Bishop's precious daughter that it would turn his stomach to hear. And you – you can't even remember all their surnames. So don't talk to me about Mr high-and-mighty James Bishop complaining about being kept at arm's length. I did what I was told to do, Mr Rivers. I might not have liked it at

114

the time, and you might not want to hear it now, but I did what I was told. And do you know what — I still came out of it stinking of shit. And before you say it — no, I'm not going to seize this opportunity to set the record straight. There isn't a record to set straight. There's nothing I can say or do now that will either change what happened five years ago or bring any one of those girls back, or that will paint me any less black now than I was painted then. I *caught* him, for Christ's sake, and that was what happened to me. What if I went out there tomorrow and found the graves of those three girls and I found another signed confession tied to each one of them? What good do you think that would do me? All it would do would be to prove to everyone else that they were right all along and that I was even more short-sighted and glory-seeking than they'd accused me of being at the time.'

It was the second time he'd used the word 'glory'.

'Why here?' I said eventually, wanting both to divert him and to push the past away from us.

He smiled. 'Nice try, but no. My wife's idea. We bought the place four years before we finally came to live here, two years before I'd even heard of Martin Roper. We lived out here in the summer. I drove into work and then back out again each night. You think it made me feel good to know that Roper's mother had a caravan less than two miles away? My blood ran cold when I heard him talk about the place, about how much he loved going there as a kid, about how special it was to him.'

'Was it why you ordered the searches of the caravan park?'

'When there was nowhere else left to look, yes. Until they decided on their smaller, watertight case and told me to stop looking. Big searches like that don't come cheap, and they waste a lot of time. No one likes making them. Mostly it's just good PR while they're waiting for the man out walking his dog to turn something up.'

115

'Hayley Forbes,' I said.

He nodded. 'Never believe anybody who tells you there's no place for luck in an investigation.'

'And, presumably, you never believed that Roper was operating alone?'

'How could he have been? Once, perhaps, when he first made himself known to us by pestering kids at the school gates, but not afterwards, not then.'

'But even in the early days they were never serious attempts at abduction or coercion on his part?'

He shook his head. 'He paid them and they were happy to do what he wanted them to do.'

'But nothing to suggest what was to come?'

'He was known to us, that's all. We always used to think him a bit pathetic, to tell the truth. Still tied to his mother's apron strings, still living at home, no real girlfriend, all those under-age kids. Perhaps he just grew up.'

'And everything got out of hand? When did he get involved with the others?'

'The so-called "ring"? You tell me.'

'So no other names came up?'

'Of course they did. We had registers, even then. But nothing ever fitted. We visited everyone, but we never found anything and no one ever incriminated themselves, not like Roper did.'

'I find that hard to believe,' I said.

'Not my problem.'

'No – your problem is living the rest of your life with the knowledge of what you should have done, but didn't.'

He smiled at the predictability of the insult. 'Like I told you, it was never my call.' He went to the window and looked out. 'What is it James Bishop *really* wants?' he said.

'Just to ensure that things are done thoroughly this time.'

'And you believe him?'

'I doubt it would matter to him what I believed.'

116

'It wouldn't. I'll tell you what he wants – what he'd happily sacrifice all that *thoroughness* for – what he wants is to hold her in his arms again, to hold in his arms the greasy stinking bag of flesh, bones and hair that his beautiful daughter has become. He wants his tears to fall on her. And he wants the world to look at him with her tight in his arms and for that watching world to bear witness to his final bout of grieving. He's a weak man, and his grief made him weaker. It was always the survival of the fittest in my line of work. The weak always went to the wall first.'

It struck me as a strange remark to make and I started to say something, but he held up a hand to silence me. 'Don't,' he said. 'You know it better than I do.'

I refused to concede the point, but said nothing.

'You can go now,' he told me. He moved to the door and then paused. 'When my wife died,' he said, and again looked slowly around the room, as though she might still be somewhere listening to him, 'all I wanted to do was to sell this place and move back into Hull. I told one or two people that it was what I intended doing.'

'And all those men you once trusted told you not to.'

'All off the record. All very subtle. All very best-intentions-at-heart.'

'Meaning they wanted you out of the way until the last of the dust settled.'

'That kind of dust never settles. How far is it? Twenty miles, less? They just didn't want to see me. They were all just sitting out the days until their own retirements.'

'And now they've all gone?'

'Most of them. And how many of *them* do you imagine still remember even the names of those girls?'

I left him.

I drove to the road's end, turned in the small car park there and drove back past his bungalow. He was still standing in the porch, watching as I drove by.

13

It was after seven when I returned to Humber Street. Late shoppers queued to get in and out of the Prince's Quay multistorey on the far side of the dual carriageway. There was a month until Christmas, and already the decorations and lights were looking jaded.

After leaving Sullivan I'd driven to the outskirts of the city and gone shopping.

In the Bilton superstore I spent fifty pounds on a week of unplanned meals, and the same on a week of unstructured drinking. I sat in the car park for half an hour before going in, trying to make better sense of all Sullivan had just revealed to me. Life would have been easier if he'd told me to fuck off and slammed the door in my face. John Maxwell may have mentioned his name a hundred times, but I'd never listened. And I'd resented Sullivan's references to John Maxwell: tangled allegiances never unravelled into straight or uncomplicated lines.

In the store, in the wine section, a demonstrator looked into my trolley and asked me if I'd like to try a small plastic cup of wine. She hoped I wasn't offended, she said, but her instant analysis of my drinking habits suggested to her that I was not fully attuned to modern trends where social drinking was concerned. She told me wines were getting lighter – whatever that meant – and that, increasingly, spirits were being drunk in heavily diluted, juice-based cocktails. I told her that the drinks in my trolley weren't for socializing. Very few people drank alone these days, she said.

I took the first of the plastic cups she held out to me and drained it. I told her the plastic made it seem like medicine. Everybody says that, she said. She asked me what I thought. I told her it tasted like water with grape juice in it. It's only 2 per cent proof, she said brightly, as though this might encourage me. I took the cup of darker liquid from her, drank it and told her it tasted even worse. She gave a short, unbelieving laugh. Her eyes flicked around me to see who might be watching. Even after drinking those two glasses, she said, I'd still be perfectly safe to drive home. It seemed pointless to suggest to her that they weren't glasses, and that between them they probably contained less than a quarter of a normal measure of wine.

She wore a sash over her tunic, upon which was written *Healthy Drinking*. A badge told me her name was Sam. She said I was the first person she'd approached not to like the drink. It was a game: it was free, and so you liked it. She told me how much she'd sold. With Christmas coming up, she said, a lot of people were looking for a low-alcohol alternative for their socializing. Surely I'd be socializing this Christmas? Of course, I told her. She asked me if I knew how many people would be killed or severely injured this festive season as a direct result of over-the-limit drivers. No, I said. How many? Hundreds, she told me, her brow creased into serious lines. Possibly thousands.

An elderly couple came to stand beside me and Sam turned her attention to them. Here was a woman, she said, picking up two more of the small plastic cups, who looked as though she knew how to enjoy herself without feeling the need to drink to excess. She held out the first of the cups. The woman said that she wasn't sure, that she normally only drank sherry, and then only because it was Christmas. You'll be pleasantly surprised, Sam assured her. She half-turned away from me, wanting me to leave her and to remove my disapproving presence from the proceedings.

The woman's husband asked me what it was. Wine, I told him. He pulled a face. His wife took the cup and sipped at it. Sam smiled encouragingly. The woman swilled it round her mouth, looked thoughtful for a moment and then smiled. Quite nice, she said. She asked Sam how much it was. Five ninety-nine, Sam told her, and the woman immediately handed the cup back to her. Please, finish it, Sam said. But in the woman's eyes that would have made her beholden, and whatever else she was about to spend five ninety-nine on, it wasn't a bottle of insipid wine that would stand in a cupboard to be dusted more than it was poured.

Sam bore this second failure better than the first, but for an instant her smile fell and she closed her eyes and looked defeated. She took the cup back from the woman and the couple moved quickly away from her.

I asked her how long she'd been promoting the drink. Just today, she said. Since nine this morning. They tell us who to target, she said. If I'm being honest, I should have ignored you completely. She laughed. She still held the second cup, and after looking quickly around her, she drained it in a single swallow. It's not exactly vodka, is it? she said. It's not exactly wine, either, I told her. Then I told her I'd take two bottles, one white, one red.

Someone else approached her and I left her.

Outside, it was dark and clear and cold. Frost was beginning to form on the windscreen, and I sat for several minutes listening to the radio and watching it clear in the feeble heat of the blower.

It was announced on the local news that Roper's appeal was due to be heard in two weeks' time. A short report recounted the crimes of which he'd been convicted. There was no suggestion of the controversy surrounding the original investigation. The only remark of any interest to me was the news that an appeal had first been considered three years ago, less than two years after his conviction, but that this had not gone ahead. There was no further explanation for this. His lawyers had probably convinced Roper that nothing would be served by returning him to the glare of public condemnation after so short a time.

Neither Bishop, nor Finch, nor Sullivan, nor Sunny had mentioned this aborted appeal. Sunny's files stopped after the first trial.

I drove back through the city centre to Humber Street.

Five messages awaited me: one from Sunny telling me to call him. One from Finch wanting to fix a time to see me again. Two from James Bishop reminding me that I'd promised to call him, but hadn't. And a wrong number, from someone called Abbot enquiring about the tickets he'd ordered for *La Bohème* at the New Theatre, but which hadn't yet arrived.

I called Sunny first, but he and Yvonne had already left. I told him I'd go and see him the following morning.

I called James Bishop and told him I'd only just returned to the office. He apologized for seeming so insistent. Did I have anything to tell him?

I told him how I'd spent the previous two days.

'You never told me about the threats you'd made against Sullivan,' I said.

'They weren't threats. I just wanted someone to look at the way he'd run the investigation. Even a blind man could see that he'd made mistakes. I didn't want them to go unnoticed, that's all.'

Or him unpunished?

'And I take it you weren't satisfied with the conclusions of the internal inquiry?'

'Whitewash. What did it say? Nothing. Every effort

had been made, every avenue investigated. They could understand the upset and the distress still felt, but blah blah blah.'

'It's the same story Sullivan tells.'

'Well, surprise surprise.'

'What did you do?'

'I tried to see him, but had no success.'

'You succeeded in making yourself look like a vindictive and revenge-fixated maniac,' I said, deliberately exaggerating the facts.

'It's what I was,' he said calmly. 'I filed a private prosecution against Humberside police.'

'Not against Sullivan personally?'

'I was told it wouldn't work. He was operating under orders, following procedure laid down by others. Others involved were only obeying him.'

'And singling out one man—'

'Would have made me look like a vindictive and revenge-fixated maniac who was unable to see things clearly.'

'I wish I'd known all this before I turned up on his doorstep,' I said.

'Is he still living out at Spurn?'

'You know exactly where he's living, so I won't pretend to answer that.'

'Right. Sorry.' He paused, then said, 'Any news on what grounds the appeal is about to take place?'

'I doubt it's the kind of thing they'd let slip beforehand,' I said. 'Tell me, did you take as big an interest in the possibility of the earlier appeal?'

He paused again, assessing. 'It was all a rumour. It never happened and it was never going to happen.'

'You seem convinced of that.'

'It was nonsense to think it would ever get off the ground. Far too soon after he'd been convicted. Rumour and hearsay in the tabloids. Why – do you think there's some connection between then and now?'

'Not particularly. It's just something that needs to be taken into account.'

He remained silent for a few seconds, and then said, 'How did he look?'

'Sullivan? Like a man stranded and alone. Did you want me to say like a man going to his grave with a terrible secret or regret still eating away at him, the revelation of which was his only hope of redemption?'

He swore at me, and I countered by telling him that Sullivan appeared to have as firm and as realistic an understanding of what was happening now as he did at the time of his original investigation.

'And if *he'd* lost *his* daughter, then I might believe him,' Bishop said. 'He pulled the wool over the eyes of the men who came to investigate him. I sincerely hope he hasn't done the same with you, Mr Rivers.' He calmed down and I waited for him to go on. 'It was hardly even an investigation. Those men brought in to undertake it wanted everything to go away, including me, as much as Sullivan and the locals wanted it. From what I've seen of the report, they colluded from beginning to end. Perhaps it was naïve of me to have expected anything else.'

'I think your priorities and concerns and the priorities and concerns of three other mothers and fathers were not the priorities and concerns of a million other people. I think you momentarily lost sight of that, that's all.'

'The report, of course, referred to my actions on insisting on the investigation as wholly understandable and done only with the interests of justice in mind.'

I breathed deeply before saying what I said next. 'Sullivan thinks you want to find and exhume the body of your daughter.'

'I know,' he said. I heard the catch in his throat. 'He told me as much to my face when I went to see him. And I honestly wish I could tell you he was wrong, Mr Rivers, I honestly wish I could tell you he was wrong.'

He hung up then, and I sat with the receiver in my

123

hand until a metallic voice told me to hang up and try again.

A few minutes later, I called Finch, but his phone was switched off.

I left the office and drove home.

I switched on the television. Somewhere on the far side of the world, a jet airliner had crashed into the side of a snow-covered mountain. The newsreader said that so far no piece of wreckage bigger than a seat had been found. Two hundred and forty people had died. There was Japanese writing on the screen.

I woke an hour later to a gunshot and a man staggering along a dusty desert street, another bullet shearing through his flesh for every step he took. I thought of the endless darkness surrounding Sullivan in his bungalow, of the sea and the estuary and the levels stretching away from him in every direction.

14

The following morning, I left the office and walked up Dagger Lane into Posterngate, bought a paper and searched it in vain for any further news of Roper's appeal, and a coffee, which I drank while I walked.

I sat on the steps beneath Andrew Marvell in Holy Trinity Square and finished reading the paper. Nothing. I looked around me for a bin, saw one at the entrance to Dock Street, and as I crossed the square towards it I saw a man come across the road at a tangent to me and then pretend to look in a shop window. I'd seen him immediately before entering the coffee shop and only remembered him because he'd been ahead of me in the queue for the paper and had been forced to wait while the vendor had cut the string from a new bundle. His back had been to me then, but I had been close enough to him, and for long enough, to recognize him now a few minutes later.

I left the square, walked down Whitefriargate and turned into Alfred Gelder Street. It was less crowded here and I crossed the traffic to stand in the old court entrance, as though this had been my destination all along. I looked at my watch and searched the entrance hall behind me as though I were waiting for someone.

The man emerged at the far side of the road, saw me and immediately started walking in the opposite direction, taking him back to where we had started. I watched him, holding the paper and pretending to read. At that distance, and with my head bowed, he would not have seen where I was looking. He stopped only once, and then went to the kerb, as though about to re-cross the road. He looked back and forth across the traffic, and then stepped back from the edge and resumed walking.

I went into the entrance, counted slowly to ten, and then went back out, hoping I would see him hurrying towards me.

But he was no longer there.

I waited a few minutes longer before retracing my steps towards Sunny's. I watched to see if the man had double-guessed me and had waited for my return, but he never came.

I walked back to my car and drove to Sunny's.

Arriving at the agency, I was convinced that the man was no longer with me.

I told Sunny what had happened.

Yvonne went to the window and looked out.

'James Bishop protecting his investment?' Sunny said.

'I doubt it.'

'No one there,' Yvonne said. 'I could go down and look if you like.'

'Call her off,' I said to Sunny.

She came back to us.

'The police?' Sunny said. I'd told him about Finch's visit.

'Perhaps you're just paranoid,' Yvonne suggested.

The youth, who still sat in the corner of the room, looked up at this. 'And even if you're not,' he said, 'it doesn't mean to say they *aren't* after you.' He smiled broadly, expecting at least one of us to laugh.

'The police might consider they had good reason to keep an eye on you,' Sunny said to me. 'Especially now that a date's been set and you've been to see Sullivan. Whatever Finch might have told you, there will be a lot of local resentment at his presence and purpose here.'

'Wouldn't a heavy-handed visit have been more appropriate?'

Sunny shrugged and remained unconvinced.

I asked him why he wanted to see me and he searched his desk for something, finally locating a clipping and handing it to me. It was a brief report of a man called Paul Hill who had tried to assault Martin Roper as he was being led from the Tower Grange police station to a waiting van upon his arrest. Hill had then gone to Roper's home and threatened his mother, after which he had smashed one of the panes in the front window. The police had returned and taken Hill away with them. He was charged with obstruction and criminal damage. Teams of investigators were already at work inside and around the house.

To account for his behaviour, Paul Hill said that a year earlier, Roper had been involved with his own teenage daughter, Angela. There was no suggestion in the report that either he or the police considered there to be anything illegal or even suspicious about this connection. The charges were not pressed, and Paul Hill was bound over to keep the peace.

'You think she was one of the girls going willingly to Roper before all this began?' I said.

'*Something* upset her father,' Sunny said. 'He has no police record and there's no mention anywhere of him before or afterwards.'

'I've seen that name before,' I said, momentarily unable to place it.

'Paul Hill?'

'No – the girl – Angela Hill.'

'I looked,' he said. 'There was no mention of her at the trial and she wasn't on any of the lists drawn up by the police in checking all those other missing girls.'

But I remained convinced I'd seen it somewhere,

and recently, and as I tried to put it from my mind, I remembered where: Angela Hill was the name of the girl standing beside James Bishop at Nicola Bishop's memorial service. She was the girl who had written the poem which Bishop had pasted into his second album.

'What?' Sunny said.

'Nothing,' I lied. 'I'm just trying to think, to remember.'

He knew I was keeping something from him, but didn't pursue the matter. He told me to keep the clipping.

Yvonne linked her arm through mine. 'I could follow you at a distance,' she said. 'See if your mysterious follower was still there. And when you didn't want him to know you'd spotted him, you could grab hold of me, pull me into a dimly lit shop doorway and pretend to kiss me.'

'Even though you were fifty yards behind me and watching my back?' I said.

'I'd run.'

The youth by the photocopier said, 'Kiss?' and 'Ugh.'

Sunny looked at me and said, 'It might just work.'

Yvonne released her grip on my arm and went back to her desk. 'You just think about it,' she said. 'Lie in your cold and lonely bed at night, every night, night after night, and think about it. "Attractive, outgoing lady, late thirties, seeks similar M for friendship and possibly more."' She lit a cigarette. '"Non-smoker. GSOH. House-trained and VGIB."'

'"GSOH"?' the youth said.

'"Late thirties"?' Sunny said.

She turned her back on us all and started typing.

15

I drove to the address on the clipping Sunny had given me. I searched my map for the street in Swanland where Paul Hill had been living at the time of his attempted assault on Roper.

The traffic was thin and I arrived in twenty minutes. It was an affluent village of large, detached houses, most styles, and all of them with something to say about the people who owned them. I had not yet visited James Bishop's house in Kirk Ella, but it was how I imagined he too lived, and I saw again the connection between his daughter and Angela Hill. The coincidence was too great for me to ignore.

A high, wrought-iron gate topped with gold-painted spikes stood locked at the end of the driveway, which curved, rising slightly to the house. The doors of a double garage, built to resemble a stable, with a dovecote on the roof, stood closed beside the entrance.

Back at Sunny's I'd searched for a phone number, but nothing was listed.

It was hard to tell if anyone was at home from that distance, and so I sat and waited and watched. Mine was the only car parked on the street, making me conspicuous. Alarm boxes and security lights surrounded all the houses.

A florist's delivery van drove slowly past me, searching out an unfamiliar address.

A woman walking a small dog tapped on my window and asked me if I was looking for someone. I indicated the folder and papers on the seat beside me and told her that I worked for the city council and that I was checking on the progress of our street-cleaning crews. I asked her if she was happy with the speed and efficiency with which the autumn leaves had been cleared away that year. She said she hadn't noticed. And you are? I asked her. She told me and then pointed to the house alongside the Hill home.

'I was hoping to visit Mr and Mrs Hill,' I said. 'But there appears to be no one at home.'

She looked immediately to the house, confirming for me that they still lived there.

I pretended to read again from one of the sheets. 'Mr and Mrs Hill and their daughter Angela.'

'Not Angela,' she said. 'Susan. Their daughter's called Susan.'

I squinted at the paper and shook my head. 'My handwriting,' I said.

'Do you have identification?' she asked me then.

'I most certainly do,' I told her and took out the false ID I carried with me identifying me as a council operative and giving a non-existent number which no one ever rang. I drew her attention to the slightly longer hair in the photograph. She handed it back to me and told me she was late for an appointment elsewhere.

Twenty minutes later, a spotlessly clean and metallic-silver Land Rover came along the road and turned towards the wrought-iron gates, which swung smoothly open at its approach. They would swing just as smoothly closed behind it, and so I left my car and approached the driver while he waited for the gates to open fully.

My rap on his window startled him, and as his window went down as smoothly and as silently as the gates that continued to open, he swore at me and asked me what I was doing there. Loud classical music filled the interior, forcing me to shout. He made no attempt to lower the volume.

A woman sat beside him, unfastening her belt. In the back seat, beside a mound of carriers, sat a girl who cannot have been more than eleven or twelve. Both of them looked pained at the volume of the music, and eventually he lowered this.

I told him who I was and that I was hoping to speak to his daughter, Angela. Both the woman and the girl looked suddenly alarmed and turned to face him.

He, too, lost his composure, but gripping the steering wheel with both his leather-gloved hands, as though to steady himself, he quickly regained it.

'*This* is my daughter, and her name is Susan,' he said. 'I'm afraid you've made a mistake.'

The girl in the back said, 'Dad?' and he immediately told her to shut up.

The gates continued to open ahead of him. Another few seconds and he would be able to drive through them and leave me behind.

'I'm working for James Bishop,' I said, hoping there might once have been some common cause between the two men.

He turned sharply to face me. 'And you think that makes a difference, do you?' he said.

'The difference it makes is that it tells me you know who he is,' I said. I indicated the girl. 'I understand how difficult this must be for you, but I'd appreciate being able to talk to you alone. I wouldn't be here if it wasn't important.'

His wife leaned across his lap towards me. 'No – you wouldn't be here if *he* hadn't been stupid enough to try and do something about that evil little bastard himself.'

He pushed her from him and told her to shut up, too.

'That's true,' I said to her. 'But he did what he did

and anybody can read about it and come looking for him. Especially now.'

'What's that supposed to mean?' she said.

'He means the appeal,' he said.

'You promised me that nothing that happened last time was going to get dragged up again,' she said.

He closed his eyes and ran a hand over his face.

Ahead of him the gates were finally fully open.

'So you knew about the appeal,' I said.

'Of course we knew. Everybody knows. It's on the news every night and in the papers every day.' It wasn't, but I let the remark pass.

'Five minutes,' I said. 'And then I'll get back in my car and drive away, and in all probability you'll never see me again.' But it was probably another lie; his excessive response had intrigued me.

He considered this, and just as I thought he might be about to agree to talk to me about the daughter he professed to no longer have, he accelerated and drove twenty yards along the driveway, breaking sharply in the gravel. He climbed out and came back to me, jabbing his key fob at the gate, which started to close between us. He stayed on his side and I stayed on mine. He'd turned the music back up and it provided a soundtrack for our exchange.

'Did she do something her daddy didn't approve of?' I shouted to him. 'Did she lie about her age to Roper? Or, worse still, did she tell him the truth and then still agree to do all those things for him?'

'You don't know what you're talking about,' he said.

Only as the gates finally swung together and locked with a loud click did he come close to me.

'You were braver then,' I said.

'If I'd got my hands on him, I'd have killed him,' he said. 'Nine months she'd been seeing him. Nine months. And for most of that time he'd, they'd—'

'He was making films of her, taking photographs,' I said.

He lunged at the gates and thrust his arm through to me. I stepped back to avoid him.

'She wasn't doing any of it against her will,' I said.

'She was only fifteen, sixteen, for Christ's sake.' Fourteen, thirteen, twelve, eleven ... 'She didn't know *what* she was doing.'

Behind him, the car door slammed and his wife stood in the driveway watching us.

'Stay where you are,' he shouted to her. 'I can handle this.'

'Just like you handled Roper, his mother and your own daughter,' I said. 'Where is she?'

'Gone,' he said.

'You threw her out?'

'The man was an animal. What did that make her? You saw what he did to those others.'

'He did it to them afterwards. As far as I know, he did nothing whatsoever to Angela that she didn't willingly consent to.'

'He still—'

'Still what? Still revealed something of her *you* weren't prepared to see?'

'Who in their right mind wants to see *that* in their own daughter?'

Behind him, the young girl climbed out of the car and stood beside her mother. The music ended abruptly, emphasizing the silence which remained.

He turned and looked at her. She stood apart from the woman, and I saw her draw away slightly when her mother reached out to hold her.

Paul Hill turned back to me. 'Just tell me what it is you want,' he said.

'To see Angela and to ask her a few questions about Nicola Bishop. And to see if she's willing to tell me anything about Roper that isn't already public knowledge.'

He shook his head.

'I'll find out where she is one way or another after all that's just happened here,' I said.

'And then what?'

'I'm just trying to find out what happened.'

'Why? So you can run back to James bloody Bishop and tell him what a wonderful, innocent and un-corrupted daughter *he* had?'

'He knows and accepts what happened to her,' I said, knowing it was only half an answer, and less than half the truth.

'No, he doesn't,' he said. He bowed his head. 'Not conclusively, not finally and absolutely and in-escapably, he doesn't.'

Not like he did with his own daughter. Not yet.

'He doesn't have the films and the photographs, if that's what you mean,' I said. 'But, then again, nor does he have a daughter still left to him, whatever she did, however she might have failed him.'

'*That's* my daughter,' he said, pointing without turn-ing to where the girl still stood beside the Land Rover.

'I wish I could convince you,' I said. I meant it.

'Wait until you see her,' he said. 'It's not a question of conviction.'

I was uncertain what he meant by the remark, but said nothing.

The girl came towards us. She said, 'Dad,' again and held her hand out to him. She was the daughter Angela had once been, and I wondered if she knew what a weight rested on her frail shoulders, what unfathomable future he gazed into ahead of her.

I said hello to her and she smiled at me.

'I didn't mean to cause any upset,' I told her.

'I know,' she said. She motioned to the papers I still held. I gave her a sheet and then the pen from my pocket. She wrote something and gave me them back.

'She sees her occasionally,' Paul Hill said, taking off his gloves and looking fondly down at his daughter's head.

The girl looked from me to him. She saw her older sister more than he knew. I was grateful for the address in her childish writing. I would take it with me when

I went to see Angela Hill and I would use it to persuade her to see me.

Paul Hill looked back to me. 'What will the appeal throw up, do you think?'

'I don't know. Not much. There's not much possibility of Roper being released, if that's what you're asking me.'

'Never believe someone who tells you a thing is impossible,' he said absently. 'You'd be surprised what's possible, Mr Rivers, under the right circumstances.' His own lost daughter.

'Right,' I said. I turned and left him and he watched me go.

He was still there when I reached my car and turned to face him, still standing behind the black and gold bars of his high gate, with his daughter still beside him and his hands still on her shoulders as though he could hold her that close to him for the next fifty years.

135

16

As I drove to see Angela Hill, Finch called again and asked if we could meet. He was then in Sheffield, but would be back in Hull by the late afternoon. He hesitated before telling me that he was bringing someone with him, as though that someone was with him now and had just prompted him to tell me this.

The address was off Beverley Road, a district of terraced streets and houses divided into student flats and bed-sits. Small shops still clung to the corners, long gone almost everywhere else. Beverley Road was busy and brightly lit, but turning down one of these streets was like turning down an alleyway. The narrow roads had speed-bumps laid across them. I struggled in the poor light to make out the house numbers.

I parked on a piece of waste ground against a high blank wall in which the outline of lost floors and fireplaces was still visible. A house had once stood there, and its absence in that abbreviated line could still be felt. Giant puddles covered the ground. Empty plastic crates stacked against the wall suggested it might belong to either a bar or a club; there were no other signs.

I walked to the house. It was larger than most on the street, as though someone who lived there a hundred years ago had bettered himself, but at the same time had been too uncertain of his new-found wealth or prestige to leave behind what he knew. It rose three floors high, with ornate woodworking around the eaves and bay windows, much of which was rotten and had been replaced. Grass grew along the high gutter.

The short path from the street to the front door had once been tiled black and white, but this pattern was now scattered and lost. A mound of ruptured black bags lay against the ground-floor window.

I looked for Angela Hill's name amid the hand-written slips attached to each of the six bells. It wasn't there. A single space remained empty. It was a long way from Swanland and the swishing golden gates.

I pressed the unmarked button and held my ear to the door. I heard the bell somewhere high in the house, and so I stepped back from the doorway and looked up.

At the highest window, narrow and set directly beneath the pointed roof, a woman drew back the curtains and looked down. She saw me and I raised my hand to her. From me, she looked along the street. If this was Angela Hill, she wouldn't thank me for calling up to her. I waved again, and she considered me for a moment longer and then withdrew. I waited. I took out the piece of paper containing her sister's handwriting.

My visit to see her was my first direct and un-directed link with the past, with Nicola Bishop and Martin Roper and all they had been involved in together. Nothing James Bishop had so far told me had remained untouched by his own memories of the daughter he had lost; nothing Sunny had told me had come unfiltered through the needs of the journalists and photographers filing copy. The same could be said for Sullivan and the demands being made on him at the time. Finch, too, was working to his own agenda, and while I wasn't entirely certain yet of what that was

– to ensure Roper's appeal came nowhere near succeeding, presumably – I had so far only been given those small pieces of unrelated information which it had suited him to give me.

It was why this direct connection to Angela Hill, who had known both Nicola Bishop and Martin Roper all those years ago, and whose name had so far not been mentioned to me by any of those others, was important to me. It was John Maxwell's solid ground; a place to start unwatched and unhindered, and from which to look directly ahead instead of through all those other tinted and refractive lenses.

Several minutes passed, and it was only as I was about to ring again that I heard someone approaching from inside.

She slid on a chain before opening the door.

'What do you want?' she said, letting me know that her options remained open.

I told her my name.

'Police?' she said.

'No, I'm not. But I am here about Martin Roper,' I said. 'I'm not a reporter, and anything you tell me will go no further.'

'You're lying,' she said.

'I'm not a reporter,' I said.

Her face was pressed to the opening. No warmth escaped from the house. She looked unlike the solitary photograph I had seen of her standing beside James Bishop and the bench and the tree with her poem in her hand. But that had been five years ago, and she had not yet properly understood all the things she had been made to understand since.

'I have this,' I said. I took out the sheet of paper and gave it to her. 'It's how I found you.'

She looked at it and was silent for a moment. I knew I had given her something precious and I waited.

'You went there?' she said eventually, little of the suspicion gone from her voice.

'I had no choice,' I said.

138

'So what are you?'

'A private investigator.'

'Working for?'

'James Bishop, Nicola's father. He wants—'

She looked suddenly up at me and pushed the door shut. I saw her back and the back of her head pressed to the glass. I saw the piece of paper she still held, close to her face.

After a few minutes, the door opened again and she took off the chain.

'You saw him, I suppose,' she said.

'Your father?'

'He's no more my father than I am his daughter,' she said. 'I haven't seen him in five years.' She opened the door wider and beckoned me inside. 'I live at the top. Three flights.'

'I'd never have found you if Susan hadn't given me that.' It was meant to reassure her. I would have found her in hours. And if I could find her, then anyone could find her. I wanted to know what she thought she was hiding from. I wanted to hear from her why her father had disowned her so completely. She had been sixteen when the photograph at the school was taken; she was twenty-one now.

'She comes here occasionally,' she said.

'With your mother?'

'My mother brings her and then waits outside in her car. He's warned her what will happen if she attempts to see me.'

She indicated the first flight of stairs ahead of us and led the way.

'What does she think he'll do to her?'

'Was she there – when you saw him?'

'Yes.'

'And did she stand ten yards behind him and keep her mouth shut?'

'Something like that.'

'That's the deal. She's neurotic. She likes to call her-self "fragile", but only so that people can act surprised,

139

deny it and tell her she's one of the strongest women they know. She's as obsessive and as self-regarding as he is.'

'And you fear for Susan?'

She stopped walking briefly, suggesting I had guessed correctly.

We reached the second landing.

I started to ask her something, but she put a finger over her lips and shook her head. Lights showed beneath two of the three doors along the short corridor ahead of us. Someone somewhere was smoking dope. Muted music filtered out into the scented half-light.

We walked silently along the corridor and through the door at its end. A flight of stairs, unlit and narrow, rose ahead of us. She bolted the door behind us and pressed a timer switch, revealing another door above us.

'I've been here almost three years now,' she said, making it sound like a lifetime. She unlocked the door.

Inside her flat, a hallway led directly to a cramped kitchen, a bathroom and a living room. The ceilings of each room sloped steeply, reminding me that we were in the attic space. In the living room was a sofa which folded out into a bed, and upon which a pillow and a rolled-up duvet still sat.

There were bookcases overflowing with books, and posters and photographs on most of the walls. Two small lamps illuminated the room. It was the kind of flat any student would be happy to own, and then even happier to leave behind them three years later.

She went into the kitchen.

I commented on how – I could think of no other word – cosy everything looked.

'Not a lot like Swanland Manor, you mean? Perhaps that's the point, Mr Private Investigator.' For the first time since her face had appeared at the door, she smiled. 'I was a student, once. English literature.' She nodded towards the bookcases. 'I never dreamed that kind of existence, well, existed. I loved it. It only lasted eighteen months. Does that surprise you, considering my background and schooling, that I never had any such' – she paused, searching – 'expectations?'

'Not really,' I said. 'What happened?'

She rubbed her thumb and fingers together. 'No money. The deeper I got into debt, the longer hours I had to work; the longer I worked, the more everything else suffered.'

'Were you kicked out?'

'I left. If you leave of your own accord, then there's always the chance you can go back and take up where you left off.'

I didn't know if this was true or not, or if it was the only delusion she allowed herself in a life bereft of the more usual dreams and expectations of a girl her age.

'I read the poem you wrote for Nicola's school memorial service,' I said.

'I used to write one a day. I even used to think they were something worth having.' It was another of her losses.

'At least it rhymed,' I said.

'Don't pretend to be a philistine, Mr Rivers,' she said.

'What did you study?'

She told me. She told me Spenser's *Faerie Queene* was her favourite book.

I remembered the opening two lines and quoted them to her.

'If they weren't the only two lines you knew, I'd be impressed,' she said.

I told her I had first editions of all Larkin's poems, books and pamphlets.

'Coffee?' she said.

I followed her into the small kitchen. A cat sat on a shelf above the two-ring cooker.

'That's Huxley,' she said.

'After the defender of Darwin?'

'After Aldous. He's half-blind. He was a gift from—'
She stopped abruptly and turned away from me.

I took a chance. 'From Martin Roper?' I said.

She considered this for a moment and then nodded.
'Was Huxley *his* name for it?'

She smiled at the suggestion. '"Number",' she said.

'Number?'

'The day he gave it me he called it "Number Nine" –
its nine lives – and each year after that it changed
– "Number Eight", "Number Seven". He just called it
"Number".'

I reached up and stroked the animal's head, relieved
that she had not been panicked into silence at the
mention of Roper's name. The cat responded to my
attention, half-rising to meet my hand and revealing
the milky ball of its eye.

We took our drinks back into the small room. She sat
on the sofa-bed and I sat in a worn leather chair facing
her.

'Your mother and father know that Susan gave me
the address,' I said. 'Neither of them tried to stop her.
Just so you know.'

'Just so I know.' She rolled a cigarette and offered it
to me. I took it and she rolled another.

I asked her how old she was.

'Good question,' she said.

'You were a year or two older than Nicola Bishop,' I
said. 'She was only fourteen when she disappeared.'

'She was three months away from being fifteen. Did
you ever see her? I mean, as she looked in those last
few months?'

I shook my head, and then remembered the photographs taken from the film of Bishop's party.

'She could pass for eighteen easily. I was just
sixteen. Fourteen months between us, that's all.'

'In some of the reports covering her disappearance,
they said she was only thirteen.'

'I know. One got it wrong and the others just copied
it and went on repeating it. I daresay they would have

corrected it if it had ever mattered for them to do so.'

'If she'd been found, you mean?'

She shrugged. 'When my father discovered what had been happening, he called me a whore. Technically wrong, I suppose, but all things considered I don't imagine I could have expected anything better.'

I wondered if James Bishop had ever thought the same about his own daughter.

'Tell me about you and Martin Roper,' I said, and then added, 'I'm trying to work out what exactly connects him to the other dead or missing girls.'

'Did I know any of *them*, do you mean? Only Nicola.' She took a long draw on her cigarette, careful to tap the ash into the glass bowl beside her. 'I met Nicola when she first came to the school. By which time it was already obvious to all concerned that I wasn't exactly turning into the doting and dutiful daughter everyone had hoped for. And so, like most other pampered and unhappy kids, I began to kick against the pricks. Prick number one, mostly. I met Martin Roper in a club in town. Lexington Avenue. I was there with a group of others, all under-age. The deal was that he took your photograph, and then when you left you could buy it from a display stand at the cloakroom door. We got talking, he let one or two things slip, and we went on from there.'

'He told you that his interest in photography was somewhat more—'

'"Somewhat more" what? Somewhat more specialized? Somewhat more exotic? Somewhat more pornographic? Say it, Mr Rivers.'

I waited without speaking.

'I was fifteen then. I told him I was seventeen. He told me I was good-looking, that I had a good body. I wasn't, I didn't – not particularly – but I was never under any illusion about what he was telling me.'

'And you agreed to pose for him.'

'He showed me hundreds of other pictures he'd taken.'

'And you knew right from the outset that he was selling those pictures, that he had paying customers for everything, that there were others beside himself involved in all of this?'

'I didn't do it for free, if that's what you're asking. He paid me. I never imagined he was a wealthy man pandering to his whims concerning schoolgirls showing their breasts, stocking tops and knickers.' She stopped. 'Have you seen any of the pictures?'

'No,' I said truthfully.

'Or the films?'

I shook my head. 'Tell me more about him,' I said, sensing her fondness for him.

'He changed,' she said.

'How?'

'You said that I knew there were others involved. Well, to begin with, there weren't. To begin with, it was just him and the girls, just him and me. They demolished his studio.'

'I know,' I said.

'Was that because of what had gone on there?'

'It was just due for demolition,' I said.

'That's what I thought. In the beginning, it was just the photographs. He had a whole wardrobe of uniforms and outfits. Schoolgirl, nurse, French maid, all the usuals and a dozen others beside. I used to make a joke of it and ask him what the point was of me dressing up as a schoolgirl when I already was one and I had a perfectly good uniform of my own. He wasn't too sure about that to begin with, but apparently his customers liked it – a touch of authenticity, I suppose. I used to open my blouse, let my bra show. And then I used to pull my tits over the bra so one of my nipples showed. I'd wear stockings, sit with my legs apart, that sort of thing. Hockey sticks and lacrosse rackets, long socks and pleated skirts. Whatever he wanted, really.'

'Do you know how many other—'

'Models.'

'—he had working for him?'

'Judging from the photographs, I'd say a fair few. Fifty or sixty, say. Some of them were only one-offs, but I suppose that was the point. Even I got tired of always being the schoolkid, and I posed in most of the other outfits.'

'And then the nature of the photographs changed?'

'Let's just say I graduated, became more daring.'

'Did you pose alone, or with other girls?'

'Both. And sometimes I posed with men.'

'Posed how?'

She looked up at me. 'I didn't sleep with them, if that's what you mean. I didn't have sex with them while Martin walked around us taking pictures. He wasn't like that. He wouldn't have let that happen.'

To begin with.

'Sometimes we posed as though we were undressing each other. He'd take a whole sequence of shots, sell two dozen instead of only one or two. And, yes, sometimes we posed *as though* we were having sex, or as though I was performing on them. And sometimes all I – all *we* – had to do was sit with them. In they came, fully dressed, and all we had to do was sit on their knees, our white socks round our ankles, our pushed-up cleavages showing, and let him get on with it.'

'So sometimes the pictures were taken to order?'

'I imagine so. Some of them. I don't know who they were, those men, but even I could tell they were somebodies. Martin behaved differently around them. He sold them the pictures *and* the negatives. They just wanted us to be little girls sitting in their laps, that's all. Nobody ever got hurt.'

'Hayley Forbes got hurt,' I said. 'Nicola Bishop probably got hurt. Lindsey Perry and Jennifer Wilson probably got hurt.'

She sat without speaking for a moment. 'I know,' she said. 'But that was later, afterwards. That was what I meant when I said that things changed.'

'Tell me.'

'I posed for him for about six months, no more. For

the first month or so it was only ever photographs of me alone. OK, so they gradually changed in themselves – but that was just as much at my insistence as his – but after those first months Martin himself changed. He got involved with those others.'

'The men you posed with?'

'Some of them. I suppose so. I'm not sure. All I know is that he started doing more and more work as part of something more organized, something bigger, something that got him more and more excited.'

'You sound as though you were fond of him,' I said.

' "Fond"?' she said.

'You felt some affection for him.'

'I know what you're saying,' she said. 'Yes, I was fond of him and he was fond of me.'

'Something beyond the photographs and the films?'

'Yes.'

'Did you love him?'

She bowed and then raised her head at the remark. 'Insofar as I knew what that meant at the time, yes, I suppose I did.'

'And yet you stopped posing for him. To all intents and purposes, you detached yourself from him.'

'I suppose I did. But not because *I* wanted to. He forced me.'

'Forced you to what?'

'To stop working with him. He told me about those others getting involved. He said that things were changing and that he didn't want me to be involved any more.'

'Changing how?'

'He had a lot of new equipment – the stuff for the films – computers, digital cameras – and most of it was paid for by these others. His business partners, he called them. He said they wanted him to branch out, to expand, to make the stuff more explicit.'

'More pornographic, you mean. They wanted him to start filming the real thing between the men and the other girls?'

146

'That's what he said. He told me he didn't want me involved in any of it.'

'Would you have agreed to do it if he'd asked you?'

'Probably. I don't know. I wasn't completely inexperienced.'

'What made you comply?'

'He showed me a film one of the men had given him.'

'The type they wanted him to start making?'

'Something like that.'

'And?'

'And it wasn't the kind of stuff I'd have been happy doing.'

'But, presumably, he had plenty of other takers, girls he didn't try to scare away?'

'Presumably.'

'Including Nicola Bishop?'

'At school, Nicola was always at the edge of things, always trying to push herself in, to get involved. One time, pissed, I blurted out to her what I'd been doing and she said she'd like to do the same. Don't believe all that butter-wouldn't-melt stuff that did the rounds courtesy of her father when she disappeared. She was younger than me and she had everything I had and more. She pestered me to take her along to meet Martin. I wasn't finding girls for him, if that's what you think. First she pestered me and then she said she'd tell somebody what I'd been up to if I didn't do what she wanted.'

'And so you introduced her to Roper.'

'I told him about her first. I told him how old she was. I knew she'd lie to him.'

'Did it put him off?'

'Are you joking? When he saw her he could hardly keep his hands off her. I'd never seen him like that. He told me that soon he would be able to handle as many models as he could get hold of. He would be making his films on a regular basis, with willing customers – he already had everything set up by then – and he'd need lots of new faces.'

'And Nicola Bishop told him what?'

'That she was sixteen and that she'd do anything he wanted her to do. He asked her what he'd asked me when we first met – if she was a virgin – and when she told him that she was, he told her not to worry, that he respected her for that. She told *me* she'd lost her virginity when she was twelve.' She drank the last of her coffee. 'To tell you the truth, I was beginning to get a bit disillusioned with it all by then. At the start I never used to feel dirty or used, but I did then.'

'And Nicola Bishop?'

'Took to it like she'd been waiting for it to happen.'

'Was all this known at the time?'

'To the police, you mean? Perhaps.'

'Roper confessed to killing her along with three others, but he himself never said anything about what had gone on beforehand.' I was thinking aloud.

'Like I said, he changed,' she said. 'He once showed me a wad of money he'd been given.'

'By his new associates?'

'Presumably. There must have been thousands. He gave me some of it.'

'But by then you'd stopped working for him?'

'He got everything he wanted from all the girls like Nicola Bishop.'

'You must have felt neglected.'

'I did,' she said. 'Still, not to worry – good practice for what was yet to come.'

'Your father?'

The half-blind cat came into the room and settled beside her on the sofa-bed. By then a pall of smoke hung around us. It was already dark outside. She rose and drew the single curtain.

'You believed him when he told you you meant something to him,' I said.

'The world's full of stupid girls.'

'How did your father find out?'

'I never asked him. Perhaps someone showed him some of the photographs, or perhaps he watched a film and there I was. It hardly matters – I'd brought shame on him and on the family; I'd brought shame on every member of the family who had ever lived.'

'Do you think he showed your mother?'

'I doubt it. She'd need protecting from that kind of thing.'

'But it wasn't until Martin Roper was arrested and charged with the murder of Hayley Forbes that everything came out and he put two and two together?'

'And he did what he always does when something is beyond his control. I told him I was sorry for what I'd done, and in a sense, I was. I wasn't ashamed of it, but I regretted how I'd let myself be used by Martin when he was only doing what the others told him to do.'

'And for having introduced Nicola Bishop to him?'

'Perhaps. We lost touch with each other after that.'

'He never once mentioned you when he was questioned by the police or at his trial,' I said.

'I know. What does it prove?'

'It proves something,' I said. 'When did you leave home?'

'He threw me out when Roper was arrested and everything else was finally made public.'

'So, presumably, because you were never mentioned in connection with the inquiry, your father must already have known that you and Roper were involved in some way.'

She nodded.

'But not necessarily *how* you were involved, not then?'

'You've seen him,' she said. 'You've seen the perfect little world he's built for himself – how on earth was I ever going to be able to tell him a thing like that?'

'You must have been concerned that the police were at some point going to make the connection between you and Roper and come to see him.'

'Of course I was, but they never came.'

'Roper himself made sure of that.'

'Presumably. And by then, of course, they'd got all those others to go looking for.'

'Including Nicola Bishop.'

'Including her.'

'Did you hate her?' I said.

'For usurping me? Probably.'

'Roper didn't try to keep *her* away from it all.'

'I know. So what does that make me – the winner?'

'What was her appeal, do you think? Was it anything to do with her father?'

'Her father? I doubt it. Roper never knew very much about any of us apart from what we were good at, what we were prepared to do for him. Look at Nicola Bishop one minute and she might be twelve. Turn your back and a minute later she'd easily pass for eighteen. According to her, the minute Roper's customers met her they didn't want to have their pictures taken with anyone else.'

'Do you think she managed to keep all this from her parents? It doesn't seem very likely.'

'I managed it for nine months. They can't have known, otherwise they would have stopped her. You'd be surprised at the excuses we managed to come up with for all the times we were with him.'

'Did you ever cover for her?'

'All the time. Usually, though, as a favour to him, not her. We joined lots of imaginary clubs and societies, did lots of non-existent homework together.'

'I just find it hard to believe that something like that would go undetected for so long.'

'What has her father told you?'

'Nothing that suggests he knew any of this was happening before she disappeared or before Roper finally made his convenient confession. Did you ever meet him?'

'All the time. He'd drop us off and pick us up, though usually it was her mother; he was always working.'

'And your two sets of parents weren't connected in any other way?'

'They met, but only through us. There was nothing else.'

'Your fathers seem remarkably similar men.'

'Perhaps that's why we did what we did,' she said.

'You never fancied the easier adolescent path via alcohol or drugs?' I said.

'All that came later.'

'Seriously?'

'Seriously enough.'

'And now?'

She pursed her lips. 'Who knows?'

'Do *you* think Martin Roper killed those girls?'

She considered this, but not for long. And then she nodded. 'I wouldn't have believed it of him when I first knew him, but, like I said, things changed. *He* changed.'

'Changed enough to make him capable of all he confessed to?'

'It's possible. Nicola once told me what she was getting up to with him in the weeks before she disappeared.'

'Such as?'

'The films she was making, what he was asking her to do for him, the men involved. Don't feel sorry for her; she boasted about it. Anything I said to try and warn her, she accused me of being jealous.'

Which she probably was, but for different reasons.

'Can you be more specific?' I said.

She shook her head and I knew not to persist.

I asked her if I could visit her again and she asked me if I was leaving. I had been about to, but told her I was in no hurry. I had three hours before I was due to meet Finch.

'Did you ever try to contact Nicola's parents after she disappeared and tell them what you knew?'

She took a while answering. 'I thought about it. I suggested it to my father.'

'And?'

'And he told me not to be any more of a stupid

fucking little bitch than I already was and then he slapped me a few times to make sure I understood him.'

'And even afterwards, after Roper was convicted, the police never came to see you?'

'No. Or perhaps they went to darling daddy by mistake and he managed to convince them that I no longer existed.'

'Not everybody was happy at how the investigation was carried out. Or at Roper's confession. The police hadn't even been aware that one of the girls he confessed to killing – Lindsey Perry – was even missing or that she'd had any connection whatsoever to him.'

'So what? They'd got him by then, and everybody who had ever known him made sure they stayed as far away from him as possible.'

I didn't press her on the remark. It told me that she had at least followed what had happened to Roper during his trial, and that her affection for him, however strained or diluted by his behaviour towards her, still connected them.

I took another chance. 'Did Roper ever talk to you about any places that were special to him?'

'Where they might be buried, you mean? Not really. Just his mother's house and the caravan she had.'

Both of which the police had taken apart brick by brick, screw by screw.

We were again close to parting, and knowing that I would want to talk to her again, perhaps in the company of Finch next time, I didn't want to say anything to her now which might make her reluctant to see me.

I had one final question to ask her.

'Whose idea was the photo and the poem at the memorial service?'

'Her father's. Who else? Her mother was still too upset to attend and so he suggested that one of Nicola's close friends might want to perform the ceremony with him. He used to make donations to the school. They jumped at the chance.'

'And no one ever knew *why* you were so close?'

She shook her head. 'The poem was my idea. I felt the need to do something for her, whatever I knew about her.'

'Her father has a copy of it in his scrapbook beside her photo. Most of it you stole from Hardy's "Death of a Maid".'

She laughed at this. 'And he kept it?' she said.

'It meant a lot to him.'

'Quite appropriate, don't you think – all those little deceptions, one inside another.'

I agreed with her.

'I don't remember seeing anything about any similar ceremonies for any of the others,' she said.

'I doubt they took place.'

'Have you visited the other grieving parents?' It seemed a cruel remark for her to make.

'Not yet,' I told her. It was my intention to visit them during the next few days.

Apart from asking her if she believed the murdered girls had died while they were being filmed by Roper, I could think of nothing else to ask her, and so I told her I'd like to come back and see her again.

'I don't go out much,' she said.

I stood up and she rose beside me.

'Can I keep this?' she said, and took out the piece of paper on which her young sister had written her address. When I told her she could, she slid it into the frame of a photograph of the two of them together which stood at the centre of the mantelpiece. The cat purred at being disturbed and she cupped its head in her hand.

17

I arrived back at Humber Street to see Finch's car parked outside. There was a second car immediately behind it. Finch sat with another man beside him, both of them studying papers in their laps.

I parked and went to them. Both men stayed there for a moment and looked out at me. Eventually, Finch wound down the window and several of the sheets on his knee blew to the floor. He swore and retrieved them. The second man continued to watch me. Finch told him who I was.

'And you are?' I said directly to him.

'My name is Smart,' he said. 'And, like DS Finch, I am NC. And, yes, I imagine a lot of people prefer to think of me as "Smart-arse". But only behind my back and only beyond my hearing. I would appreciate the same courtesy from you, Mr Rivers.' He gathered up the papers in his own lap and returned them to the slender case he carried. He was clearly Finch's superior. 'I imagine we might be more comfortable and considerably less conspicuous in your office,' he said.

I looked around us. 'Are you being followed or watched?' I asked Finch.

'It wouldn't matter if we were,' Smart said.

He was the first to leave the car. He crossed the road

and stood looking up at the half-demolished or half-refurbished building.

'Very characterful,' he said to me, pausing between the words.

Inside, the office was cold and we stood in our coats. Our breath clouded in the air.

Finch arranged two chairs facing my desk.

Sitting, Smart said, 'I'm pleased to meet you, finally, Mr Rivers.'

He was five years older than either Finch or myself. Six inches taller, and with what little hair he still possessed cut close to his scalp. The skin there was darkly tanned, the hair silver, and unlike almost every other balding man I knew, he never once ran his hand over his own head.

'I won't waste your time,' he said. 'Our shared interest is in Martin Roper and his forthcoming appeal. Our own concern in this matter, I imagine, goes considerably further than your own, but I'd nevertheless be extremely interested and gratified to learn anything you yourself might discover which relates to the case, and which might have some bearing, however tangential or indirectly, on our own investigation.'

' "Tangential"?' I said.

He considered me for a moment, looking quickly at Finch and then back at me. 'You won't get in our way, Mr Rivers. We're *this* big.' He opened his arms. 'And you're *this* big.' He closed his finger and thumb until they almost touched.

'At least now I know how big I am,' I said.

'It's a wise thing to understand from the very start,' he said.

Beside him, Finch flicked his eyes at the ceiling.

'So, you want me to tell you everything I've discovered about Martin Roper, about what he was up to, how he killed those girls and where he buried them?' I said.

Smart smiled. 'The chances of you having

discovered anything we aren't already long-since familiar with are very slim, Mr Rivers; whereas what I am about to reveal to you has been disclosed to no one not already involved with the case at a senior level.'

'Don't tell me anything that might compromise my own investigation,' I said.

' "Compromise"?' he said.

Finch shook his head at this. 'Just listen to him,' he said to me.

'Thank you, Detective Sergeant,' Smart said. 'I'm sure Mr Rivers appreciates my directness and honesty in this matter.' He kept his eyes on me as he spoke.

'Perhaps Detective Sergeant Finch could wait outside,' I said. I said 'Detective Sergeant' the way Smart had said it, and Finch smiled.

'I'd prefer it if he stayed,' Smart said. 'I'd hate for there to be any misunderstanding concerning what passes between us here today.'

'My interests still being tangential to your own,' I said.

There was a long pause before Smart spoke again.

'I understand you have been in contact with James Bishop, the father of Nicola Bishop,' he said.

'If you know that, then you also know what he wants from me.'

He nodded. 'What has he told you regarding his own feelings where Martin Roper is concerned? What does he believe will happen? What does he hope to achieve by your involvement, and, via you, his own? And please, don't tell me what you've already told Finch – that he's a seeker after the truth, desperate to avenge the death of his daughter.'

'She was killed,' I said, as though this simple reminder might stop him.

'We don't know that for certain,' he said. 'And we certainly don't know with any degree of certainty that Roper was wholly or solely responsible for her death.'

'Are you denying any connection whatsoever?' I said.

He turned to Finch.

'Of course we aren't,' Finch said. 'You know that.'

'I'm merely trying to understand James Bishop's true motivation,' Smart said. 'As, I imagine, you yourself are. He knows as well as anyone, Mr Rivers, that this appeal will not succeed and that Martin Roper will rot where he sits.'

'Perhaps, but it would still be reassuring to know that for certain, wouldn't it?'

Smart sat back and folded his arms.

Finch took out his cigarettes and offered us both one. I began to wonder if it was a pattern they worked to – not exactly good cop–bad cop, but something just as disarming and productive.

'If, like you suggest,' I said to Smart, 'I don't understand James Bishop's true motives for wanting to know what might be about to happen to Roper, then tell me something that *you* know that might make me see things differently or more clearly. That, presumably, is why you're here.' I waited for them to exchange another glance, which never came.

'Perhaps,' Smart said. 'But first I would appreciate being brought up to date on what you may have uncovered.'

'Even if it's only to confirm what you already know?'

'Perhaps.'

'I know that this is far bigger and involves many more men than just Roper,' I said.

'I think that's more or less understood by everyone now.'

'I think it was understood at the time of the original trial, too,' I said. 'And it was certainly understood afterwards, during the slipshod investigation into Sullivan's case against Roper.'

'Your evidence for this being what, exactly?'

Finch nodded imperceptibly.

'Presumably you already know that I've been to see Sullivan,' I said.

'Yesterday morning. His beautiful seaside retreat. Hardly Cannes, is it?'

'You knew five years ago that he was railroading Roper and that he was leaving gaps wide enough for everybody else concerned to saunter through and never be seen again.'

'Not *me*, Mr Rivers. One of my distant predecessors. Who will, no doubt, also be long gone by now.'

'So none of this would have happened if you'd been in charge?'

'Let's just say that things would have been done very differently and that times have changed.'

'Why don't you go and see James Bishop yourself?' I said. 'Tell *him* all of this.'

'I may yet do that,' he said.

'No, you won't. You'll send somebody else. If you know I've seen Sullivan, then presumably you were following me this morning as well.'

He seemed genuinely surprised at this remark. 'No one is following you, Mr Rivers.'

'*Are* you being followed?' Finch asked me.

I told him I was and what had happened. I left out that I'd been visiting Sunny.

'I told you, no one is following you,' Smart said again, but without conviction.

'No one local,' Finch said.

I believed him. And if it wasn't one of them following me, then they must have had Sullivan under surveillance, probably from one of the empty bungalows lining the road to his own.

'I'll see what I can find out,' Finch said to me. 'As you can imagine, the locals aren't particularly friendly; but nor are they clever enough to keep us completely in the dark.'

'See,' Smart said. 'We really do have your best interests at heart.'

'What's in the case that you're going to show me?' I said.

'That can wait. To be entirely honest with you, Mr Rivers, I'd expected a little more from *you*.'

I took a chance. 'I've seen Angela Hill,' I said.

'Angela Hill?' Smart looked again at Finch, who shook his head, and then both men looked at me.

'She was one of Roper's models before he got involved with the others, before the killings. She was the one who introduced Nicola Bishop to him.'

Both men seemed disappointed by the revelation.

'So, this was what, six, seven years ago?' Smart said. 'Mr Rivers, let's forget the past and concentrate on the present.'

'What did she tell you?' Finch asked me.

'How Roper worked. How things changed when all those others – the men you are now carefully omitting to mention by name – became involved and took control of what Roper had already built up.'

'Was she interviewed at the time?' Finch said.

'No. Roper erased every single reference to her, though I daresay if you look hard enough at the films or photos you're bound to find her somewhere.'

'They ignored everything that wasn't in some way tied in to his confession,' Smart said, and for the first time he was unable to keep the exasperation from his voice.

'Did her father know Sullivan personally?' Finch said. He took a piece of paper from my desk and made a note of the name.

'Only through the investigation,' I told him.

'We are not here to build a case against Sullivan,' Smart said.

'*Are* Hill and Bishop connected in any way?' Finch asked me.

'She didn't think so.'

He made another note.

Smart looked at his watch to suggest to us that we were wasting his valuable time. 'You've made your point, Mr Rivers,' he said to me.

'*You're* the ones who went after the evidence which would secure Roper's conviction for the killing of Hayley Forbes,' I said.

'Not us, Mr Rivers. Not us,' Smart said. 'And we can

tie Roper to every one of those other girls. Every one of them had been filmed or photographed by him. Every one.'

'But he still made some kind of deal with his "associates" which allowed them to walk while leaving his own head squarely on the block,' I said. It was a clumsy way to say it – and I regretted that in front of Smart – but it was the only half-guessed conclusion I had so far arrived at.

'Allowed them to escape prosecution?' Smart said.

'That's what it amounted to. And all *you're* interested in now is working out why Roper would do something like that – something which, on the face of it, seems so unlikely. It was hardly in his own best interest to confess to those killings, even if there was no concrete evidence to prove he'd done what he said he'd done.'

Smart held up his hand. 'And, presumably, if you understand that much, then you'll have worked out that Roper had some kind of insurance policy.'

'For if his appeal failed,' I said.

'Which these so-called "associates" of his had assured him it would not.'

I remained silent. The fact that Smart felt secure enough to indulge himself in all this ground-levelling told me everything I needed to know.

He paused briefly. Our breath continued to cloud in the cold air of the room.

'Then let me tell you something you don't know, Mr Rivers.' Smart looked briefly at Finch, who gave him no sign. 'What Roper didn't know when he made this deal or arrangement with his "associates" was that we already had a bucketful of his DNA in our evidence files relating to Hayley Forbes. Sadly, the law as it then stood was running to catch up with the advances in technology concerning DNA sampling and matching and its use as evidence. But that wasn't a problem. We had it, and we had lots more besides to connect him to the killing of Hayley Forbes. It didn't matter that we couldn't use it.'

'But you can use it now?'

'A way can be found. Like I said, whatever else he might try – whatever he and his friends imagined was going to happen, and whatever they promised him in return for taking everything square in the chest while they slipped through all those loopholes – forgive my scrambled metaphors – Roper is going to rot where he sits.'

'*Is* it admissible as evidence?' I asked Finch.

'I've told you,' Smart said angrily. 'We'll *make* it admissible. These things happen. It saves a lot of time and money. Think about it. Roper knew all along how much the case against him concerning those other girls was missing. He must have believed everything the others told him. Only the case against him in relation to Hayley Forbes was ever tight. Perhaps they persuaded him that it was in his best interest to confess to the others as well. He knew there wasn't any proof – certainly nothing that would stand up in court. His confession concerning the other girls would never be proved, and eventually it could be used to cast doubt on the single secure conviction.'

'He must have known you had the DNA evidence against him where Hayley Forbes was concerned,' I said.

'He'd been told it was inadmissible. It wasn't used or needed to convict him. Perhaps he thought it would be destroyed when the trial was over.'

'Or go missing like most of the rest of the evidence?' I said.

Smart blew out his breath.

'So the whole point of the DNA is that it will be secretly used to confirm his conviction and quash his appeal,' I said.

'No, Mr Rivers, the whole point of the DNA is that *we* know it still exists and what use it might serve. Roper doesn't know that. And the men who backed him into the corner where he had no choice but to agree to what they suggested to him certainly don't know it. Unfortunately for them, what they *will* know by now is that Roper was clever enough while all this was happening to set his little insurance package aside.'

'And if they are as convinced as you are that the appeal will fail . . .'

He applauded me. 'The last thing we want now is for them to get to Roper before he finally comes to us with *his* evidence of their involvement in everything, begging to make a deal.'

'Which will never happen,' I said.

'What – the begging or the deal?'

'The deal,' I said.

'Of course it won't happen, but *he* doesn't know that, and *they* certainly don't know it. For all they know, Roper might already have opened negotiations.'

'Before the outcome of his appeal?'

'It would make sense. Why do you think he abandoned his first appeal three years ago? I'll tell you. He abandoned it because he had no one to sell the deal *to*, because people like me and Finch here weren't yet sufficiently interested in what he had to trade or to say.'

'And now you are?'

'Now we are.'

It made sense.

'But presumably those negotiations haven't started, otherwise you wouldn't be here now, wondering how and where I might fit into it all.'

He applauded again. 'I have to leave,' he said. He opened his case and took out a bound and sealed file. 'You are being shown this for one reason, Mr Rivers, and one reason only.'

'To convince me that whatever the outcome of all this, Roper is the monster everyone wants him to be?'

'The outcome is in no doubt, but, essentially, yes.'

And because you are still suspicious and uncertain of James Bishop's involvement. And because you might best understand and keep an eye on that through anything new I might uncover on his behalf.

'And because, when Roper's "associates" – men whose names and whereabouts you presumably already know – learn of any deal he might be trying to make with you, you will have to act quickly and comprehensively if you want to catch them,' I said.

'Say it – "Unlike the last time." And to act swiftly, yes, we may require your co-operation, though I am not yet entirely certain how; and, in all honesty, I am considerably less convinced of that need than Finch is. I am here, never forget, at his urging.' He rose and laid the file on the desk. It was unmarked. He held his forefinger on it and said to Finch, 'As per our agreement.'

Finch nodded once. I expected him to rise and leave, too, but he remained where he sat.

Smart held out his hand to me. I waited for him to tell me what a pleasure it had been to meet me, but he said nothing. Our handshake was short and efficient. It sealed a bargain. He tapped the file again and left us.

Finch lit another cigarette and leaned forward in his seat, resting his face in his hands.

' "As per your agreement"?' I said.

He nodded to the folder. 'Just look at it.'

'Who is he?' I said, meaning Smart.

'He worked for six years at setting up the Child Protection Unit and bringing it properly into line with law and procedure. He's hard work and up his own arse sometimes, but he knows what he's doing. After the CPU he worked at Serious Crime for three years. The powers at NC have been interested in Roper and the others ever since his less than convincing conviction and the outcry at Sullivan's methods. They wanted Smart and they got him.'

'So all that stuff about Roper's DNA was true?'

'If they need to use it, they'll use it.'

'Because Smart knows which ears to whisper in, which laws will bear a little bending?'

'It happens. You're going to have to start trusting him.'

'Because he'll blame you for getting me involved if I start to mess things up for him?'

'He won't let that happen. Tell me about Angela Hill.'

I told him everything I knew.

Since Smart's departure, neither of us had touched or mentioned the file. Eventually, I asked him what was in it.

'The reason Roper will stay where he is, and the reason why Smart is so determined to get the others.' He picked it up and tore the seal.

It was mostly photographs, and a few typed reports.

I looked at the pictures and found myself holding my breath. Smart had chosen them well. Some were of young girls alone, exposing and fondling themselves, grinning at the camera because they were being told to smile while they did this. Some of the girls might have been Nicola Bishop's age, but some were much younger. In group shots they touched and fondled each other, kissed and licked each other. Everything that needed to be shown was shown.

And after these came the pictures of the girls with men.

'Have you seen all these before?' I said to Finch.

'Often enough not to want to see them again if I can help it,' he told me.

'And they're all directly traceable to Roper?'

'Every single one of them.'

In some of the pictures, the men were engaged in sex with the girls, vaginal, oral and anal. In some, they held their own penises and rubbed them against the young bodies, against their cheeks and lips, their breasts, their buttocks. In some, two or three men performed with a single girl; in others two or three girls clung to a single man. In none of these photographs were the faces of the men identifiable.

'Do you know how old the girls are? Have you identified them?' My voice was dry.

He pulled a list from the bottom of the file. 'Oldest

fifteen, youngest barely ten,' he said. 'And before you ask, no Nicola Bishop or Angela Hill.'

'But you do have pictures which include Hayley Forbes and the other two?'

'Lindsey Perry and Jennifer Wilson. Yes.'

'Do you think James Bishop knows they exist?'

'I doubt it. He'd have stamped his feet long ago if he'd known about them. Anyway, if he did know about them, the story he's been feeding you would hardly hold up, would it?'

'And you and Smart think that Roper's insurance — if it exists — is another file like this one but with the faces recognizable?'

'Something like that.' He yawned and stretched his arms. 'Were you serious about being followed?' he said. 'Describe him.'

I tried, but like most descriptions of someone so fleetingly seen, I quickly realized how inadequate it was.

'No chance of Bishop having arranged it?'

'The watcher watched? I doubt it.' I continued turning through the photos as I spoke, hoping he was wrong, and that one of them would reveal either Nicola Bishop or Angela Hill to me. But neither of them was there. 'How much of this is there?'

'That times a thousand,' he said. 'Then there are the films.'

'And much of it worse?'

He nodded.

'What does Smart think showing me this will achieve?'

'If nothing else, it means you owe us. It means you'll stop having doubts about Martin Roper. It means that every time somebody talks to you about him or the others, that all you'll see will be those pictures. Smart would call it being "focused".'

The last batch of photographs revealed older girls in the outfits Angela Hill had spoken of. Some revealed only their breasts, some their genitals and buttocks. Some posed with the men, some alone.

'And you had all this at the original trial?' I said.

'Sullivan did. Which made what happened all that much harder to swallow. Smart wants you to keep them for the night. Look at them again. I'll come for them tomorrow. He likes people to dwell on things.'

'To consider the error of their ways? He doesn't think much of you,' I said.

'He thinks I made a mistake in coming to see you in the first place, that's all,' he said.

'But if you hadn't, then he would have had to go to James Bishop directly,' I said. I finally stopped looking at the pictures. 'Are the others, the ones who slipped away, still involved in all of this?'

'It's a very profitable business. Especially if you're catering to specific tastes. And especially now the Internet exists.'

I asked him if he'd ever heard of Alison Menzies.

'Is she another of the girls?'

'One of James Bishop's legal team. He brought her with him at our first meeting. He seems to tell her everything that's happening.'

'And?'

'It just struck me as strange, that's all, considering why he was employing me. Why her and not his wife?'

He considered this. 'It might suggest that he knew more about his daughter's involvement with Roper than he was prepared to reveal to you.'

'Or that he was covering his own back for when I finally brought the subject up and accused him of having misled me?'

'Perhaps he's just that kind of man,' he said. He yawned again and rose from his chair.

The photographs were spread across the desk by then, and I gathered them together and returned them to the file.

'You might as well take them now,' I said.

'He'd rather you had them to yourself for a while. Everything's accounted for; he signed them out at the

166

station. They're copies.' He looked absently at the card folder, as though now that its awful secret had been revealed, he was incapable of touching it again. 'What next?' he said to me, buttoning up his coat.

'I'm not sure,' I admitted. 'Patricia Bishop, Nicola's mother.'

'They got nothing useful out of her five years ago.'

'Then I shall endeavour to be at my most persuasive,' I said.

'You're beginning to sound like Smart,' he said.

We shook hands and he left.

I pressed the broken adhesive seal on the file, and as I did this I saw the pen and piece of paper he'd used to make his notes about Angela Hill on the desk, and as I reached across for it, he returned, stood at the door for a moment, knocked and came in.

'You forgot these,' I said, picking up the pen and paper and turning to give them to him.

A muffled voice said, 'I forgot nothing,' and then I felt an instant of searing pain against the side of my face and I blacked out. I saw a man's leg and then his foot and then the floor. And then nothing.

18

The next thing I knew, I was surrounded by women in leotards and wearing headbands. Someone asked me over and over if I was all right, and someone else tried to lift my head to put something beneath it, which caused me a second excruciating pain. I cried out and my head went back to the hard floor. The dance instructor crouched beside me, her hands moving back and forth close to my face. I thought at first that she was trying to comfort me but was uncertain where to touch me because of the pain.

She told me that they had called for an ambulance, and that the police were also on their way.

I tried to push myself upright, but the pain in my ribs was equal to that in my head and so I let myself back down.

'Don't try to move,' the woman told me. She pressed the tips of her fingers against her own forehead and let out a long, low hum. My mouth felt wet, but it was beyond me to ask if I was bleeding, or how badly. I passed out again and the humming was the last thing I heard.

When I next came round someone was holding my eyes open and shining a light into them. I groaned and a man immediately started talking to me. He asked me if I knew who I was and where I was. I started to tell him, but the words would not form, and again the pain of even trying was too much for me. I guessed that the ambulance had arrived and that I was in hospital before blacking out again.

The night passed, but I knew nothing of it.

I woke for a third time at six in the morning. I remained in my clothes, screens around my bed. It was still night outside, but fluorescent lights shone above me.

Someone said, 'Don't try to move,' and I recognized Yvonne's voice. She shifted her chair so that I could see her without raising my head. 'They think you've got a fractured cheek or jaw or something. And three fractured ribs. Nothing serious. Not for a man like you.'

'Just painful,' I said.

' "Gaingul"?' she said. She showed me the time. Twelve hours had passed. 'Somebody will be here to see you at nine. Don't try to talk.'

'Yes, mother.' By clenching my teeth I could talk and the pain was bearable.

'They've given you some pain-killers. And I'm not your mother. I'm an angel come down from heaven to watch over you.'

I realized then that she was holding my hand in both her own. She released her grip and laid my arm by my side.

'Look,' she said, and she lifted the cardigan she wore over her shoulders to make a pair of wings. It was a pale cardigan, almost translucent in the overhead light.

I looked at her. She wore a dress beneath it. Her hair was fastened up and she wore more make-up than usual.

'For me?' I said.

At first she didn't understand me, but then she looked down at herself and shook her head.

'I was about to go on a bona fide date when your

169

friend Finch called. Sunny was out. He told me you'd been attacked and that you were on your way to hospital. I told him I'd meet him there.'

'A date?' I wanted to talk, to bring myself round.

'Don't,' she said, and then pulled a face.

'Miss Lonelyhearts?'

'Something like that. I phoned him and cancelled. He wasn't too pleased. Probably already forked out one ninety-nine on a forecourt bouquet. I told him my father had fallen downstairs.'

'Cheers,' I said. One word sentences were best.

'Finch has been here most of the night. They sent him outside to use his phone.'

'Who did it?' I said.

'Who attacked you? Nobody knows. All I can deduce personally – is that the right word, "deduce" – is that it must have been someone incredibly stealthy, skilful, silent and strong to have surprised you in your own office and sitting at your own desk.'

I remembered the file, and groaned.

'Finch told me you had a harem of scantily clad women clucking round you when he arrived. I take it he means the barely synchronized stompers from upstairs.'

'Yes.'

'Pity they couldn't have come down sooner. Perhaps they could have disabled whoever it was with some Reiki.'

'Reiki?'

'No,' she said. 'Me neither.'

I reached out to hold her hand. 'Thanks,' I said.

'They only let me stay because I told them I was your partner.' She pulled a face at the word.

' "Gartner"?'

'I know. But it worked.'

She was about to say something else when Finch appeared beside her. He looked down at me for a moment and then sat beside her.

'How are you feeling?' he said.

I tried to laugh.

'I spoke to Smart,' he said.

'And?'

'He's fully aware of the situation and all it might imply.'

There were things neither of us wanted him to say in front of Yvonne. She understood this and told us she was going for coffee. She held out her hand and he gave her some money. 'Ten minutes,' she told him. 'After which, no more of this Men Only stuff.'

'I appreciate it,' he said.

'Of course you do. Milk? Sugar?'

'Neither.'

She left us.

'I thought it was you,' I said. If the sentences were going to be long, then the syllables were short.

'Whoever it was must have known that Smart and I were there and then waited for us to leave. The real question is, did they know *why* we were there, or was finding the file a bonus?' He knew this was as unlikely as I did, and said, 'We'll work on the assumption they knew.'

'Which means . . .' I didn't know what it meant.

'That someone told them, and that they were watching either us or you. Your follower, perhaps. Did you see anything?'

I remembered only the man's leg and his foot. I started to shake my head, but quickly thought better of it. 'No,' I said.

'He hit you hard with something harder.'

'I know,' I said. 'Smart?'

'As you can imagine, he isn't the happiest man in the world.'

I looked at him and closed my eyes.

'What? You think he set you up? You think he brought the file knowing or hoping this would happen? Not very likely. In fact, I'd say it was impossible. Why would he? Why would he need to?'

'OK,' I said, but I remained unconvinced and I made sure he knew it.

'I'll think about it,' he said. He looked over his shoulder in the direction Yvonne had gone. 'She cried when she saw the state you were in,' he said.

'It looks bad?'

He nodded. 'I'll assume by "it" you mean you. Your face looks like a bowl of rotten fruit.'

'Why Sunny?' I said.

'Why did I ring him? Because I knew you and him were close. Because I knew he'd have been the one to put you on to Wallis the warder in the first place. Because I knew there'd be something in this for him if it ever came out into the open. Because you and him have probably already struck a deal about revealing everything eventually. And because, knowing all this, I was intrigued to hear that Sullivan had once had him thrown out of a press conference for repeatedly asking a question Sullivan had no intention of ever answering.'

'At Roper's arrest?'

'At Roper's arrest. Yvonne answered, told me Sunny wasn't there, and when I mentioned your name she told me to tell her everything.'

I closed my eyes again. 'Who?' I said.

'I've spent most of the night trying to find out. It's nobody we're already watching. No one saw anything. Smart was on his way back to Sheffield. Nothing suspicious reported. Whoever it was could easily have parked in the darkness, probably in the multistorey, waited there and then come to you without anyone seeing them. I'm going to go over the car-park videos for the hour or so before our arrival until the time you were attacked. We had to wait for you, remember. If there was anyone following either us or you, they'd have had plenty of time to sit and wait.'

'And find something hard?'

'We're looking, but don't hold your breath. Luckily for us, if we do find something, the chances are it will have some of your blood or hair on it.'

'That's good news,' I said.

Yvonne came back to us, carrying two styrofoam cups with a bar of chocolate held between her teeth.

'Finished with all that secret stuff?' she said, letting the chocolate fall on to my bandaged ribs. She gave Finch his coffee and held her varnished nails out to him. 'Is this me, do you think?' she asked him.

'I thought last year's mauve was this year's lilac,' Finch said.

'It's pale plum,' she told him.

They sipped their coffee.

'You cried,' I said to her.

'I was looking forward to being wined and dined. I'd been looking forward to it since five o'clock when Mister Wonderful called me from the garage forecourt to confirm our "arrangement".' She turned to Finch. 'I know you're a policeman, but don't ask.'

'Where's Mr Summers?' he asked her.

I tried to work out if it was a serious question – something connected to what had happened to me – or just something to say.

'He went out about three, said he was unlikely to be back.'

' "Pig With Two Heads"?' I said to her.

'Probably.'

'Where's Smart now?' I said to Finch.

He looked at his watch. 'He's on his way.'

Yvonne looked at each of us. 'It's good to know you're both actually scared of someone,' she said. 'Perfect men worry me.'

'Even ones with flowers?'

'I make exceptions.' She put her cup on the bedside cabinet and stood up. 'I'm going home,' she said. 'Work to do and I don't want Sunny to see me like this.'

'You could tell him you stayed out all night,' I said.

'I did,' she said.

'Can I get in touch with you?' Finch asked her.

'I'm on my way to the East Carr Estate. A twelve-year-old girl is about to have her first baby. Just imagine, she could be a grandmother at twenty-four.'

I held out my hand to her. 'I owe you,' I said.

She laughed at the words. 'I'll tell Sunny what happened,' she said. She leaned over to kiss me, came close, said, 'Ugh,' and stood up again.

'It can't be that bad,' I said.

'It is,' she said. 'When you stop having to liquidize all your food you can take me out to dinner.' She leaned back down and kissed my forehead.

I cried out at the pain.

'I'm used to it,' she said to Finch.

He stood up and held his hand out to her. She looked at this and then hugged him and whispered something to him.

'What?' I said when she'd gone.

'She told me that if Smart and I were going to keep on fucking using you, then we'd fucking well better keep a closer fucking watch on you from now on.'

'Police protection?' I said. 'Great idea.'

'What would be useful', he said, 'would be knowing at what point whoever attacked you knew precisely what you were up to.'

I considered this, but said nothing.

Smart arrived several minutes later.

Finch rose at his appearance and Smart acknowledged this with only a sour glance.

'We were followed,' he said immediately. 'Someone at the station knew we had that file with us.'

You were the one who insisted on going through the proper channels and signing it out, I thought. *You were the one who insisted on me keeping it overnight.*

'It's the most likely explanation,' Finch said, though doing little to disguise his own lack of conviction.

Smart sat in Yvonne's chair and studied my face. 'You'll mend,' he said. 'I spoke to the doctor. It'll hurt for a while, but they won't keep you in too long.

They'll strap up your ribs and give you something to hold your mouth shut while you're sleeping.'

'Great,' I said.

'It could have been a lot worse.' He saw Yvonne's half-drunk coffee, picked it up, sniffed it and dipped his finger into it. Neither Finch nor I said anything.

'They took the file,' Finch said eventually, as though the words needed to be spoken. Smart already knew this and said nothing. 'You don't seem too concerned about its loss,' Finch added.

'Don't I?' Smart said. 'And so now you want to suggest to me that I agreed – that I insisted even – on taking it to poor Mr Rivers here with the sole intention of getting someone – one of Sullivan's old cronies, pre-sumably – to finally come out of the woodwork and make a grab for it?'

Finch said nothing.

'Apart from that little far-fetched scenario leaving me as the one with most egg on his face, it was *you* who wanted him to see the stuff in the first place. All *I* did – and imagine here that I'm talking now to a Police Board of Inquiry – was point out to you the likely consequences of your actions.'

'All I meant was that you seem—'

'What I *seem* to be may be of very little consequence now that the file has been taken,' Smart said. 'I imag-ine all our energies might be better spent now in keeping abreast of whatever happens next and not wasting time on pointless speculation. I suggest we leave Mr Rivers here and that you go and examine the car-park videos. Be thorough.' He rose, told me he genuinely regretted what had happened to me and that he'd be in touch soon.

Finch remained sitting, and Smart told him it was time for him to leave, too.

They went together, leaving the screen at the bottom of the bed open.

I saw the ward beyond, and the other beds and patients and the machinery surrounding them. In a glass cubicle by the entrance, two nurses sat watching a small television.

It was not yet seven in the morning.

I thought I might like to sleep, but it remained only a thought.

19

The doctor arrived to see me mid-morning. He had with him the X-rays of my face and ribs. He held these up to the light and showed me the fractures.

'Another two inches higher, and whatever hit you would have taken out your eye,' he said. 'You still don't know what hit you?' he said.

'Or who.'

'Quite.'

'Would it make a difference?' I asked him.

He considered this and shook his head. He prodded the side of my swollen face and when I flinched at the pain in one place, he moved to another and prodded the pain there. He told me he had arranged for a CAT scan for me later in the day.

'There may be damage we have yet to discover,' he said.

I asked him how long I would have to remain there.

'No one can keep you here against your will,' he said. 'But it would certainly be my recommendation that you stay with us another twenty-four hours at least.' He told me the swelling would soon go down.

Earlier, talking to Finch and Yvonne, I'd hardly felt the pain from my fractured ribs, but now, presumably as the pain-killers wore off, they were beginning to hurt. I told him this. He took the chart from its sleeve at the bottom of my bed and read it.

'Pain-killers,' he said. 'They kill pain. Let someone know when it becomes unbearable. We'll keep you strapped up; it should help.'

'Recovery through suffering,' I said.

'People forget what suffering is,' he said, and left me.

An orderly brought me a late breakfast, which I couldn't eat. She straightened the creases in my sheets and asked me if I needed anything. She said I looked as though I'd been in the wars.

A nurse came shortly afterwards with a carrier. 'Your partner dropped these off,' she said. A white T-shirt and a navy-blue dressing-gown, both still in their wrappers. 'She told me to tell you the receipts are in there.'

I slept for most of the morning and was woken at noon by the same nurse telling me there was someone to see me. My ribs hurt worse than before.

James Bishop and Alison Menzies stood beside me, vying with each other to look the most concerned at my injuries.

I propped myself up on my pillows, helped by the nurse.

'We came straight away,' James Bishop said. 'As soon as I heard.'

Sweat beaded on my brow at the effort of pushing myself upright.

'*How* did you hear?' I said.

'Someone called Finch called me.'

I'd hoped he might somehow reveal that he'd had someone watching me.

'Why did he do that?'

'He was concerned. He said it was a brutal and deliberate assault.'

As opposed to an inoffensive and accidental one?

'I take it, therefore, that this happened in connection with the enquiries you are carrying out on my behalf.'

178

He was speaking like he had spoken in front of Alison Menzies at our first meeting, and she again stood and listened as though she were making notes of our conversation for future reference.

'Don't worry,' I told him. 'My insurance will cover it.'

He looked at the room around us. 'Exactly,' he said.

He was about to say more when his phone rang. The nurse, who had moved on to talk to the man in the next bed, came quickly back to him and told him to turn it off.

'Off?' he said. 'Surely not?'

'Off,' she repeated. She held out her hand as though she were about to take it away from him.

Bishop checked to see who had called and then switched it off. He held the screen to Alison Menzies.

'Sorry,' he said to me. 'I have to take it.' He turned to the nurse. 'Where?'

'Outside. Right out. There's a notice at the entrance, another at reception, others in the lifts and corridors, and one on the ward door.'

'I must have missed them,' he told her. He looked pointedly at her security identification, and in response she angled it directly at him.

'Just as you missed the notice telling visitors to wait until after lunch before coming,' she said to him.

' "Except in Exceptional Circumstances",' Alison Menzies said.

'Mr Rivers's case is hardly exceptional,' the nurse said.

I remained silent. The sweat on my brow ran into my eyes.

Bishop left us and Alison Menzies pulled up a chair to sit beside me. 'I was with him when he heard,' she said. 'We have a meeting. Negotiations are at a critical stage.'

'They always are where he's concerned,' I said. 'It was good of Finch to call him.'

She understood my meaning.

'Then, like you, I can only assume it serves his purpose to tell Mr Bishop.' She looked more closely at my swollen face. 'Does it hurt?' she said.

'Only when I laugh in scathing disbelief at how it happened,' I said.

'*Why* did they do it?'

'Finch didn't tell you?'

'He didn't tell *me* anything. And all he told James was that you'd been attacked. Were they after something, were you robbed? They surely weren't trying to kill you.'

'No, no, and I seriously hope not,' I said.

James. It was the first time I'd heard her use his first name.

'Who exactly is Finch?' she said. It was easy to imagine the conversation she and Bishop had had on their way to see me.

'National Crime. He's here to build the case against the men they believe Roper was involved with.'

'And who avoided prosecution during his trial?' If she knew that much, then she knew everything. And all of it from Bishop. She was making no effort now to disguise the fact. 'And none of whom have been prosecuted since then,' she added, making the remark sound uncertain, a careless thought.

'Finch thinks Bishop might be having me followed,' I said. It wasn't strictly the truth, but I knew that everything I said to her would be repeated to Bishop and that his response would be interesting.

'He's convinced that this will slow things down,' she said, indicating my face and chest.

'It will certainly rule out any Jackie Woo-style gunfights or high-speed car chases,' I said.

'The bits you look forward to most,' she said.

I almost laughed.

'He still has great faith in you,' she said. She glanced at the door through which James Bishop had disappeared. 'He told me that hiring you was the best thing he'd done as far as finding out about what happened to Nicola was concerned. He wishes you'd tell him more, but he's happy to let you get on with things.'

'I won't leave anything out,' I told her.

'He knows that.'

'Do you know his wife well?'

'Patricia? Not really. I've met her once or twice, of course, but I wouldn't say I *knew* her.'

'I just wondered about *her* feelings concerning her daughter's disappearance and murder.'

'I can probably guess.'

'Of course. Please, don't tell him I was asking.'

'I won't. And just in case you're wondering about me and him—'

'I wasn't,' I said. She had been about to tell me that, despite my suspicions, they meant nothing to each other, but now the option for her to say nothing existed, and because it was the lesser deceit, she chose it.

'I have a great deal of respect and admiration for James,' she said. 'And if the thought ever crossed anyone's mind, then it crossed mine long before it ever crossed his.'

I tried to understand what she was trying hard not to have to deny.

'I'll tell you something,' she said. 'A long time ago, before his daughter disappeared, I worked with James on one or two small corporate take-overs. I wasn't actually employed by him then, but he knew one of the partners of the firm I worked for and they agreed to me going to him on a month's attachment. One night we were working late, on our way back from somewhere, and when we arrived at his offices – it must have been almost midnight – we overheard one of the security guards there, a young man, twenty or so, on the phone to someone – probably his girlfriend – telling them that James and I were in his office together again. I'll spare you the more lascivious and imaginative details of what he said, but I'm sure you can imagine.'

'What happened?'

'James apologized to me for what I'd heard. He said he hoped I didn't feel personally compromised or my position to be jeopardized by it. I told him to think nothing of it and not to make anything of it with the guard. Like I say, it was midnight; we were both exhausted.'

'To keep silent because, for you at least, some kind of involvement was still an option? He had other affairs.'

'I know. Perhaps.'

'But nothing happened?'

'No. It was a long time ago. And I'm telling you this instead of telling you to mind your own business because I don't want it to cloud your feelings or thoughts concerning James and everything he's been through.'

'Just as you've not allowed it to cloud yours,' I said.

'Precisely.'

'What happened to the guard?'

'James sacked him. He paid him off the next morning. He even gave him a reference. He made no mention of what we'd heard the man say and pretended his dismissal was for something else entirely. Apparently there were lots of other reasons for getting rid of him.'

'And so he did what he does best and bought himself out of the problem.'

'If that's how you prefer to see it, then nothing I say is going to change your mind.'

'And you prefer to believe that Bishop did it to spare your feelings.'

'And to prevent it from becoming public knowledge, yes. I finished working for him the following week. We didn't meet up again for almost three years.'

'Will he ask you to tell him what we spoke about?' I asked her.

'Probably.'

'Will you tell him about this?'

'No. You neither, I hope.'

'My lips are sealed,' I said. If nothing else, the anecdote told me that Bishop had lied to me at our first meeting when he'd told me that he'd only known Alison Menzies for two years.

'He told me you had integrity,' she said.

'I do,' I told her. 'And a fractured cheek and three fractured ribs.'

She smiled. Laughter was a long way up the scale, but I felt she'd told me something important – important to her. And something she had never before told to anyone else.

'Does he still talk about her?' I said.

'Nicola? Occasionally. More frequently now that all this is happening, of course.' Now that everything that was once long-dead had been brought back to life.

'He knows as well as anyone that the appeal won't succeed,' I said. 'Finch will already have made that much clear to him.'

'He's still the only one of you to have lost a daughter,' she said. 'And under those circumstances.'

The simple remark silenced me.

Bishop came back into the ward behind her and paused for a moment at seeing us so close together. I indicated to her that he was back and she turned and rose to meet him.

He came and sat beside us.

'They want us there now,' he said to her. Turning to me, he said, 'I really am very sorry, Mr Rivers. Sorry for what's happened to you, and sorry that I don't have more time to spend with you. I must appear very callous to you on occasion.'

'On occasion,' I said, but in a tone that let him know I understood he had his own priorities.

'If there's anything you need. Anything at all.'

'I'm fine,' I told him. 'I have a T-shirt and a dressing-gown and a pain in my chest that feels like three hot knives stuck into me. What more could a man want?'

He held his hand out to me.

'It would hurt even more,' I said.

He and Alison Menzies left me.

At the door, she half-turned and half-waved to me. James Bishop held the door for her and watched her. I was left alone for several hours.

At two, Yvonne returned, accompanied this time by Sunny.

Yvonne lifted the sheets and inspected my bandages. I had been given some more pain-killers an hour earlier and they were beginning to take effect.

'You needn't have come again,' I told her.

Sunny sat close to my head. 'You've no idea at all?' he said, his voice low.

'None.'

'Yvonne told me about the file,' he said. 'Do you think you were set up with it?'

'What do *you* think?'

'To kick over the ants' nest and to set things in motion before Roper himself decided that the time was right?'

'Something like that.'

'Can you afford to wait and see what happens next, where the pictures turn up, what use they're put to?'

'If one of Roper's former associates took them, then they probably won't turn up at all, ever.'

'And you think that's why Smart is so unconcerned about it all?'

'He let Finch call Bishop,' I said.

'Only to find out if Bishop *had* employed someone else.'

I told him what Angela Hill had told me.

'And you believed her?'

'Everything she told me made sense. She had nothing to gain and a lot to lose by telling me what she did.' I asked him what he'd been up to in connection with Roper's forthcoming appeal.

'I thought there might be a story in visiting the parents of each of the missing girls,' he said. 'Everyone else appears to have ignored them ever since.'

'Whereas Bishop just went on attracting attention to himself in trying to keep the case open. Was there any resentment, do you think?'

'Of Bishop? Possibly. I doubt if any of them will want to have anything to do with this, though.'

'I'll try and find out from Finch if their original interviews are still around.'

Yvonne said that Roper's appeal was being mentioned more and more often on the local radio and television news stations. The agency was already receiving requests for background articles and information. I asked her if she could keep a note if anyone out of the ordinary asked for this and to let me know.

'So what else can you do now?' Sunny said.

'Not much,' I admitted. I asked Yvonne if she'd heard from her disappointed date.

'He called this morning,' she said. ' "Disappointed" isn't the word. He thinks I led him on and then deliberately pulled out at the last minute.'

'What happened to his own Friendly, Romantic Nature and GSOH?' I said.

We were interrupted by an orderly pushing a wheelchair who announced that he'd come to take me for my scan.

Sunny and Yvonne rose to leave.

'See if any other names cropped up at the time of the original trial,' I said to Sunny.

'Roper's evil cohorts?'

The orderly helped me into the chair, complaining that no one had told him of my bandaged ribs. It was an old chair, he said, and it was a long journey.

'It always is,' I said.

Yvonne told me to shut up and she kissed me again on my forehead.

The orderly pushed me along a mile of corridors. I arrived and then waited a further hour for my scan. The pain from my ribs was almost gone.

I was slid into the scanner and then pulled back out again.

'All done,' the woman at the controls said to me.

I waited for the same orderly to return and wheel me back to my bed.

We stopped at an open fire door for a cigarette and he warned me against drawing on it too hard on account of my lungs. I ignored him and then sat gasping at the unexpected severity of the pain.

'Told you,' he said.

It was six by the time I was returned to my bed. I felt suddenly exhausted and wanted only to sleep. But it was a busy time in the ward and I was woken every few minutes. A television was turned on and showed a succession of soap operas. I waited for the news, but it never came.

I was brought a bowl of soup, which I did my best to eat.

At seven, the activity decreased and the ward was made ready for the second influx of visitors. I switched off the light above my bed and hoped only to be left alone and to sleep at last. This second visiting period would last only an hour, after which I had been promised more pain-killers.

I watched the men and women and children coming and going from the ward.

At quarter to eight, as the first of these newcomers started to drift away, their conversations exhausted, the door opened and Richard Sullivan came into the ward. He stood for a moment, uncertain of whether or not he would find me there, and then he saw me and came to me.

'This is a nice surprise,' I said to him.

He unfastened his coat to reveal the same shirt, tie and blazer beneath.

'I heard what happened,' he said.

'Was I on the news?'

'Very funny.'

'One of your little spies in the department?'

He acknowledged this in silence, looking around him.

'And you were concerned about me?' I said. 'Why? Because I'd been attacked or because I'd survived?'

'I know exactly what you think of me, Mr Rivers. You made yourself clear enough on that score. You don't need to keep telling me.'

'Why are you here?' I said.

'Just to tell you, so there can be no doubt in your own mind, that no one on the force did this to you. It was no one acting out of some misplaced sense of loyalty to me.'

'You know about the file?'

'The pictures, yes. Everybody at the station knows about them. I thought that once you'd seen them you might understand a bit better why I did what I did in making the best possible case against Roper.'

'I do,' I told him. 'What puzzles me now, though, is why *you* should think I might think that someone on the force had done this to me just to get them back.'

He sighed heavily. 'If I had anything to hide, why would I be here saying any of this? I'm telling you so there's no doubt in your own mind and so you don't waste too much time looking in the wrong direction.'

'Or watching my back?'

He smiled. 'I never said that.'

'And are you going to tell me that Smart made too much noise in checking out the photographs?'

'There's plenty who think it.'

'Which leads me to conclude that someone who knew what he was doing passed the news on to someone whose interests would be best served by getting them back, or by preventing me from seeing them.'

'Copies,' he said. 'Nothing lost.'

'So you think there was something in one of the pictures that someone didn't want me to see?'

'It's the more likely of the two,' he said.

I'd looked at each of the photographs and seen nothing.

Behind him, the last of the other visitors left the ward.

Sullivan rose from his chair. He pulled that evening's *Hull Mail* from his pocket.

'I also thought you'd want to see this,' he said. He indicated the quarter column reserved on the front page of the second edition for late news, usually filled with that afternoon's football or racing results, but which today contained a single small headline announcing, 'Local Woman Killed In Fall'.

'Who is it?' I asked him.

He shook his head, dropped the paper on the bed and left me without speaking.

20

The few words which followed told me little more. A 21-year-old woman had died following a fall at her home in the Beverley Road area earlier that afternoon. A police spokesperson was unable to comment further on the incident. A full inquiry was under way.

I shouted after Sullivan, but he was beyond my hearing, or if he heard then he ignored me and carried on walking. Anyone who bought the paper would know what he knew, what I knew. Everyone else on the ward turned to look at me. Someone told me to stop shouting.

I pressed my button to summon the nurse. I waved the paper at her, as though this suggested some urgency.

I told her I needed the phone and she said she didn't like patients making calls after the second visiting period. The man who had called to tell me to shut up called to tell her to tell me to shut up.

I started getting out of bed and she asked me what I was doing.

'Going to the public phones,' I said.

She waited until I'd swung my legs from the bed and was standing upright for the first time in twenty-four hours before telling me to stay where I was. It surprised me to see how little pain it caused me to stand. I'd taken my last pain-killers two hours ago. I walked around my bed and back again.

I was sitting where she'd left me when she returned wheeling the phone, refusing to plug it into its socket until I was back in bed.

I realized I had no money and asked to borrow some. She fetched her purse from the glass cubicle and gave me her change. I apologized for having disobeyed her.

'Good,' she said, then told me to keep my voice down. Along the ward, sick men were watching a programme about a beached and dying whale.

I called Finch and he picked up immediately.

'I'm there now,' he said.

'Then it's her?'

'Yep.'

'I just saw the paper.'

'It didn't make the early edition.'

'What do they mean by "fall"?'

'From an attic window.'

'To the ground?'

'It's the usual way.'

'Does Smart know?'

'Of course he does. He isn't here.'

'How are they doing it?' I said.

'No one seems to have decided. Some want suicide; some want suspicious circumstances.'

'What's suspicious?'

'That she should have done it at all. That she should have done it like this. That her arms and legs and body should be covered in bruises. It's not the biggest drop in the world. She's just as likely to have broken something and survived.'

And I'd been to see her the previous day and talked about something no one had talked about with her for five years.

'And presumably everyone in the know is already aware that she was once connected to Roper?'

His voice dropped to a whisper. 'Not really. You, me

and Smart know. Her name never appeared anywhere else, remember?'

Sullivan knew.

'Do they know I visited her?'

'No. It was the first thing Smart told me not to tell them.'

'I might be accused later of withholding evidence.'

'You might. I take it you're still in hospital.'

'Was I there at the time of her death, do you mean?'

He said nothing. I knew that he was either keeping something from me, or that he was reluctant to talk openly in the presence of the men around him, any one of whom might be continuing to inform Sullivan of everything that was happening.

'Tell me,' I said.

'Two things. The window didn't look as though it had been opened for a long, long time. Someone had painted over the crack between it and the frame.'

'Meaning it was forced.'

'I've known suicides back down because they couldn't get the cap off a bottle of pills. It's all some of them need, sometimes. Or because while they stood on the bridge waiting to jump, the sun came up.'

'And the second thing?'

'In her pocket,' he said. 'A piece of paper with her own name and address on it. Looks like a child's writing.'

'Her sister. I showed it to Angela Hill to get in to see her. She asked me if she could keep it. When I left her it was tucked into the frame of the photo of her and her sister on the mantelpiece.'

He told me to hold on.

'There's no photo there.'

'It was there when I left her.'

'I can see the space and the marks in the dust where it was,' he said.

'The suspicious circumstances,' I said.

'If she was killed, then you're saying that whoever

did it put the paper in her pocket solely to make the connection with you?'

I could think of no other reason. 'They're just letting us know, that's all,' I said.

And if they knew enough to know that, then presumably they also knew where I was.

'First you,' he said. 'And now this. Smart thinks the ball's starting to roll. Those were his exact words, incidentally.'

'He knows the two things are connected,' I said.

'Of course they are.' He misunderstood me.

'No – directly connected,' I said. I told him about the paper and the pen he had left on my desk the night I was attacked.

He said nothing for a minute. 'I wrote her name and address down,' he said, remembering. 'You think your attacker saw it and went there? They might just as easily have followed you to her beforehand.'

'It's a possibility,' I said. 'But think about it. If my attacker is who you and Smart think it is – someone once connected to Roper who knows what's happening now and who buys into Smart's insurance theory – and he saw the paper and the name, he's hardly going to ignore it.'

'You think they'll have recognized the name after all this time? Roper never—'

'Roper never mentioned her in connection with the murders in his confession or at his trial, that's all. I think the others will have records more comprehensive than yours on everything Roper was up to, even if he'd managed to convince himself that he was doing it without being watched by them. They were getting him ready for a fall, remember. They were never going to risk knowing less than he did. I think whoever attacked me for the photographs saw the paper and the name, checked it out or remembered her, and then went in search of her themselves.'

'And we destroyed all those years of anonymity by our carelessness,' he said.

I could think of nothing to say. Certainly nothing that would reassure either of us or make us any less responsible for her death.

'Do her parents know?' I said eventually.

'An hour ago. They're on their way here.'

I asked him if he'd stay to talk to them. They were bound to mention my visit to them. Whatever they thought of their daughter, and however callously and cruelly they themselves had treated her, they would still want someone to blame for her death.

'How do you want me to handle it?' he said.

'I don't know,' I told him.

'I'll call Smart.' He told me he had to go; someone had just arrived.

I heard the noise in the house and the street around him. A siren whirred briefly into life and then died. I heard voices and engines and I imagined the metallic silver Land Rover negotiating that narrow street. She would not be in it, but I saw the small girl sitting in the back, her face pressed to the glass.

Finch told me he would visit me first thing in the morning and hung up.

A minute later, the nurse returned to unplug the phone. I gave her back what remained of her change and she slid it into her pocket without counting it.

She stood beside me for a moment and then told me that my hand was shaking. She held it briefly, and at first I thought she was checking my pulse, but then realized she was holding it simply because it was what I needed and she understood that.

'Bad news?' she said.

'Someone died,' I told her, and she nodded once and said nothing and put her other hand on my arm and rubbed it gently. Someone might have said exactly the same to her every day of her working life.

She left me a moment later. She told the men around the television to turn the volume down.

I closed my eyes and replayed over and over everything Angela Hill had said to me and everything I had said to her. In the morning, I knew, Finch would tell me how painfully or painlessly she had died, how quickly or how slowly. Just because no one had heard screaming didn't mean that no one had screamed.

One way or another, and however hard we might try to frame our reasons and excuses, we were both responsible for Angela Hill's death, and we would both now have to live with that understanding as best we could until someone even more responsible was caught and convicted of killing her. And even then the reduction in our shame or regret would be so small as to be imperceptible.

21

He arrived the following morning before I woke. The same nurse said my name and shook my arm. Finch sat with an unlit cigarette in his mouth. She told me that he was a policeman and that he had insisted on seeing me. Everyone else in the ward remained asleep. She spoke in a whisper and told us to do the same.

I asked Finch if he had a five-pound note and he took one from his wallet. I told him to give it to her, wanting to repay the money she'd given me for the phone.

'She gets paid just for waking you up?' he said.

'It's too much,' she said.

'I'd pay a hundred,' Finch told her.

'I'd wake you for free,' she told him.

'I doubt I'd be asleep,' he said.

She shook her head and told us again to keep our voices down.

I thanked her for the previous evening.

'I'm a nurse,' she said. 'I have to do it.'

She left us.

'I went back to your office last night,' Finch said. 'The note I made definitely wasn't there.'

'At least it didn't show up at the scene. Have you told Smart?'

'Everything. I couldn't risk him finding out later. If connections exist, he needs to know.'

I asked him what else they'd found.

'They took the body away after I spoke to you, shortly after her father arrived.'

'He came alone?'

'He left his wife looking after their other daughter,' he said. 'He made a big thing about how upset they all were.'

'Two days ago he denied she even existed.'

'Then he can stop pretending, can't he?' He signalled his apology for the remark.

'Did you speak to him personally?'

'I said, "Is this your daughter, sir?" And he took a long time answering me. He cried.'

'Did he ask you what had happened?'

'Later. He seemed convinced she'd killed herself.'

'She was dead five years ago as far as he was concerned. Did he mention my visit?'

'I mentioned it first. He seemed surprised that I knew about it. He said his daughter had killed herself because she couldn't bear to have all that stuff with Roper brought up again.'

' "All that stuff"? Good to see him facing up to everything. Again.'

'And when he learns about the suspicious circumstances, that his daughter was probably murdered?'

'Let him.'

'Keep your voice down,' he said. He looked around us at the sleeping men. He looked at the nurse in her office and she looked back at him. 'Why don't we wait until we know for certain,' he said, knowing that I would not agree to this.

'Because we already know what's happened,' I said. 'She was murdered by one of the men who might just as easily have put his hands around her throat five years ago.'

'I know,' he said. 'Even Roper will have worked that much out by now.'

I hadn't considered Martin Roper in any of this. Angela Hill had spoken of him with affection. In her eyes, he had cared for her, too, and had spared her from whatever had happened to those other four girls. Perhaps she had even lived all those years with the belief that he had somehow also sacrificed himself for her, that in keeping her away from his 'associates' he had allowed himself to be ensnared and persuaded by them. It was an imperfect understanding, but it might have been what she had believed, especially in light of all that had happened to her since then.

Both Finch and I considered this in silence for a moment.

'You think it's going to prod Roper into action?' I said eventually.

'Too soon. His appeal's in a week. It'll just make him better prepared, more determined, that's all. Smart thinks—' He stopped abruptly.

'Smart thinks what?'

'I told him what Angela Hill had told you about her working with him.'

'And Smart thinks what – that Roper might still harbour some feelings for her?'

'Something. Perhaps. I don't know.'

'And what? That he can now use this and her death as leverage with Roper?'

'It wouldn't hurt. Especially if she was telling you the truth.'

'She was,' I said. 'And how does Smart intend to find out what Roper might or might not think or feel? He can't approach him, not with his appeal so close. Roper's lawyers would have a field day. Their wrongly convicted client helping the police. A new crime just like the old ones and their man – the police's main – the police's *only* – suspect still behind bars when it happens. If Roper felt everything else was slipping through his fingers, he'd seize this and hold on to it.'

We sat without speaking for a few minutes, considering the implications of all he had suggested.

People came and went in the corridor outside. Phones rang, buzzers sounded, and somewhere further away a floor-polisher hummed.

'Was there anything else at the scene?' I asked him.

'We're more or less certain the window was forced. None of the other tenants remember ever seeing it open before. There's something that might be the impression of a heel on the bottom of the frame, and when I closed it, it didn't sit flush in its surround.'

'Would she have fitted through it?'

'That's another thing. There's a window at the front of the house that would have suited her better. The one at the rear meant she would have had to pull herself through it. Jumpers like to sit. It's against human nature to throw yourself head first.'

'Even if you're trying to kill yourself?'

'Even then, apparently. She was wearing two T-shirts, a top and a fleece.'

'On her way out somewhere?'

He shrugged. 'Cold rooms.'

'But no indication of her having been sexually molested?'

He shook his head. 'Just all those other bruises. No damage in the flat that we can see. The door untouched, unlocked from the inside.'

'Someone waited for her to open it.'

'Or knocked, being someone she knew.'

'Or perhaps someone who said he knew me,' I said.

'Her bag and purse were on the kitchen table. Nothing was taken.'

'And still no sign of the paper with your writing on it?' I said.

He bowed his head. 'Christ. I'm a fucking Detective Sergeant, for fuck's sake.'

'If they'd wanted to get to her, they would have got to her.' I sounded nowhere near as reassuring as I'd hoped to sound.

'They didn't need you and me making it so easy for them, though.'

198

'No, but we now have two small advances on them. One – we can make the connection between what happened in my office and her killing.'

'They left the address written by her sister in her pocket. *They* pointed that out to *us*. And two?'

I was less certain of myself on this one. 'And two – we know or suspect that Angela Hill and Roper were perhaps closer than anyone else ever suspected. As far as they know, Roper might have forgotten her completely; she might have meant nothing to him.'

He thought about this. 'Which is why Smart wants us to use the connection now?'

'And by "us" – your hands being tied where Roper is concerned – he presumably means me. What does he want? For me to apply to visit Roper? Not very likely to happen, is it?'

'You could say you were acting solely on behalf of James Bishop, who only wanted to learn the truth about his own daughter. You wouldn't even have to let on to Roper that you knew he and Angela Hill had ever known each other.'

I saw what degree of wishful thinking all this reasoning contained and said nothing. He told me that the swelling on my face had gone down since he'd last seen me. Then he asked me if I'd had many visitors. I wondered if he'd had someone watching the hospital and if Sullivan's visit had already been reported to him.

'Sunny and Yvonne, Bishop and Alison Menzies.'

'No strangers coming in pretending to be lost, asking you for directions?'

'Why would they come here? Surely, they'd assume I had police protection.'

He laughed. 'What did Bishop want?'

'I'm not certain. Just to express his concern? He left me alone with Alison Menzies for most of the time.'

'Perhaps Paul Hill called him and told him you'd been to see him.'

'And Bishop thought that was unwise?'

'He sees these little things slipping through his fingers. It unsettles him.'

'When will the autopsy take place?' I asked him.

He looked at his watch. 'A few hours.'

'Whoever killed her will have mentioned her sister to her,' I said. 'They'll have taken the photograph down and asked her who the pretty little girl was. They'll have told her that the aptitude for posing and acting might run in the family and that it would be a shame to let a talent like that go to waste.'

'You don't know any of that,' he said.

'I do,' I said. 'And so do you.'

He conceded the point in silence.

'Do you think they'd have killed her if they'd known the truth about her and Roper?' he said.

'Either that, or use her like you and Smart want to use her.'

He wiped a hand across his face. 'Smart's already talking about it as though it's the best thing that could have happened,' he said. He put the unlit cigarette back into his mouth and drew on it as though, even unlit, he still gained something from it.

22

I discharged myself later the same day, taking with me enough pain-killers to last a fortnight. A taxi delivered me home, where I stood in the shower for ten minutes, and then another took me to Humber Street.

I checked the waiting messages.

James Bishop had called twice prior to his visit with Alison Menzies. Sunny had called, said he'd called, and left no message.

It was all old news, yesterday's history — as simultaneously intriguing and as useless as yesterday's weather report. In addition, there were two further calls from someone who neither spoke nor left a number to be traced. I imagined this to be either Sunny keeping his eye on me, or Paul Hill calling to tell me how little he thought of me in light of what had just happened to his daughter.

I called Finch and asked him where he was. He was anxious that I'd discharged myself so soon and I told him I doubted if Smart shared his concern. I told him I wanted to see them both as soon as possible. He told me he was in Leeds, and that Smart was either still in Hull, or had gone to Sheffield. He said he'd call me back when he could arrange something.

'Make it in the next hour,' I said.

'What's the urgency?'

'No urgency. I just think that in light of recent developments, it's time for either you or Smart to start telling me everything you've so far been meticulously careful to avoid telling me.'

'Such as?'

'At least try and sound convincing,' I said. I regretted having to say this to him, and not directly to Smart.

'It's not much,' he said.

'I think it's time for me to be the judge of that,' I said.

'Not while Smart's in charge,' he said. His voice was low, as though Smart might hear him over all the miles that separated them.

If Smart did want me to attempt to see Roper, then I needed to be better informed than I currently was on all the background between Roper and his 'associates' and Smart's involvement now. With the death of Angela Hill, the pace had suddenly quickened, and everyone involved knew that. And if everyone else already knew, then they were all going to be watching their own backs and I needed to start watching mine.

'Give me an idea of what you want,' he said.

I told him that I'd tell Smart to his face, implying that I didn't want him and Smart to work something out between themselves and then to tell me where I fitted in to their plan.

'Anything on the car-park cameras?' I asked him.

'Not much,' he said. 'No familiar faces or significant matches.' Meaning they had a list of known registrations to check against. 'We're looking at arrivals and departures an hour either side of everything. It was a busy time – end-of-work Christmas shoppers – and the cars going in had to wait for cars going out. We've eliminated as many as possible, but there are still eight or nine cars that we can find nothing for.'

'What does that mean?'

'Not much. Their registrations are still being

processed. It could be anything. We'll do quick visits to everyone who has an address registered, see what they turn up. Nothing looks very likely, but we'll see it through.'

'Have you spoken to the car-park attendant?' I asked him.

He sighed. 'The guy gets three quid an hour and sees nothing.' He paused.

'What?'

'We showed him a few faces.'

'And?'

'He knows Wallis.'

'Knows him how?'

'They once worked together. Car-Park Man failed the warders' test.'

'And Wallis didn't. Do they still see each other?'

'He says not.'

'But he might be lying?'

'I suppose that might depend on *why* they still saw each other.'

'Did Smart tell you not to mention this to me?'

'I couldn't possibly comment.' Another long breath. 'He resents the fact that you're involved in places where he can't even afford to be seen.'

'Which is exactly why he keeps feeding me just enough to keep me interested while he works out what use I might be to him,' I said. 'Smart didn't even know Angela Hill existed until Sunny showed me the clipping about her father trying to get to Roper.'

'She was somewhere in our files,' he said.

'Along with how many hundred others?'

'None of whom have had anything to do with either Roper or any of the others for over five years, who did what they did with him because they wanted to do it, and who came to no harm as a result.' He was shouting.

'Four of them had something to do with those "others" and ended up dead,' I said. 'And one of them died now.'

203

'And that's what you imagine you're going to ask Smart about, is it?'

'It might be worth suggesting to him that if he continues to keep all the good stuff from me, I might stop agreeing to be so very helpful myself and go back to blundering around looking for Bishop's daughter alone.'

He considered this. We both knew I was behaving unfairly.

'I'll do what I can,' he said.

I regretted treating him like this – I trusted him – but I needed Smart to get the undiluted message.

It was my belief now that whoever had killed Angela Hill had done so because they too had known about her closeness to Roper, and that they'd killed her with the express purpose of trying to get Roper to reveal what proof he still possessed of the others' involvement before it was in his own best interest to do so – at his appeal – and that this, the killing of Angela Hill, was *their* message to him.

It made no sense to me just to kill her because Finch and I had led them back to her after all those years. We might just as unwittingly have led them to any one of a dozen others. They killed her because someone somewhere remembered her and Roper together, and they had seized this opportunity to act. And in killing her, they achieved the unexpected bonus of implicating both Finch and myself in her death.

'The autopsy came through,' he said.

'Anything?'

'Threads inside her mouth.'

'A gag.'

'And a skull fracture consistent with a blow from something heavy and sharp.'

'As opposed to a fall?'

'The damage from that is on the other side of her head. There was nothing on the ground or on the way down to account for the spread of other injuries.'

'And the gag suggests she wasn't struck and knocked

unconscious immediately. Somebody wanted to talk to her, for her to know what was about to happen to her.'

'Looks that way.'

'And you still think she might have known her killer, might have remembered him from her time with Roper?'

'It's a possibility, no more than that,' he said.

'No — it's a strong possibility. It's the same people involved, the same people clearing up after themselves and doing all they can to get their hands on Roper's little bomb before it blows up in their faces.'

'Do you think they might have followed the trail to Angela Hill and thought she was still somehow involved with Roper, that he was about to act *through* her?'

It wasn't something I'd considered, but even as he said it, I saw that it was a possibility we could not afford to ignore.

'And when she wouldn't talk, they killed her,' I said. 'Or, perhaps having uncovered her, they believed she might already have been to see Roper now that he was back here.'

'Unlikely,' he said. 'Not if Wallis is watching him and selling everything he can to whoever's willing to pay. Besides, Roper hasn't had a single visitor for years and if they're watching him, they'll know that.'

'If Roper did agree to take the fall for all of them in some sort of reciprocal arrangement whereby they guarantee the success of his appeal, then Roper himself would presumably have promised to remain silent. All the killing of Angela Hill will tell him is that they've gone back on their word and that the agreement no longer stands. And if they did believe Roper was about to act through Angela Hill against them when his appeal failed, then they must also believe that Roper's back is now against the wall.'

'We came to the same conclusion,' he said. 'Which is why Smart wants *you* to apply for a visiting order to see him.'

Without Roper and the evidence of his insurance – and there was still no proof that this actually existed; or if it did, then exactly what it was that he planned to reveal – Smart's case against the others would crumble and vanish.

'It makes sense,' I said, wanting to sound conciliatory. 'We'll discuss it when I see you with him.' I asked him if the threads found in Angela Hill's mouth gave them anything.

He read to me from the autopsy report. 'A cotton–linen mix. Probably a man's white handkerchief. Whoever used it, retrieved it.'

'After knocking her out and before pushing her through the window.'

'Presumably. Smart thought it might be an idea for you to return to the flat with one of us, see if anything strikes you.' He asked me how I was feeling, meaning my face and my ribs, and when I'd finished telling him, he hung up.

23

Yvonne arrived to see me an hour later. She studied my bruises and said I looked as though a child had been practising face-painting on me.

'*Cats* has a lot to answer for,' I said.

She took several bottles of pills from her bag and told me to carry them with me. I showed her the ones I already had and she said they weren't as strong as the ones she was giving me.

She asked me about Angela Hill and I told her what I knew. She went to the window, then the mirror, then came back to the desk.

I asked her what she was trying to avoid telling me.

'Sunny's convinced there was a man watching the agency yesterday.'

'Which means there probably was.'

'I know.'

'The same man who followed me in the city centre?'

She shrugged.

'Does he have any idea why?' I said.

'The North-east's premier independent news agency?' she said. She pronounced premier 'premeer'.

'Someone who thinks Roper might want to tell the world what he knows through you?'

'Why not?'

I knew from her voice that she considered this as unlikely as I did.

'Chances are, it's the local law,' I said.

'Sunny's not so certain.' She finally sat down.

'Tell me why you're really here,' I said.

'Sunny,' she said.

'What about him?' I already knew what she was going to tell me.

'He's treating all this Roper stuff like it's his last big chance,' she said.

'It's just a good opportunity for him to get ahead of the competition, that's all.'

'It's more than that,' she said.

'The appeal will be news. It'll last for a few days and then it'll be over. Nothing will have changed, but for those few days you'll have the Nationals begging you for stuff. Court reports, human interest, peripheral perspectives, spin-offs.'

'Is Angela Hill a spin-off? Is your face a spin-off?'

'I'm in the middle of things. I got too close to something, that's all. I can have a word with Sunny if you like.'

'It'll only encourage him. It's practically all he does, all he talks about.'

'Because he knows how short-lived everyone's interest is likely to be once the appeal's over and done with and Roper disappears for good.'

'These are peoples' lives you're raking over.'

'That's not an argument,' I said. 'Especially not for you and him. It's what you do.'

She said nothing in response.

'I can try and find out if the police *are* watching the agency,' I suggested.

'You know it's not them.'

If someone were watching, then it might be of some use to Smart to know.

'Perhaps I could get someone to keep an eye on the place,' I said.

'And how are *you* going to do that? Sunny's there

208

twenty-four hours some days. This is his little crusade.'

'I didn't—'

'You're no different,' she said.

I waited a few minutes before telling her that the difference between me and Sunny was that something I'd done had led Angela Hill's killer to her.

'God,' she said.

'I'm not making any excuses; I just wanted you to know. I don't know why Sunny is as involved as he is, but I don't think that I personally have any choice now but to see it through.'

'No one's going to come back to life,' she said. She was talking as much about Sunny's dead wife and daughter as about Nicola Bishop and Angela Hill.

'They might,' I said. I asked her what the man watching the agency looked like, but neither she nor Sunny had seen his face. She wondered aloud why James Bishop didn't just back off and let the appeal run its course.

I told her I agreed with her, but that, like Sunny, Bishop saw this as his own last opportunity to find out the truth about his lost daughter, and that he would be unable to live with himself if he let it pass. She accepted this and asked me about his wife and how *she* felt about it all.

'I was going to see her the day after I'd visited Angela Hill,' I said. 'And then all this. Has Sunny said anything?'

'Only that he knows her, met her at the time of the trial.'

'Tell him not to go near her until I've had a chance to talk to her, although I doubt she'll say anything she hasn't already been primed to say.'

'By Bishop?'

'It's how he works.'

'Sunny reckons she's as big a mover and shaker as he is, or at least she was until they lost their daughter. Forever calling the agency for someone to cover some

209

event or other, lots of charity work, civic societies, lunching ladies, that kind of thing.'

'And after her daughter's death?'

'Nothing, according to Sunny. According to him, she was the one who did all the real grieving, not Bishop. All this jumping up and down and demanding action didn't happen until Roper's trial a year later. If you ask me, Bishop only makes a song and dance when he knows people are looking and listening, and when he looks good doing it.'

I couldn't agree with this, but said nothing.

She asked me if I'd spoken to Kelly McLean yet, and the name meant nothing to me, until, prompted by my blank stare, she reminded me that Kelly McLean was Wallis's girlfriend, the mother of his child.

'Wallis was a false start,' I told her. 'I only went to see him because Sunny told me he might be prepared to talk about Roper. Now that the appeal and his own disciplinary hearing are due, he'll be keeping his head down.' I left out what Finch had suggested about Wallis keeping an eye on Roper for someone else on the outside, and his connection to the car-park attendant. Finch had given me the man's name. I asked her if she recognized it, but it meant nothing to her.

'Go and see Kelly McLean,' she said. She picked up her bag and took an envelope from it, hesitating before handing it to me. 'I want this straight back,' she said. 'Kelly's mother showed it to me. She was worried in case it got into the wrong hands.' She handed the envelope to me.

Inside was a single six by four photo of a girl posing topless. She wore fingerless lace gloves to her elbows and a slip which had fallen to her waist and been carefully arranged there. She had on stockings and suspenders and sat with her hands on her knees. A single shiny black high heel hung from one foot.

'Kelly McLean?' I said.

She nodded. 'Turn it over.'

I turned it over and stamped across the back of the

210

picture was Martin Roper's name and a telephone number. It was not a Hull number, but somewhere close, somewhere in East Yorkshire. Kelly McLean had written 'For Your Eyes Only' and the date, Summer 1995.

'Meant for lover-boy Wallis?'

She shrugged again. 'Her mother doesn't know.'

I looked again at the girl. 'Roper's earlier work,' I said.

'She never did anything pornographic with him, if that's what you mean. It's called "Boudoir Photography". A lot of women have them taken.'

'And you're certain she never went on to other things with Roper?'

'Her mother was convinced that this was all she had.' She gestured for me to give her back the picture.

I made a note of the telephone number and asked her again for Kelly McLean's address.

'Has Sunny seen it?' I said.

She shook her head.

'Will she talk to me if I guarantee her anonymity?' I asked her.

'You can't do that,' she said bluntly. She put the photo in the envelope and the envelope back in her bag. 'I'll see what I can do.'

I told her about Smart's suggestion that I apply to see Roper on Bishop's behalf.

'Is he likely to agree to see you?' she said.

'Only if he thinks it might help him in light of everything that's happened.'

She considered this and shook her head.

'I might be able to—' I started to say.

'No – I don't want to hear it,' she told me. 'Whatever it was, it would be an excuse.' She rose from her chair.

I thanked her for having shown me the photograph, even if I wasn't certain of what it proved, or how it might now be of some use to me.

'Nobody's going to come out of this smelling of roses, are they?' she said.

' "Let justice prevail or the Heavens fall",' I said.

She continued looking at me without speaking and then left me without kissing me.

I dialled the six-year out-of-date number and a recorded message told me that the number I had dialled had not been recognized. It was what I had expected.

My cheek started to ache and I studied the labels of the bottles standing in a row on my desk.

24

'I understand you have reservations concerning information you believe me to be withholding from you, Mr Rivers.' Smart leaned forward in his seat.

We were sitting in the Baltic Wharf, overlooking the marina and its ranks of yachts. He got the emphasis on 'me' and 'you' just right. As though the whole idea of him having to reveal anything to me was ridiculous and hilarious in equal measure.

It was not yet midday. I drank from my glass.

'That's a very concise statement,' I said. 'Identifying me, why we're here, and followed by your very own pre-emptive conclusion,' I said. 'Almost as though you were recording the conversation.'

Finch looked at him to ascertain whether or not this equally ridiculous suggestion was true, but Smart refused to be drawn and ignored him.

'Mr Rivers . . .' Smart paused, and having leaned forward, he then sat slowly back in his seat and stretched his arms. 'This conversation isn't taking place, so why would I want a record of it that might later be used to compromise or embarrass *me*?'

'Good,' I said quickly, tapping my breast pocket. 'Then you'll have to rely on my own considerably inferior technology.'

Smart smiled. 'I'll assume that was a joke,' he said. I signalled to Finch that it was.

'*Why* isn't this conversation taking place?' I asked him.

'You know perfectly well why.'

Because if I did apply to see Martin Roper, then both his defence and prosecution teams would call it, at best, interference and manipulation, and, at worst, behaviour likely to prejudice the outcome of his appeal. And even if he refused to see me, the request alone – a stranger working for the father of one of the girls he had confessed to having killed – would alert Roper to my involvement and perhaps push him into doing something that neither he nor Smart was yet fully prepared for.

'Mr Rivers.' My name at the start of all his sentences like a finger prodded into my chest. 'What makes you think that I consider it incumbent upon myself to tell you anything?'

I understood his purpose in taking this stance. He had allowed me to come too close and now he was re-establishing the distance between us.

'Because you came to me,' I said. 'Because without my independent concern and interest in Roper on behalf of my client, you would have no way of getting any closer to him. Or of keeping an eye on all those others supposedly waiting to get closer to him.' I was going to say more, but he interrupted me.

' "Concern"? Mr Rivers. You're being paid to do a job, that's all. I'm still not entirely certain what that job is – just as you yourself appear not to be – but, please, let's not dress it up with notions like "concern".'

'My client wants—'

'Bishop wants his hands around Roper's throat. And because he can't have that, and because he's a man accustomed to getting what he wants, he wants someone else's hands around Roper's throat. Don't talk to me about his dead daughter, Mr Rivers, because it doesn't wash. It's *him* you should be talking to about

214

"withholding information", not me.' He had over-reacted, and the instant he finished talking, he subsided. He ran a hand down his tie and looked around us.

I wanted Finch to say something and keep Smart off-balance, but Finch – perhaps because he had never seen Smart like this before; or perhaps because he *had* seen him like this and knew better than I did what it meant – remained silent.

'I've known from our very first conversation that James Bishop has known things he's pretended not to know,' I said to Smart.

'I still don't see *him* sitting at the table,' Smart said.

No one spoke for a minute, after which Finch took an envelope from his pocket and gave it to me. It contained an Instamatic photo of fifty other photos laid out untidily on the floor and photographed from above.

'The stolen file,' I said. 'Why this?'

'Because whoever took them wants us to know he's got them,' Smart said. 'Because he knew you should never have seen them in the first place and that I should never have shown them to you. Call this collateral damage.'

Finch shook his head slightly at the phrase.

'Everything goes wrong, everything ends, and they can still hurt you?' I said.

'I don't imagine they believe we're going to back off just because they've confirmed they have the pictures,' Smart said. He looked again around the room at the few other drinkers.

Finch took a second envelope from his pocket. 'From the car park. A list of plates and owners. Nothing to tie in anyone we already know about.'

I looked at the list. 'Will someone check each name?'

'They're doing it already. Wallis, incidentally, doesn't even own a car.'

'Which means nothing,' I said.

Several garages were listed as owners and I asked what this meant.

'Either they were hire cars, courtesy cars, or they were still in the process of being registered. It happens. Don't worry, we'll get to all of them. We don't even know if the person who attacked you and took the file used the car park.'

I looked again at the list, at the makes and colours of the cars. Still nothing.

'Keep it,' Finch told me.

'See,' Smart said. 'We're not withholding *that* information.'

'Tell me what you know – what you knew then – about the men Roper was involved with,' I said.

Smart considered this for a moment.

Finch rose and went to the bar.

'When we understood the connection between Roper and the others, and the paedophiles they supplied, we compiled a list of all known suspects – those involved, those who bought – living locally,' Smart said. 'Except by then, of course, the necessary technology was rapidly becoming available and affordable, which meant that it no longer mattered where those people lived.

'Five years ago, Sullivan and his team had neither the technology nor the expertise, nor even a basic understanding of how to go about putting a net round those involved. To compound matters, the proper legislation didn't yet exist – not as it exists today – to ensure that we could get our hands on the right people for the right reasons. It's why Sullivan went for Roper. It was also why Roper, knowing he was well and truly on the hook for the killing of Hayley Forbes, made his deal with the others, and why they, ultimately, and with what today seems like surprising ease, slipped away.

'There were things Sullivan could have done, but didn't. Every step he took, they were ahead of him – dismantling and disappearing. And once Roper made his confession, then Sullivan considered he had good cause not to waste his time elsewhere. He had what the public and his own superiors had been baying for all that time.'

'Are all the men who were involved with Roper then still involved in some way?'

'Most of them. Some considered they'd had a close enough shave and that things were getting beyond them.'

'But presumably there are enough of them still active for Roper's insurance to do you a lot of good.'

'If I didn't believe it existed, then none of this would be happening now. There are those among my own superiors who consider me to be on a fool's errand.'

'How many men do you still have in your sights?'

'Half a dozen, eight at the most. I can't tell you their names, and I have no intention of doing so.'

'Do you think the man who attacked me and stole the file was one of them?'

'It's unlikely. These are now powerful, wealthy, careful men, all with legitimate business interests. We've spent the best part of three years making all the connections between the legitimate and more salubrious parts of their business empires.'

'The latter still making them the most money, presumably.'

'The most money for the least effort. And before you ask me why we don't arrest them and charge them if we already know all this, you have to understand that after their close call with Roper at the very start of all this empire-building, they all suddenly became very clever and sophisticated, and made sure that nothing they did would ever again be connected to them directly. And nothing we know about now ties any of them to the missing girls. If we prosecute them for something recent, then all that will finally get left behind and no one will give a toss about what happened to those girls.'

'Making you no better than Sullivan was then.'

'Thank you, Mr Rivers. The thought had occurred to me. Roper's new-found greed and commitment to his

217

own burgeoning little empire, and getting everything they wanted from him, came as a bit of a shock to them. It made them realize a lot of things, and the first thing they realized was the need to distance themselves from him before he went too far and everything blew up in their faces.'

'And whether Roper has his insurance or not, what matters now is that *they* believe he does,' I said.

'That would be my personal understanding.'

'And what happens to your case against them if nothing exists?'

'If Sullivan and his team had held off, waited, done their job properly, let someone who knew about these things come in and work alongside him, then all our eggs wouldn't be in that one particular basket now.'

'And these others knew that. It's another reason why, when Sullivan finally got close to Roper, Roper was persuaded to make his all-inclusive, final offer of a confession.'

'Put up his smoke-screen, yes.'

'And none of them had guessed that Roper had been a lot smarter than any of them had ever considered him capable of being?'

Finch returned to us with more drinks.

'Roper', Smart said, 'got carried away with himself, that's all. I don't care what Angela Hill told you – Roper got what he deserved. The only thing he didn't deserve was *all* the blame.

'I can show you a film, made by Roper, of an eleven-year-old girl being abused by three men simultaneously. I can show you a film of a girl only a year or two older being sexually abused by a man and a German shepherd. I have photographs of a girl, the same age, being penetrated anally and vaginally at the same time. I can trace all these back to Roper.

'This is what I'm withholding, Mr Rivers. We have a roomful of this stuff. If you want to see it, I can arrange for that to happen. I've seen it all. Finch has seen it all. We've searched for those missing faces. We've searched for Nicola Bishop. We've looked in places it would make you sick to your stomach to have to start searching. I've seen a girl possibly as young as seven being abused by men old enough to be her grandfather. I've seen sleeping babies – and I mean babies – being masturbated over. If I withhold something, Mr Rivers, it's usually with very good cause.

'I don't apologize for any of this. I don't apologize for wanting to use you while James Bishop is still paying you. I don't even apologize for stretching the law on occasion because the law is sometimes so out-of-date and inadequate that it works against itself.

'So, yes, if you seeing, or even trying to see, Roper makes him or any of those watching him break cover and do something, then, yes, I'll use that to the best of my ability to make sure he stays where he is and for everyone he ever knew to join him there.' He stopped speaking and drained his glass.

'Sullivan saw most of the stuff that was seized,' Finch said. 'He knew how much of it existed. He knew Roper couldn't have been working alone.'

'Are you suggesting he was motivated by something other than the need to make a quick arrest or to ensure that his own reputation didn't slip so close to his retirement?'

'We're saying it's always a possibility, that's all,' Smart said.

He asked me when I'd last seen James Bishop and I told him about Bishop's fleeting visit to the hospital.

'We want you to suggest the Roper visit to him,' he said. He watched me closely. I understood what he was telling me.

'Hopefully, Bishop will jump at the opportunity,' Finch said.

'Even if it means that the man he's held responsible for his daughter's death all these years turns out not to have done it?' I said. 'Even if it means he has to go through everything all over again for another five years? Or do you imagine he'd take that chance just to

219

learn for certain how she'd died or where she was buried or how she'd been disposed of?'

'It's what *I'd* want,' Smart said, avoiding my eyes. He picked up his case and laid it on the table. His second drink stood in front of him untouched. He took out an addressed envelope.

'An application to see Roper,' he said. 'Just sign it, add the details where necessary, and send it. It'll receive priority treatment.'

'Who else will be notified?' I asked him.

'What do you mean?'

'If I send this form, presumably Roper will tell his legal team. Who will *you* inform?'

'Nobody,' Smart said. 'And if Roper wants from us what I think he wants from us, then he won't be telling anyone about your visit.'

'Bishop will know you're involved,' I said.

'So what? He's still getting what he wants. And he's certainly getting more than he ever considered possible when he first picked you up and started stirring. In fact, looking at it from his point of view, I'd say that so far you've been something of a disappointment to him. This should more than make up for everything.'

There was some truth in what he was suggesting.

Smart looked at his watch and told Finch that it was time for him to leave. He indicated the envelope I still held.

'Post it. See Roper,' he said. 'Once his appeal gets under way nobody will get within a mile of him except his legals. And between you and me, Mr Rivers, it could all be over in a matter of hours rather than days.'

'Oh?'

'Trust me,' he said.

I laughed. 'I'm laughing in your face,' I said.

'I'll call it healthy scepticism,' he said, picked up his case and left us.

Finch and I sat for several minutes without speaking.

Outside, the yachts rocked and their rigging rattled in the wind.

'Why do you think there was no film of Nicola Bishop among everything Sullivan seized?' I said eventually.

'Perhaps Bishop got to him and bought it all from him,' he said. 'Believe what you like.'

But I could see that he was intrigued by the suggestion; either that, or he and Smart had already considered it and decided it meant nothing.

'Angela Hill could have been lying to you about Nicola Bishop's involvement with Roper,' he said. 'Perhaps Roper transferred his affections to Nicola Bishop, and Angela Hill just got jealous and decided to make up stories to make Roper's new girlfriend look bad.'

' "Girlfriend"? She was fourteen,' I said. I asked him if he was married.

'Why? Because all of this would somehow make more sense to you if I had a couple of young daughters of my own and every time I looked at one of Roper's films I saw them instead?' He rubbed his face. 'Yes, I'm married. And I've got kids.'

It was clear to me that he didn't want to talk about them.

'Look,' he said. 'The films are every bit as bad as Smart says they are, and everything he's just told you is true.'

I took a piece of paper from my pocket and gave it to him. It contained the unavailable telephone number I'd taken from the photo of Kelly McLean.

'And this is?'

'Non-existent. Five years old, six. Is there any way of finding out where it might once have been?'

I'd considered attempting to do this myself, but knew how unlikely I was to succeed, or without attracting even more attention to myself.

'I can look through all the numbers we've gathered, see if there's a match. I take it there's some connection to either Roper or Nicola Bishop.'

'It was a number Nicola Bishop once had for Roper,' I lied.

'The demolished studio, perhaps?'

'Not a Hull exchange. The East Riding.'

'Don't hold your breath,' he said. 'Not after six years, not these days.' He was already making the connection with Sullivan's retirement home and Roper's mother's caravan.

He asked me to go to Angela Hill's flat with him to see if anything had changed since my visit.

We arrived to find strips of police tape still fluttering from the gate posts.

He had a key and let us in.

Arriving at the attic flat, he showed me the window that had been forced, and I looked out to see where Angela Hill had been thrown.

I went back to the centre of the room. Unheated since her murder, everything in it was cold. He put on the overhead light. I told him I'd only seen it with the lamps on and with the fire lit. This new, stark light made everything look different.

'It was on,' he said. 'And the lamps.'

I looked around at the few pieces of furniture and the ornaments, the books and plants. Nothing was broken, nothing lying on its side. I told him the room looked larger than when I'd been there before.

'How?'

I went to the sofa-bed. It was pushed back against the wall. The throw and cushions which had covered it were stacked against one arm.

'Was the bed out?' I asked him.

'No. Like that.'

'It was pulled away from the wall, closer to the fire,' I said.

'So you think someone opened it out and closed it up again.' He pulled the sofa open. For it to extend fully, the back of it needed to be flush with the wall. He closed it again.

Everything else seemed exactly as it had been.

He stood by the bed and looked around the room. In the electrical socket by the bed a three-way adaptor held a single plug to one of the lamps. He pointed this out to me, but it suggested nothing and I could remember nothing of it from my visit.

He took out his phone and dialled. He spoke to someone who had been involved in collecting samples from the flat and asked if the bed and everything on it had been examined. Whatever he was told disappointed him. He thanked whoever he was speaking to and hung up.

'Hair, skin, make-up, oil, all hers,' he said.

I showed him where the picture of Angela Hill and her young sister had stood on the mantelpiece.

'We've told everyone to keep an eye out for it,' he said, and as he spoke, the door to the flat slowly opened and we both fell silent.

No one entered, but looking down I saw the cat come purposefully along the short corridor.

'We were wondering about all the cat hairs,' he said.

I told him the cat was half-blind, but said nothing about it having been a gift to Angela Hill from Roper.

We both watched the animal continue slowly towards us, saw it lift its head and stop as it finally sensed our presence in the room, perhaps momentarily mistaking us for the only person in the world who had ever cared for it, and who was now as lost to it as any one of its own nine lives.

25

The address Yvonne had given me for Kelly McLean was at the far side of the Bransholme Estate. I took a bus to the edge of the city, walked to where people congregated at a precinct of shops and asked directions. My request was treated with suspicion by the first man I asked, who wanted to know why I was there. The woman beside him waited until he'd walked away without answering me before pointing to the avenue I wanted. I told her who I was looking for and she immediately brightened at the name.

Kelly McLean, along with Bishop's wife and the parents of the two other missing girls, were still people I needed to talk to before I attempted to visit Roper himself.

Until Yvonne had shown me the photograph of Kelly McLean taken by Roper, it was unlikely, following my only encounter with Wallis seven days earlier, that I would have gone to see her to find out what part, if any, she played in all of this. Even then, standing outside her home, I was not hopeful of anything other than being able to cross her off my list of all those peripherally involved people whose five-year-old ties to Roper had long since frayed and parted.

Knowing from Yvonne that Wallis didn't live here

with Kelly McLean, and that, following the birth of her child, times were hard for her, had persuaded me further that she would be the easiest of those old connections to see and to eliminate.

I rang the bell and waited. A satellite dish pointed out into space above the door.

I heard children inside, shouting and crying.

A woman in her early twenties, holding a baby, answered.

'Kelly McLean?' I said.

She looked over my shoulder to the street beyond.

'I'm a friend of Yvonne's,' I told her.

She held the door for me to go in.

Inside, the noise made conversation impossible, and she closed the door to the room from which most of it came. She told me to wait where I was, went into the room and half-drew the curtains to the window over-looking the street.

'We can go through here,' she said, coming back out to me and indicating a room at the rear, to which a small conservatory had been attached. The garden beyond was narrow, fenced and filled with toys, a swing, a slide and a sand-pit.

'I look after their kids for some of them,' she said. 'Pound an hour.'

'You've got your work cut out,' I said.

'I don't mind, not really.' The baby she still carried was asleep and she laid it beside her on the cane sofa.

'Yvonne said you might be able to help me,' I said.

'She's a friend of my mother's,' she said.

In a small city like Hull it was an easy enough con-nection to make, and people were always willing to make them. Go back a single generation, when the place was still a major freight and fishing port, and hundreds of these links could be sought and found; people felt reassured by them; it meant they might trust you, lower their guard, forget their suspicions. It was why I had already mentioned Yvonne's name twice.

'Is it about Sean?' she said.

'Sean?'

'Sean Wallis. I know you went to see him.' She searched for something.

'Sean, yes,' I said. 'I thought he might be able to clear a few things up for me.'

'About Martin Roper?'

'Yes, Roper,' I said, intrigued that she had used his Christian name and hoping that she might reveal more about her own distant connection to the man without me having to mention the photograph Yvonne had shown me.

Six years had passed, and Kelly McLean had changed beyond all recognition. She had gained weight. Her well-cut blonde hair had grown out brown and now hung shapelessly over her shoulders. She wore no make-up that I could see. Her skin was pale and her face bloated. Dark lines of exhaustion ringed her eyes. She looked nearer forty than twenty.

Perhaps Roper's photo was all that remained of her girlhood dream of beauty, ease, wealth and success. It was a lot to have lost in so short a time. Some people, John Maxwell once told me, were better defined and understood in terms of their losses and emptinesses than their achievements or their belief in themselves. It had been a long five years for Kelly McLean.

'He told me you'd seen him,' she said. 'He give me that thirty quid you give him.'

'That was generous of him,' I said. If Wallis was as greedy as both Sunny and Finch had suggested, then he was more greedy for himself than for his child or its mother.

'Told me to buy something for Ellie Marie,' she said, looking at the sleeping baby. She slid a hand behind one of the cushions and drew out an inhaler. 'Asthma,' she said. 'Nothing serious.'

I looked back into the small room through which we had come into the conservatory. One corner was dominated by a giant television, beside which stood a computer, a VCR, a DVD player, and a video camera mounted on a tripod with wires trailing into the television.

'It belongs to a mate of Sean's,' she said.

Of course it did.

'Sean's just looking after it all for him.'

Of course he was.

'He's going to be a real father to her.'

'Sorry? A real father?'

'You know – to Ellie – me, him and her. Just like a real family. Just because he doesn't live here, he says, doesn't mean he's going to miss out on her growing up. He takes her out, and everything, brings her stuff. She's five months and three weeks.'

I wondered when she'd last seen him. Probably when he gave her the money.

She sucked on the inhaler, her eyes closed.

'What was it you wanted?' she said.

'I'm not really sure,' I said. I told her about James Bishop and his concern at Roper's appeal. 'Just loose ends, really.'

Her disbelieving glance told me she knew I knew about the photograph.

I remarked on how peacefully the baby girl was sleeping.

'She's good like that,' she said. She removed the hood from around the child's face so that I might see her more clearly. 'I give him ten back,' she said.

'Ten?'

'Of that thirty. Out with his mates.' She smiled again at this reference to Wallis's generosity. 'He said he only agreed to talk to you so he could bring a bit more money in. I've got a pram, but it's second-hand. I want one of those American things with three wheels. They're expensive, but you save in the long run.'

She expected me to pay her, too, and understanding this, things became easier for me.

'Does Wallis know about you and Martin Roper?'

She made no attempt to deny what I'd suggested.

'Why would he?' she said. 'All that was years ago. I only met Sean two years back, less.'

'You must have been surprised when Roper turned up here again, especially with Wallis working as a warder in the prison. Weren't you afraid that something might be said, that Wallis would find out?' I was asking primarily to discover how much Wallis had already told her.

'Not really,' she said. 'There weren't nothing in them pictures connected to what Roper got done for afterwards. I was never into any of *that* stuff with him, if that's what you're thinking. We all had them took. Just a laugh. Apart from which—' She stopped.

'What?'

'I'd never seen myself like that before. Even then I hardly recognized myself. What was I, sixteen, seventeen? And now . . . well, you can see for yourself.'

'How did you find out about Roper?'

'I'm not sure. I worked in a supermarket. One of the other girls had her picture done and showed it to the rest of us. There were three or four of us went.'

'And Roper never even suggested that you or he might want to take things a bit further?'

She laughed at the suggestion. 'No. Getting even that much kit off was as daring as we ever got. He was a professional photographer, proper studio, the lot. We might have had a laugh about it among ourselves, but none of us ever took it any further. I remember thinking about it when they arrested him and all that other stuff came out. Some reporters came sniffing around us, but nobody said nothing.'

'And the pictures?'

'Got rid of them. Burned them. I thought the police might find the negatives or something and come to question me, accuse me of being involved in all that other stuff. I don't know how the picture my mother's still got survived.'

Because you'd been unable to destroy it, because it was what all your dreams of the future were founded on.

'What did you think?' she said, her voice low.

'I think he did a good job. You made a good model.'

'Sean would go mental if he knew I'd posed like that, even all that time ago, and especially for Roper. He thinks they ought to hang him. That what he told you?'

'Something like that.'

'I keep telling him he ought to keep his mouth shut, that he's only making it worse for himself with his Prison Board and everything.'

'It's not the first time he's been in trouble,' I said.

'I know. That's why he says he's got to make a bit of money while he can. He's a dreamer, always has been.'

'Did you ever know a girl called Angela Hill?' I said.

Nothing registered. 'Never heard of her. Who is she?'

'Just another girl who had her photo taken by Roper.'

The police had so far released no further information about their suspicions concerning how Angela Hill had died. I'd hoped for a connection to her via Wallis and whatever he might have known.

'She was in the papers,' I said.

'Then good luck to her.' She turned to look out over the scattered toys. Rain pooled on the seats of small chairs and in the sand-pit. 'Me and Sean are going to get married,' she said. 'Probably at the Register, but I'll have a dress and everything, do it right.'

I rose and went to admire the equipment beside the television.

'You'd better not touch it,' she said. 'He'll go mental if he thinks I've been messing with it. Press the wrong button, he said, and you can do a lot of damage.'

The sound of something being dropped or thrown came through from the other room and she told me to watch the sleeping baby while she went to investigate.

She returned a minute later.

'No harm done,' she said.

I told her it was time for me to leave and repeated that I didn't really know why I'd come there in the first place. She was relieved that I had asked her – and that she had disclosed – so little. She remarked for the first time on my fading bruise.

'Steering wheel,' I said.

'Right. Never learned myself. No point. Sean takes us everywhere we need to go.'

I told her I was grateful for all her help.

'I've not really told you nothing,' she said, prompting my reassuring confirmation.

'I know,' I said. 'But I had to ask – Yvonne, Roper, the picture and everything.'

'You won't tell Sean, will you?'

'That I've been to see you?'

'Anything.'

It was what I wanted her to say. I took out my wallet.

'I'm working for James Bishop,' I said. 'Not the police, not anybody else.'

'Sean says he's not saying nothing everybody else in the prison doesn't already know.'

'I won't say a thing about seeing you,' I said. I gave her forty pounds.

'What's this for?' she said, the words no more than a reflex, her fingers already closing round the notes.

'For the new pram,' I said.

'Sean will want to know where I got it. I'll hide it.'

'Our secret,' I said, and then added, 'Before I forget – where did Roper take the photos, the Anlaby Road studio?'

'Behind a chemist's shop. Nothing to look at from the outside, but, like I said, a real professional set-up once you were in. I think they knocked it all down.'

'Right,' I said. 'Did he work anywhere else that you knew of?'

She shook her head. 'I was only there for less than an hour.'

'I'd be grateful if you remembered anything else,' I said, holding my wallet between us.

'Sorry,' she said.

She checked the sleeping baby and walked with me past the room of noisy children back to the front door.

She opened this, looked out and then immediately closed it again.

'What is it?'

'Nothing,' she said. 'Just somebody I don't want to see. Just wait.'

I pulled her hand off the catch, opened the door and looked out. There was no one there. Along the road an old-design green Polo turned the corner and disappeared.

'The neighbours keep threatening to send the inspectors round,' she said. 'You need licences to look after kids these days, proper training. Anyhow, it probably wasn't even them.' She asked me which way I was going, and when I pointed to the shops in the opposite direction taken by the car, she seemed relieved.

As soon as I stepped outside, she closed the door behind me.

I walked back to the shops and waited at the bus shelter there. I watched to see if the car reappeared, but it never came.

If nothing else, I'd learned four things: I'd learned that Wallis had lied to her and that his own investment in their future together was considerably less gilt-edged than her own; I'd learned that the photograph taken of her by Roper had been intended for someone other than Wallis; I'd learned that Wallis had frequent access to a car that wasn't his own; and I'd learned that the number on the photograph was not connected to Roper's long-demolished studio. I didn't know for certain what any of it meant, or where it might lead, but I'd learned it.

26

The next day I went to visit Patricia Bishop in Kirk Ella.

The house was less than a mile from where Angela Hill had once lived and, like hers, it was large and surrounded by a well-established garden and a high wall and gates. Unlike hers, it did not reveal itself to the street, and nothing of it was visible from the entrance to the driveway, which curved sharply and was bordered by tall, dark pines. The entrance to Hull Golf Club lay a short distance away across the road.

The gates were open and I walked to the door, knocked using the ornate lion's-head knocker, and waited.

There was a click from the white box beside the door and a woman's voice told me to press the button beneath this. I pressed and a buzzer sounded inside. At the same time, the small camera mounted above the door whirred gently. I turned to face it and spoke into the box.

Patricia Bishop opened the door several minutes later. She apologized for the delay, but made no attempt to sound either convincing or concerned.

'The knocker's for show,' she told me. 'You press the

button, the camera takes your picture, and when that happens the automatic lock awaits my response and then I press it, or don't press it.'

'You can't be too careful,' I said.

'Under the circumstances,' she said, 'I find that remark both facetious and offensive. I know who you are, Mr Rivers, and I know why you're here. I've never met a private investigator before, but, please, do try to live down to my expectations.'

'I'll do my best,' I told her.

'When Nicola was taken from us my husband vowed never to leave us so vulnerable or exposed ever again.'

By 'us' she meant her. And their daughter had been abducted from somewhere in Hull city centre, five miles away, another world.

'You know by now what a thorough man James is. Thorough and devoted.' And by that she meant devoted to her, which was still not an easy thing to believe. She spoke about her daughter as though she were a jewel that had been stolen from her. Daughter, door, vulnerability, locks, husband, devotion, camera: her tone remained evenly pitched.

'I don't know what you expect me to tell you, Mr Rivers. I suppose I should ask you if you have some means of identification.' She held out her hand.

'Perhaps I should go back outside and hold it up to the camera,' I said.

'James has told me about you, of course, but you *might* be an impostor.'

'Someone pretending to be *me*?' I said.

'I suppose so,' she said. She walked ahead of me and paused at the end of the long hallway, as though deciding which of the four rooms leading from it best suited her purpose. I heard a vacuum cleaner upstairs.

'Our cleaner,' she said. 'She's usually long gone by now. Running late.' She spoke of the woman as though she disapproved of her. She stopped walking. 'I think in here,' she said, and led me into the kitchen. A radio played, which she switched off. 'Noise,' she said.

Apart from the distant vacuum, the house was silent. 'Fire away,' she said.

She sat at the table and brushed non-existent crumbs from it with her palm. Then she wiped her palm clean with the other.

'I've not come to question you,' I said.

'Oh?'

'I doubt if there's a single aspect of your daughter's abduction that you haven't already considered a thousand times over.'

'A million,' she said. 'So what is this? Something you promised my husband you'd do, something *he* insisted on?'

'I just wanted to see you,' I told her, hoping my honesty might temper her hostility towards me. 'To see you and to see where Nicola lived.'

'None of which will bring her back to us, Mr Rivers.'

'No, but—'

She held up her hand. 'I apologize for that last stupid remark. These things tend to follow a pattern.'

I told her I understood and she sagged a little.

'Our daughter was abducted, used and murdered,' she said. 'And we've known all that ever since the man responsible was arrested, charged and convicted. We had a year to prepare ourselves for the worst, and even when that confirmation came, I'd say we were about 0.1 per cent ready for it.'

'I don't want to go over that same painful old ground,' I said.

'It will be painful for me until the day I die, Mr Rivers,' she said. 'Nothing will ever change that.'

'Your husband told me you were pregnant again, soon after Roper was convicted.'

'Briefly. But I willed the baby to die, and it died.'

This harshness surprised me, and she looked up at me to see how her words had registered.

'No – not really,' she said. 'But I will admit that the thought of another baby, another child, so soon after all that had just happened to us did not inspire me with any true hope for the future. Anyhow, it wasn't to be.'

'Would you have had other children if you hadn't lost Nicola?'

'Absolutely not. Her birth, and afterwards, was not a particularly pleasant experience for me, not a pleasant time at all.'

'You suffered from depression?'

'How reassuringly simple and straightforward it sounds when you say it like that. Yes, I suffered from depression. It lasted a year, and afterwards I was fine, cured, the happy mother of a beautiful daughter. What more could I ask for? James's businesses were going from strength to strength, and everything we had ever wanted, or thought we ever wanted, we got.'

'Before Nicola disappeared,' I said, 'did you have any idea, any idea at all, that there were parts of her life she was keeping from you, that you never even suspected?'

'She was a teenage girl. Of course she kept things from us. That's what teenage girls do.'

'And until Roper was arrested and made his confession, you had no idea whatsoever that there was any connection between them, let alone what Nicola might have been involved in with him?'

'The man was a paedophile and a pornographer. What are you suggesting?'

'I'm not suggesting anything,' I said. 'I just need to know what you and your husband knew, what you honestly knew.'

She believed I'd tried to trick her and she became angry.

'I'm just trying to understand why he chose Nicola and those others – why he named them in his confession – why *them* out of all the others he might have named – why them out of the dozens available to him,' I said.

'Why does there need to be a reason? The man was sick. It's why he did what he did. Why go looking for a reason when it's the last thing *he* needed? And you're right – we have gone over this at least a thousand times. My husband went to see all those other poor parents in an attempt to understand better what connected us, what tied us all together in this, but there was nothing, absolutely nothing, nothing at all.'

'Did they talk to him?'

'Not really. They accused him of interfering. They just wanted to be left alone with their own grief. I can't even remember their names – Hayley something – she was the one whose body they found, but not the other two.'

'Lindsey Perry and Jennifer Wilson,' I said.

'See,' she said. 'They mean nothing to me. If they'd meant something, I would have remembered them. Wouldn't I?'

'Angela Hill?' I said.

'Who's she?'

'She was Nicola's friend. The girl photographed with your husband at Nicola's school memorial service.'

'I never attended.'

'I know.'

'No, you don't – I'd miscarried less than a week earlier. Stop fooling yourself that you know me, Mr Rivers.'

I apologized. 'What happened when your husband tried to see the other parents?'

'Like I said, they told him to leave them alone.'

'Did he think they were keeping something from him?'

'You know James, Mr Rivers. If he wants something, he usually gets it. More than anything, I suppose, he was angry at their refusal to share in his outrage and condemnation of Roper.'

'It seems unlikely,' I said.

'They weren't our kind of people, Mr Rivers. You might say that their own grief rendered them

236

inarticulate as well as inconsolable. They would rather have lynched Roper and then chopped him into pieces than find out from him what had happened to their own missing daughters. You might also say that James has been on the same hopeless quest ever since.'

'Hence my involvement now,' I said.

' "Involvement"? You're *employed*, Mr Rivers, not involved. James and I are involved; you are employed for money to do what he tells you to do.'

Neither of us spoke for a moment.

'They were entitled to grieve, to mourn, to get angry in their own way,' I said eventually.

'I understand that,' she said. 'But I could never convince James of it. It didn't help, of course, that Nicola's body was never recovered. I think if we'd been able to have her back, even then, even knowing what we knew, I think things would have been different for us.'

'For you or for your husband?'

'Mostly for James.' She paused. 'It took me a long time, three years perhaps, but I think I finally found some peace, some respite from it all. I think I finally stopped dwelling on it to such a great extent.'

'Were you ever able to confide this to your husband?'

She shook her head. 'How do you tell someone that *you're* getting over something that is continuing to shake *them* to their core?'

I was still not convinced that Bishop had been wholly unaware of what his daughter was involved in before her abduction. Perhaps it was this knowledge which prevented him from moving on, which drove itself into the first of the opening spaces between himself and his wife. They were like two rotten trees that had become uprooted and then fallen against each other in a storm.

'Did coming to terms with Nicola's death make you feel guilty?' I said.

'Because my own anguish was not as great or as all-consuming as his? Because I wanted everything to pass and to fade away, whereas all James ever wanted was to keep everything alive and constantly agitated? Because he thought more of his dead daughter than—' Again she stopped abruptly. 'You get the picture, Mr Rivers.'

'You stayed with him,' I said.

'Is that the best you can do? Yes, I stayed with him, went on living here surrounded by everything I thought I'd ever wanted.'

'You could have gone.'

'I could have done a thousand things, but for years I wouldn't have been able to convince myself that any one of them was what I truly wanted. And, afterwards, well, everything seemed too late. The world had turned on its head.'

'And you just clung to the wreckage.'

'I just clung to the wreckage.'

Just like Angela Hill had clung to the wreckage of her own life for so long.

Above us, the vacuum fell silent. She looked at her watch and then at the ceiling.

'Did my husband tell you about the grave?' she said.

At first I thought I'd misheard her. 'Whose grave?'

'A grave for Nicola. When it became clear to us that her body might never be retrieved and returned to us for proper burial he went to the local vicar and asked if he could create a grave for her in the churchyard. I think he thought the circumstances were so exceptional that the vicar, the church authorities, would bend their rules and make an exception for him, for us. He just wanted somewhere he might be able to imagine her to be, somewhere he could go and pretend he was with her again.'

'What did you think to the idea?'

'I seem to remember that I didn't have much say in the matter.'

'What happened?'

'The vicar told him it couldn't be done. He

238

suggested a compromise – a memorial plaque inside the church itself.'

'But it wasn't enough for your husband?'

She shook her head. 'He accused them of failing in their duty – their obligation – to Nicola. We used to go to the church quite regularly beforehand, but never afterwards. Afterwards, James turned his back on them.'

We were interrupted then by a woman coming backwards through the door dragging the vacuum.

'This is Mrs Ellison,' Patricia Bishop said to me. And to the woman, she said, 'This is Mr Rivers. He's an associate of James's.'

The woman looked at me, said, 'Oh, right,' and then told Patricia Bishop that she was finished for the day.

'Yes, Mrs Danvers,' Patricia Bishop mouthed as the door closed behind the woman.

27

On my way back into the city centre, Finch called me with the news that he'd been able to trace the telephone number on the back of Kelly McLean's photo. The good news, he said, was that it was a pay phone which stood at the entrance to the Easington caravan park where Roper's mother had had her caravan, and where she had died. The bad news was that, according to Finch's contact, the phone had been taken out of service in November 1997, a year before Roper's arrest, and two before his mother's death. No one knew why this had happened.

'Perhaps Roper and Kelly McLean had something going and it was a one-off number where she might have been able to contact him,' Finch suggested. 'Perhaps Roper had gone to the caravan and she was supposed to call him there at a prearranged time.'

None of which sounded convincing.

'Do you know exactly where the phone stood?' I asked him.

'My contact faxed me a map with the information. It's marked. Do you think there's something there for us to find?'

'The place meant a lot to Roper.'

'Until his mother died there.'

240

'He was already convicted and serving his sentence when that happened. Whatever it is, it's something we can't ignore,' I said.

'You still think Roper might have hidden something there – at the camp or the caravan?'

'The caravan was completely destroyed in the fire. And what wasn't burned beyond recognition was probably shovelled into a skip and disposed of a long way beyond Roper's control.'

'In the camp, then?'

'It would make as much sense as anything.'

We arranged to meet the following day. He insisted on visiting the place with me.

'So anything we find you can report immediately to Smart?' I said.

'No – because you can't drive yourself there. Besides, you'd tell him yourself.'

'Of course I would.'

'Even if it meant telling Smart before you reported to Bishop?' he said.

This reference to Bishop only minutes after leaving his home made me cautious.

'Bishop?' I said.

'Plus,' he said, avoiding answering me, 'you're probably still as unhappy as we are about the fact that Sullivan retired to somewhere so close to somewhere which meant so much to Roper's mother and to Roper himself as a boy.'

'Meaning you think Sullivan might also have been interested in the place as somewhere Roper might have hidden something? Something he might now discover and use to redeem himself?'

'It's not beyond the realms of possibility,' he said.

'Ah,' I said, ' "the realms of possibility",' and hung up.

I looked behind the bus on which I was travelling. There were a dozen cars which might have been following me, but nothing I recognized.

Finch called me again later to say that he'd been

unable to find out anything else about the disconnected phone, except that the campsite had been sold earlier that same year and that the new owners had subsequently redeveloped and upgraded it, and that several buildings, including the old clubhouse, had been demolished as part of this work. In all likelihood, the phone had been in this lost building.

The following morning, he arrived at eight, and by nine we were at the Easington caravan park.

It was bitterly cold on the coast and there was snow in the air. Finch had arranged for the owner of the camp to meet us there, and to bring with him any old plans he had of the place.

The man was there before us. At our arrival, he came to us and climbed into the back of Finch's car. His name was Reece, and even before he had finished shaking the damp from his coat, he told us that he had no idea why we were there, and that whatever it was we might be looking for, we were unlikely to find it.

Finch asked him when he had bought the camp.

'Winter, ninety-nine,' he said, making it clear to us that it had not been one of his wisest investments. He had with him a carrier of old maps and outline plans of the site, which it was difficult for him to show us in the car. He indicated a building a short distance away and said we could better examine them there. He remained suspicious of everything either Finch or I said, and after he had left the car and run through the wind and the watery snow, Finch told me not to reveal anything to him.

We followed him into a room overlooking the camp entrance. The caravans stretched away to the low clay cliff behind us.

'There was a fire here,' Finch said.

'Apparently,' Reece said. 'Just before my time.'

'But you knew about it?'

' 'Course I did. It was one reason the previous owner

decided to sell up. A fire like that brought a few too many Health and Safety inspectors into the place. You'd be surprised how many rules and regulations there are these days.'

'And the previous owner hadn't kept everything up to scratch?'

'Something like that.'

'And so you were able to take advantage of the situation,' Finch said. 'And buy the place cheap.'

'I paid a fair price,' Reece insisted. 'There was a lot needed doing.'

'And, presumably, if you knew there was a fire, then you also knew whose caravan had burned.'

Reece admitted this reluctantly. 'One of the other caravan owners said that once the connection had been made between that guy in Hull and his mother here, some of them wanted her evicted.'

'So she might have been burned out by an angry mob? Is that what you're suggesting?'

'Look, just who are you?' Reece said.

Finch showed him his warrant card. 'And this is Rivers.'

Reece finished laying out the maps.

'Where was the fire?' Finch said.

'E44,' Reece said, tracing his finger along a row of numbered rectangles. 'The site was cleared up straight away. We had a lot of other work going on at the same time. It was the start of the closed season. We had to work fast before the following March when the site opened up again.'

'But you were also aware that some of the owners came in during the few days after the season officially ended to get things sorted out for the winter?'

Reece nodded.

'Must have come as a great shock to you to discover that a woman had died in the fire. Even if she was the mother of a convicted paedophile and murderer.'

'Yes, well . . .' Reece said.

Finch took out the blueprint upon which the

243

telephone had been marked. 'Was this building part of the demolition work?'

Reece studied it. 'That's the old clubhouse. Been up since 1956. It would have fallen down by itself if we hadn't seen to it. People expect a bit more these days.'

'And what about the public phone in it?'

'No idea. Presumably the phone people will have come and taken it out.'

I was beginning to wonder what more we might learn from the removal.

'What sort of phone was it?' Finch said.

'It was a phone box, a red metal and glass phone box just outside the door. Put there when the clubhouse was built, probably. Afterwards, we had others installed inside the new building. You can't have just one public phone on a place this size. Come to think of it, I don't even think it was working when I first came here. In fact I'm certain it wasn't. It had been disconnected beforehand.'

'Before the fire?' Finch said.

'What's that got to do with anything? It might not have worked for years.'

'Show us where it was,' I said.

Reece looked outside. 'In this?'

'In this,' Finch told him.

We followed him to where the old clubhouse had once stood, and where there was now a car park. Reece studied the map and moved back and forth over the empty space. Finally, he called us to him at the edge of the land.

'The car park's built along the line of the old frontage,' he said, pleased with himself at what he had discovered. 'So the phone would be about' – he walked away from us, judging his position against the new building – 'here.'

We went to him.

'That's the old path running up to the door,' he said, indicating a disused track leading to the edge of the car park. 'The booth would have been just here.' He stamped his foot on the ground.

There was nothing to see. Finch and I searched a few yards in every direction. There was still nothing.

'What were you hoping to find?' Reece said.

And only then did it occur to me that Finch might have believed that this was where one or more of the missing girls might have been buried.

I took him to one side. 'You didn't think any of the girls might have been brought here, surely?'

'Look around you. Can you think of anywhere better to hide them? A place practically deserted for half the year. All that rebuilding, all those new foundations.'

But I knew by the way he said it that he was not convinced of what he was saying.

'And you think that's why Roper left a record of the phone number – to keep us pointed here?'

' "Us"?' he said, then, letting out his breath, 'No, not really. The number might just as easily have been lost or destroyed with the photograph. It never turned up anywhere else in Roper's evidence.'

'So all it does is confirm his connection to the caravan site.'

'Which everyone knew about already.' He asked Reece to take us to where Roper's mother's caravan had once stood.

Each of the rows of caravans was lettered, each caravan numbered.

We came to E44. The new caravan was identical to those on either side of it. A wooden stairway had been built up to its door, a platform attached beneath its window looking out over all the other caravans.

'What would the caravan that burned have looked like?' Finch asked Reece.

'Not like this,' Reece told him. 'Top of the range, this. The old ones would have been a lot smaller, less well equipped. It had been here since 1972, apparently.'

'He's been doing his homework,' Finch whispered to me.

'Five years before Roper was born,' I said.

If there had once been a mark on the ground to indicate where the old caravan had burned, then there was nothing now. The wet snow touched the grass and collected in thin drifts.

'It's a dead-end,' Finch said eventually, having walked all around the new caravan.

And overhearing him, Reece said, 'I could have told you that and saved you a journey.'

'I know,' Finch told him. He looked around him. 'Which direction is Spurn?'

Reece pointed.

Then Finch and I left him and walked back to his car.

'Would finding the phone booth still here have made any difference?' I said.

'We might have dug beneath it and found a sealed box containing Roper's insurance,' he said, smiling, and then added, 'When the inquiry into Sullivan's investigation was under way, they dug out the foundation of the caravan on the off-chance. It seemed too good and too obvious a chance to miss.'

'And?'

'They found a few metal toy cars that Roper might either have lost or buried there as a boy. Apart from that, nothing.'

We both watched as Reece came back out, walked to his car and drove away.

'They checked him out, too,' Finch said.

'Hoping to find what?'

'That he was a member of a consortium that included one of Roper's known associates.'

'And?'

'Less than nothing,' he said.

'So why did we come?'

'Because I still think there's something here that everybody's missing, something Roper himself wanted us to at least be aware of.'

'Do you want me to ask him about it if he agrees to see me?'

'If he sees you, he'll have his own reasons for doing so. And whatever he wants to tell you, he'll tell you.'

We returned to his car. I knew what he meant about the place; I felt something similar, and something equally inexplicable and elusive.

'Why the question about Spurn?' I asked him.

'I might want to go there one day when all this is over,' he said.

'Right,' I said.

28

Three days later, Monday morning, I arrived at Humber Street to find both Smart and Finch waiting for me. They were parked directly outside the main entrance. Smart was the first to leave the car. He carried an envelope, which he gave to me.

'Roper has agreed to you visiting him,' he said.

I took the envelope.

'And you were informed before me?' I said. 'The applicant?'

'Your confirmation will have arrived Saturday morning,' he said. He indicated the mail-boxes inside the door.

Finch got out of the car and came to stand beside us.

'You don't sound too surprised that he agreed to see me,' I said to Smart.

'A week ago, he wouldn't have looked twice at the application.'

Angela Hill. I stopped trying to provoke him.

'Whatever it takes, Mr Rivers.' He motioned to the door.

I opened the envelope he had given me and read the few details of the single sheet it contained.

'Thursday,' Finch said. 'Two o'clock.'

We went up to my office.

'I want Finch to go with you,' Smart said to me once we were inside.

'No,' I told him. 'Roper has agreed to see *me*, and whether or not it's because of some long-held affection he might or might not have had for Angela Hill, he's refused every other request you or anyone remotely related to you has ever made to see him over the past five years, and whatever you've pretended to promise him.'

'During which time we could have *insisted* on talking to him,' Smart said.

'And learned what?' I turned to Finch, annoying Smart even further. 'Have the cars all been checked?'

'They're still on it. The weekend slowed things down.' He shrugged to signal his own disbelief and disappointment at the speed with which things were being done by the local men to whom the task had been given.

'Forget the cars,' Smart shouted. 'If Roper talks, we won't need *any* of that.'

'Everything he says will be part of a deal,' I said. 'Because that's why he's agreed to see me.'

'Do you still honestly think Angela Hill has some part to play, knowingly or otherwise, in Roper releasing his evidence against the others to us?' Finch said to me.

I wasn't convinced one way or the other. If she and Roper had been in contact, then she had lied to me; besides which, Smart would already have been aware of the connection. What mattered to me now was that my enquiries had led her killer to her, and that her murder had caused Roper to break his silence and see me.

'I'm seeing him on behalf of Bishop, remember?' I said. 'I made that clear on my application to him. There was no mention whatsoever of Angela Hill. He has no idea I even know she exists.'

'He'll know everything there is to know by now,' Finch said.

'He'll know that you've taken practically every step with me,' I said. 'He'll know that his being brought back here so close to his appeal was no coincidence.'

'So what?' Smart said. 'He'll also know that his conviction for the murder of Hayley Forbes will still stand, whatever else he's banking on. The only thing that's changed is that now he's just as ready to jump as we are to push him.'

Considering Angela Hill's death, the remark was in poor taste, and Finch looked away as Smart made it.

'What?' Smart said, realizing. 'Respect for the dead? Don't make me laugh. You hardly knew her. Get Roper to tell you where those three other girls are buried, get him to tell us who else was involved and how many other young girls they might have abused and then killed who we don't even know about, and *then* you can talk to me about respect for the dead.' He held up his hands. 'OK, I'm sorry. It was a thoughtless thing to say. But if her death is to count for something, then what we need now is to work out exactly what kind of pressure to apply to Roper, and how best to apply it. OK, I agree – Roper is as far ahead of us as he's always been, but up until now there's never been anything we could do to close that gap, let alone force his hand where the others were concerned. Whatever you think *you* might want, Mr Rivers, *I'm* not going to throw away that opportunity now.'

'Which is precisely what will happen if anyone other than me turns up to talk to him. Roper knows Angela Hill and Nicola Bishop were connected, and you don't believe any more than I do that Roper alone killed Nicola Bishop, or even that he had any involvement in her death other than perhaps procuring her for the men already taking over his operation.'

Smart remained silent for several seconds. 'We know all this,' he said. 'My concern – *our* concern – now is just to keep Roper moving in the right direction, and to be in a position to act on anything he might reveal the instant he does so.'

It was almost nine o'clock, and lorries came and went among the stores below. Smart rose and went to the window and looked down at those manoeuvring close to his car. He came back to us.

'I accept that we have no chance of talking to Roper ourselves,' he said. 'And you know he isn't talking to you out of remorse for the death of a girl he might or might not have had a hand in killing all those years ago. All I want to do between now and Thursday is to make sure we all know exactly where we stand and what we all need to get from this. Roper's making us a one-off offer here. It won't be repeated. And regardless of our differences on this, we both know that for any-thing useful to come out of your visit, we've all got to be at least as aware of what's happening here as Roper is, and as his erstwhile so-called associates certainly are.'

He pre-empted my next question by saying, 'It wouldn't be in any of our interests for me to tell you the names of those men, Mr Rivers. If you know them, you'll give something away to him. Everything now has to come from Roper. But remember – he knows all about this investigation and he'll be watching you for any indication that you're working on our behalf at the expense of James Bishop. If you think *we've* been using you, Mr Rivers, then it's nothing to what he'll attempt to do.'

'And you already know what the others are capable of,' Finch said.

Smart rose to leave. 'If it makes you feel any better, talk to Bishop about what's going to happen. There's still something that will connect his daughter's dis-appearance and death to Roper other than Roper's confession. Like I said, we've never been ahead on this one, and nor have you, Mr Rivers. Who knows – Roper might yet see that his main chance lies elsewhere and cancel the visiting order. We have to do something while the opportunity exists.'

Without mentioning that I'd been to see Kelly

McLean, I asked Finch if he knew when Wallis's disciplinary hearing was being held. He didn't know.

'Forget Wallis,' Smart told me. 'He was a way in, that's all. He's as stupid as he is greedy.' He motioned to Finch and the two of them left.

'I'll speed up the cars,' Finch said to me in the doorway.

I stood at the window and watched them go. It had been six days since I'd last spoken to James Bishop. I'd been expecting him to call me following my unannounced visit to see his wife.

I called him and told him about Martin Roper agreeing to see me. I asked if we could meet. He was in London, he said. Business. He'd be back in Hull by the early evening. He asked me why I thought Roper had agreed to see me after remaining silent for so long. I told him we could discuss all this later. We fixed a time and a place, and I sat listening to the distorted rasp of his breathing for a few seconds before he hung up.

29

I told him as soon as I saw him that I did not believe that he had been completely unaware of his daughter's involvement with Roper prior to Roper's confession, and that one of his reasons for coming to see me upon hearing of Roper's appeal was to satisfy his need for revenge on the man. I also told him that I believed he knew about Angela Hill and his daughter – how, in his mind, Angela Hill had led his daughter to the man who had killed her – and that this was the reason for the continuing hostility between himself and Paul Hill. And I told him that I believed Smart had used him – Bishop – just as he was now using me.

He waited silently as I said all this, and then said, 'What else?'

'Nothing,' I said.

'You're right in some of what you surmise,' he said. 'Though I doubt "revenge" is the right word. I merely wish to ensure that Roper stays where he is and that he isn't released as part of some deal he is allowed to make in return for selling his associates to Smart.'

We were again in the bar of the Royal Hotel, where he had come directly from his train.

'I need to be straight on all of this because I can't sit and talk to Roper without knowing everything he knows concerning Nicola,' I said. 'I need to know, for instance, what contact you had with him at the time of his trial.'

He drained his glass and held it up to one of the waiters, indicating that we both needed a refill.

'None,' he said. 'My overriding concern and purpose then was to discover what had happened to Nicola, and to keep Patricia from the worst of it.'

'*She* didn't know, did she?' I said.

He shook his head. 'I honestly don't know what made Nicola do those things. Boys, alcohol, drugs I could have understood, but not that. How can any father believe that his daughter was sexually active at that age?'

'You didn't see what everybody else saw,' I said.

'Obviously. But *that*? The things Roper said she did, the things she'd agreed to do.'

'We only have his word for all that. He had reason to lie, remember?'

He looked up at me. 'I appreciate what you're misguidedly attempting to do, Mr Rivers, but I'm beyond all that. She *did* those things they said she did. I might have been the last person in the world to want to accept it, but I finally did accept it.'

The waiter brought our drinks and Bishop paid for them.

'I used to be so proud of how strong-willed our daughter was. Daughters are supposed to be like their mothers, but not Nicola – she was always more like me. I used to despise Patricia for what she'd become – greedy, ostentatious, lazy, always getting everything for nothing. Afterwards – after the trial – I wanted to blame *her* for everything that had happened, to believe that it was *her*, and not me, that Nicola was rebelling against. I was the one out at work, away from home on business all the time; *she* was the one who was supposed to be keeping a close watch on our daughter. I couldn't believe that she hadn't known what was happening.'

'Perhaps she did,' I said.

He shook his head. 'No, she saw nothing. All that, and she saw nothing. Too full of herself and all her socializing, all her good works.' He paused, then looked at the men and women around us. 'Shall I tell you how I discovered something was happening, Mr Rivers? I saw her play-acting on her bed, lying there, caressing herself, moaning and groaning, pretending, rehearsing what Roper was asking – paying – her to do. And do you know what – she was good at it. She made herself up, dressed herself like a woman five years older, and then behaved like one. I *saw* her, saw it all.'

I realized only then what he was saying.

'On a monitor, you mean,' I said.

'She never knew. There were security cameras all over the house.'

'Even her bedroom?'

He bowed his head and nodded. 'You'd never know they were there. I took them all out afterwards.'

'Did anyone else know?'

'Mrs Ellison.'

'Your housekeeper?'

'I had to show her how to set the alarm. The cameras were only supposed to be operational when the alarm was set. Everything was wired up to the single monitor in my study. She turned it on once in error after I'd keyed in the alarm code. She didn't know what to do and so she showed me. I passed it off as Nicola growing up, copying something she'd seen in a film, living in a fantasy, whatever.'

'But she didn't believe you?'

'Tell me, is that how *you* would want to remember your own dead daughter? I kept a closer watch on Nicola after that. I still had no idea, of course, that she was doing this for anyone else, that anyone else was involved. This was only three weeks before she disappeared. What could I do? I'd seen what I'd seen, but can you imagine what either Nicola or Patricia would have done if I'd told them about it, if I'd brought it out into the open? Every week there seemed to be some fresh row between the two of them, with Nicola always threatening to leave home and her mother always threatening to throw her out.'

'At fourteen?'

'You'd be surprised how often it happens,' he said. 'I thought it would all pass – that whatever she was doing, and whatever she got out of it – would pass, and that she'd leave it all behind her.'

'And during those three weeks, you envied your wife her ignorance?'

He nodded. 'Of course I did. And eventually I came to despise her for it, too. There was one occasion, after the trial, when I asked her if she believed everything that had been said about Nicola was true, and she slapped me across the face, hard, over and over, and screamed at me, asking me how I could possibly even begin to imagine that anything Roper had said might be true.'

'What happened?'

'I let her go on hitting me. Even now there's still a part of me that wants to be convinced that I've got it all wrong – that the film lied and that Patricia was right all along.'

'That's not going to happen,' I said.

'I know.'

I asked him about his trip to London. Alison Menzies had accompanied him, but had gone straight from the train to a taxi.

'You could have told me all this from the outset,' I told him.

'No, I couldn't. What father could tell anyone *that* about his own daughter?'

'You don't need me to tell you this,' I said, 'but I'll do everything I can to get something out of Roper concerning what happened to Nicola.'

'I know,' he said. He raised his glass again and beckoned to the same waiter.

'Tell me what you want me to ask him,' I said.

He thought about this and ran a hand over his face before answering me.

30

Prior to being attacked, I had intended visiting the parents of both Lindsey Perry and Jennifer Wilson, the remaining two girls named by Roper in his confession.

I knew from Sunny's files, from what Smart had told me, and from what I had read of the controversy surrounding Sullivan's early retirement, that many other teenage girls were then listed as missing; some, presumably, still were. Finch had calculated there to be between eight and twelve girls aged between thirteen and sixteen, all of whom lived within a thirty-mile radius of Hull. Most were assumed to have run away from home. There was an appeal at the time of Roper's conviction for all these girls to contact their families to let them know they were safe, and for them to be eliminated from the police inquiries. Only three responded.

However the sums were done, there was considerable scope after Roper's trial, in both the inquiry into Sullivan's methods and Smart's inquiry now, for the boundaries to have been widened to include at least some of these other missing girls. I did not anticipate there would be any conclusive connection made between the four girls named by Roper and these others, but I remained intrigued as to why those four particular girls were named and none of those others, especially when naming them would have further served Roper's purpose in adding to the uncertainty surrounding his confession and subsequent conviction.

Lindsey Perry had gone missing at least a year before her involvement with Roper came to light. She had been put up for adoption at birth, and since the age of eight had lived in a succession of council-operated homes. Prior to that, she had been fostered by six different couples. She had absconded from most of the council homes. At twelve, she had spent ten months in a secure unit in the Midlands following a succession of juvenile offences, including theft and arson, and upon her release she had come to Hull to live with yet more foster-parents.

At fourteen, she had run away from them, and up until the time of her final disappearance less than a year later, she had lived in a hostel on Marfleet Lane. She was there for seven months, and with the exception of the juvenile detention centre, it was the longest she had ever stayed in one place during the past nine years.

While at the hostel she had attended Archbishop Thurstan school, but her attendance there had been intermittent and disruptive and there was little real expectation that she would achieve anything academically. For her first few months in the city, Educational Welfare Officers visited her at the hostel. After that they appeared to have abandoned her completely to her own devices.

It had come as a surprise to everyone involved in Roper's prosecution that he had insisted on naming her as one of the four girls he had used, killed and then disposed of.

At the time of her disappearance from the hostel, no one who knew Lindsey Perry was unduly concerned by her absence, and it was assumed by most that she had returned to the Midlands.

It was not until her name appeared on Roper's list and he remained adamant that she was one of his victims, that one of Sullivan's officers began looking into her background. As a result of this, it was suggested by Sullivan that Roper had seen a list of the missing and had chosen these names at random from it. He was playing games, Sullivan said, knowing that some of these girls would remain for ever elusive. It was his belief, Sullivan said in an equally unguarded public moment, that they might attempt to extend the case against Roper to include the killing of Lindsey Perry only then to have her appear alive and well a hundred miles away a few months later. It was another reason, he said, for concentrating their case on the murder of Hayley Forbes alone. At least with Hayley Forbes, the assumption went, they had the body and the evidence to prove conclusively that Roper had murdered her.

When I arrived at the Marfleet Lane hostel, having called to confirm that there would be someone there to whom I would be able to talk, I was met by a woman who introduced herself as Claire Madison, and who immediately held up her laminated identity card which she wore on a chain around her neck. She told me that she was in the middle of a crisis and that she would be grateful if I got straight to the point.

I began to explain to her why I was there.

She held up a hand to stop me. 'So you're not Child Protection or Educational Welfare?' she said.

I told her I wasn't, but it seemed like an admission of a great deal more.

'Then I can't talk to you,' she said.

'You were in charge of the hostel when Lindsey Perry went missing,' I said, uncertain how she might respond to this.

'And?' she said brusquely. 'I gave a full account of everything I knew about Lindsey Perry and the circumstances of her disappearance. These things happen all the time. They happened then and they happen now.'

'I understand that,' I said. 'But you told Sullivan's men what you knew in the light of Roper's confession. I'm just trying to understand how differently you might have responded if you hadn't known what Roper had already told them about Lindsey's association with him.'

'Meaning what?' she said.

'Meaning most people probably believed what Roper was telling them because it was what they wanted to believe. Meaning that of all the four girls he named, Lindsey Perry was probably the one most likely, in most people's eyes, to fit the bill and—'

'I made no judgement of her whatsoever,' she said. 'And if you are accusing me now of professional laxity or indifference towards a client, then I assure you I was cleared completely of even the suggestion of such a thing at the time.'

'I'm not,' I said, noting her retreat into this imprecise and deflective language.

'You're certainly *behaving* as though you suspect me of having failed in my duty to Lindsey Perry.'

'She had no one else looking out for her interests,' I said.

'Nor would she have appreciated anyone else "looking out" for her. I knew her, Mr Rivers; you didn't. I don't mean to sound dismissive, but it's a fact. Lindsey Perry did not endear herself to a single person who tried to do anything for her. In fact, she was violent, abusive, deceitful and malicious. And yes, to tell you the truth, when they told me what Roper said she'd been involved with, then I for one could easily believe everything he said.'

'And what you told the police, presumably, only reinforced their own beliefs.'

'If by "beliefs" you imply prejudices, Mr Rivers, then you're probably right. If Roper was looking for girls to do his bidding, then he wouldn't have had to try too hard to persuade Lindsey Perry to participate in whatever that was. She attacked other residents here; she stole from them; she was known to use drugs regularly – despite all our warnings and threats of eviction – and she was known to be sexually promiscuous.'

Beside us, a phone rang and she picked it up, looked at her watch, said, 'I know. I'm on my way,' and put the phone down.

'Like I said,' she said to me. 'A crisis.'

'Just tell me one thing,' I said as she began to gather together her belongings.

'What?'

'Would you honestly have believed all the things Roper revealed about Lindsey Perry if you hadn't heard it from the police themselves?'

She considered this. 'Honestly? Yes, I would.' She pushed me out of her office and set the alarm at its door. 'If you have a problem, Mr Rivers, then believe me, it isn't with me or with anything that happened here or with what Lindsey Perry might or might not have been – it's with society at large refusing to accept or even to see that some fourteen- or thirteen- or even twelve-year-old girls are capable of doing those things, that they can happily behave like that – that they aren't the perfect little creatures all too many people want them to be. Ask Roper. *He* knew.'

'Thanks for the speech,' I said.

I followed her to her car.

'Think what you like,' she said. 'You can even think what you like of me, but it's my guess that you're employed now by one of those people who refuses to confront the truth.'

'Almost,' I said.

She went on as though I hadn't spoken. 'And whatever else you do, don't try to convince me or yourself that you're doing any of this for Lindsey Perry or any of the other girls like her. People stopped caring for Lindsey Perry on Day One.'

Her car peeped, flashed and unlocked itself ahead of us.

I turned and saw that we were being watched from several of the hostel windows.

'You didn't say any of this in your statement at the time,' I said, guessing.

'I wasn't asked.' She climbed into her car and sat for a moment to compose herself before switching on the engine.

I waited where I stood.

She wound down her window. 'I'd like you to leave the premises, please,' she said. 'More specifically, you do not have my permission to remain or to return here during my absence to question any of the other residents. Anyone who might have once known Lindsey Perry is long gone by now.'

It had not been my intention.

She left me and I stood at the entrance and watched her go. A girl passed me on her way into the building, her bare arms folded across her chest. She considered me for a moment and then continued walking. She pressed a number into the coded lock and let herself into the building. I saw what attraction the place might hold for a man like Roper.

31

I visited the mother of Jennifer Wilson the following morning.

The address I had found was off Southcoates Lane, an extension of Preston Road, where Roper had lived. The quickest route to his Anlaby Road studio from his mother's house would take him along Southcoates Lane and Holderness Road.

In his confession, Roper said he met Jennifer Wilson outside a fast-food outlet at one of the Holderness Road junctions. She had been alone and had accepted his offer of money to accompany him to his studio to have her photo taken. At his trial, the details of this meeting were recounted in great detail by Roper, and everything he said about Jennifer Wilson, her appearance and her habits, was confirmed by her mother, who lived with Jennifer and her two younger sisters less than a hundred yards from where Jennifer and Roper met.

I knocked at the door and waited. A woman answered and I told her who I was looking for. A man's voice called from behind her to ask who I was.

I told her, and why I was there, and she immediately looked anxious.

'Who is it?' the man called again, this time from

somewhere closer, and a moment later he pulled the door fully open and stood beside her. He was several inches shorter than Jennifer Wilson's mother, and dense tattoos braided his upper arms.

I remembered what Sullivan had told me about all the other parents and step-parents and boyfriends and acquaintances.

I told him who I was and asked if they could spare some time to talk to me. It was mid-morning; Jennifer Wilson's two younger sisters would be at school.

'Wondered how long it would be before the rest of you came sniffing round,' the man said.

'This is Damien,' the woman told me.

'And before you ask me – no, I ain't Jennifer's father. I ain't the father to none of them. I care for them like they was my own, but I ain't their father. So you can say what you've got to say to me and not give her any more fuckin' grief. You'd think people like you would show a bit more consideration, but they never do. Have you got any idea – any fuckin' idea at all – how hard all this is for her? Have you? Have you?'

I wondered who had been there before me.

'I do understand how painful all this must be for you,' I said directly to Jennifer Wilson's mother.

'*I'm* the one you're talking to,' the man said.

'Leave it, Damien,' she said softly, and he looked at her as though even that was provocation enough for him to hit her.

He left the doorway and then reappeared at the window directly beside us.

It was clear to me by then that the woman did not want me in her home. Equally evident was the fact that she was considerably more aware of the man's watching presence beside us than I was.

I lowered my voice and explained to her again why I was there. She recognized James Bishop's name immediately and remembered the names of the other girls.

'Were any of them familiar to you before Jennifer went missing?' I said.

She shook her head. 'Damien's only doing what he thinks is best,' she said. 'After what happened to Jennifer, her real father walked out on me. Said he couldn't stand to be with me, said I was to blame for what she'd been up to. Damien's only been living here a year; I don't know where I'd be without him. They need a man around, firm hand, that sort of thing.'

'That sort of thing,' I said. 'Did you never wonder about or challenge anything Roper said about your daughter at his trial?'

'Did I ever deny that any of it had happened, you mean?' She shook her head. 'I'd have been lying if I'd said any of it was beyond her. Her father was away a lot; one thing or another. She was off the rails a long time before all this happened.' She fell silent as someone passed behind me in the street. 'Do you think he'll win?'

'Roper?'

'They're already saying it was an "unsafe" conviction. What does that mean, "unsafe"?'

'It means that things may have come to light which—'

'So what you're really talking about is finding them, isn't it?'

This sudden change of direction made me wary.

In the window, Damien had half-turned away from me to watch a television. He hadn't heard what she'd said.

'Is it not what you want, too?' I asked her, my voice even lower.

Her eyes stopped moving around me. She looked as though she was about to cry.

'I used to think about nothing else,' she said.

'But not now?'

'Ever since she went, I've been on tablets. Every now and then I try to come off them. I don't ever seem to get very far. Damien says it's all to do with how other people have treated me, how they look at me because of what happened. He says people have treated us no better than animals.' She faltered as she said the words. 'That's what he says,' she repeated.

'It's not how I see you,' I said. I asked her if she had ever heard of Angela Hill.

The name meant nothing to her, but she made the effort to try and remember.

'Another of Roper's, was she?'

'I think so,' I said.

At the window, Damien was again watching me intently.

I told her I was grateful for her time and for what she'd told me.

'I've told you nothing,' she said. 'Not really.' She gestured at the house behind her. 'You could have imagined all this without coming to see.'

I gave her my card and asked her to call me if she wanted to tell me anything more.

At the window, Damien put his hand to the glass at the sight of my wallet.

I thanked her again and told her I'd let her know if I found out anything new.

'Will you?' she said, disbelievingly, as though a hundred similar promises had already been made to her and then broken.

I told her I would, and then left her.

I followed the street to its junction with Southcoates Lane and from there to Holderness Road. It was the same short journey Jennifer Wilson would have made the morning she met Roper.

In truth, I had expected to learn nothing new from the woman, but I had been surprised and then affected by her calm and lasting grief. I had long since learned that the public expression of grief was no true indicator of the depth or intensity of the suffering it created, and in her I had found the counterpart of all James Bishop's concern and outrage, his endless insistence in his belief that he alone of all these grieving others was in a position to rectify or resolve the injustice perpetrated against them all.

I wished I'd been to see her sooner; I wished I'd been able to say to her that she, too, would one day be reunited with her daughter, and that she, too, might then be able to reconsider all those things about her daughter that others had insisted on telling her, and which she now wore like blemishes on her own skin.

32

The following morning I was woken in the darkness by someone repeatedly ringing my bell and knocking on the door. It was not yet five o'clock, and my first instinct was that it was either Smart or Finch and that something had happened to make Roper change his mind about seeing me in two days' time.

I'd been up late the previous evening, preparing a list of Bishop's questions for Roper. If I showed these to Finch and Smart, I reasoned, they might be able to add something to them to learn more from Roper without him suspecting that anyone but James Bishop was waiting for his answers. It was a pretence in which none of us could afford to wholly believe, but one in which we were all now participating, Roper included, for our own individual reasons and to our own different ends.

I put on the dressing-gown Yvonne had bought me and went downstairs, leaving off the lights. The bell was no longer being rung, but I could still hear the dying echo of its chime in the cold hallway.

I waited at the bottom of the stairs, crouched down and looked at the front door, which contained two vertical glass panels. There was no one there. I moved closer. I heard a car drawing away, but nothing else.

Still certain that I could not be seen by anyone outside, I went into the sitting-room, where I was able to look out.

There was a frost on the ground, and a line of scuffed footprints ran from the street to the door and back again.

I went back into the hallway and switched on the light. It was what anyone watching would have expected to see. A padded envelope lay on the floor beneath the letter-box.

I rang Finch and was surprised when he answered immediately.

'Go on,' he said, and then, 'Who is this?' when I didn't answer immediately. He was in a moving car.

I identified myself and heard him repeat my name to whoever was beside him. I assumed this to be Smart, otherwise he would have said nothing.

I told him what had happened.

Smart took the phone from him and said, 'When was this? Exactly.'

'Ten minutes ago, less.'

'Leave it where it is.'

'You think it might be incendiary?'

'Unlikely,' he said. 'You'd probably know about it by now.'

'Where are you?' I asked him.

He asked Finch the question. 'On our way through Keyingham,' he said.

On their way to see Sullivan.

'At this time in the morning?'

No one answered me. I heard Smart tell Finch to stop and turn the car.

'We're coming back to you,' Finch said. 'Just don't touch anything.'

I told him about the footprints in the frost. Beside him, Smart spoke into another phone.

'Get dressed,' Finch told me, and then the line went dead.

I got dressed, trying to second-guess all that was happening.

And then I called Sunny at home, but got no answer, not even his machine. I knew it was unlikely, but I called him at the agency and I was again surprised when Yvonne answered.

'How come I'm the only person asleep?' I said.

'Sunny called you last night,' she said. 'He wanted to move on it then. He called me at half past midnight. We've been here ever since.'

Sunny picked up another phone. 'Are you coming in?'

I was confused. We were obviously talking at cross-purposes.

'What's happened?' I said.

'The red-tops,' he said. 'I assumed that was why you were calling.'

'What are they saying?'

'Nothing they haven't already said a thousand times before, except this time they're saying it with pictures and with promises of lots more to come. "Hull Monster. New Pics".'

'From the stolen file,' I said.

'If this is all news to you, why *are* you calling?'

I told him about the package lying in the hallway and my call to Finch and Smart.

'You think they're going to see Sullivan because of something in the papers?'

Neither of us spoke for a moment.

Then he asked me how big the package was and I told him.

'Big enough to hold a videotape,' he said. Another phone rang beside him.

I told him I'd appreciate either him or Yvonne being with me when Smart and Finch arrived.

He considered this. They were still working to produce copy for the local papers that might want the tabloids' left-overs. If I insisted on one of them being present at the showing of the video – if that was what it was – then the story would stop being second-hand and become considerably more valuable to him.

'Yvonne's on her way,' he said, and hung up.

I finished dressing, left the house by the back door and went round to the front. There were no marks on either the path or the overgrown grass at the rear.

I waited in the cold for only a few minutes before Yvonne arrived. I signalled to her and she parked further along the road and came to me. As she did so, the first of two silent but flashing police cars arrived, followed immediately by Smart and Finch.

Smart came to me, saw Yvonne and asked me why she was there, already calculating how much I might already have told either her or Sunny.

'A bit rich,' she said. 'Considering what ten million breakfast tables will shortly be full of.'

It was clear by his response that Smart already knew what had happened. 'Nothing we didn't expect or anticipate,' he told her.

A man in a white disposable suit carrying a case approached us and Smart told him what to do. I pointed out the house to him.

'You responded to Mr Rivers's anxious plea for help pretty swiftly,' Yvonne said to Smart. 'Already out prowling the streets, were you?'

He lied to her. 'I daresay we saw the papers the same time you did. We've been going through them for anything they might reveal.'

'And?'

'And you'll be the last to know.' He left us, calling for Finch and several uniformed officers to join him.

I waited with Yvonne in her car.

'Where else would they have been going at that time in the morning?' she said.

'What do the reports say?' I asked her.

'Not much. Everything's wrapped around the pictures. And even there they've all been careful to promise more than they've actually revealed.'

I knew from what I'd already seen of the pictures in

the file that a great many of them could never be printed in even the most salacious of the tabloids.

'Sunny thinks there'll be some reference to a website somewhere and that all the really bad stuff will turn up there.'

'Provided by whoever stole the file and then sent the pictures to the papers?'

'I can see why you became a detective,' she said.

There was a rap at the window and Finch called in to me.

'The footprints are no good,' he said. 'You didn't see anything of the car you heard?'

'Nothing.'

'There's no writing on the package, it's a common bag, unsealed, no saliva, a single videocassette, probably a more common make than the bag, no other inclusions.'

'Damn, it'll probably mean having to actually *watch* the thing,' Yvonne said to him.

Finch rubbed his eyes. 'I'll suggest it,' he said.

Along the road, lights had come on in some of the adjoining houses and a few of my neighbours stood at their windows watching the man in the white suit. Tape had been strung across my doorway. The two police cars had blocked off the road.

'We'll be finished in a few minutes,' Finch said. 'How long between the car pulling away and our arrival?'

I guessed at fifteen minutes.

He asked Yvonne if she'd passed anyone driving quickly, but she too had seen nothing.

Smart came back to us. 'We're finished here,' he said. 'You'll no doubt want to come to the station,' he said to me.

'Me, too,' Yvonne said.

Smart shook his head. 'This has nothing to do with you,' he told her.

'I'd like her to be there,' I said.

He turned his back on us and spoke to Finch, after which he walked away.

'He wishes me to convey to you that he graciously accedes to your entirely reasonable request in view of your valuable assistance with our enquiries so far,' Finch said. He told us to follow him to the station.

On the way there, Yvonne called Sunny and told him what had happened, relaying to me everything Sunny said to her.

'He wants to know why they were on their way to see Sullivan and why none of them told you about the papers. He thinks they'll have been watching for the contents of the file to resurface, and that there might possibly have been some forewarning of what was about to happen.'

I took the phone from her. 'Martin Roper has agreed to see me,' I said. 'On behalf of James Bishop.'

'I know,' he said immediately.

I looked at Yvonne and she avoided my eyes.

'I would have told you afterwards,' I said to Sunny.

'No need. Roper's not going to tell you anything. And no doubt Smart's already tried to get in on the act.'

'He knew about it before I did,' I said.

'Just like he knew about the newspapers and everything else that's happened,' he said, and hung up.

I dropped the phone in Yvonne's lap.

'Warder Wallis,' she said. 'Making hay. It was why Sunny wanted to work through the night on all this. It's no coincidence, is it, that all this happens less than thirty-six hours before you and Roper get all nice and cosy with each other?'

We arrived at the Tower Grange station.

Smart and Finch waited for us in the main entrance. Smart held the padded envelope in an evidence bag. I watched as a man took this from him. He beckoned us over to them.

'Whoever pushed it through my letter-box knew that I was going to see Roper,' I said.

'You're guessing,' he said. 'Come inside.'

We followed him to the top floor and to the far end of a corridor to his temporary office.

The instant the door clicked shut behind us, Smart turned to Yvonne and said, 'You're here against my wishes. Don't forget that. And don't abuse the privilege. Anything gets repeated that shouldn't get repeated, and I can make life for you and Mr Summers very difficult.'

'Threats,' Yvonne said.

'I just need for there to be some understanding between us, that's all,' Smart said. It was the most uncertain of himself I'd ever seen him. Even Finch seemed ill at ease seeing him like that. 'I need your permission to examine and then to watch the film,' Smart said to me.

'Granted,' I said.

He sat at the desk and indicated for the rest of us to sit, too. Someone arrived with a tray of hot drinks.

'We'll get the cassette back in half an hour,' Finch said. 'Though no one's hopeful of finding anything.'

'Plenty of time to tell us why you were on your way to see Sullivan at five in the morning,' I said.

Yvonne took out her notebook and pen and laid them on the desk out of reach.

'And the recorder which already contains my allegedly threatening remark,' Smart said.

She took this out too, and opened it to reveal that it was empty.

Smart laughed.

'You should laugh at yourself more often,' Yvonne told him. 'You're a funny man.'

Smart sipped from his cup and pulled a face. He put it down and started talking.

'At four twenty-three this morning, a vehicle identified as a black Nissan Micra, but with a mud-covered registration plate, approached the home of ex-DCI Sullivan and a man – no clear description – got out of the car, approached the door and pushed a package through it. Upon receiving this news, I told the officer on observation duty there to stay where he was. Apparently, there had been no response from inside the bungalow, and as far as the officer watching could determine, there was no attempt made to wake ex-DCI Sullivan and alert him to the fact that a delivery had just been made.'

'You think it was the same man who delivered my tape?' I said.

'That's our understanding. We've been thinking on our feet so far. That's why we were on our way to see Sullivan. Fortunately, *en route*, two other things happened. One – you called Finch with the news of your own delivery, and, two, the man watching Sullivan's bungalow called in with the news that a light had just then come on in Sullivan's bedroom, followed by one immediately behind the front door. After which, the porch light came on and Sullivan came outside for a moment with something in his hand to search the empty road.'

'He was phoned and told to look,' I said.

'At exactly the same time as you yourself were on your way downstairs. If the same person delivered both packages, he might easily have driven from Sullivan to you in forty minutes at that time of the morning.'

'What purpose would it serve – us both receiving them simultaneously?'

'I don't know. But what we must assume is that Sullivan knows that Roper has agreed to see you tomorrow, and that by the time both of you received your packages the tabloids would already be full of all those details of the stolen file fit to print.'

'What does Sullivan have to say?'

'Nothing yet,' Finch said. 'We changed our minds about confronting him.'

'We thought it might be more revealing if he contacted us,' Smart said.

'Either way, we'll learn something.'

'And so far?' I said.

'Nothing. Either he's been warned against telling us, or he's taking some time to consider what's happened and what he now stands to gain or lose.'

'He'll know he was being watched,' I said. 'In which case, he'll know you know about the package and act accordingly.'

'He'll need time to watch whatever's on the cassette.'

'He has a player,' I said, remembering the VCR beneath the television.

'The downstairs lights remained on after he'd gone back indoors,' Smart said. He looked at his watch. It was almost six. 'If he calls, I'll be informed immediately.'

'Are you working on the assumption that what he's been given to watch is the same as I've been given?' I asked him.

'I can't say. It seems a likely assumption. We'll have to wait and see if he volunteers the tape, and, like I said, either way we'll learn something useful.'

'You think he's involved with the people trying to stop Roper revealing what he may be about to reveal?'

'I won't insult your intelligence or powers of deduction by officially denying or refuting such an outrageous and unfounded allegation,' he said.

'It was only a suggestion,' I said.

Smart shared a glance with Finch. 'We honestly don't know, but it's important that we continue to see all this in that wider context.'

'Whoever delivered mine must have known that I'd contact you,' I said.

'They might believe you'd watch the video first, though,' Finch said. 'And even if the two tapes are identical, they would each be intended to serve a different purpose.'

'Perhaps the fact that Sullivan and I were informed of our deliveries simultaneously is unimportant,' I said. 'Whoever delivered mine made enough noise to wake the dead. Why not just phone me instead? At least then he could be certain that I'd acknowledged the delivery.'

'Meaning they gave Sullivan alone the option of keeping everything to himself?' Finch said.

'Which would suggest', Smart said, 'that whoever delivered it had no idea that Sullivan was being watched.'

'Or perhaps they did know,' Finch said. 'Hence the obscured registration and unidentifiable man, and they wanted us to know either way – whether Sullivan told us or not – and for us to act independently of whatever he might later bring to us.'

'Meaning he would be little more than a diversion,' Smart said. 'Diverting our attention from elsewhere.'

'You can't know any of this for certain until you know what's on the films,' Yvonne said, exasperated at their guessing. 'For all you know, they might be blank tapes, and at this very moment half a dozen hardened criminals might be playing at mummies and daddies with Martin Roper prior to tying a noose made of sheets round his neck.'

The remark stopped all our speculation.

Smart held up his hands. 'He's still in isolation with a twenty-four-hour watch. If anything had happened, I'd have heard.'

There was a knock at the door and a man came in carrying the videocassette.

'Nothing,' he said. 'Possibly leather gloves. There's a trace of some cream on the envelope, but it might be anything. Nothing on the sleeve. Brand new. Sold within the last three months along with several million others at possibly a thousand outlets in the city.'

'We get the picture,' Smart told him. 'And the film?'

'Short. Seventeen minutes. Edited stills, mostly. Some hand-held live shots.'

'Is the editing professional?'

'Hard to tell. We're still trying to work out which particular piece of software was used.'

Smart reached out and the man gave him the cassette.

Beside me, Finch switched on a small television. Smart hesitated before handing the film to him.

'No call yet from Sullivan?' he asked the man about to leave.

'Nothing. He's still at home, lights still on. He was standing in the window for some time.'

'Anxious in case anybody else was coming to visit him while he was being watched?'

'His phone's on the front window-sill,' I said. 'Sea view.'

Someone else knocked and entered, a local WPC.

'Message from Thompson,' she said to Smart. 'DCI Sullivan called him a few minutes ago. He wants to bring something to show you.'

'*Ex*-DCI Sullivan,' Smart said, surprising her. She looked hardly out of her teens.

'Who's Thompson?' I said.

'One of his team of old fuck-ups,' Smart said, the WPC still waiting to be dismissed.

'The last of them,' Finch said. 'He'll be retiring within the year. Obviously someone Sullivan still feels comfortable about calling to pass on his messages.'

'He'll be covering his own back,' I said. 'Making sure everybody else knows what's happening before he sees Smart.'

Smart considered this, but not for long. He indicated for Finch to put the cassette in the player. He finally told the WPC to leave us, and she went.

Smart remained uneasy about showing the tape in Yvonne's presence and he warned her again about revealing anything of what she saw. Yvonne put her hand over her heart and promised him.

'I might just as easily have taken the tape to her and Sunny in the first place,' I said.

'Not once I'd suggested it might be incendiary,' Smart said, and laughed. He pointed the remote and started the film.

The first few minutes showed a compilation of stills, all of them connected to the murder of Hayley Forbes.

Some of the photographs had already been revealed at the time of the first trial, and some of them had come from the stolen file. There were school photographs, pictures used by the police in their appeals, and then photographs of her performing a variety of sexual acts with a succession of unidentifiable men. And then several photographs of her dead.

Smart stopped the film.

'So far, it's only telling us what we already know. It's putting Roper where they had him five years ago. There's no point to it.'

'It might make more sense considered in the light of his appeal,' I suggested. 'Suppose other copies have been sent. What if the parents of Hayley Forbes were to see all this again?'

'It still wouldn't alter the facts of the matter.'

'There's another nine minutes,' Finch said, prompting Smart to restart the film.

The collage soon ended, and was followed by a succession of shots of the remaining three girls, each of them revealed only in the photos given by their parents to the police. Nicola Bishop was shown last of all, which might have been significant.

Smart rewound the tape to the start of the three faces. He timed the duration of each. Nineteen seconds in total for the first two; twenty-five seconds for Nicola Bishop alone.

'He's tailoring the tapes,' Finch said.

Smart stopped the film again. 'Which makes seeing the tape he delivered to Sullivan all the more important.'

In the corridor outside, someone called out and someone else cheered.

Smart raised the blinds and we looked out to see that Sullivan had just arrived in the larger room next door. Several men rose to greet him.

Smart went to the door and called to Sullivan. He told him to wait where he was.

He returned to the desk. Finch lowered the blind.

'He brought the tape,' Smart said. 'I want no indication to him that we already knew it existed.'

'He'll know I'm here,' I said.

'And if his own delivery has worried him, then we'll use that to prise something out of him.'

He restarted the film. Only five minutes remained.

Five minutes of live footage showing the murder of Angela Hill, showing her punched and kicked and beaten with a length of wood. Showing her trying to avoid these blows and cowering in a corner of her attic room trying to cover her head.

'Two men,' Finch said, his voice dry.

There was no sound, only silence, but we could all hear her screams of pain and her unheard and unanswered cries for help. I felt tears form in my eyes at all I saw.

A man's foot kicked her back against the sofa, forcing it to the wall.

The film stopped unexpectedly, and then resumed with Angela Hill lying unconscious on the floor with a lamp beside her head, the bulb still shining.

'I'm running it again,' Smart said, warning us all.

Beside me, Yvonne began to catch her breath at what we were seeing.

Smart gave her his handkerchief. 'You don't have to watch,' he told her.

'I think I do,' she said. She wiped her eyes.

He ran the film again.

The lamp on the floor had been stripped of its shade and deliberately placed so that we might clearly see Angela Hill's face once she had been beaten unconscious.

'It's definitely my tape, isn't it?' I said, and no one spoke to tell me I was wrong.

There was still noise from outside, and Smart still paid attention to it.

The final minute of the film showed Angela Hill being picked up and then being slapped and having water thrown over her face to partially revive her.

The last shot was of her body, dimly revealed, in the yard below.

The film ended.

Smart rewound and removed the tape. Then he raised the blind again and watched the men outside, Sullivan still at their centre.

Sullivan looked up as the blind rose and the two men considered each other.

After a moment, Smart turned back to Yvonne and me. 'You two should leave. I want to watch whatever he's been sent alone with him.'

'Walk past him,' Finch said to me as I rose. 'Let him know you were here with us.'

'He already knew,' I said.

'We know,' Smart said. 'But I want him to know that we know.'

The men standing around Sullivan withdrew from him as the four of us left the office and walked towards him.

'Never forget,' Smart said loudly as we got close, 'he knew those other missing girls were probably already dead and he did nothing in his prosecution of Roper to take them into account. As far as *he* was concerned, they could rot where they lay, just so long as Roper was convicted and he, Sullivan, was presented to the world as the man who caught the monster. Roper's associates probably couldn't believe their luck when they saw who'd been put in charge of the investigation.'

Even Finch began to look uneasy as we drew level with Sullivan and the men around him.

Smart went on. 'This force spent too much time and effort and money protecting itself and its own self-interests instead of the people it was meant to protect.'

We finally arrived where Sullivan blocked our path to the doorway behind him.

Smart extended his hand. 'Mister Sullivan. Good to see you. Good, too, to know that you finally feel able to co-operate with us, whatever your reasons for doing so.'

Sullivan felt the 'Mister' like a blow in the face, and he looked at Smart without speaking.

'I'll be back to see you in a minute or two,' Smart told him. 'I'd appreciate it if everyone else was allowed to get on with what they're being paid to do.'

'I brought—' Sullivan began.

'You brought your tape to show me. I know. I'm looking forward to seeing it and to hearing your views on it.'

'I'm here because it's my—'

Smart turned sharply so that his face was only inches from Sullivan's. 'Please don't tell me that you're here because it's your *duty* to be here, Mr Sullivan. You had a duty to those girls. You had a duty to ensure that the people responsible for their deaths were sought and convicted. You had a duty to the people of this city and to everyone else on this force.' Smart looked at the men still gathered around Sullivan. 'And please, make no mistake, Mr Sullivan, if I uncover any instances of criminal negligence or find the slightest shred of evidence which suggests to me that you are somehow *still* involved in any of this, then I will arrest, charge and prosecute you. You may imagine yourself to be fire-proof, invincible, salt-of-the-earth, above and beyond it all, but that's just another of your own pathetic, sanctimonious delusions. As far as *I'm* concerned, you had a job to do and you failed to do it, and because you failed to do it, all this is happening now. And even if this wasn't happening now, I would still see all those dead girls clinging to your back wherever you went.'

He pushed past Sullivan and continued walking to the door beyond. Yvonne and I followed him. Finch came more slowly behind us.

Everyone watched us go. Phones rang unanswered. No one pretended to return to their work.

Outside, Smart waited for us on the stairs.

'Nice show,' I said. 'He couldn't have saved any of the murdered girls.'

'I know. But for one fucking minute of the investigation he might have considered them before himself.' To Finch he said, 'Get his film. Wait until the lab gives us everything before we watch it. Some indication of that same polish or cream would be good. Identical packaging proves nothing, but it would reassure me. And get a car to check the route between the two houses. Speed cameras, security cameras on buildings, anything. Black Micra. Don't talk to Sullivan. Let him think about this. I want him to be only too aware that by simply getting the tape he's still in this up to his neck, whether he likes it or not.'

'But you're still convinced it's more than that?' I said.

'And you're not?'

I wasn't, but said nothing.

'I think he knew things five years ago which he either ignored or allowed to slip away from him,' he said.

'Will Roper know about the tapes?' I said.

'Probably not – at least not yet – but he'll probably be learning about the pictures in the newspapers just about now.'

The same man ran up the stairs holding Sullivan's cassette. 'The same polish or cream,' he said to Smart. 'We still don't know exactly what it is, but we're working on comparisons.'

'How long does the film run?'

'Thirty-one minutes.' A different film.

'Anything else?' Smart said.

'A rectangular trace of something on the side of the cassette. Probably a Post-it note.'

'But no sign of the note itself?'

The man shook his head.

'It's something,' Smart said.

'No one would be stupid or careless enough to write anything,' I said. 'Not after taking all those other precautions.'

'Not unless they knew for certain that Sullivan would destroy it before showing us the tape.'

'It's a big risk.'

He clicked his lips. 'That would all depend,' he said.

He motioned for Finch to follow him back into the room of hostile, waiting men. He took the envelope from the man who held it and took the cassette from it.

Yvonne and I continued down the stairs, through the entrance and back out to her car.

It was by then almost nine o'clock and the traffic around the station was slow-moving and it took her twenty minutes to drive me back into the city centre.

33

Before returning to Humber Street, I walked to the nearest newsagent and bought all the tabloids. The 'discovery' of the photographs was on four front pages. Three of the papers suggested that it was as a result of their reporters' 'endeavours'. Only the best interests of their readers were being served in publishing the pictures. More were promised. Whoever had stolen and then dissected the stolen file had done their work well.

Each paper showed a different picture, and while there might have been something to gain in impact had they all shown the same picture, this diversity did at least allow each editor or crime writer to claim an exclusive. The reports accompanying the pictures were sharpened by constant reminders of Roper's imminent appeal.

I sat with all the pictures and stories for an hour and tried hard to understand what effect these allegedly new revelations might have on Roper's appeal, and what the men promoting them – presumably his one-time associates – might thus achieve by them. It seemed a contradictory thing to do, something that might work against them if Roper failed to react to all these new and unexpected pressures being suddenly placed on him.

I read each of the reports several times over. They revealed little that the articles of five years earlier hadn't already made public.

Only one of the broadsheets in which this manufactured storm of outrage was reported bothered to point out that what was happening now was what had happened then – namely that the unconfirmed murders had been used to add ballast to the one for which Roper had been convicted. What the tabloids were all careful to suggest – presumably at the insistence of their lawyers – was that all these terrible 'new' photographs were being shown now because they were 'connected' to that first trial, not because they were previously undisclosed or unseen evidence, and certainly not because it could be proved that Roper had actually taken them. There was sufficient elsewhere in the reports – photographs submitted by the families at the time, police quotes, old headlines and unofficial judgements – to help keep every other distinction between valid evidence and hysterical condemnation unclear.

After an hour of reading and re-reading, I was convinced of only two things: firstly, that the purpose served by the selling of the pictures to the press was not as self-evident as many, including Smart, might now want it to be; and, secondly, that whoever did it must have known how uncertain that outcome was likely to be.

In fact, the more I thought about it, the less sense the theft and sale of the pictures made. If it was intended as a winning hand, then it was being played too soon, and by someone who must have understood that. The pictures represented only a fraction of what the stolen file had contained. All of the reports suggested there was more to come, but, equally, the writers must have known that, in light of the appeal, they were all likely to have injunctions placed on them to prevent them from revealing anything more. Similarly, Roper's legal team would use this to his advantage by suggesting that it created a hostile environment in which his appeal could not now be fairly heard.

My final guess was that it was in the interests of whoever had stolen and sold the pictures to have the appeal delayed while a more lasting solution to the problem of Roper and his revelations could be found.

I was cutting pages from each of the papers when Finch rang.

'Two things,' he said. 'The chemical analysis of the adhesive says it was definitely a Post-it note.'

'Which could have been stuck on the cassette long before it was delivered to Sullivan.'

'Brand-new cassette. Same as yours. First time it was used. And the same polish on both envelopes. Faint, but it's there. And there's an even fainter trace of it on your letter-box. We've sent a team to Spurn while we know where Sullivan is.'

'Is he still with Smart?'

'Two hours twenty minutes, and counting.'

'And *his* film?'

'A compilation of much the same as yours, but omitting the killing of Angela Hill and concentrating instead on the actual police investigation. Rubbing Sullivan's nose in it. Headlines about what a wonderful job he was doing followed by a few photographs, some of the missing girls still alive, and some of the body of Hayley Forbes when it was found and retrieved.'

'So the films were definitely compiled specifically for Sullivan and myself?'

'Looks that way.'

'Where's all the material from?' I asked him.

'Most of it was made available five years ago in one form or another.'

'Some of it from all those boxes of evidence which went missing?'

'Perhaps. But unlikely. What's your point?'

'What if the videos and all the tabloid stuff were being done by two separate people?' It was an idea that had half-formed as I read the papers.

'Bit of a coincidence,' he said, but I could tell that he was already considering it.

'Think about it,' I said. 'All the pictures in the papers come from the stolen file. The videos, which are both compilations, contain none of that. Surely they would have had more impact if they'd contained something that no one outside the investigation at the time had ever seen before. It would certainly have made you and Smart take them more seriously. Whoever had that file would have used it to best effect. You said it yourself – the photographic material could have been gathered together by anybody.'

'In addition to which,' he said, speaking slowly and thinking as he reasoned, 'the videos are aimed specifically at two individuals.'

'And the stuff sent to the newspapers was scatter-shot.'

'Go on,' he said.

I admitted that that was as far as I'd got.

'What would it prove or confirm?' he said.

'That whoever sent the tapes to Sullivan and me knew what weighed heaviest with us – me especially – and that both he and I would come directly to you.'

'Perhaps the same person wanted the best of both worlds,' he said.

I was about to ask him what else Sullivan might have revealed when he was interrupted and he told me to wait. He returned a minute later.

'The polish is definitely leather polish. We have a brand. Sold everywhere.'

'How many people polish their gloves?' I said. I remembered Paul Hill climbing out of his Range Rover and peeling off his gloves as he came towards me at his gates.

'Who even *wears* driving gloves these days?' he said.

'It was a cold morning. Perhaps the car was too old to have reliable heating.'

'The camera at Garrison Road has a black Micra heading into the city at four forty-three,' he said.

289

'Which makes it a more-than-likely candidate.'

'Sullivan has confirmed that he was called at four fifty-five, and that whoever was calling hung up when he answered.'

'Suggesting Sullivan might have recognized a voice?'

'Not really the kind of mistake the delivery-man would make, is it?'

'Anything from the newspapers yet?' I said.

'An anonymous phone call to ensure further payment.'

'How much?'

'Ten thousand from each. Same again when further pictures were delivered. Naturally, they jumped at the offer. None of the calls have been traced. Envelopes all delivered through the mail. They're the actual pictures from the file, not copies. That's why they all got something different.'

'And why no trail back to a photocopier or scanner exists.'

'It might also suggest that whoever sent them didn't really know what he was doing and how much more the pictures might be worth if we ever did discover the whereabouts of the missing girls.'

'Or if Roper's associates were caught and convicted,' I said. 'Reprints of pictures the papers already own will cost them nothing.'

'And presumably their lawyers are already closing their contractual fists.'

'What are you going to do with Sullivan?' I said.

'Not much we *can* do. He came in voluntarily. He probably still knows as much about everything that's happening as anyone here.'

I told him I thought Sullivan was living burdened with his regret and that he was searching for some way to redeem himself.

'Good,' he said.

'You're missing my point,' I said. 'If he'd found a way to do that before now, he would have done it.

You're right – he does know more than most about what's happening now, and more than anyone about the original investigation. All I'm saying is that—'

'All you're saying is that we should get over our own feelings about what happened and begin to consider what use Sullivan might still be to us. Look, if there was anything Sullivan wanted to tell us, he's just had two and a half hours to do it.'

'And?'

'Precisely.'

'Any idea yet why he might have had a message stuck to his tape and I didn't?'

'No mention of it so far. He knew the compiler? He knew he was being prodded in our direction?' Again, someone spoke to him. 'I have to go. Smart still wants us to get together tomorrow before your visit.' We agreed a time.

I finished gathering the cuttings from the papers and then went out to clear my head.

I walked to the disused Minerva Pier and then along the railings above the river to where the statue of William de-la-Pole stood with his hand on his hip and his snapped dagger, dressed like Hollywood's idea of Robin Hood. I looked out over the water. The tide was low and beneath me there was no clear divide between the sluggish, muddy water and the glutinous, watery mud.

After a night of frost and the earlier threat of snow, the day had become clear and bright, and from where I stood I could see along the shore towards the mouth of the estuary, past the city and the docks and refineries.

A barge passed upriver, looking more like a floating slab of wood than a vessel. Its sides rose little more than a metre above the water. Two men stood, one at each end, and looked up at me as they passed. The wake from this pushed the waves further into the absorbing mud.

A woman with two small children, both girls, six or seven, arrived beside me to look across the River Hull at the giant glass aquarium there. Her enthusiasm for everything she pointed out to the girls was forced, and none of it was shared by her daughters, both of whom complained of the boring building, the boring river and the cold. She pointed out the barge to them, and the distant vessels waiting on the deeper water, but all they told her in return was that they'd seen it all before and wanted to leave. She became angry with them and shepherded them ahead of her back to their car.

It was then, watching her return to the Victoria Pier, that I saw the dark green Polo which had arrived and parked beside her, its engine running, its wiper blades moving back and forth. A single figure sat in the driver's seat. Pale smoke rose from an inch of open window. I looked away, back out over the river. The car had not been there upon my arrival. The driver would have had a clear view of me where I stood, and, close to Pier Street, he would also be able to drive away long before I reached him. I could not be certain, but it looked like the same car that had approached and then driven away from Kelly McLean's house on the day I had visited her. The front off-side wing was a replacement, ochre, yet to be sprayed.

I continued to watch it without appearing to. I turned to look upriver after the barge, I stretched my arms, I walked back and forth and looked at my watch. Nothing of the car's registration plates was visible to me.

After several minutes, the driver's door opened and the man inside flicked out the stub of his cigarette. Then he lowered his foot out of the car and rubbed the smoking stub to nothing. The gesture seemed excessive. He sat with the door open for a moment, perhaps to allow the rest of the smoke to clear, before pulling the door shut. Again, the gesture seemed excessive, as though the door was faulty and needed to be slammed hard to be closed properly. There was an unidentified Polo on the list of cars recorded leaving the multistorey on the day I was attacked and the file was stolen.

I walked back towards it, took out my phone and went through the motions of making a call, and as soon as I did this, the driver immediately pulled away, almost colliding with the departing woman, forcing her to brake and then sound her horn.

34

I slept little that night. At eleven, I resumed work on bringing up to date the report I was compiling for James Bishop. It was long overdue, and though he had not insisted on seeing it, I knew that my meeting with Roper would mark a turning point, and I wanted him to know all I had learned regarding his missing daughter before Roper himself was finally in a position to confirm or deny anything I might put to him.

I had neglected Bishop's own interests in favour of Smart's investigation. But since the killing of Angela Hill the two were now inextricably bound together, and the three of us – Smart, Bishop and myself – were all now complicit in our actions and deceits, and we all moved forward and around each other in each other's shadows.

At two I went to bed and slept until six.

I was in my office at eight, and at half past Smart and Finch arrived and stayed until noon. I showed them the questions I had prepared, and they showed me theirs. We corresponded on most things. Where we differed were the questions concerning names, events and places relating to Smart's overall investigation, about which he had so far told me almost nothing. He

made it clear to me as he divulged this new information that it was only to be used in my conversation
with Roper and never to be repeated elsewhere. I
asked him about the new names he mentioned, but all
he would tell me was that Roper would know them
and might respond in a manner which revealed something to me.

'He'll know you've primed me,' I said.

'Not necessarily. I could have told you all this
already. Or Sullivan could have told you, or you could
have found it out for yourself.'

I was unconvinced and let him know this.

One of the names he mentioned was a man called
Charles Abbot, and I'd heard it before, but couldn't
remember in what context. I presumed it was another of
Sullivan's discredited officers.

'He'll know you're there partly at our bidding, anyway,' Finch said.

'But any overkill, and his legal team—'

'Will descend on us like the supercilious and self-
righteous bastards even they must know themselves to
be,' Smart said.

When this long meeting was over, and just as they
were about to leave, Smart said to me, 'You can tell us
now if you want. It might be easier than afterwards.'

'What?' Finch said, pulling on his coat, uncertain
what Smart meant.

'I'm talking about the things he intends to discuss
with Roper about which he's so far managed to say
nothing,' Smart said.

'I still have to emphasize the James and Nicola
Bishop angle,' I said. 'That's what he'll expect. If I go
in there asking him only what are all too obviously
your questions, he'll either refuse to answer me or
walk out on me.'

'He'll expect it,' Smart said. 'It's all part of his
strategy. It's why he's agreed to see you. You give him,
he gives you, you give us, we give him. He's waited a
long time to be able to make this deal. It's why all this

is happening. You get to learn a little bit more about what he knows, and he gets to confirm a few suspicions of his own concerning our inquiry and who we might have in our sights and what we now need from him to pull the trigger. We're all over the same big uncomfortable barrel here.'

'And if he sees the obvious imbalance in all of that?'

Smart shrugged. 'His choice. He's already told us a great deal just by agreeing to see you, and he'll want something in return – something he was never going to get before or from anyone else.'

As the two of them finally left me, and as Finch wished me luck, I asked Smart what concessions he would have made to Roper if he and not I had been chosen to see him.

'None whatsoever beyond the demands and requirements of the law,' he said, but with a note of resignation in his voice. 'I can't tell you that,' he added. 'Because I don't know. Too much depends on what Roper gives to you – us. Don't get your hopes up. Perhaps you do no more than intrigue him or he's getting bored.'

'I'm an intriguing man,' I said.

He looked at me and shook his head. 'Personally, I'd rather spend a minute with him than let you in there for an hour.'

'Perhaps if you'd found Angela Hill before me and gone to see her and offered her some sort of protection, then she might have talked to you instead and Roper *would* be seeing you.'

'Like you protected her, you mean?' he said, and the two of them left me.

They would return at six. Smart had arranged with the prison governor for Roper and I to spend as much time together as we needed.

At one, I walked to the station and took a taxi to the prison. I asked the driver to pull up a hundred yards short of the entrance, beside the abandoned bus shelter in which I had spoken to Wallis ten days earlier.

By the time I reached the prison, a short queue of other visitors had formed and I joined them, hoping to enter without being spotted by Wallis or anyone else who might now be selling information to the press.

At the head of the queue, the door was finally unlocked and we moved forward.

We crossed a yard and waited at another door. A warder came and unlocked this, greeting those visitors with whom he was familiar.

Once inside, we were all searched and asked to identify ourselves and who we were there to see. I held back until I was the last to be approached. Upon telling the warder my name, he looked along to the corresponding name on the list he held and then looked back at me.

'You're through there,' he said, indicating a door at the far end of the room, and towards which no one else had been directed. Being singled out from the others like this made them suspicious of me, and I went to the door hoping to suggest to them that I was as mystified by this as they were.

'Knock,' the man called to me, further focusing their attention. I understood then that Smart's rules no longer applied.

I knocked. Nothing happened.

'Louder,' the man called to me.

'Yeah, louder,' the warder beside him said. They both smiled at me.

I knocked again. This time the door opened and I was confronted by Wallis himself, and beside him stood the blond-haired man – Carl Boyd – I had seen with him at our first meeting. The governor stood immediately behind the two men.

I started to explain why I was there, but the governor stopped me and told me to follow him. Wallis and Boyd stepped aside and then followed close behind me.

We passed along a succession of corridors and through four further sets of locked doors.

At the last of these, the governor turned to Wallis and Boyd and told them to return to their duties elsewhere. I wondered why he'd felt the need for them in the first place, but said nothing. I wondered, too, about the coincidence of Wallis himself being involved so publicly in my arrival. It was unlikely that the governor was aware of my acquaintance with him. I was only grateful that Roper knew none of this.

Twenty yards along the final corridor, the governor stopped and turned to me and indicated a door ahead of us, beside which another warder waited.

'You are probably already aware that I am not in wholehearted agreement with Smart concerning what's happening here today,' he said. 'For Roper to break his silence like this so close to his removal and his appeal leaves me feeling less than comfortable, less than comfortable.'

I almost laughed at the words and all they told me about him, and I resisted the urge to remark on how much supposedly confidential information concerning the man under his charge had already been leaked.

He went ahead of me and spoke to the warder at the door. The man unlocked it and pushed it open. The governor returned to me.

'I have complied with Smart's request to allow you as much time as you require, Mr Rivers. But please remember that you are here at the behest of another and against my own better judgement.'

He expected me to say something about being grateful for his assistance, but I said nothing.

'Mr Roper awaits you,' he said. 'Again in accordance with Smart's wishes, I have asked my officer to remain outside while the interview takes place. The door will remain unlocked. Loud or violent language will not be tolerated, and should my officer see fit, then he has the authority to enter the room and terminate the interview. My own office is only a short distance away. Rest assured, I shall be informed of anything untoward.' He turned and left me.

I thanked the man on the door and went inside.

The room was small, little larger than a cell, with a central bulb in a mesh cage and a solitary high window of thick glass showing nothing but the pearly grey of the sky above. There was a small stainless-steel sink in one corner of the room, a table and two chairs.

Roper was standing beneath the window as I entered, smoking, letting the smoke drift up and out of the room. Several crushed filters lay in a foil ash-tray on the table.

He was shorter than I had imagined him to be, and slighter. The last photograph I had seen of him had been taken only a year earlier, but it was a prison photo, and it showed.

I held my hand out to him and he reciprocated.

He saw my surprise at this, and said, 'I understand Mr Smart has arranged for us to take as long as we need, Mr Rivers.'

'Have they kept you waiting here long?' I said.

'Long enough. It's what they do. I'm hardly likely to win the prisoner-of-the-month award, am I? Not here.' There was a bruise at the side of his mouth. He looked pointedly at the faint mark on my cheek, causing me to wonder if he already knew what had happened to me.

'Sean Wallis made sure he was there when I arrived,' I said.

'I imagined he would. There's a few of them. Ignore him.'

I went to the table and sat at it.

He came and joined me. He stubbed out his cigarette, leaned back in his chair and folded his arms. He wore a vividly red bib, fastened beneath his arms, which he removed and lay on the table.

'You have the advantage over me,' he said. 'So before you start asking me Smart's questions, tell me why *you're* here, you specifically.'

'Because Angela Hill was killed,' I said. 'And whatever else you might be about to deny or pretend to

299

dismiss, you once felt affectionately towards her, and she you, and you came to the same unavoidable conclusion I came to – namely that the men who set you up and then abandoned you five years ago were the ones who killed her. Until then, you'd been in control of everything – or thought you were – and now everything is less certain. And, possibly – just possibly – you now want to avenge her death as much as you want any reckoning for the past.'

He considered all this without speaking, and without betraying any emotion. It was not how I had intended to start, but I knew immediately upon seeing him that nothing would be served by avoiding the matter.

'"Avenge"?' he said. 'Is that what I am, an "avenger"?'

'You're a man who played some part in the murder of at least one girl.'

'Which I have never denied.' He indicated the cigarettes I had put on the table and I told him to take them.

'Only because your denial would have served no purpose, not then, and because your associates had already convinced you that sufficient uncertainty existed concerning those other girls – all of whom were known about by everybody at the time of your trial – that any subsequent appeal—'

He held up his hand and I stopped speaking.

'You worked all this out, what, a couple of weeks ago? I've lived with it for five years, longer.'

'And with the knowledge that you alone were made to pay for what happened?'

'How is Sullivan?' he said.

'Enjoying life better than you,' I said. 'I don't care about Sullivan.'

He smiled. 'Lie number one. Of course you care about Sullivan, and so you should, Mr Rivers. You should care just as much about Sullivan as Mr Smart cares about him. There's nothing gives a good copper

300

more satisfaction than nailing a bad one.' He stood up and returned to stand beneath the window. 'Tell me about the man who employed you.'

'James Bishop,' I said, wondering why he had asked this. 'Nicola Bishop's father. You met her through Angela Hill. For some reason, Angela stopped doing what you had been paying her to do, and Nicola Bishop took her place. There were always plenty of others, of course, but I can see you know what I'm talking about.'

'It's what Angela told you, that's all,' he said. 'They needed dozens of them by then, the more the merrier.'

'And that wasn't how you'd been accustomed to working?'

'Angela wanted me to write on some of the head-and-shoulder shots I'd taken of her when we first met. I told her she might change her mind about that later.'

'Because you were already involved in the killing of Hayley Forbes?'

He refused to answer me.

'There must have been thousands of photographs,' I said. 'I've seen plenty. Smart has most of them on file.'

'Not all of them,' he said.

I conceded the point.

I told him how I had come across Angela Hill's name in the report of Nicola Bishop's memorial service, how I had looked for her and first found her father. I told him I felt responsible for what had happened to her.

'Whoever killed her had a choice,' he said.

'And you didn't?'

'I had as much choice as any man.'

'You tried to contact her after your arrest and then again after your trial,' I guessed.

'She wrote back, just the once, but never really said anything.'

'I know; she told me,' I lied. '*Is* her killing the reason you're doing all this now?'

'By "all this" I take it you mean a little more than "avenging" her death.'

301

'Smart believes you have sufficient evidence hidden away somewhere to convict the others involved in the deaths of the other girls.'

'And is that what you believe? Is that what you've been sent here to find out?'

'If that's what you think, then why don't you go directly to Smart with it. If what you've got is as good as he believes it to be, then—'

'Then what? He can go and arrest them and they can all come and join me in here?'

'They could be kept away from you.'

'What, because Smart says so, or because some judge or governor or warder says so? Even you can't be that blind to how everything works.'

'It would still be a way forward for you,' I said.

'Forward?'

'From here, this,' I said. 'In getting the others convicted. In getting your own conviction re-examined.'

'The appeal will take care of that.'

'But Smart can help.'

'Like he helped the papers yesterday? Like he helped you?' He looked again at my cheek. 'This is happening *now*, Mr Rivers, because for the first time I'm in a position to do myself a bit of good with what I know – with what I can *prove* – instead of just helping Smart and his team feel good about themselves. Three years he's been applying to see me, ever since the plug was pulled on my first appeal.'

'I never discovered why that happened,' I said.

'Because it was too soon. And because if that appeal had failed then, which was likely, I wouldn't have been able to submit the same evidence again. Who was going to listen to me after everything that had happened?'

'Sullivan retired nearly two years before the appeal would have happened.'

'He was kicked out, but he was still a player in it all. Never forget that, Mr Rivers. Anything I gave the police then would have been either wasted or lost.'

'Like the bulk of the evidence they gathered?'

'What a surprise that was.'

'And so you needed to wait until someone was actively engaged on an independent investigation to make what you knew—'

'What I can prove.'

'—start working in your favour.'

'Whatever they said in their reports into his methods, Sullivan still had public opinion on his side. Everything his successors did, he still got to hear about. Besides, there was never any real appetite then for a serious investigation into what had happened. For all Sullivan ever cared, those girls could rot where they were buried as long as *his* reputation and pension were secure.'

'Smart said exactly the same to his face yesterday,' I said. 'You could have agreed to see him before this. Why didn't you?'

'Because however hopeless everyone else might have considered my appeal to be, *I* still needed to be reasonably convinced of the outcome.'

'Meaning you wouldn't be handing over any of your evidence until the appeal had failed.'

'You know as well as I do by now that I was backed into a corner.'

'And you agreed to something because you had no choice? And because you once believed the men who backed you into that corner?'

'Sullivan knew me. He knew what I'd been up to in the past, and he knew what I was getting myself involved in then. They might have handed me to him on a plate, but he didn't have to snatch me off it so fast and then give the plate back to them.' He breathed deeply to calm himself. 'He was probably as surprised as anybody when my name first came into the frame.'

'You would never have been successfully prosecuted for the killing of Hayley Forbes without the forensic evidence against you,' I said. 'They said you were involved and you were involved. In all likelihood, you even filmed the events leading up to her death and her death itself. You'd filmed Angela Hill, you'd filmed Nicola Bishop. You weren't *not* involved in any of that. You weren't standing innocently or unknowingly by while all *that* happened. And if nobody else could be caught and convicted for it all, then you can't really blame the police for making a good case against the one man they knew they could prove something against.' I fell silent as abruptly as I had started.

Roper came away from the wall and sat back at the table. He took another cigarette. It was not until the door opened and the warder standing outside looked in that I realized I had been shouting.

'Everything all right?' the man said. He looked directly at me.

'Fine. Sorry. My fault,' I told him.

He glanced briefly at Roper and withdrew, closing the door behind him.

'You knew all that from the outset,' Roper said quietly. 'How much better do you feel now for having said it?'

I apologized to him.

'You would have felt the need to say it at some point,' he said. 'Sullivan once shouted at me for forty-eight hours non-stop.'

'Did it never occur to him that the body of Hayley Forbes was discovered out in the open where anyone might have found it, and where it certainly wouldn't have stayed undiscovered for too long, whereas the others have never been found?'

'He might have mentioned it. How hard do you think they looked for the others?'

'Plus she was found beyond Goole, to the west, suggesting to anyone even remotely concerned that she'd been dumped along a route used by the killer in that direction.'

He watched me closely. 'Your point being?'

'My point being that practically everyone who has so much as expressed an opinion on the three missing

304

girls has pointed in the opposite direction completely, towards Easington.' I used the name deliberately.

He applauded me slowly. 'I wondered how long it would be before that came up,' he said. 'They searched hard enough there. Sullivan saw to that. Funny that he should have gone to live so close by when they kicked him out.'

'It was his wife's choice,' I said.

'Don't kid yourself. She counted for nothing as far as he was concerned. Job first, mates second, her and the family last and least. Always used to make out he was this big family man — kids, grandkids, all that. He didn't give a toss. Made out that it was because teenage girls were concerned in his investigation of me that he went after me so hard. And everyone swallowed it.'

I remembered the pictures on Sullivan's mantelpiece and shelves and television.

'You think he moved out there to go on looking, to make amends?' I said.

'Forget it. He went out there because he was causing a bad smell in the city. He might have had most of his old team still on the force, but even they were beginning to distance themselves from him. He went to Spurn because there was nowhere else for him to go.'

I doubted this, but said nothing, noting only his vehemence in making the remarks, and knowing that this was in some way connected with his own childhood association with the place.

'I knew all along that your holidays at Easington were precious to you and that you didn't want anything to spoil those memories,' I said.

'Oh?' And for the first time, he seemed caught offbalance, uncertain of himself, of whether to agree or disagree with me, of my reasons for making the observation. This surprised me: of all the topics he knew I might raise with him — on my own behalf or on Smart's — the caravan camp had been a priority. There had been packets of photographs taken at the place each summer, each year carefully labelled and dated.

He started to speak, but, seizing this small advantage, I interrupted him.

'Just as I know it was a big leap from taking dirty photos of schoolgirls and selling them locally to producing pornographic films with a distribution network far beyond anything *you* might be able to control. Sullivan might not have seen it – or not wanted to see it – but as far as I can understand it, you were a man suddenly out of his depth, involved in something before he really understood that he was involved, or what he was involved in. You never even touched those schoolgirls. They were as willing as you were. And then all of a sudden there you are killing them and filming them being killed.'

'Not—' he said.

'Not what?' I said. 'You woke up one day and realized the sports bras and knee-length socks were no longer enough and you wanted to see one of them getting what she'd wanted all along – if not from you, because *that* was never what you really wanted, was it? – then from one or two or three of your new friends?'

He slapped both his palms down on the table. Again, it surprised me to see him so easily unsettled by something he had had long enough to consider before seeing me.

I waited without speaking while he composed himself.

'You and Smart have worked it all out between you,' he said eventually. 'You're right. The devil took the hindmost, and that was me, out of my depth and too slow-moving.'

'What I still don't understand is why you agreed to it all so readily, why you let yourself get talked into something as big as that so easily. You must have known what would happen to you.'

'Why – because, unlike them, I hadn't been clever enough to keep myself anonymous? Because my trademarks were all over everything that happened?

Because Hayley Forbes had already been working with me for almost a year before she was killed?'

'Added to which,' I said, guessing again, 'they threatened to kill Angela Hill if you didn't go along with the plan, which, in theory, was foolproof and would see you released after, what, two years, on appeal?'

He sat with his head down and said nothing for several minutes.

'In theory,' he said eventually.

And now they've killed her anyway. I didn't need to say it.

He looked up at me. 'She asked me once if she was my girlfriend, and I told her she was. I still went on taking the pictures, that kind of stuff, but I let her go on thinking all those things she wanted to believe.'

'You wanted them as well,' I said.

'She was sixteen.'

'So? You were only four years older.'

'What are you saying – that if all this hadn't blown up in my face, then she and I might have . . . you know?'

'It's a possibility,' I said.

He shook his head. 'Nothing lasts for ever, Mr Rivers.'

'That's just something people say to account for something coming to an end. Things last for as long as you want them to last. It's an excuse, your excuse. You never tried to get away from them or to stop them. You just went along with everything they told you to do because they paid you well to do it. And, eventually, even you stopped caring about what happened to the girls you procured for them.'

He smiled at these probing remarks, understanding perfectly why I was making them. 'Nice try,' he said.

'Not really,' I said. 'You know well enough that Smart and his team already know most of what you know. All I'm doing is confirming it for you.'

'Nothing ventured, nothing gained?' he said.

'Something like that.'

Any more questions about Angela Hill would push him further away from me.

I waited a moment and then said, 'Smart gave me a list of names.'

'So?'

'He wanted me to see how you reacted upon hearing them.'

'You mean he doesn't know for certain who they are? I'm disappointed in him.'

'He knows,' I said. 'But he needs *something* out of all this.'

'He got that the instant I agreed to see you. What he needs to work out now is what *I* stand to gain by talking to you. It would be an even bigger disappointment if you – *you* personally, Mr Rivers, not Smart and you together – were to make the same mistake *they* made.'

'Meaning your associates?'

'Is that what they were?'

'It's what Smart calls them.'

'I can see how easy that must make things for him.'

I recited the list of names I had memorized, and as I did this he turned away from me and began humming to himself.

When I fell silent, he said, 'Finished?'

'At least I can tell him that I did what he asked of me,' I said.

'Added to which, both you and he will now assume that no one was missing from the list.'

'And that, presumably, there were some names that Smart made up just to make sure of your response.'

'If I'd made one.' He asked me the time and I told him. We'd been together an hour.

I told him I'd been to the caravan camp at Easington with Finch.

'And?' he said, betraying and then disguising his interest.

'Looking for a long-lost phone,' I said.

'Phone?'

'Now who's being disingenuous?' I said.

He smiled.

'I know the place meant – means – a lot to you,' I said. 'And I know there's still some connection with it that you're telling no one.'

He refused to be drawn, convincing me even further.

'I imagine we all have *somewhere*,' I said. I told him about the rusted toy cars that had been found there when the site was searched after the fire.

'No one ever mentioned them,' he said. 'I remember playing with them there.'

'If you won't tell Smart, then tell me,' I said.

He shook his head. 'Same thing,' he said. He pulled himself closer to me. 'Would it have been easier for you if I'd been the monster they said I was?' he said.

'Monsters sell papers,' I said.

'Still do, apparently.'

'Tell me about the mistakes,' I said.

'Mine or theirs?'

'They underestimated you,' I said. 'They got greedy and then overexposed. Somebody needed to fall. You got pushed. They burned their bridges and you were still standing on one of them wondering why no one was waiting for you. Did you know Hayley Forbes was going to be killed before they killed her and you joined in sufficiently to leave Sullivan all the evidence they intended you to leave him?'

He looked at me, but said nothing. 'No,' he said eventually.

'I know how your mother died,' I said.

'I don't recall it ever being a secret,' he said, but there was something in his sudden attentiveness which made me go on. It was something I'd given some thought to since learning of the circumstances surrounding her death.

'You think she was killed by one of those names,' I said.

' "Accidental death",' he said.

'But you still think the caravan was destroyed

because of what someone thought it might contain, what might have been hidden there. She went to clear out the caravan a few days into the closed season, missed the last bus back into Hull and so she stayed over. It wasn't allowed, but who was to stop her? She'd done it before, hundreds had. One night, in and out, no harm done. Instead, someone else turned up, turned on the gas canister and flicked in a match completely oblivious to the fact that your mother was asleep in there. Or', I said, seeing that I had kept his interest, 'they turned up hoping to search the caravan, find what they were looking for, and *then* destroy it. Instead, they found your mother there and altered their plan slightly to get rid of this secondary obstacle.'

'Is that what Smart thinks?' he said.

'He's never mentioned it.'

'The coroner said she was probably unconscious when the fire started. Called it a blessing.'

'I'm sorry for her death,' I said.

The remark surprised him and he nodded his acceptance. He leaned forwards again, slowly connecting the fingertips of both his hands.

I decided to press what small advantage I might have gained in talking about his mother. I even imagined it was what he wanted me to do. 'When I first heard about it, I thought that her death had perhaps had some bearing on your decision not to withdraw your confession,' I said.

'It didn't,' he said, but with neither disbelief nor hostility in his voice, adding, 'It broke her heart when she found out about everything, when she had to sit and listen to everything everybody told her.'

'She didn't know what you were up to even when you were working alone?'

He shook his head. 'I told her it was all family portraits, weddings, anniversaries, baby stuff. It was how I started out, and to begin with there was always enough of that kind of work to provide a cover.'

'It must have hit her hard.'

'She probably felt as though *I'd* hit her. The bastards were all over her when Sullivan came to arrest me.'

'The police?'

'And the press. They took her home to pieces. It was never the same for her after that. Then the neighbours decided to get in on the act.'

'I went to see the house,' I told him.

'I'm surprised it's still there. They called it the "Monster's Lair", wanted it knocked down, levelled, carted away.'

'Didn't they offer to re-house her?'

'Once. But she wouldn't have any of it. She started going to the caravan more and more often.' He paused. 'You're right – it was probably the only place I ever was truly happy. My father walked out on us when I was seven and died a year later. She used to make a big thing of it only ever being me and her there, just the two of us, our special place. When he was still with us we used to go out there for practically the whole of the summer holidays – me and her for all that time, him for just a few days of his week's holiday. I was born on the twentieth of May, Mr Rivers. I must have been conceived during one of those holidays. She took me there when he finally walked out on us, said it would help us to get over everything.'

'Just the two of you.' There was nothing of this in any of the reports I had read; there, every reference to the caravan was in connection with the police searches, the fire and his mother's death. If my visit there with Finch had served no other purpose, then it at least kept Roper talking to me now.

'I'll tell you something else,' he said, as though surprised by what he had just remembered. 'When I was born they got the date wrong on my birth certificate – either that, or the O looked too much like an eight. She went to all the hassle of making them change it. She had to get a letter from the hospital, the midwife, everything. It didn't make much sense to anyone else, but it was what she wanted and what she did.'

I told him it was the kind of thing I could imagine my own mother having done. It was the truth, and he saw this.

'She once said—' He stopped abruptly and drew his hands suddenly apart, as though the gesture might break a connection, another memory that had come to him unexpectedly.

'You don't have to tell me,' I said.

He waited before speaking. 'I almost had a sister,' he said. 'Three years after my father walked out, she met another man. He insisted on coming to the caravan with us. It ruined the entire holiday.'

'Because it was meant to be just the two of you?'

He nodded. 'I can't even remember his name. He was working on the containers in the docks. One minute he was there, the next he'd gone.'

'And your mother was pregnant by him?'

'She lost it at five months. January.' He glanced up at me, knowing the calculation I would be making. 'Something went wrong and the baby was induced, stillborn. A girl. She even had a name for her – Gina. I remember how she used to tell me that the three of us would be just as happy at the caravan as the two of us had been all those years.'

'But you weren't convinced?'

'I don't know. All I know is that I used to look forward to our time there together too much ever to risk spoiling or losing it.'

'How did your mother take the loss?'

'Badly. But then she managed to put it all behind her and get on with things. These days, a thing like that happens and they'll have a proper funeral and everything, counselling, all that.'

'But not then?'

He shook his head. 'We went back to Easington two months later, start of the season. I remember her saying how much Gina would have liked it there, how much I would have enjoyed taking care of her and playing with her on the beach.'

'Did any of this ever become public knowledge?' I asked him.

'No. Why should it? I was almost ten when it happened. When I was arrested and when Sullivan insisted on parading me in front of all the cameras, I remember her, my mother, crying in the background, still in the house, and shouting to someone that I was the only child she had. I heard her shout it, and then I heard by the way her voice changed that she'd remembered the daughter she'd lost. I remember thinking that it wasn't the time to remember a thing like that. He destroyed us all, Mr Rivers, he destroyed us all.'

This final remark caught me unawares. 'Who did?'

'Sullivan. He did what he did, and he did it all for his own self-serving ends, and it destroyed us. Everywhere she went, people pointed at her, whispered about her behind her back. She didn't even feel secure at Easington any more.'

'Was she able to visit you?'

'Hardly. Dartmoor? The Isle of Wight? They kept me as far from this place as possible. Procedure, see? With just enough calculated indifference thrown in so as not to show. And if the people at Easington weren't enough to put her off, then Sullivan and his team paid enough visits to the place, looking for whatever it was they hoped to find there, to make her even more unwelcome.'

'Did they never consider that the caravan was a bit . . . obvious? As a hiding place?' I said.

'Perhaps they'd already looked everywhere else.'

'Or perhaps it was just another of those loose ends they couldn't afford to leave dangling,' I said.

'Perhaps,' he said, finally suspicious of where all this was leading us.

I changed the subject. I told him about the poem Angela Hill had written for Nicola Bishop's memorial service.

'It was something she used to do,' he said.

I promised to send him a copy of the clipping.

'I'd appreciate it,' he said.

'Tell me about Nicola Bishop,' I said.

'Is that why you mentioned Angela – to bring us back to her?'

'No. Because I'm partly responsible for what happened to Angela.'

'Perhaps you and I should swap places,' he said. He pushed the bib across the table to me.

'I won't make any excuses for what happened,' I said.

'Like I do, you mean?'

'Nicola Bishop.'

'I can't tell you anything you probably don't already know,' he said. 'And certainly nothing her father will ever want to hear.'

'She was a willing participant in everything you wanted her to do?'

' "Willing" is a good word. She revelled in it, started acting like she was indispensable, as though she had something none of the others had.'

'Did you try to warn her like you warned Angela Hill?'

He considered this. 'Not really. Besides, it was too late by then. What they wanted, they got.'

'And you're still not prepared to give me anything to take back to him now?'

'You've got all you need, Mr Rivers,' he said, looking directly at me as he said it. 'Perhaps we should leave it at that.'

Neither of us spoke for several minutes, after which there was a single rap on the door, and this time the governor came in to us.

'I was wondering how much longer you might require, Mr Rivers?' he said. 'As you will appreciate, there must be a limit to these things. My shifts are due to change in twenty minutes.'

'Meaning if I'm not back in my cell by then,' Roper told me, 'he'll have the inconvenience of finding someone on the late shift to escort me back there.'

'It doesn't matter to me one way or the other,' the governor said, angry at being confronted like this by Roper.

I rose and said that I was ready to leave.

'Good, right, well,' the governor said.

Roper rose and stood opposite me.

The governor called for the man outside to come in to us.

I held out my hand to Roper, which he considered for a moment and then took. I thanked him for having spoken to me.

'Give my regards to Mr Smart,' he said.

'And Sullivan?' I said.

Roper looked at the governor and the warder. 'Chances are he'll already know everything there is to know,' he said.

The governor made a noise, turned sharply away from me and went outside. The warder told Roper to sit back down and to put his bib on. He would be made to wait in the small room until I had been escorted out of the prison.

The governor waited for me and we walked together back along the same corridors and through the same doors.

'I hope your meeting was a fruitful one,' he said.

'Not particularly,' I told him, careful of what I might reveal.

'It concerns me that he might have had his hopes raised a little too high concerning the outcome of his appeal,' he said.

'I imagine he's prepared for every eventuality,' I said.

'It was not my decision to have him returned here – here, of all places,' he said.

'I know that.'

'Then be aware, also, Mr Rivers, that I also know that his being returned to Hull was an act of deliberate provocation on the part of whoever chose to make it happen.'

I knew that, too.

Sean Wallis and Carl Boyd stood at the door leading out into the first of the yards. The governor saw them ahead of us and stopped walking.

'I shall say goodbye to you here, Mr Rivers.'

'Goodbye,' I said.

He looked from me back to the two waiting men, before turning and leaving me.

I went alone to Wallis.

'Tell you everything you came to hear, did he?'

'As far as I know, my visit here was a confidential one,' I said.

'Yeah, right, confidential.'

Carl Boyd held the keys to the door, but was in no hurry to open it and let us out. He listened intently to everything Wallis and I said.

'We're off shift now,' Wallis said, as though this might mean something to me.

I had always assumed that Smart had arranged to have Roper brought back to Hull at such a sensitive time because he knew what Roper might be about to reveal, and because some of the others still involved still lived and operated here. I was beginning to understand now that there might have been other, less obvious reasons behind the decision.

Wallis repeated his remark about being off-duty.

'And?' I said to him.

'You could give us a lift back into town.' They both carried coats, which they put on over their jackets.

I told him I'd come in a taxi, that my ribs were still too sore for me to drive.

'Your ribs?' Wallis said.

'I fell.'

He looked puzzled by the remark. Beside him, Boyd laughed and finally opened the door.

'So neither of you drive?' I said to Wallis.

'If you're asking us what cars we got, then forget it,' Boyd said.

'I wasn't,' I said.

'What you talking about?' Wallis said. 'We haven't neither of us got a car.'

'See?' Boyd said. He gave his keys to a man at the outer door and the two of them accompanied me out of the prison and on to Hedon Road. I felt suddenly vulnerable in their presence. They separated and walked one on either side of me. They went on talking to each other as though I wasn't between them.

It was already dark, and while a continuous stream of cars passed us in both directions, there were few other pedestrians. A light rain was falling.

We passed the Sportsman and Wallis asked loudly if they ought to go in for a drink, to which Boyd replied even more loudly that the place was full of snitches. Both of them burst into laughter at this.

Beyond the bar we approached the used-car lot, where two men were erecting wire panels for the night. One of them saw Wallis and Boyd beside me and called out to them. The man beside him stood looking pointedly at me, grinning and sliding an iron bar in and out of his fist.

Wallis's phone rang. He ignored it and it went on ringing.

I was considering whether or not to run – perhaps through the slow traffic, across the road and into the darkness – wondering how many seconds' start I might gain on them were they to chase me, when I heard a siren approaching us from behind. All five of us turned to see the flashing light on the roof of an unmarked car on the far side of the road.

The siren stopped. Finch wound down his window and shouted to ask if I wanted a lift.

The man with the iron bar moved closer to me, and all four of them looked hard through the darkness and the rain to see who had shouted.

The car stopped. Smart got out and walked slowly around the front of the car, holding up a hand to stop the traffic as he came to us. Our arrangement had been to meet back at Humber Street later.

He took out his warrant card and pointed it briefly at the man with the iron bar. 'Bang,' he said. 'That looks like a deadly weapon to me.' Turning to me, he said, 'Mr Rivers, what a coincidence. Here we are following these two corrupt warders, and who should turn up, but you?'

No one was expected to believe him; his meaning was clear.

Wallis finally answered his phone, which had continued to ring throughout all this. He spoke into it briefly, listened for longer and then came back to where we stood and pulled Boyd away from us.

Behind Finch, other drivers sounded their horns, angry at being held up.

Neither he nor Smart paid any attention to this.

Smart then turned to Wallis and Boyd. 'I'd offer you two a lift,' he said. 'But the car would stink for days afterwards.' He held my arm and the two of us walked to where Finch waited for us.

35

'I assume there was some reason for all that,' I said to Smart, who sat beside me in the rear.

'We saved you,' he said, his face away from me, watching the four men, who were easily able to keep pace with us in the slow traffic. They crossed the road to walk even closer to us. The man with the bar made threatening gestures with it. Eventually, as the succession of lights ahead of us changed, the traffic started to flow and we left them behind. Seeing they were about to lose us, the four men turned back towards the car lot.

'Roper was attacked,' I said.

'What a surprise,' Smart said, his gaze still on the men disappearing behind us.

I caught Finch's glance in the rear-view mirror.

'He seemed to know a great deal about you and what you were up to,' I said to Smart, finally getting his attention.

'Oh?'

'In addition to which, he has no faith in your assurances, sitting in there.'

'Just as well he's already on his way somewhere else then,' Smart said.

'Are you serious?'

'As opposed to what?'

'Where?' I said, knowing he wouldn't answer me.

'Guess what we found today,' Finch said. 'Back on the car lot.' He motioned behind us.

I almost said, 'A green Polo.'

'A black Micra.'

'We could barely contain our surprise,' Smart said.

'Can you prove it was the one that visited Sullivan and me with the tapes?'

Smart shook his head. 'Cleanest car on the lot. Spotless inside and out, registration clear as a bell.'

'But . . .' I said, waiting.

'But we spoke to the boy who washes the piles of junk and he told us that the owner of the lot makes as much money by renting cars out – no questions asked – as he does by selling them.'

'Did he give you any names?' I remembered the boy I had seen while waiting for Wallis.

'A lot of customers from the prison, apparently. When all this is over, we're going to get the locals to go through the place.'

'It might account for why nothing ever came back to us from Swansea,' Finch said.

'So it probably ties Wallis to Sullivan and the videos,' I said. 'And if the newspaper revelations and the videos are connected, then it makes Wallis the man most likely to have attacked me and stolen the file.' I knew it could not be so straightforward. Wallis had seemed genuinely surprised at my cracked ribs. Neither Smart nor Finch showed any enthusiasm for what I suggested.

'Greed and intelligence is a dangerous combination,' Smart said. 'It gets Wallis off the hook on at least one count.'

'Roper didn't kill those other girls,' I said, determined, despite all their attempts, to return to Roper.

'I think we already knew that,' Smart said, unconcerned, knowing that I too had long understood and accepted this.

'Also, he's convinced his mother's death wasn't the accident everybody else was happy to believe it to be at the time.'

'He can't know for certain either way,' Smart said.

'Perhaps not. But if *he* believed the fire was started by one of the others, it might give you a little more leverage in getting him to help you to get to them.'

The remark disappointed Smart and he continued to look through the window as we drove. 'He can think what he likes,' he said. 'No proof, no evidence, no deal.'

And again I knew that I was deliberately being diverted from my course.

'Did you know Wallis coming off his shift would coincide with my leaving?' I said.

'We guessed he might want to keep an eye on you for someone. Plus it got him out of the place while Roper was being taken to the proverbial unmarked vehicle.'

'His belongings, presumably, having been gathered up and taken there while he was talking to me.'

'If he'd known, he would somehow have used it and probably lied to you. What else did he tell you?'

'It was mostly what I inferred,' I said.

'OK, what did you mostly *infer*?' He was beginning to lose patience with me.

'That he has a good understanding of what you're using him to do, and that he knows precisely what cards he still holds and how easily they might be lost if he plays them too soon at your urging.'

'"Cards"?' Smart said, understanding me perfectly.

'Tell me honestly,' I said to Finch. 'Did you know he'd been attacked?'

'It happened the same night you were taken to hospital,' he said, disregarding the loud tutting sound Smart was making beside me. 'Did he tell you who did it?'

Smart laughed at the question. 'Finch here thinks it's about time we became a little more pro-active in all of this.' He gave a disparaging emphasis to the word. 'And regardless of my own preferences, I have to say that, recent developments considered, I tend to agree with him.'

'You sound like the governor,' I told him. 'And if, regardless of your own preferences, you tend to agree with Finch's suggestion, then I can only imagine that something's happened to make you want to get your hands dirty.'

He considered this remark carefully before saying, 'Not dirty, Mr Rivers. Not dirty.'

'Because anything that might be interpreted as interference by Roper's legal team would—'

'Something like that.'

'Meaning, presumably, that even tame judges know they have to draw the line somewhere.'

He turned away from me again and looked at the passing shops and traffic. We were approaching the city centre. I had assumed they were accompanying me back to Humber Street for our arranged de-briefing, but instead they turned onto the inner ring-road.

'We thought we might go and see Mr Summers,' Smart said.

His tone made me cautious. I tried to catch Finch's eye in the mirror, but he refused to look up.

'No particular reason,' Smart said. 'Except he seems to be gaining a great deal from all of this at very little cost to himself. And because he called your office a couple of hours ago saying he had something important to show you.'

'We were there,' Finch said. 'We were going to wait for you.'

'Three hours?' I said.

'We let ourselves in,' Smart said. 'What about the names?'

'He made no response to any of them, even the made-up ones.'

'Nevertheless, he'll have been pleased to have had them all confirmed,' he said.

'Which was the whole point of my visit,' I said.

'Did he say anything about Sullivan?'

'Not really.'

'At the time of his mother's death, he wrote a letter to the Home Secretary saying that her death wasn't being properly investigated because of who she was, because of who *he* was. As you might imagine, there wasn't much sympathy for the woman at the time of the trial. Sullivan was still effectively in charge of the detectives. All Roper could see was a continuing conspiracy. We thought at first that it was the death of his mother and the realization that, yet again, justice was unlikely to be served that made Roper consider making his first appeal. Far too soon, of course, but the seeds of doubt were being sown in his own mind.'

Finch braked sharply, throwing us both forward. A car stopped inches behind us and the driver sounded his horn.

Finch was slow in moving off. The driver flashed his lights at us.

'When you're ready, DS Finch,' Smart said.

'In what way "pro-active"?' I said.

But instead of answering me, Smart looked at his watch and smiled. 'It won't surprise you to learn that injunctions have already been served on all of the editors who printed the stolen photos.'

'So whoever was hoping for a delayed pay-out might not now get it, not even for the pictures already delivered and published?'

'These are not men of scruple,' Smart said. 'On either side.'

'I'm glad I'm with you two, then,' I said, and he laughed, stopping abruptly.

'One day,' he said. 'You'll get to see one of those films and all your confusion about scruples and legality and doing the right thing will become a lot clearer for you. Either *they* win or *we* win, and however ridiculous or melodramatic that might sound to you, it really is *that* simple. It would be easier if we didn't endlessly have to watch a press that on one page calls for men like Roper to be castrated, and on the next shows us all a topless sixteen-year-old looking forward to a long and lucrative career in modelling and helping those less fortunate than herself, but that's the reality, and some of us are made to face that reality a little more forcibly and a little more often than others.'

We crossed Ferensway and into more traffic.

I asked Smart what belated advantage he hoped to gain by the injunction.

'It all depends on what whoever stole and sent the pictures hoped to gain from them in the first place. Finch believes that they were stolen by or on behalf of Roper's old associates, and that by sending them to the press they would either invalidate the photos as evidence – which is hardly the point considering how little they achieved the first time round – or that something in them would make someone other than Roper jump too soon.'

'Meaning they might not have been stolen by the men who set him up, and that, for once, they themselves might be the targets?'

'That's the theory.'

Finch half-turned to me. 'The file might have been stolen by someone who didn't at first understand the value of what he was being paid to steal.'

'Someone like Wallis, say,' Smart said.

'But who then saw an opportunity to make a lot more money, and who only handed over half of what was in the file to whoever paid him to steal it,' Finch said.

'And you are the only ones who knew for certain exactly what was in the file,' I said.

Smart patted the case beside him. 'A replica of which speeds along beside us.'

'And if the stolen photos *did* contain something other than—'

'We've been over them a hundred times,' Finch said.

'None of the men is 100 per cent identifiable, and none of the pictures contains any of the three missing girls.'

'Which, of course, and to extend your card-playing analogy,' Smart said, 'remains Roper's trump ace.'

We turned out of the main flow of traffic and made our way towards Sunny's.

'What did Sullivan tell you?' I said.

'Nothing we didn't already know. He was very careful on that score.'

'Proving what – that whoever compiled the films had either saved everything from five years ago or that they still had access to everything they needed.'

'It would suggest one of those things, yes,' Smart said, rubbing his face and seeming suddenly exhausted by all that had just happened.

We arrived at Sunny's.

Yvonne answered the bell and told us to go up.

'Mr Smart,' she said, curtsying slightly. She touched my cheek and asked me how it felt.

I told her it hurt only when I smiled wryly or ironically.

'I could never tell the difference,' she said.

Sunny lay asleep at his desk, his head cradled in his arms.

'Wake him up,' Smart told her.

She leaned over Sunny and gently shook him. He woke slowly, lifting his head a few inches and pushing his arms through the clutter of his desk.

'Christ,' he said. 'It's the Untouchables,' and let his head fall back down.

Yvonne brushed the hair from his eyes and then plugged in the kettle.

'Busy days, Mr Summers,' Smart said to Sunny.

'What do you want?'

'We're here in a spirit of mutual and beneficial co-operation,' Smart said.

'Again?' Sunny looked from Smart to me to Finch. 'Tell me your plan,' he said to Smart, 'and I'll tell you what's wrong with it.'

325

'If only it were that straightforward, Mr Summers. Nobody has plans these days. We search for patterns and tenuous connections, that's all. One tiny inconsistency is worth a dozen plans. What do you want – a blackboard with names, arrows and photographs? A few giant question marks dotted around? A line of villains above the naked and mutilated body of a dead child?'

Yvonne distributed coffee.

Sunny took the bottle from his desk and passed around clean plastic cups.

'Roper is on his way to London,' Smart said.

Sunny looked at his watch. 'He left at four minutes past five,' he said.

'I shall endeavour to contain my surprise,' Smart said.

'Meaning you already know that the story's been filed.'

' "Filed",' Smart said. 'How . . .' He sipped from his plastic cup. 'Meaning that in less than twelve hours' time, everyone with even the slightest interest in him will know he's gone.'

Sunny drained his own cup. 'Meaning that whoever might have been waiting to get their hands round his throat has missed their first chance.'

'Possibly,' Smart said. 'Although the thing about being in prison is that someone somewhere always knows where you are to the nearest foot every single minute of your life there.'

'And when Roper's appeal fails and you lose interest and stop watching him, they'll have all the time in the world to catch up with him.'

'Unless, of course, Roper succeeds in his daring plot to reveal all and incriminate everyone and he reaps some fabulous reward as a result.'

'Which is what?' Sunny said. 'Likely? Unlikely? Possible? Probable?'

Smart fluttered his hand at each of the words, and only then did it occur to me that what he was suggesting was that it would be best all round if Roper, having revealed his incriminating evidence to Smart, was then himself killed as a consequence of Smart, like Sullivan before him, not arresting everyone else quickly enough.

The thought occurred to Finch, too, and he looked to me with a mixture of uncertainty and disbelief in his eyes.

No one spoke for a moment as the implications of all this were considered.

Then Smart held out his cup for more drink from Sunny. Sunny poured it and offered the bottle to me.

'OK,' Smart said eventually. He took out his phone, dialled and was answered immediately. 'Where are you now? And the other end? Everybody? And after that? Good. Hold on, I'm putting Rivers on.' He handed the phone to me.

I took it, uncertain what to say.

' "To whom do I have the pleasure of speaking?" ' Smart said.

The man on the phone identified himself as DS Oliver, a member of Smart's team. He told me he was accompanying Roper to London and that they were just leaving the M18 to join the M1. I heard the noise of traffic behind him.

'Can I speak to Roper?' I said.

'Not a chance.'

Smart gestured for me to give him the phone. 'Yes, I know,' he said. 'No, don't stop. Let me know when you arrive.' He looked at his watch. 'What, ten? And knowing something of Mr Rivers's terrier-like tenacity, I may still be with him.' He closed the phone and put it on the desk. 'I know that proved nothing,' he said to me, 'but at least you've got two witnesses who heard it all.'

'Three,' Finch said.

Smart smiled. 'You're one of us,' he said.

Sunny started searching through the papers on his desk and sorting them into piles.

'I imagine you have a busy night ahead of you, Mr

Summers,' Smart said. 'Feeding all this into that insatiable public maw.'

'What's "insatiable"?' Yvonne said, and took the papers Sunny gave to her.

I rose to leave, telling Sunny I'd call him the following morning.

' "Monster Arrives Safely",' Sunny said. ' "The Waiting Begins".'

' "Waiting"?' Smart said. 'I imagine that is one particular luxury neither you nor I share or can afford to indulge in.'

'Your friend', Sunny said to me, 'is considerably more predictable than he imagines. And his loquacity is not the servant he fondly believes it to be.' He turned to face Smart, who looked back at him.

'Boys, boys, boys,' Yvonne said. 'All these long words in one evening. No wonder you're all wound up.' She motioned for me to go.

Finch rose beside me.

'Aren't we forgetting something?' Smart said.

'Such as?' Sunny said, but even I could see that he was lying.

'What we came here to see,' Smart said. 'Whatever it was that you wanted to show Mr Rivers.'

'The "terrier-like" Mr Rivers,' Yvonne said.

Sunny looked to me and I signalled to him that I had not told Smart of the call. He made his own silent calculation. The moment was heightened by the passing siren of an ambulance as it sped along Spring Bank into the city centre.

Sunny slid open a drawer and took out a nine by six photo.

'I came across this in one of our original files.' He handed the photo to me.

Smart leaned forward, as though he might be the one to receive it.

In the picture, Sullivan stood with at least two dozen others, mostly men, most out of uniform, and in front of them a long table lay piled with pieces of equipment and stacks of video cameras and cassettes. Along the front of the table someone had pinned an enlarged headline which read PORN MURDERER CONVICTED. It was Sullivan and his original team. Most of the men smoked and held up glasses to the photographer. The men on either side of Sullivan held champagne bottles above their heads. The grin on Sullivan's face looked considerably more forced than the grins on the faces of the others.

I passed the picture to Smart.

His disappointment was evident. 'Their trophy picture,' he said. 'Everyone Sullivan ever shook hands with above the level of DI, he made sure there was a photographer present.'

The results of which still hung along the hallway walls of his bungalow.

Smart handed the picture to Finch and turned to look at me. 'What?' he said. He took the picture back and pushed it into my hand.

I pointed to everything displayed on the table, most of it still bagged and labelled from the trial. 'It shows us what existed before most of it went missing,' I said.

'All of it useless,' Smart said. 'Spent. No appeal judge is going to look at any of this again. What else?'

'That was it,' I said.

'You're as bad a liar as Mr Summers here,' he said.

'The man to Sullivan's right,' I said. 'The one holding the bottle by its base. There's something familiar about him.'

He took the picture back, studied it, tapped it with a finger and said, 'Detective Sergeant Lloyd. Sullivan's right-hand man.' He passed the photo back.

The man held the bottle in one hand and his other was firmly round Sullivan's shoulder, his head inclined towards Sullivan's. He looked to me like a man who had grabbed Sullivan, pointed him firmly towards the camera and then hissed 'Smile' in his ear.

'Familiar how?' Smart said.

'I don't know. Just familiar. What do you know about him?'

Smart thought for a moment. 'Only that he and Sullivan had worked together for the best part of twenty years, and that he had only a year left to live when this picture was taken, assuming it was the day of Roper's conviction. Cancer.'

'Did he know?'

'Must have done.'

'Did Sullivan?'

He shrugged. 'It wasn't a good year for Lloyd. Once all the omissions and inadequacies of the investigation started coming to light, he was the one hung out to dry. He was ten years younger than Sullivan, though you wouldn't think it to see him here.'

'Sullivan became the hero everyone wanted, and—'

'And Lloyd caught the first of the flak. Sullivan got his early retirement with pension and accolades intact, and Lloyd was left behind to start fending off the allegations. There were calls for a re-trial even then, but, like I said, it was too soon, unthinkable.'

'Did they keep in touch once Sullivan retired and moved to Spurn?'

'Yes would be my guess. They'd had twenty years of watching each other's back, remember. Once a bent, self-serving copper, always a bent, self-serving copper.' He looked to Sunny, who had been surreptitiously writing in shorthand on a pad.

He looked up at us. 'Except for the words with more than two syllables,' he said.

'What happened to Lloyd?' I asked Smart.

'From what I remember, his treatment became less and less effective. He was forced to retire on the grounds of ill-health in' – he closed his eyes – 'March or April of ninety-nine. He died three or four months later. His wife had left him ten years earlier. He lived with his son. He wrote letters to Sullivan asking for his help, but Sullivan was beyond helping anyone by then.'

'Did the police authorities know Lloyd hadn't got long to live when they retired him?'

'I imagine so. He became embarrassing – writing to the papers, insisting that he and Sullivan had done a good job, that they were being unfairly persecuted.'

'Except that Sullivan *wasn't* being persecuted,' Yvonne said. 'He was still the golden boy, enjoying his retirement.'

'And who could do without Lloyd yapping at his ankles,' Smart said.

'Another dog reference,' Yvonne said.

Smart smiled at her. 'I like to theme each day.' He turned back to me. 'Sullivan went to two funerals in the space of ten days – first his wife's, and then Lloyd's.'

'We looked into everyone on the original team,' Finch said. 'Lloyd did next to nothing off his own back. Sullivan pulled the strings hour by hour. Anyone who didn't like the way he operated was soon taken off the case. There was always a waiting list to join.'

'Forget Lloyd,' Smart said.

'Because he sleeps with the fishes?' Yvonne said.

'In the Eastern Cemetery, to be more precise,' Smart said, again confirming his thoroughness.

'I thought the stuff on the table might be of more interest to you,' Sunny said. 'See what's there, see what you've still got, and then when you know what's missing you might gain some idea as to how or why it went missing.'

None of us followed this reasoning.

'I'm cutting down on his Benylin,' Yvonne said.

'Just a thought,' Sunny said, and perhaps only I understood that the remark had not been made for nothing. Smart was right – the evidence was all old evidence and would be ruled inadmissible by an appeal judge, especially one already sitting on a verdict.

I passed the picture back to Sunny.

'Keep it,' he said. 'It might come in useful.'

Smart, Finch and I left shortly afterwards.

At the door, Smart turned to Yvonne and said, 'Would you like me to spell "loquacious" for you in case the *Tatler* or *Country Life* give you a call?'

'No need,' she said. 'I've got my *Reader's Digest* dictionary. You could have a shot at "diphtheria" before you go, though.'

It was the only word no one in the world ever knew how to spell correctly. It was also the coded password she and Sunny used for their confidential files.

Sunny made no response to the remark other than to glance quickly at me. 'Just go,' he said eventually.

36

The three of us returned to Humber Street. I told Smart that there was nothing more I could tell him about my conversation with Roper, but he and Finch insisted on accompanying me and then waiting with me until we received confirmation of Roper's safe arrival.

My office was much colder than usual, and the muted rhythms of the dance class again filtered down to us. I switched on the heater and put Sunny's photo in a drawer. Finch asked me where the nearest take-away was.

'What sort of food?' I asked him.

'*Food* food,' he said.

'Dinner on the tax-payer,' Smart said, taking out his wallet.

I gave Finch a leaflet and he ordered three pizzas.

While we waited for these, Smart suggested that I check my messages. 'Sunny called at two forty-five,' he said.

I checked the machine and heard Sunny's voice.

There was one further message.

I pressed for it to play as Smart and Finch took off their coats, but at the sound of the caller's voice, both of them stopped, exchanged a look and came immediately to the desk.

'Mr Rivers,' the man's voice said. 'Just a courtesy call to say I hope this afternoon's little visit was to your satisfaction. A rare privilege to be able to talk to a man like that. An even greater privilege when you consider that you might be one of the last people to talk to him at all.'

'Switch it off,' Smart said. He finished taking off his coat, and he and Finch drew up chairs to sit close to the machine. He rewound the tape and played it again. He checked the phone, but the number had been withheld. 'The man himself,' he said to Finch.

'One of Roper's old associates?' I said.

The tape continued. Distantly behind the voice, music played. Music and then someone singing. A foreign language. Opera.

The voice went on: 'I imagine you'll be conveying everything you learned to Mr Smart at some point in the near future. In fact, I wouldn't be surprised if he wasn't sitting there with you right now following his dramatic intervention on your behalf.'

'He was watching us,' Smart said.

'Or Wallis told him what happened.'

'He was *there*.'

'Like I said,' the voice continued, 'this is just a call to reassure you that a close eye is being kept on things. We didn't want you to be misled by Smart into thinking that just because he says something is private and confidential it necessarily is. That's really all I had to say. Oh, and that you might extend my regards to James Bishop. I don't know him personally, of course, but I knew someone who did. We'll talk soon.'

The message ended abruptly.

Smart took the tape from the machine.

'No mention of Roper having been removed from the prison,' Finch said.

'Which probably means they don't know. He was talking because he likes the sound of his own voice. What did he tell us that we didn't already know?'

'He knew I'd been to see Roper,' I said.

334

Finch clicked his lips.

'Do you think they were watching me come out?'

'To make sure that Wallis and Boyd and the thugs from the car lot did what they'd been told to do? I doubt it.'

'You think they came, saw us, and considered it too much of a risk to be spotted by us?' Finch said to Smart.

'After all this time, Abbot probably thinks he's fire-proof.'

'Abbot?' I said. It was one of the names on the list I had recited to Roper.

Smart looked at me. 'Abbot.'

Unexpectedly, the name struck another chord. I remembered the wrong-number call upon my return from seeing Sullivan at Spurn thirteen days earlier. A man called Abbot enquiring about tickets for a per-formance of *La Bohème* at the New Theatre. I told Smart about it. The tape had already been recorded over.

Smart looked at me as though he believed I had deliberately withheld information from him, as though I already knew who Abbot was. I also remembered the two silent, untraceable calls awaiting my return from the hospital.

We were interrupted by the arrival of the pizzas.

'Do you think he'll call again when he discovers Roper is gone?' I said to Smart while Finch was downstairs.

Smart considered this unlikely.

When Finch returned, we listened to the tape six more times.

'Can you trace the call?' I said.

'Not from here back to the caller.'

'Then from him to here?'

'He won't have called on a phone traceable to him.'

'He didn't make any threats to speak of,' I said.

'You think so?' Smart said to me. He wiped his lips with his handkerchief. 'It sounded threatening to me.

And it proves that our investigation here is as leaky as it's always been.'

Then something occurred to him and he played the tape again. 'The music's from *Madame Butterfly*,' he said. 'Abbot's an opera buff. They used to dub excerpts over their films.'

'Does it tell us anything?' Finch said.

'Only that he feels safe enough to reveal himself like this.' To me, Smart said, 'Being a private investigator, I don't suppose it occurred to you to investigate whether or not *La Bohème* was actually being performed at the New Theatre?'

'I'm not *that* good,' I said.

'When exactly did the first call come?' Finch said.

I thought hard about the exact time and told him.

Smart shook his head. 'We should have known all this then.'

'What difference would it have made?'

'For a start we would have known that Abbot was keeping a close eye on things and that he was still up to scratch.'

'Via Sullivan?'

'Unlikely.'

'Do you think he knew I'd been to see Sullivan? Was that why he called me on my return?'

'It's a possibility. Your visit was hardly a secret.'

'A bit like today's,' I said.

'If he was watching,' Finch said slowly, 'then he knew then and now that you wouldn't be here to answer when he rang. He called to leave messages, not to talk to you.'

'Which, presumably, he thought you would relay to us,' Smart said.

'Almost a two-week gap,' Finch said. 'Why?'

'Perhaps he realized Rivers hadn't made the connection and felt he needed reminding.'

'People usually overestimate my intelligence,' I said.

Smart looked at me hard and smiled. 'Never make

336

the mistake of including me among those people,' he said.

'If he'd genuinely wanted to talk to Rivers, then he'd have called back,' Finch said.

Smart shook his head. 'He had no intention of talking to him.'

I told him about the two silent calls.

'Where did he stand among Roper's associates?' I asked him.

'The major player,' Smart said immediately. 'Him and six others, and all of them still doing what they think they do best. But now, of course, they do it *and* keep their hands clean and their heads down.'

We listened to the tape again.

'He's just batting a few balls back at us,' Finch said.

'It might mean they're keeping an eye on Sullivan as well,' I suggested.

'Which, if true,' Smart said, 'means that by now they certainly know that we're watching him, too.'

'Then why no call immediately after the videos were delivered?' I said. 'If my two calls were acts of confirmation, surely they'd have wanted some kind of connection made then.'

Smart considered this. He took the tape out of the machine. 'May I?'

I told him to take it.

'What now?' Finch said, dropping a crust into one of the grease-soaked boxes.

And as though in answer to this, his phone rang. He identified himself and then said nothing for a minute before clicking it shut and saying, 'He's arrived safely.'

I looked at my watch. It was not yet eight. 'Meaning that all your talk of Roper being taken to London was a lie.'

'Misleading,' Smart said.

'The leaks?' I said.

'Precisely.'

They left me shortly afterwards.

I watched them drive away before taking Sunny's

photo of Sullivan and Lloyd's victory celebration out of my drawer. I looked hard at the face of Lloyd. I remained convinced that I knew him or that I'd encountered him elsewhere. He'd died over four years ago, and I guessed that I'd perhaps seen him while he was still working in connection with John Maxwell. It was as close as I could get.

I looked at each of the other faces and at the mounds of evidence used to convict Roper, all of it arranged along the table like the prize bag of a hunting party. There were computers and video recorders, cameras and lighting equipment. The press had been quick to make something of this 'Crime of Technology', as though human pain and loss and suffering were somehow no longer worthy of their consideration.

The men at the table, particularly the older ones like Sullivan and Lloyd, had no true idea of the potential or capability of the equipment they crowed over. It might have been modest by today's accelerating standards, but it was still more than enough then to outrun them and their twenty-year-old methods.

The room around me smelled stronger than ever of molten cheese and congealed meat. I wondered where Roper had been taken that could be reached in three hours.

At ten I called John Maxwell to ask him about Lloyd. The interest he showed in the case was for my benefit alone. He told me all he knew of Lloyd, but couldn't remember me ever meeting him. He didn't like the man, he said. Lloyd's wife had left him because he was violent towards her. No one had been surprised when their son had chosen to stay with his father. The boy and the man were very alike, John Maxwell said. The boy had enrolled at the Hendon Police College, but had been expelled following allegations of violence against other cadets there.

John Maxwell had no idea what had happened to the boy, but assumed he still lived in the house he had shared with Lloyd at the time of his father's death. He thought that it was in North Hull somewhere, but couldn't be more precise.

'Lloyd also used to partner a man called Lynch,' he said. 'He retired early and went to live in Spain shortly after Roper was arrested. The pair of them were as bad as each other.'

I mentioned the name Abbot and he fell silent for a few seconds.

'It was never made public,' he said, 'but those urging Sullivan to slow down and to spread his net wider always believed Abbot to be the one they ought to have set their sights on alongside Roper in the first place.'

'He called me,' I said.

'I wouldn't want a man like Abbot calling *me*,' he said, his even tone a warning to me. 'What did he want?'

'Just to let me know that he knows I'm involved, presumably.'

'He knows Roper's appeal will fail,' he said.

'Either way, Roper's still angling for a deal with Smart to hand over his evidence against Abbot and the others directly to him when Smart's in a position to do something about it.'

'He's been in that position for months,' John Maxwell said.

'But not Roper.'

'Perhaps. But Smart still let you put yourself between himself and Abbot. And Abbot will know by now that Roper has temporarily slipped away from them.'

I told him what Smart had half-seriously suggested about the convenience of Roper being killed after his evidence was handed over.

'It wouldn't stop with Roper,' he said. He said he'd considered coming to visit me in the hospital, but that it would have brought back too many bad memories for him.

I told him that I had borne my suffering with dignity, silence and grace.

He laughed. He rarely laughed. 'It's a ridiculous way to bear suffering,' he said. 'Take care of yourself, and let me know, either way, when it's all over.'

I said I would, but he hung up before I'd finished speaking.

Either way.

When his wife of thirty-five years had died in the same hospital, his legs had given way beneath him and he had been unable to stand for several hours. And so he'd knelt beside her bed, holding her dead hand, crying into the sheets and cursing everyone who came and tried to take her away from him. Later, when he was able to stand, he'd apologized to everyone he'd shouted at and then thanked them all for what they had done for her.

37

The next day I met James Bishop in the Portland Hotel and told him all I knew. I gave him my report and he considered the envelope in which it was sealed with a look that told me he would not read it.

Twenty-one days had passed since our first meeting, and we seemed to each other like two exhausted men who had been labouring at the same unsuccessful task for years. I told him that everything had happened too quickly and that I'd been left behind. He saw this for the excuse it was and then quizzed me half-heartedly on the likely outcome of Roper's appeal. I made all the obvious guesses and remarks – small cushions for his own long fall.

'You still don't believe that Roper killed her, do you?' he said.

'No,' I told him. 'Her involvement with Roper led to her involvement with the men who used them both, and who then pushed him aside. That's what killed her,' I said.

We sat together in the mostly empty bar, where he was meeting Alison Menzies before the pair of them flew to Amsterdam later in the evening. He told me the business deal he had been working on for the past four months was close to being completed. He would feel empty afterwards, unfulfilled, he said, and then told me to ignore him. He was remembering his daughter.

It would have been a good place and a good time to leave him. I could have sent him my bill and he could have sent me a cheque and we need never have seen each other again. And one night, in his Kirk Ella home, his wife asleep above him and dreaming of all she would never now have, his daughter's face would suddenly appear on a silent and flickering television screen at the news of the outcome of Roper's appeal, and James Bishop would see her and be made to understand again all that he had lost.

He paid the waiter for our drinks, taking the money from a wallet I knew to contain her picture.

'Let me see,' I asked him.

He gave me the wallet and there she was, amid the credit cards and the crisp new Euro notes.

'Are we ready to pay for all our sins, do you think, Mr Rivers?' he asked me unexpectedly.

'One way or another,' I said. 'But nine times out of ten we get to keep everything to ourselves because there is no way of paying.'

'Checks and balances,' he said. He held out his hand for the wallet and I gave it back to him. 'Patricia still accuses me of having affairs – though, as you might imagine, the word itself is seldom used – or of wanting to have affairs with most of the women I meet. It's her way of keeping herself apart from me.'

'Did you once think that finding out about Nicola's death might bring her back to you?'

'Closer, yes. I see now, of course, that I was deluding only myself.'

'It surely can't hurt to know,' I said.

He shook his head. 'I doubt if that will help anyone, not now.'

I asked him about the deal he was about to close and he told me about it, but without enthusiasm.

I asked him if the name Abbot meant anything to

him, and he considered it, shook his head and said it didn't.

I had a copy of the phone tape and I played it to him on my miniature player. I asked him if it sounded like the voice of the man who had first called to alert him of Roper's appeal and presence in the city.

He listened to it several times, but again nothing registered.

'What will you do now?' he asked me as I put the player away.

'See the thing through?' I suggested.

'Because it's what Smart wants you to do?'

'Among others.' I wanted to tell him that Smart believed Roper might still reveal something to us that might finally make clear to everyone what happened to the missing girls, but I said nothing. He would have seen the remark for the false assurance it was, and he had heard too many of those in the past five years to hear any of them repeated now.

Instead, I asked him about something Alison Menzies had told me during our brief time alone in the hospital.

'She said you fired a security guard for spreading malicious gossip about you and her.'

At first the remark puzzled him. 'Recently?'

'When you first met her, before she worked for you, before all this happened.'

He closed his eyes. 'I remember,' he said. 'We came back to the office from somewhere – a flight, I think – and there was something I wanted to put in the safe there. Alison was with me. I let us both in. It must have been eleven, twelve at night. No one spotted us or challenged us, which surprised me, and when we came to where the guards spent most of their nights, there was this man, a recent employee, holding forth on the phone about all he believed was happening between Alison and myself. It was more embarrassing for her than for me. Needless to say, there wasn't anything I was supposedly doing to and with her that the

343

man couldn't imagine doing to her himself. I'll spare you the details.'

'What happened?'

'I told her I was going to fire him and she persuaded me to wait until the following day, not to let the man know we'd overheard him, and then to get rid of him on some other pretext.'

'Can you remember his name?'

He thought hard, but shook his head. 'It'll be on our employment records. I could ask Personnel – sorry, Human Resources.'

'And the man?'

'He made a few threats and then went. I learned afterwards that he was never very popular among the other guards. He had a few scams going that they wanted no part of. They were probably as pleased as I was to see him go.'

'And that was the last you saw of him?'

'Yes, thank God.' And then his face changed and he said, 'God, no, it wasn't. I saw him once more – though purely by coincidence. There was a party at the house soon afterwards. Patricia had hired her usual caterers. A big do. Foreign clients. We had a marquee and everything.' He stopped as suddenly as he had started.

'What is it?'

'You saw the pictures,' he said, his voice much lower, his mouth barely moving. 'The stills from the video.'

The last pictures of his daughter.

'Christ, I'd forgotten all about it,' he said.

'And the man?'

'That's what I was about to tell you. He was one of the waiters employed by the caterers. I didn't even recognize him myself until half way through the afternoon. I told the man in charge that I wanted him off my property immediately. The man said they were short-staffed, that they'd only managed to hire the necessary help earlier that same day. But I insisted on

344

him going. Most of the guests had eaten by then and the caterers were beginning to clear up.'

'And he went?'

'I assume so; I never saw him again. We used the firm on a regular basis. I doubt they'd want to upset me.'

'Did you imagine he might cause trouble when you spotted him?'

'With Patricia, you mean? I suppose so. To tell you the truth, I had a lot on my mind that day, needed to see a lot of people.'

'But he went without saying or doing anything?'

He nodded. 'I assume they paid him off. He probably never even knew who he was being hired to cater for if they took him on at such short notice.'

'No,' I said. I asked him if it would be possible to see the whole film from which the stills had been taken.

He told me how long he would be away, and that he did not want me to see his wife again.

As he spoke, about to arrange a time when we might watch the film together, Alison Menzies entered the room and came to us. She was surprised to see me with him and did nothing to hide this. She kissed James Bishop on his cheek and shook my hand.

He repeated to her some of what I had earlier told him and she rubbed his arm and said she hoped as much as he did that everything would soon be over, however inconclusively.

And I saw in that simple act of kindness that she loved him, that he allowed her to love him, and that he loved her back in equal measure. Her glance to me told me to say nothing more of that sacked guard or that summer's day five years ago when the world must have seemed as perfect and as fulfilling a place to James Bishop as it had ever seemed.

She sat beside him, careful to maintain an exact distance between them.

I rose. 'I'll call you,' I said.

'Do, please.'

345

And I left them there, understanding for the first time what a simple, narrow and well-lighted path she was to him through the darkness in which he had groped and stumbled for so long, knowing that each day, each hour even, he might finally seize upon some awful understanding of himself which made that clean and comfortable world he inhabited suddenly too much for him to bear.

I looked in at them from outside and saw that she was again rubbing his arm and listening attentively to what he was telling her.

38

The next day I called Claire Madison at the Marfleet Lane hostel and asked her if she'd see me again. I lied and told her I'd uncovered something new concerning Lindsey Perry's disappearance. She was busy and so we arranged to meet later in a city-centre bar.

An hour later, Finch called to ask if anything had happened that he and Smart needed to be aware of. I told him of my meeting with James Bishop, but nothing of what we'd discussed. Likewise, I told him nothing of my conversation with John Maxwell and what little he had revealed to me.

He told me that Smart remained convinced that my meeting with Roper, especially in light of what had happened immediately afterwards, would remain the catalyst for whatever happened next.

I told him I'd arranged to see Claire Madison and he told me immediately that I shouldn't have. When I asked him why, he said that all these peripherally involved people dragged everything back to the past and insisted on keeping it there. I imagined Smart sitting across the desk from him. I asked him if there was anything Smart wanted me to do in readiness for whatever was supposed to happen next, and his pause confirmed Smart's presence for me.

He told me to contact him if anything happened.

I told him I was surprised he hadn't said 'Claire who?' and I hung up.

I left to see her shortly afterwards.

She was waiting for me, a case stuffed with paper on the table in front of her.

I told her I appreciated her coming and asked her what she wanted to drink.

'Water,' she said and slid the case onto the seat beside her.

At the far end of the room a group of a dozen men in suits sat around a long table and laughed and shouted at each other. The jukebox played a succession of Christmas songs.

'When we last spoke,' I said, 'you suggested that no one took Lindsey Perry's disappearance seriously, that her disappearing acts were a frequent occurrence. Why did *you* think this time was different?' I hoped she would tell me something before asking me what I had uncovered.

'I shouldn't be telling you anything,' she said.

'You knew she was participating in Roper's films, didn't you? Did you ever see any of them? Is that why you wouldn't talk?' I saw by the way she avoided my eyes that my guesses were right.

'Like I said, Lindsey Perry did nothing to help herself, but everyone she ever turned to for help or support or just some guidance let her down. By the time she came to the hostel, you could see how completely adrift she was.'

'And presumably she was already known to be using drugs.'

'You say that as though it might have been a rare occurrence.'

'In the hostel, I mean. I assume you have strict rules about that sort of thing.'

'Don't threaten me, Mr Rivers, or I get up here and now and walk away. I'm only here because I was angry at the fact that when Lindsey went missing, no one took her disappearance seriously, and even when Roper was caught and made his confession which included her, *still* no one did anything to find out what had happened to her, to find out if what he was saying was true.'

'Except you?'

'Me? What did I do?'

It was another guess. 'I don't know. You tell me.'

She was silent for a minute before going on. 'Lindsey Perry was a user. She couldn't help herself. Heroin, mostly, but she wasn't particularly choosy. It's probably why she agreed to participate in Roper's films.' She rubbed her thumb and fingers together. 'I saw her once or twice with this young guy. She always waited outside the hostel with him. She was never particularly close to anyone. I saw him with her three or four times.'

'Was it Roper?'

'No,' she said. 'I know what *he* looks like.'

She described the man to me – early twenties, shaved head, average build, average height, perhaps an inch or so below – but it suggested no one and everyone.

'What makes you think there was any connection between what Lindsey was up to with Roper and this man?' I said.

She shrugged. 'I'm not sure. He turned up, she went off with him, and when she returned she was always flush. It wasn't a secret, what she was doing, Mr Rivers. When she was drunk or stoned, she'd tell everyone where the money was coming from. She enjoyed what she did. They made a fuss of her, treated her well, told her how good she was, how important. I once caught her showing a film to some of the other residents.'

'One she'd brought into the hostel?'

'I assume so.'

'And you thought that she was perhaps trying to get them involved in the same kind of thing, that the man might have been using her to find more girls?'

'Something like that.'

'And what – you took it off her and watched it yourself?'

She drained her glass. 'A few days before she finally "disappeared", I came back and found her with this man and another at the hostel entrance. They were arguing. The other man was older, and he had hold of Lindsey by her arm. Like I said, they were arguing. When I showed up, he let go of her. She was the worse for wear. She hadn't been around for two or three days. I asked her if there was any problem and the younger man – the one I'd seen before – told me to keep my nose out. The older man apologized to me and said he was sorry for any disturbance they were causing. All they wanted to do, he said, was talk to Lindsey. He said she had something that belonged to them.'

'The film?'

'I assumed so.'

'Do you still have it?'

'I gave it back to her later that same day. I thought it might get her out of whatever trouble she was in with them. A week later she was gone again and never came back. My superiors had just about had their fill of her by then. Me, too, if I'm honest.'

'Was there anyone else in the film whom you recognized, then or later?'

'No. It only lasted twenty minutes. Lindsey and another girl about the same age and a dozen or so men. Both the girls looked stoned; Lindsey certainly was. The men's faces were all hidden.'

'How?'

'What's it called? Pixilated. Lindsey and the other girl were dressed as schoolgirls. The film started with them coming out of a schoolyard surrounded by lots of other kids and then getting into a car. That lasted all of twenty seconds. The next scene, they were both on all fours on a mattress surrounded by the men. You can imagine the rest.'

'And you watched it all?'

She nodded.

'Was it because you knew about all this that you insisted that something more be done to find her, or because you felt guilty at what you'd seen?'

'Both.'

'But you never told anyone else you'd seen the film?'

'No.'

'Why do *you* think Martin Roper included the killing of Lindsey Perry in his confession when everyone else was inclined to dismiss her from the case? There were plenty of other missing girls of that age who never turned up again.'

'I don't know. But in a strange way I was pleased he did.'

'Because you felt vindicated in insisting that an effort should be made to find her?'

'I just wanted her to get a fair deal for once. Notices were put in fifty different papers appealing for information from anyone who might once have known her. Nothing.'

'Whereas when Nicola Bishop went missing . . .'

'Exactly. When all this was happening, I overheard someone who should have known better remark that even if Lindsey hadn't become involved with Roper, then something else would have killed her before too long.'

'Did you ever work out why Roper included her in his confession? Surely the police must have asked you the same question at the time?'

'The police?'

'When they were making their case before his trial.'

'They came once, listened to everything I told them – and, no, I never confessed to having seen the film – and that was the last I ever saw of them. I daresay it was a different matter where Nicola Bishop was concerned.'

'I daresay,' I said. 'I appreciate you telling me all this.'

'Will Roper's appeal be successful?'

'There was never any solid evidence that he killed Lindsey or the two other girls.'

'Just the films.'

'Just those. If it's any consolation,' I said, 'I would probably have done exactly the same.'

'It's no consolation whatsoever,' she said. 'You asked me earlier why I was so convinced she'd gone for good, that this time she wasn't coming back.'

'Was there something specific?'

'She had a small jewellery box – no real jewellery to speak of, just a few studs – a cheap laminated box which she took with her everywhere she went. She told one of the other residents, another of the girls, that it had been given to her by her real mother – don't ask me how or why she thought this, or what the rest of the fantasy involved – and that it was the most precious thing she owned. She kept bits and pieces in it. It was this big.' She made a rectangle with the thumbs and index fingers of both hands. 'It had a flimsy lock, a red velvet interior, and when you opened the lid music played and a little plastic ballerina popped up and started turning. She told this other girl that she remembered the music from being a baby, and that she still sometimes played it if ever she woke in the night, unable to sleep.'

'And when she went for the final time, she took it with her?'

'She left a few clothes and books and CDs, but the box went, yes.'

'Do you think whoever persuaded her to go with them told her to bring it along?'

'It's possible. Especially if she had no intention of coming back.'

'Did you tell the police all this?'

'I think so. Like I said, they didn't seem too convinced that she had anything to do with Roper, and that she'd just gone off again, like every other time.'

She rose to leave.

'If I find anything out . . .' I said.

She considered the remark. 'I'd probably prefer not to know.'

When she'd gone, I went back to the bar and then returned to my seat.

It was unlikely that the two men she'd seen with Lindsey Perry had been there solely to retrieve the video when the films were already being sold to and downloaded by thousands of others. It was equally unlikely, given the technology Roper was using, that anything resembling a master-copy even existed, let alone that Lindsey had been able to get her hands on it. I should have asked Claire Madison about the girls who had been watching the film with Lindsey. I should have taken the photograph of Sullivan's team to show her to find out who had questioned her about Lindsey's disappearance.

The men at the far side of the bar grew even louder. One of them climbed onto his seat, took off his jacket, loosened his tie and started to sing along to the 25-year-old song, and the men around him applauded him and spurred him on. The bar manager watched them closely. It was two in the afternoon. He caught my eye and shook his head.

39

And two days later, three days before Roper's appeal was due to begin, Smart called me at home at six in the morning, woke me and told me that Roper had been found dead in his cell less than ten minutes earlier. I was only half-awake as I took all this in and I told him to tell me it all again.

They were on their way to get me, he said. They were twenty minutes away. I told him I'd be ready.

They arrived on time and I went out to them.

We drove to the city centre and parked overlooking the fountain at Prince's Quay. Smart turned off the police radio.

'Do you have any idea who?' I asked them. I didn't even know where Roper had been killed. 'Where?'

'Durham,' Finch told me. 'Not yet.'

'How?'

Neither of them spoke for a moment, then Smart said, 'Forty stab wounds to his stomach, chest and groin.'

'He bled to death. They were supposed to be watching him round the clock. He was mutilated. Only one of the wounds killed him.'

'Mutilated after or before he died?' I said.

'Hard to say just yet,' Finch told me. 'Too many

wounds and a lot of blood. It must have happened in his cell. He was wrapped in blankets by whoever did it.'

We sat in silence for a few minutes longer.

'Don't say it,' Smart said eventually.

'What?'

'Eggs and basket.'

'There must be a fair number of men in Durham with nothing to lose and a lot to gain by getting to him,' Finch said.

'But nothing that will connect whoever did it with whoever wanted it done. They'll charge someone eventually, and he'll say he had a thing about child murderers.'

'And a month or a year later somebody somewhere gets a nice fat packet of completely untraceable money.'

'What happens to the appeal?' I asked them.

'Guess,' Smart said. He wound down his window and turned his face into the cold air coming off the water. A street-sweeping machine came close to us, leaving its pattern in the frost on the road. The man who drove it looked in at us, his yellow jacket fluorescent under the streetlights. An empty bus waited behind him, fumes billowing from its exhaust.

'We should have insisted on you wearing a wire,' Smart said, winding up the window.

'Only if you'd known this was likely to happen.' The remark sounded more accusatory than I'd intended it.

'It would have left us holding more than we have now,' he said.

'Whatever it was that Roper was about to make his deal with must still exist,' I said. 'It must all still be hidden away somewhere. Surely, now, it's just a question of finding it?'

'Where do you suggest we start looking?' Smart said.

'Roper knew it was a possibility,' Finch said. 'Especially after what happened to Angela Hill and all the newspaper stuff.'

When I said nothing in reply to this, Smart turned to me and said, 'What?'

I shook my head. 'How did they know where he was?'

'It wasn't the drivers. They were ours. It must have been someone already inside and waiting.'

'Inmates or staff?' I said.

'Someone in Hull must have known he was being taken away, even at that speed and short notice. Perhaps they'd worked out that it was likely to be one of six or seven other locations and contacted them all as soon as they knew he was gone.'

It was something they had long considered. And they knew better than I did that there were never any secrets in a prison. Both of them looked exhausted.

'What are you going to do?' I said.

'Whatever we can.'

'Have any of the other men you're watching made a move?'

'Run, you mean? Why should they? That's what all this was about – so they could all now live out their comfortable, profitable lives without fear of ever again being connected to Roper and being dragged down with him.'

Finch turned back to me. 'You mean was Roper tortured to reveal where the stuff – his evidence – was hidden and has someone made a move to collect and destroy it?'

'Do you honestly believe one of them would be stupid enough to do something like that knowing we were watching them?' Smart said.

'No, but they might make a call for someone else to do it not knowing you were monitoring their phones.'

'We aren't,' Smart admitted. 'It never added up for the judges.'

'Were you watching them last night?'

'Between then and now? Yes.'

'And?'

'Nothing.'

'Which suggests that either Roper died before talking or took a long time to die and said nothing,' I said. 'If you could find out how many of his wounds were made post-mortem, it might suggest an angry, thwarted man.'

'You're beginning to sound like the prison quack,' Smart said angrily.

'Perhaps, but like I said, whatever he was going to give to you, it's still there, it still exists.'

'You can't be certain of that,' Finch said.

'What "certainties" are *you* still clinging onto?' I asked him.

'Go on,' he said.

I hadn't made the point with anything further in mind. 'All along,' I said, 'we've been assuming that what Roper might have been about to hand over was a film or films incriminating the others. It's what he knew how to do, what he did; it was why they employed him in the first place, why they *needed* him; it was what *he* knew about and *they* didn't.'

'They needed him for the girls and for everything he'd managed to build up for himself in the years before they muscled in on him,' Smart said.

'It was more than that. He understood the technology. When the time came, he would know how to use it in his favour. He would know how to keep things from them.'

'You're saying that Roper was the one who understood all about digital cameras and computer link-ups and Internet distribution, that they were following *his* lead and using him in that way, too? I don't buy it.' But there was a rising note of uncertainty in his voice as he considered what I had just said.

'Perhaps they never fully appreciated what a hotshot Roper already was when they closed in on him for his girls,' Finch suggested. 'The girls might just have been a bonus as far as Abbot and the others were concerned.'

'Plus they flattered him and paid him more than he'd ever been paid before,' I said.

'They put their hands over his eyes,' Smart said. 'And when everything turned bad they made sure there was enough evidence on Hayley Forbes's body to convict him, and then they pushed him through all those loopholes before they were pulled tight on him.'

'Roper went one way and they went the other through the same holes,' Finch said.

We'd run ahead of ourselves in this leap-frog reasoning, and in truth there was little in any of it that they hadn't already considered before.

I looked at my watch. Ten to seven.

At nine, I'd arranged to collect a copy of James Bishop's video from his Park Street office.

'So you're saying what?' Smart said, interrupting my thoughts on what the film might reveal to me. 'That we're not necessarily looking for something tangible, that it's *information* we're after, something on a disk or a hard drive somewhere?'

'It's a strong possibility,' I said. 'It's the kind of thing Roper would know how to hide.'

'And what no one else involved would know how to start looking for,' Finch said.

'It's not what I want to hear,' Smart said. 'It could be anywhere.'

'So could a buried videocassette,' I said.

He thought about this. 'Do you think Abbot and the others have already worked this out?'

'It might account for why none of them picked up a spade and drove off into the countryside when they knew Roper was dead,' I said. 'They might have known hours before you were finally informed. Perhaps now they don't care what he might or might not have had that would incriminate them. Perhaps everything *did* go to the grave with him. Either way, it's not something you can afford to ignore now.'

'In which case, we're all fucked,' Smart said. 'But you, Mr Rivers, are fucked after an exciting and well-paid fortnight paddling around in the shallows; whereas we, on the other hand, have wasted –

expended – considerably more time, men and money on this.' Meaning he was already considering his report on Roper's death to his own superiors.

And knowing this, though not entirely knowing why I said it, I said, 'What if we already knew all we needed to know? What if Roper has already given us everything we need to find whatever it is he's hidden?'

'Hey, that would be great,' Smart said. 'I could be played by Brad Pitt and Keanu Reeves could be cast as you. Perhaps now we'll get to have a car chase and a shoot-out.' He switched the radio back on and we sat for several minutes listening to the drivers and the controllers talking to each other. There had been an accident on the A63 and this occupied most of the dispatches.

Throughout Smart's outburst, Finch had said nothing, and had sat looking directly at me, starting to consider what I had suggested. He switched off the radio. 'So tell us – what do *you* think we've missed?' he said.

I confessed that I didn't know.

Smart's phone rang and he left the car to answer it.

When he returned, he signalled for Finch to turn on the engine and asked me where I wanted dropping.

'Any news?' Finch asked him.

Smart shook his head. Something he didn't want to discuss in front of me. We'd gone up all the ladders and now we were starting to go down all the snakes. 'Just everybody screaming to know what went wrong,' he said. 'Looks like we're going to have a post-mortem of our own. Leeds.'

I left the car.

Smart wound down his window. 'I hate to say this, Mr Rivers, but anything you turn up, I'd appreciate it if you'd let me know.'

'Will they close down the investigation?'

'It depends on what – if anything – remains to be salvaged from it.'

I watched as they drove away from me and along

Carr Lane over the pedestrian cobbles. When they were out of sight, I walked to the nearest bench and sat on it.

I'd visited Angela Hill and she'd been killed, and then I'd been to see Martin Roper, and he, too, had been killed. It was what Smart had had the good grace not to mention to me in the car.

The street-sweeper returned on his noisy machine and manoeuvred his spinning yellow bristles to capture the single smoking filter thrown down by Smart.

40

The tape was waiting for me at the reception desk of James Bishop's office. The woman who sat there asked me to identify myself before handing it over.

Sunny's office was closer than my own, and he possessed a VCR. I opened the envelope as I walked. Inside was an unmarked tape and a cheque from James Bishop for almost twice what he owed me. I wondered if the two things were connected.

At Sunny's, I told him what I had with me and he told me to play it.

Yvonne was with him. I asked her to lock the door. The youth who had been with them had left almost a week ago, she told me.

'Couldn't stand the pace,' she said.

I looked around the room. 'What pace?' I said.

'She means the pace of the photocopier,' Sunny said. He quizzed me on what I expected the film to reveal.

I told him I didn't know. It was clear to me that neither of them knew about Roper's death.

Sunny pointed and pressed the remote, and we watched together the short film of James Bishop's summer party and saw his lost daughter moving among his guests, only once, and then briefly, the sole focus of whoever was holding the camera.

'Looks to me as though the thing was passed around,' Sunny said.

I agreed with him and then told him to pause the film as a line of waiters and waitresses emerged from the marquee carrying trays of food and drink. There was an equal number of men and women, and when Sunny saw that I was paying close attention to these, he came closer to the screen. I told him then about the man James Bishop had fired.

'Is it one of them?'

The faces were indistinct, the camera moving from them to where the guests awaited their food.

'Which one?' Sunny said.

The film moved on to a long shot of the house and then to Patricia Bishop and the women surrounding her.

Nicola emerged from these and walked towards the pool. The camera followed her briefly, registering her displeasure or unease at being filmed, before turning back to the main body of the guests.

'Camera-shy,' Sunny said. 'That's interesting.'

Yvonne hit his arm.

I ignored them and went on watching, knowing that the short film was close to its end. The cameraman walked in a full circuit of the pool and returned to the marquee. He looked briefly in through the open doorway. Two waiters stood together. One of them was smoking, and the instant the camera appeared he held up his hand to it and turned away.

'A smoking waiter,' Yvonne said.

But I saw in that instant of briefly revealed anger that this was not why the man had held up his hand to try and hide himself: his hair was cut differently, a different colour even, and he was dressed in a way which further concealed his identity, but there was no doubt whatsoever in my mind that the man I had seen working as a waiter at James Bishop's party was the dyed-blond, crop-haired warder, Carl Boyd, whom I'd seen with Wallis – first on my visit to find Wallis, and

362

then again, four days ago, when I'd been to visit Roper.

I rewound the film and paused it the instant before his hand went up. The lines of silent distortion across the screen lay above and below his face.

'Who is he?' Yvonne said.

Neither she nor Sunny knew the man.

'He worked briefly as a security guard for James Bishop, who sacked him for spreading rumours about James Bishop and—'

'Somebody who wasn't his wife,' Yvonne said.

'Why didn't you watch this before?' Sunny said.

'James Bishop had stills made of his daughter from it. It's the last thing he has of her. It's all he – we – were looking at.'

'And you think this joker had something to do with her death?'

'Think about it,' I said. 'He's a warder at the prison where Martin Roper is brought back to, a close friend of Wallis, an ex-employee of James Bishop, a man with a grudge against him, *and* he turns up accidentally on a film which also contains the last recorded sighting of James Bishop's murdered daughter. What am I supposed to think?'

'Do you have a name, a history?'

'He's called Boyd. That's all I know. Bishop's employment files might have more.'

'Do you think Nicola Bishop recognized him from somewhere else? *Something's* obviously upset her.'

I looked again at the frozen face.

I started to run the film forward, but Sunny stopped me. 'I've seen him somewhere else,' he said. 'I'm certain.'

The same vague and unsettling thought had just then entered my own head, but I let Sunny go on trying to identify where he might have seen the man while I thought again of the two occasions I had seen him while my attention had been on Wallis.

Neither of us reached any conclusion.

Yvonne made us coffee.

Sunny asked me if there was anything in the story that he might write up in time for the afternoon editions, reminding me of the valuable secret I was still keeping from him. He saw my expression change.

'What's happened?' he said.

I drank a mouthful of my coffee. 'Roper was found dead this morning,' I said.

'Jesus fucking Christ.'

'I don't think it's public knowledge,' I told him.

'Where was he?'

'Durham.'

He turned away from the television screen and made a call. 'The Roper latest,' he said. 'Yes or no? Two hundred.' He hung up immediately afterwards. 'At least it didn't come from you,' he told me.

'I'm sure Smart will be happy to believe you.'

'Smart will be eating shit for the rest of his career,' he said. 'And even if he isn't, he's going to be too busy over the next few days to worry about what does or doesn't happen here. You have too much respect for men like him.'

'He reminds me of John Maxwell,' I told him.

'Fair enough,' he said. 'The point is, he's going to be busy elsewhere, watching his own back for a change, which gives *us* a bit of time and space of our own.'

' "Us"?' I said.

'I've just remembered where I've seen that face before,' he said.

'Boyd? Where?'

'And it isn't even him,' he said.

I looked at Yvonne.

'Don't look at me,' she said. 'He's "Intrigue and Cryptic Revelations". I'm more "Leisure-time Activities" and "Searching For Love".'

I asked Sunny what he meant.

His phone started ringing, but he ignored it. He picked up his coat from behind his chair and told me to take the tape from the machine, which I did.

I could hear Smart's voice telling me that it proved nothing.

'Where are we going?' I asked him.

'Your office,' he said.

'To do what?'

'To look at something we should both have looked at a little harder a lot earlier.'

The phone went on ringing until Yvonne answered it.

'Don't mind me,' she said to us, her hand over the mouthpiece.

41

Sunny said little on the walk to Humber Street. He was quickly out of breath, and each time we stopped, he lit another cigarette.

We sat beside the war memorial.

'Is this the end, do you think?' he said.

'Your guess would be better than mine.'

'Smart's superiors will want everything to stick to him. The longer this drags on, the more chance there is of some of the crap flying over his shoulder and hitting them.'

'He has Finch to stand in front of him,' I said.

'No, he doesn't. He wouldn't do that to Finch. Finch will get pushed to one side and forgotten. Smart will see to that.'

'Then what – Finch finds himself doing the legwork for another Smart?'

'And then another and another. The shit might not stick, but the smell of it will certainly linger.'

'I can see why you're a journalist,' I said.

Two hours had passed since I'd been in the car with Smart and Finch, but the temperature had not yet risen above freezing.

Sunny resumed walking ahead of me.

At my office he asked to see the photograph he had

given me of Sullivan and his team and all their trophies on the day of Roper's conviction.

I took it out and laid it on the desk.

He pointed to Lloyd.

'Anything strike you?' he said.

I saw it then. 'He's related to Boyd?'

'Lloyd and Boyd. Think harder.'

'Boyd is related to one of Sullivan's bent coppers.'

'Possibly the bentest. Keep thinking.'

'His son,' I said eventually. Lloyd and Boyd were father and son. Boyd had changed his name.

I was unable to play the video again and make the connection any more convincingly, but looking at the man with his arm across Sullivan's shoulders and holding the bottle above his head, I knew that the two men were far too alike for them *not* to be father and son.

'Boyd dyed his hair, that's all,' Sunny said.

'Is that what you were trying to tell me in front of Smart and Finch the other night?' I said.

'Funnily enough, it wasn't. It was only when I saw the video that the similarity struck me.'

I was only half-listening to him, already trying to understand the connections now suddenly growing outwards from this solid centre: a connection to Sullivan and the original investigation; a connection, via Wallis, to Kelly McLean, to Angela Hill and the missing file; a connection to James Bishop and his daughter; and, finally, because of what had happened outside the prison, a connection to the man called Abbot and his own distant involvement in all these other lives.

None of this was verifiable, but at least a few dotted lines were already starting to re-appear on the page which had been wiped clean with Roper's death.

'I ought to let Smart know,' I said. 'It might be something he can use to keep the investigation alive.'

'He might not want to,' Sunny said.

I considered this unlikely, but said nothing.

'As I was saying,' Sunny went on, waiting for my full attention.

'Go on,' I said.

'This,' he said. 'All this.' He ran his finger along the evidence-loaded table in the photograph.'

'Most of it disappeared,' I said. 'Years ago. Before Smart got started.'

'I know that. Who's going to throw their arms up in surprise at the disappearance of a few hard-core videos? Even policemen need to relax.'

'Are you suggesting they might have been returned to whoever made them?'

' "Sold" might be a better word. But that's not really what I'm saying, either. I can understand everyone involved helping themselves to a few videos here and there. I can even see how a few hand-held cameras might go missing. But some of this stuff is big and heavy, state of the art at the time. The computers, the scrambler boxes, the copying equipment.'

'None of it's still there. Anyone could have taken it during the past five years. It might even have been thrown out as old evidence.'

'Unlikely. Whatever was taken was taken between the trial and Smart's arrival three years later. The first thing he'll have done is to have called for it all to be gathered together again, and then to be held some-where secure while he had another look at it all. It might not have been part of his official brief, but getting something to stick to Sullivan and his team – Lloyd included – after all these years was always just as important to Smart as getting Roper to finally reveal all he knew about his associates.'

I remembered Smart's outburst at the appearance of Sullivan at the Tower Grange station the day we received our videos.

'Sullivan's out of it,' I said. 'They won't go back after him, not now.'

'You think so? I think if Smart can prove any active involvement or duplicity, they'll stop worrying about

Sullivan's local-hero image and stuff his pipe and slippers and all those beautiful commendations down his throat on the way to the court.'

I was still not convinced by what he was suggesting, but I knew that if the opportunity arose to officially and publicly discredit Sullivan, then Smart might seize it, especially if it could now be used to fan the embers of the dying case against Abbot and the others.

'Are you suggesting we identify some of this equipment and then go looking for it? That's ridiculous. All this stuff looks the same. It's in every home in the city, and God knows what percentage of that's knock-off.'

'You're still not listening to me,' he said. He took out a cigar, lit it and drew on it. The room around us filled quickly with the curling blue smoke. 'Martin Roper was a smart boy – a lot smarter than anyone – including Sullivan – gave him credit for. He might not have been smart in the beginning in allowing himself to get involved with Abbot and the others, but he was smart afterwards, when he began to understand what was happening. And he was certainly chewing on big slices of smart when Abbot went to him with diagrams of the hole he was about to be pushed through.'

'The films were all stolen from the police evidence stores and returned to Abbot because that was Roper's incriminating evidence?'

Sunny let out a sigh, a solid plume of smoke which punched towards me like a ghostly fist. 'The technology,' he said. '*That's* what made Roper smart.'

'So you think there was something hidden away in one of the computers?' Again, I considered this unlikely. 'Surely he'd be more likely to keep it all apart from any of this.' I ran my hand over the photo. 'Somewhere he could keep a proper eye on it, even from inside.'

'The best place to hide something', Sunny said, 'is the last place anyone searching for it would think of looking. All this stuff was seized and bagged as evidence. It sat on a dark shelf somewhere for a year before it was brought to court.'

'Someone must have checked it all. Sullivan might have been behind the times where all this was concerned, but there were already others on the force who knew what they were doing.'

'And suppose Sullivan kept a tight lock on everything, suppose he kept all these other so-called experts away from his case? He never struck me as a man with much time for anyone who operated differently from him. "Computer Experts Finally Solve Solid Copper's Case"? I don't think so.'

I was still not convinced, and he saw this.

'OK,' he said, this time tilting back in his chair to aim the smoke at the ceiling, which it hit, and where it spread outwards in a near-perfect circle. He watched this for a moment before going on. 'Just suppose Roper *did* hide what he had in the way I'm suggesting. A secret file, coded, and not only with nobody else knowing the code, but with nobody else even knowing how to go about looking for it.'

'The file or the code?'

'Both. Suppose that. There'll be back-ups, of course. You're still going to find your disks and tapes hidden away somewhere – your hard copy – but just suppose the only way to get to that was through a nice little secret file somewhere that only *he* could ever gain easy access to.'

'Something he would do only *after* Smart had made a deal with him.'

'It all makes perfect sense.'

Some of it did.

I picked up the photograph again and counted the pieces of equipment arranged in front of the celebrating men like dishes at the Last Supper. There were at least a dozen computers, twice that number of screens and video recorders, and another hundred pieces I couldn't identify, but which I assumed to be either receiving, transmitting or decoding equipment, any one of which might have contained Roper's hidden file, if it existed, and if it was still there.

But even finding the machine in which to start searching would be a near-impossible task, and was unlikely to tempt Smart into making the effort.

'Well?' Sunny said.

'It's a good theory,' I said.

'It's a probability, not a theory.'

'It's a good probability,' I said.

'But you still prefer to concentrate on Lloyd-turned-Boyd and how he ties into all of this?'

'He used Wallis as a smoke-screen,' I said, only then properly understanding this.

'Wallis?'

'Wallis came to you. You sent me to him. All Boyd had to do was stick close and watch. Which is precisely what he did.'

He shook his head, still convinced that I was looking in the wrong direction.

'Boyd would be a better bet to give to Smart,' I said. 'He's going to need something that helps him to tie all these things together.'

'You're like Yvonne,' he said. 'All this one-thing-leading-to-another stuff. It's not how the world works. Then again,' he added, 'she's also an accomplished line-dancer.' He rubbed out the final quarter of his cigar, adding a final, acrid note to the room's other smoky aromas.

42

I anticipated that either Finch or Smart would call me later in the day to let me know what had happened in Leeds, but there was nothing. If Smart had stretched himself to his limit and the investigation was about to be closed down, then all I could do now was complete my report to Bishop and tell Smart that my connection to him was over. I doubted if Bishop had read what I'd already given him, and understood now that he had perhaps been the first of us to lose heart at everything that had been revealed to us in the past few days.

I worked in the office until seven, checking my messages each time I went out. I caught up on the paperwork from jobs I had abandoned following Bishop's first visit. I phoned clients I had promised to call a fortnight earlier and listened to their complaints. I banked Bishop's cheque.

At six I called Sunny and asked him how much of the story of Roper's killing was already news. 'Everything that's fit to print,' he told me, meaning everything. The following morning's papers would be full of it. According to him, none of the editors was any longer concerned about the injunctions placed on them. The story had changed. The monster was dead. His killing was news, and everything they had recycled before they could recycle again at little extra cost to themselves.

There was a rumour, he said, that a photo existed of Roper's bloody corpse. Most of the editors were playing their 'Natural Justice' and 'Taxpayer-Saved-Expense' cards.

'What about you?' I asked him, and he said nothing. He asked me if I'd heard from Smart, and then told me to go home when I said I hadn't.

I waited another hour.

I had just turned off the light when the phone rang, and I answered it in the dark, my coat hanging on my shoulders.

I waited for Smart to tell me the worst.

Instead, I heard only music, and I felt a sudden knot in my stomach. I waited without speaking.

After half a minute, Abbot began humming. 'Still not a fan?' he said abruptly.

'No,' I said, my voice as even as I could make it. 'But I can see why its overblown, pretentious and crass sentimentality might appeal to a man like you, Mr Abbot.'

'Very clever, Mr Rivers. Is that, like, a means of identifying me for the record?'

'You're Charles Michael Abbot,' I said. 'You've called me at least twice before, same shitty soundtrack and message I still don't get. And somehow you were involved in the abduction, abuse and murder five years ago of at least four teenage girls and, more recently, in the deaths of both Angela Hill and Martin Roper.'

'Very good. That should make everything nice and clear for whoever might give a toss for all your slanderous and unfounded allegations. My lawyers, for instance.'

'What do you want?'

'Want? I just considered it the done thing to call you and offer you my condolences regarding your friend Roper. And to thank you.'

'Go on.'

'I can tell you're a disappointed man, Mr Rivers. As I imagine Smart and his own little band of so-called detectives must be. They should be back from Leeds soon. Or perhaps they're back already and haven't bothered to let you know.'

'Turn the music down,' I said.

'Anything to oblige.' He turned down the volume.

'You called Wallis outside the prison,' I said.

'Did I? What I did, Mr Rivers, was save you from a beating. I don't expect your gratitude, but perhaps some acknowledgement of my noble intentions would not go amiss.' He laughed.

Which meant he *had* been waiting for me to emerge with Wallis and Boyd.

'You should have called Boyd directly,' I said. 'Or would that have given the game away too soon?'

He considered this for a moment. 'I hardly think it matters any longer, do you? Very brave, though, of Smart to jump in like that. And as for Boyd, I don't think we need to concern ourselves over him for much longer, do we? Especially now, with friend Roper so tragically lost to us.'

'I could almost hear you having your little fit when Wallis didn't answer you,' I said. 'You let it ring because you were watching him, and because you knew something was happening back at the prison and you wanted him and Boyd to get back there and find out what.'

'Did I?'

'Do you have a tape for the car, too?'

'Tape, Mr Rivers? You really should keep up. Mini-disc. MP3. Entertainment for the twenty-first century at practically no cost.'

'Who killed Roper for you?' I said.

'What a question. I know nothing about how Roper died.'

'Of course you don't. Just as you know nothing about Sullivan or Lloyd or Lloyd's son, Boyd. Because just as we were all supposed to keep our eyes on Wallis and not Boyd, so five years ago everyone was meant to be watching Sullivan and not Lloyd, because Lloyd was your special greedy little friend on the force, and everything that happened in connection with Sullivan's investigation you got to hear about from Lloyd. You took advantage of his closeness to Sullivan at the centre of things. And then you even worked out how to play his illness to your advantage. You must be very proud of yourself.' I stopped abruptly, conscious of how much I had just revealed to him.

'Again, I can only repeat that nothing of what you're talking about makes any sense to me, Mr Rivers.'

'And so you called me – why? – to find out what Martin Roper had told me?'

'He told you nothing, Mr Rivers.' But his tone had changed.

'Play all the games you like,' I said. 'You're still going to be convicted on charges relating to the deaths of those girls and go to prison for the rest of your life.'

'You make such rash accusations, Mr Rivers. Nobody is going anywhere. Let's leave the past where it belongs and look to the future. That's the trouble with men like you, Mr Rivers – you're tethered to the past, earthbound.'

'And men like you are what?'

'We're men reaching forward, Mr Rivers. Men who seize opportunities, men who make things work.'

'You make money for yourselves, that's all, and you destroy other people's lives in the process.'

'We create momentum, Mr Rivers.'

'You're a disgrace,' I said. 'You're convinced you're off the hook and yet you're still not brave enough or certain enough to confess to what you did.'

He laughed at the remark.

'Is this where I get angry?' he said. 'Is this where I'm supposed to lose control and shout something at you that implicates me? Perhaps I should be just as obvious as you are and say, "Nice try."'

'*You* called *me*,' I said. 'You obviously feel safe enough now to do that.'

'Meaning?'

'Meaning you knew about the deal with Roper and Smart, and now you think you can stop worrying about it.'

'There was never going to be any deal between Roper and Smart. That was all a little fantasy in Smart's head. Smart fans the flames of a dead fire and Roper throws on some more fuel? Face it, Roper was never going to talk – not without something a bit more positive from Smart – something, incidentally, that Smart's superiors were never going to allow him to give to Roper – and without either Roper's testimony or proof, nothing was ever going to happen. Roper should have taken his chances with the earlier appeal. But he didn't. He waited until his chances improved. He waited too long, and then Smart got too desperate. That's where you came in, Mr Rivers. Roper was always Smart's line of least resistance. Shame – I credited you with more brains than that. Smart used Roper like he used you. He didn't want to stick his own fingers into the door, so he stuck yours in instead.'

'We can finish this conversation at your formal interview,' I said. 'It's getting late. I'm expected somewhere else and you're probably off to the opera or the ballet, so I won't keep you.'

'You talk as though you believe you still have some control over what happens next, Mr Rivers.'

'And you called to gloat because it was something you were incapable of *not* doing, Mr Abbot.'

'There's that name again.'

'I don't see—'

'Nicola Bishop,' he said unexpectedly, causing us both to fall silent.

'You had a hand in her death,' I said. 'I know that for a fact and I want you to know that I know it. Nothing you tell me now will alter that, so if that's what you were about to do, then save your breath.'

'And you wouldn't get a nice fat bonus from James High and Mighty Bishop for telling him for certain what happened to his precious little girl?'

'If you imagine that anything you tell me will put me in your debt, then, again, save your breath. In fact, tell me where you're calling from.'

'Why? So that someone can pounce on me and arrest me?'

'No. So that I can check what you tell me with the man sitting in the car outside watching you. You're a liar, Mr Abbot. Everything you say is a lie, and everything you do is a lie. You lie as easily as other people draw breath. But, happily for me, you lie to yourself just as much as you lie to everyone else. Just because Martin Roper died doesn't mean everything ends. Whatever gave you that idea? You say Smart depended too much on what Roper might have given him, but I think *you* were the one who had too much resting on Roper. I think *you're* the one who's going to be the next to stumble and fall, and then after you, all your own little band of pornographers, paedophiles and child-killers. Where will you hide, Mr Abbot? No, don't tell me. I don't need to know, because before too long there will be at least half a dozen others only too willing to tell Smart where you are.'

'Fuck you, Rivers,' he shouted.

'*Mister* Rivers, to you,' I said, and hung up.

It was only as I lifted my hand back to my face that I saw how much it was shaking. I could feel the blood pulsing at my wrists. I looked at my reflection in the window. The man in the glass looked back at me even harder, and beyond him, the frozen darkness of that December night went on for ever.

43

The following morning, I told Smart and Finch about the call. Finch showed some interest, but Smart's concerns remained elsewhere throughout our brief meeting.

As Sunny had warned me, the news of Roper's killing was in all the papers.

I told Smart and Finch what I'd learned from Bishop's video and they both considered this without speaking. The film proved nothing other than that Boyd had been present at Bishop's Kirk Ella home five days before Nicola Bishop disappeared.

Smart's superiors were already demanding to know why so much of his investigation had been allowed to rest on Roper's as yet unrevealed evidence. Some, Finch told me later, had even questioned the existence of this evidence. They had given Smart until the end of the year – sixteen days – to wind everything up, which, Christmas being so close, meant he had a little over a week.

Finch also told me that some of their superiors, and the men working in parallel with Smart in other forces, were already beginning to distance themselves from Smart and the methods he had used, in the hope that their own names and reputations would not be tarnished when the collapse of the inquiry was eventually announced. Some were already saying that they had never agreed with Smart's methods, that they had questioned these from the outset, and that his reliance on all that Roper might have revealed had now somehow jeopardized their own work. They were all excuses, and Smart understood this better than anyone.

'What are you expected to salvage?' I asked Finch.

He looked at Smart before speaking. Smart motioned for him to go ahead. 'They think we've already given too much away to achieve anything now. They think Roper's revelations died with him, and that now would be a convenient point to call a halt to an investigation that some consider has been going on far too long already, and which has grown uncontrollable.'

'Because there were too many suspects involved?'

Smart intervened. 'Perhaps we could have adopted Sullivan's solution and thrown all the evidence at Abbot and waited for some of it to stick. The rest of them would have ducked out of sight for a few months and then have been back in business more confident than ever that they were beyond our reach.'

'We spent all last night looking at what we've got,' Finch said. 'We'll lose the manpower and the observation teams in a week.'

'Is that what Abbot guessed would happen?' I said to Smart. 'Is that why he called me?'

'He certainly didn't give anything away, did he? It isn't enough for him to win; he wants everyone to know he's winning.'

'Especially the losers?'

'He called *you*,' Finch said. 'Not us.'

'Only because he's a coward.'

Smart told me to tell him again everything Abbot had said to me, as though he alone might recognize the value of this.

I told him as best I could, but nothing struck him as

forcibly as he had hoped, and so he repeated the few obvious connections I had already pointed out to him.

'He was watching as you came out of the prison,' he said. 'He saw what happened. My guess is that he arranged for it to happen.'

'Which at least connects him to Boyd and the two men from the car lot,' Finch said.

'He saw me approach you,' Smart said. 'And the minute I was in the picture he called Wallis and told him to call everyone off. Why do you think that was?'

'He got wind of what was happening back in the prison?' I said. It was what I'd already suggested to Abbot.

'He wouldn't have been there in the first place if there wasn't a reason for it,' Finch said.

I thought hard. 'The first thing Wallis did after talking to Abbot was to pull Boyd away.'

'Suggesting Abbot knows Boyd,' Smart said, 'and that he didn't want you or us to make that connection between them.'

'Of course he knows him,' I said. 'He must do.'

'Are we absolutely certain that Lloyd and Boyd are father and son?'

I showed them photographs of the two men.

'We should have known or worked it out sooner,' Finch said. 'The locals were onto Boyd for something completely unrelated to our interest in Roper. We were doing them a favour by staying away from him and concentrating on Wallis.'

'Let's stop worrying about what we've missed and start tracing lines from Lloyd back to Roper,' Smart said sharply.

'And from him to Abbot?' I said.

'*Shit*,' Smart said. 'Why didn't any of the locals see fit to point this one fucking thing out to us?'

Neither Finch nor I said anything, our answers all too clear to him.

I let Smart consider his options regarding Wallis for a moment, and then I told him what Claire Madison had told me about Lindsey Perry and the two men who had argued with her, and about the perfunctory nature of the police investigation into her disappearance.

Finch shook his head at most of what I said. But Smart held my gaze, and when I'd finished, he said, 'We could have done with all this a couple of days ago.'

'A couple of days ago,' I said, 'Roper was still alive and probably getting ready to make his deal with you.'

'If I lay on the floor, perhaps you could kick me,' Smart said, then turned to Finch. 'Call Oliver. Everybody stays where they are. Everybody. Tell Brownlow not to move. Tell Victor we've found some leverage. And the ob-squad stays as close to Abbot as it's always been.'

'He knows you're watching him,' I said.

'I know he knows,' Smart said, listening to his own unanswered dial tone. 'And better still, he knows I know he knows.' His call was finally answered and he turned away from me.

A moment later, Finch's phone rang, and he handed it to Smart, who put his own call on hold. After only a few seconds he handed the phone back to Finch and told whoever he had been speaking to on his own phone that he would call them back.

He turned to Finch and me and said, 'Well, well, well.'

'What?' Finch said.

'Someone just fired the starting pistol,' Smart said. He picked up his coat. 'Car,' he said.

44

We drove into the city centre and out along Anlaby Road before Smart told us what had happened.

'The fire brigade phoned in a suspicious house fire. Someone from Tower Grange went along. Howdale Avenue, North Hull.'

The address meant nothing to either Finch or myself.

'It's where Boyd lives,' Smart said. 'Petrol through the letter-box and more squirted down the hallway for good measure.'

'Was Boyd in?'

'Certainly was. He's been on early shifts. He'd been home an hour, in bed.'

'So whoever did it probably knew where he'd be.'

'Probably.' Smart almost sang the word.

'Who do you think it was?' I asked him.

'Who else?'

I remembered what Abbot had said about Boyd no longer being of any use to him.

'Makes sense to me,' Smart said. 'With Roper out of the way Abbot can start to wipe everything else off his shoes.'

'Hardly his style,' Finch said. 'Even now.'

'I'm not saying the noble Mr Abbot stood at the

letter-box himself with a Fairy Liquid bottle and a glowing Lambert and Butler.'

I considered what he was suggesting.

'I notice our first concern is not for the health or condition, satisfactory or otherwise, of Boyd,' Finch said.

The hospital appeared ahead of us.

In the car park, Finch drew up and then turned to Smart and said, 'We can't do this.'

'Can't do what? It's a suspicious arson attack. We're concerned for poor Mr Boyd's safety. Who could have done such a terrible thing to him?'

'You know what I'm saying. Boyd will know exactly why we're there. He hasn't been charged with anything. In all likelihood, he won't even agree to answer any questions. He'll accuse us of harassment. We push him now – whatever his condition, however scared he is of Abbot and what's just happened to him – and we'll jeopardize anything we might still have left worth hanging on to.'

'*This*,' Smart shouted. '*This* is what we've got left to hang on to. To hang on to and then to start shaking.'

Finch slapped his hands against the wheel. He sat looking directly ahead of us, breathing heavily. Everything he said made sense, and Smart knew this.

We sat in silence for several minutes.

'Who's with him?' Finch said eventually.

'An investigating constable.'

'Who will know nothing about anything else, and who will only be there to get what Boyd knows about the arson attack.'

'Has Boyd asked for protection?' I asked Smart.

'Not that I'm aware of.'

'Would he get it?' I said.

He fluttered his hand. 'He's burned his forearms and hands. Nothing too serious. The fire started at the front. He tried to put it out and then escaped through the back. There was petrol there, too, but the fire burned out without taking hold.'

'You think they were flushing him out, that someone was waiting for him?'

'Either that, or the fire was just intended as a warning, a statement of intent.'

'It's a thought,' Smart said. 'Especially if Boyd himself was sharp enough to consider it.' He looked at his watch. 'I still want to see him before all this starts to pan out, and before he has time to start wondering about his own rapidly diminishing options.'

'You could search the house,' I suggested.

'It's being done. Nothing so far.'

'Perhaps the fire was supposed to destroy something.'

'Like it destroyed the caravan, you mean?' Smart said dismissively. 'I'd rather Boyd took it more personally.'

After a further silence, I said, '*I* could go and see him.'

It was what Smart was waiting for me to suggest.

'I'm still employed by Bishop, and Boyd, via Abbot and his father, is still tied up in the death of Bishop's daughter.'

'And that's what you'd say to anyone looking to charge me with procedural irregularities, is it?' Smart said.

'Presumably Boyd will still be unaware of any direct connection we might have made between him and Bishop,' Finch said.

'If you turn up now, so soon,' Smart said, 'he'll know we've put you up to it.'

'But against that, he'll also know that Abbot just tried to roast him in his sleep. I know you,' I said. 'And I know Abbot. And I know who scares *me* the most.'

'You'd have to be careful what you said,' Finch said. 'Anything that ties him to Abbot and the killings that we already know about, you'll have to avoid.'

I understood that. 'I was the one he knocked unconscious and whose cheek and ribs he fractured,' I said.

'None of which we can prove.'

'*He* knows it and I know it,' I said. 'And he knows I'm not going to press charges on it. Besides, he might be in a confessional mood. He must surely be feeling a little exposed by now.'

'If we had more time, I wouldn't countenance this for a minute,' Smart said. He showed me his crossed fingers.

'I know,' I said. 'But Abbot is already wiping his tracks clear – Angela Hill, Roper, now Boyd – and you're nowhere in sight of him.'

'Thanks for that vote of confidence.'

'Look on the bright side,' I said. 'At least this time someone tried to kill Boyd *before* I got to talk to him.'

Only Finch smiled.

'So I should agree to you seeing him because it will make you feel better about yourself?'

'It's something I could add to that procedural irregularities hearing,' I said.

'Meaning we aren't even here.'

'Meaning I was with you when you received the news of the fire and that I acted independently.'

'No one will believe it.'

'No one will need to believe it. It's just something to hold onto while you wait for a better break with Abbot.'

I opened my door.

'Call me in two hours, no later,' Smart told me. He put his hand on my arm. 'I have a good idea what you want to talk about with Boyd, Mr Rivers, but if anything you say or do in there compromises my own investigation, whatever that might be rapidly turning into, then I have to warn you . . .' He trailed off.

'I know,' I said.

'We'll go to the house,' Finch said. 'If Abbot still has someone watching, it might cheer him up to see us there, let him go on thinking he's still pulling some of the strings.'

Smart continued looking at me as Finch spoke.

Eventually, he released his grip on me. 'I'll call the station and get the man with Boyd taken away for an hour, leave him feeling a little more vulnerable.'

I climbed out and they drove away.

A receptionist checked on her computer and told me where to find Boyd. She didn't ask me who I was or why I was there, or tell me what I could or couldn't do.

I saw the constable in the corridor outside Boyd's room.

'You Rivers?' he said to me. 'They told me to leave you alone with him but to stay close.'

'Has anyone else turned up to see him?'

'Not so far.'

'Is he awake?'

'I think they gave him something but he's been awake on and off for the past hour.'

'Does he know you're here?'

'I don't think so.'

I told him I'd find him before I left, and went in to Boyd.

There were three beds in the room, but only Boyd's was occupied. I sat beside him and watched him sleep, wondering if it was an act. Both his arms and hands were coated in lotion and enclosed in loose-fitting plastic gloves. There were smaller marks on his cheeks and forehead. I was studying these when he opened his eyes and looked up at me. From me he looked around the room.

'There's no one there,' I said. I slid my chair back from the bed.

His arms lay flat by his sides on the mattress. He started to raise one, then flinched at the pain this caused him.

'There's supposed to be a copper,' he said. His voice was hoarse from the smoke. A plastic bowl covered by a cloth stood on the cabinet at the far side of the bed.

'Didn't see one,' I said. I caught his glance at my cheek. 'Practically healed,' I said.

'What you telling me for?'

'Because it was you who hit me, stupid.'

'I never—'

'While you were still of some use to Abbot. Before he felt the need to start squirting the petrol.'

Everything I said alarmed him further. He started to cough. I took the cover from the bowl and he spat into it. His phlegm was flecked with black. The effort and pain of this exhausted him and he sank back onto his pillows.

'Funny,' I said. 'Not that long since I was in here myself. You'll never guess who came to see me.'

He opened his eyes instead of talking.

'Good old Sullivan. You remember Sullivan, don't you? Him and your dad were like that.' I held my crossed fingers close to his face. 'But you knew that already, didn't you? Well, friends, that is, until Sullivan went off into retirement under a well-earned golden glow and your father got to field most of the shit flung at Sullivan even while he was dying of cancer. Shame, that, but very convenient for Sullivan, of course. Show your father his gratitude privately, did he? No, thought not.' I took out a cigarette, put it in my mouth, and then returned it to the pack. 'So, you see, I probably do understand a little bit more than you give me credit for.'

'That fucker,' he said.

'You and your father visited Lindsey Perry at the hostel. My guess is that you already knew her – probably because she bought drugs from you, or perhaps just because some people get so desperate for whatever it is someone else might offer them after a lifetime of being abused and ignored that they grab what they can. You went to see her, you got her into your debt, and then, knowing no one would miss her, and how unreliable and ungrateful everyone already considered her to be, you told her what a big favour she'd be doing you by getting involved with Roper and Abbot and their films. Except that by then Abbot was already planning to get rid of Roper and take everything under his own control. You turning up with Lindsey Perry was what? A way of proving something to him? I'm presuming you told him how all alone in the world she was.'

I stopped talking, letting all this sink in, needing to be sure of his reaction before going on. I rose and walked around his bed, went to the window, looked out over the car park and then went back to him.

'The thing was, of course,' I went on, 'you were also helping Abbot to set up Roper, and at the same time helping good old Sullivan to find his way to Roper via Hayley Forbes. Whose idea was that – your father's or Abbot's or Sullivan's? Did Sullivan persuade your father to use Lindsey Perry so that he could get a conviction based on more than one killing, or was it your dying father's one last favour to Sullivan?'

'Sullivan's,' he said.

'I doubt that,' I said quickly. 'I think that was what *you* wanted to believe. I don't think Sullivan had anything to do with it. I'm not saying he didn't take full advantage of it once it had happened, but I don't smell his distinctive stink on it. In fact, I'd go a step further and say it was *you* who got your father interested. He didn't have much to lose, did he? Stop me if I've got this all wrong, but I'm betting your father knew more clearly than anyone how long he'd got left to live. Oh, except for his great and loyal friend of twenty years, Detective Chief Inspector Sullivan.'

'My father watched that bastard's back for longer than twenty years,' he said, almost choking at the effort.

'They watched each other's. Except Sullivan always kept a better eye on his own back than on your father's. He wanted Roper, and you and your father helped him to get him. Except the girl you chose as bait became superfluous to requirements once Hayley Forbes's body was found and all the incriminating evidence Abbot had planted on her led straight to Roper. No one could ever understand why Roper insisted on including Lindsey Perry in his confession when no one else was convinced she was even involved. But then it occurred to *me* that she was Roper's way of keeping that finger pointed at *you*, at your father and at Sullivan.'

'Even when my dad saw what was happening to him – all the criticism and other stuff—'

'What Sullivan was *making* happen,' I said.

'He still told me to leave Sullivan alone, that at least one of them should come out of it looking good.'

'And in return Sullivan would make sure that what you and your father had done with Lindsey Perry would remain in the outer darkness of the investigation? *You* were the one who fucked everything up, Boyd, by thinking you were clever enough to kill two birds with one stone. *You* were the one who handed Abbot Lindsey Perry on a plate to get yourself into his good books. And then you thought Sullivan might be able to use her disappearance to get to Roper. But your father didn't like what you were doing, did he, and Sullivan liked it even less because by then he'd decided to concentrate on the killing of Hayley Forbes. And if your father and Sullivan didn't like what had happened, then Abbot himself must have certainly considered it a completely unnecessary risk to have taken, however profitable the filming of her abuse and murder turned out to be for him. But, of course, it did put you and your father in the palm of his hand, where *you've* been ever since.' I missed a beat. 'Until now.'

'They didn't even give him a proper police burial,' he said.

'Of course they didn't,' I said. 'I imagine it wasn't only Sullivan who thought they'd all had a lucky escape. The monster was in prison, the girls stopped being killed, everyone was happy. And afterwards, once everything had cooled down and the investigation was wound up, you were back on Abbot's payroll and so you, too, had something to show for all your hard work. Christ, I bet Abbot wet himself when he found out that Roper was being brought back to Hull just before his appeal and there *you* were, already working as a screw.'

'I didn't have nothing to do with what happened to Roper,' he said. He was convinced it was the truth, but only because he hadn't stabbed Roper himself.

'But you and Wallis managed to make his life a little more intolerable while he was there, right? Roper knew you. He could have talked to Smart about you. It must have caused you a few sleepless nights.'

He turned away from me briefly. 'He didn't talk to nobody,' he said.

'He talked to me.'

'Only to tell you fuck-all.'

'Perhaps he didn't need to tell me anything,' I said. It sounded like an excuse – it was meant to – and he smiled. 'Is that what you, Wallis and the two from the car lot were waiting to find out before Abbot called you off?'

'You got out of that because Smart showed up.'

'No – I got out of that because Abbot knew better than you what bad news Smart was. What happened – did you wait for Sullivan to retire and then go and see him to try and get him to exonerate your father? It must have seemed like some kind of natural justice when his wife died like that. I don't suppose you helped matters, hounding him; her, too, probably. Making threats to the pair of them.'

'This is all just guessing,' he said.

'I know,' I told him. 'But it's what I'm good at.'

He became more confident, probably because he knew that, as yet, there was no proof of anything I had so far suggested to him, and because, like Smart and Finch before him, he had just then begun to consider the legal implications of what I was doing.

I rose as though about to leave him, and then sat back down.

'I'm completely forgetting James Bishop,' I said.

He knew it was an act, but waited for me to go on.

I heard Smart telling me to shut up, that I was revealing too much to him.

'First he sacks you and the next thing you know you're lackeying for him and all his big friends,' I said. 'That must have pissed you off. I'm surprised you didn't make more of a show when he told your boss he wanted you off his property. If that had been me, I'd probably have pushed him into his own pool. "Mayoral Candidate in Punch-Up with Scum". Bit of an embarrassment all round, I'd say. And it would certainly have hurt him a lot more than it would ever have hurt you.'

He smiled at the distant memory.

'But of course you didn't need to do anything so crude or obvious to get back at him, did you? Because you'd already spotted Nicola, whom you recognized as another of Roper and Abbot's willing starlets.'

I was careful to make no reference to Angela Hill.

'Christ, that must have come as an even bigger surprise – to see her there and then to realize who she was – the rich, spoilt daughter of the bastard who'd sacked you, and who was getting her kicks doing the one thing daddy would never in a thousand years believe her capable of. No wonder she looks unhappy on the day of the party. Recognize you, did she?'

He grinned again, but remained silent.

'I imagine your first plan was to send Bishop some photographs, to get something out of him like that, but then I imagine your twisted little mind went into overdrive and you went directly to Abbot with a different proposition altogether.'

'You're still guessing,' he said. 'So far you haven't—'

I turned suddenly away from him and watched the door.

'What?' he said.

'Nothing,' I said. 'I thought I heard someone outside.' I put my hand on his arm and he cried out with the pain.

'You did that deliberately,' he said.

'Just like the man who squirted the petrol through your letter-box knowing you'd be asleep upstairs.' I leaned closer to him. 'Between you and me, I personally wouldn't want to be on the wrong side of Abbot.' I sat back from him. 'Which, of course, begs the question – was he trying to get rid of you because you've become such a liability to him, and because now that the even bigger threat of Martin Roper has been removed, he doesn't want *any* of you other bottom-feeders hanging around? Or was he hoping to get rid of something you had in the house which might somehow still have incriminated him? Just imagine how annoying that must have been for him – first Roper puts a little something aside which will put him away for, oh, the rest of his life, and now *you* go and do something which will have exactly the same result.'

'Such as?' The words dried in his mouth.

'Such as stealing all those photos in the file when you knocked me out and then not handing them all over to Abbot as arranged. No one apart from Smart knew exactly what was in the file, so who was to know if you took a few out for yourself to sell to the newspapers? But, being the greedy moron that you are, you stole them and sent them to the papers without properly working out how you were going to get paid without revealing yourself as the thief in the process. You thought you were clever in telling the editors to defer payment until you contacted them later. When? When Abbot was convicted and locked up? But then you weren't clever enough to foresee the injunctions which were slapped on the pictures because of Roper's appeal. I suppose that's the real problem with men possessed of what we private investigators like to think of as "evil cunning" – that in addition to being evil, they are also cunning. Perhaps we should consider a new category of cunning to include idiots like you.'

I raised my hand, as though about to touch his arm again, and he pulled it away, this time crying out at the pain he caused himself.

'Tell me what happened to Nicola Bishop?' I said.

'Fuck off,' he said immediately.

I'd asked so that I could later tell James Bishop that I'd asked.

'You think Abbot's going to be happy to leave you here like this?' I said. 'You're as stupid and as pathetic as your father was when he covered Sullivan's back, and when he listened to you in the first place. Whatever else happens, I'm going to see you convicted for your part in Lindsey Perry's death – and I'll drag your father back into it – and on top of that I'm going to make sure you spend a second lifetime in prison for what you made happen to Nicola Bishop just because of the grudge you bore her father. Who knows, you might even get to play happy families with Abbot.'

I closed my eyes and clicked my fingers.

'What?' he said.

'I'm forgetting. No one actually has anything on Abbot yet. It's just you, really. Not to worry, I'm sure they'll be happy with one of you behind bars. Who knows – they might even get Sullivan back in front of the cameras saying he knew all along that you and your corrupt and conniving father were perverting the course of justice, and that he only did what he did in not exposing your father at the time out of respect for his lifelong friendship for a dying man. I'm assuming, incidentally, that it was Sullivan who put in a word for you when you applied to join the Prison Service after you were kicked off your police training course. Was that when you also decided to change your name? Smart move.'

I left the bed and went back to the window.

He waited for me to return to him before speaking again.

'Suppose I gave you something on him?' he said.

'Something on Abbot?'

'Sullivan.'

'Too late. Smart already has everything he needs on that score.'

'Something else. Something nearer home.'

I knew Smart would be interested in whatever Boyd might reveal, and that this might be a way for Smart to talk to Boyd alone.

'You'd have to talk to Smart,' I said. 'My interest is in Nicola Bishop.' I tried hard to imagine what he might have to reveal that Smart hadn't already uncovered or considered. Sullivan was beyond the reach of most old allegations, and after what had just happened to Roper, there would be no enthusiasm whatsoever for another inquiry into Sullivan.

I pulled on my gloves and made a show of flexing my fingers and forming a fist.

'I meant what I said about Lindsey Perry and Nicola Bishop,' I said. 'You've got nothing whatsoever to deal with where either of them is concerned. My only worry now is that you live long enough to face trial.'

'On what evidence?' he said. 'You've got nothing.'

'A pity, then, that you weren't clever enough to get something on Abbot which didn't incriminate you alongside him.'

'Who says I haven't got something?'

'Me,' I said. 'And everybody else who knows you.' I paused. 'Will it be Wallis, do you think?'

'Will it be Wallis what?'

'Whom Abbot promotes up into your place. Hey, perhaps it was even Wallis with the Fairy Liquid bottle?' I pretended to consider this, but knew it was unlikely. Boyd, too, despite his initial unguarded alarm at the mention of Wallis, smiled at the suggestion and shook his head.

I went to the door, opened it slightly and looked out. The constable stood in the corridor.

I turned back to Boyd. 'Hurry up and get well,' I said. 'Nothing looks more pathetic than a bandaged man standing in the dock.'

45

I saw Smart and Finch an hour later and told them everything I'd said to Boyd. As I'd expected, Smart was angry that I'd laid everything out for Boyd without first going over the ground with him. But I'd revealed nothing to Boyd that he didn't already know, and which anyone looking at the events since the file was stolen couldn't have worked out for themselves.

My only true guess was that Boyd and his father had been the two men Claire Madison had seen with Lindsey Perry and that they had coerced her into working with Roper and Abbot, each for his own ends: Boyd to ingratiate himself with Abbot; his father to provide Sullivan with the bait to connect the murders with Roper. In neither case had either man given a moment's thought to what would almost certainly happen to Lindsey Perry.

Smart remained sceptical that I had guessed correctly – or that I had thought through the fuller implications of this vital connection – but he said nothing.

'Boyd seemed pleased that I knew how his father had been treated by Sullivan,' I told him, hoping that this, too, might be of some use to him.

'I don't care about his father,' Smart said. 'Anything

that we might throw at Boyd in connection with the murder of Lindsey Perry he can turn around and say it was all his father's idea and that his father was working with the blessing of Sullivan. Whichever way you look at it, and whatever the truth of it, nobody's going to want to rake over that particular shit-heap again.'

'He said he had something on Sullivan that he could give you.'

'He'll *give* me nothing.'

'I told him he was going to prison for the murder of Angela Hill and Nicola Bishop,' I said.

'Somewhat rash of you, I'd say. Until we turn up Roper's little stash we've got a mountain of circumstantial and nothing that'll stick.' He rubbed a hand over his face. 'There was another fire while you were out consoling the injured. Guess where.'

'Wallis's?'

'Close. The used-car lot. Someone allegedly broke in there and mysteriously selected just two cars from the fabulous array of bargains on offer and torched them.'

The green Polo and black Micra.

Finch spoke next. 'You may be right about Lloyd, Boyd and Lindsey Perry. But suppose *Lloyd* instigated the approach to her. Suppose he did it because he knew he was dying and he knew it would give Sullivan what he needed to arrest Roper. He can't have known that Roper had already been measured up by Abbot. And suppose Lloyd told his son they were working with Sullivan's blessing, but they weren't.'

'And all the time never guessing that his loving son was already on Abbot's payroll,' Smart said.

'And, presumably, Roper knew what they were up to, and so there will be something to tie *them* to Lindsey Perry instead of himself, as Abbot intended,' Finch went on. 'Whatever Boyd wants to tell us now, it will only be part of his revenge on Sullivan for what happened to his father after Roper was arrested. Suppose Abbot convinced him to keep an eye on Roper by telling him that Roper's so-called new evidence would finally convict Sullivan and exonerate his father.'

'Do you think Abbot got wind of Boyd's plan to blackmail James Bishop and so *he* arranged for Nicola Bishop to be killed, putting Boyd well and truly in the frame and ensuring he kept his mouth shut?' I said.

'It might not make perfect sense,' Smart said. 'But looked at through either Boyd's or Abbot's eyes, it makes some kind of sense. It gave Boyd the opportunity for his revenge on Sullivan, and at the same time it tightened Abbot's stranglehold on him.'

'And Angela Hill?' I still wanted to be told that my own clumsy visit to her had not led directly to her being found and killed.

'Who knows?' Finch said. 'Perhaps Abbot convinced Boyd that she and Nicola Bishop had been close, and that Roper had already told her about his insurance.'

'So they still believed she was the key to it all?' I said.

'Whether they believed it or not, it wasn't something they could afford to leave hanging out in the open,' Smart said. 'And whatever their reason for killing her, Abbot saw that Boyd had his own double-sided agenda – avenging his father and punishing Sullivan – and so he went on using him to keep an eye on Roper.'

'But then Boyd stole the file for Abbot, guessed that Abbot didn't know for certain what was in it, and decided to cash in on the pictures himself,' Finch said.

'Except he wasn't smart enough to think it through and do it properly.'

'All of which made him a big liability,' I said.

'A very big one,' Finch said. 'Hence the fire.'

'He's terrified of what Abbot might do next,' I said.

'But probably not as terrified as Angela Hill was,' Smart said. 'Or Lindsey Perry. Or Nicola Bishop. Or Hayley Forbes. Or Jennifer Wilson. Apart from which, he's got nothing. He's their sacrifice. First Roper, now him.'

It was what I'd already told Boyd.

'We're expected at the car lot,' Finch said. He asked me if I wanted to go with them and I said I did.

In the car, Smart said that Boyd's theft of the photos explained why they'd been used in such an un-controlled way, whereas the two videos delivered to Sullivan and myself had been carefully tailored to serve their specific needs.

'The tapes were from Abbot to Sullivan and you; the photos were from Boyd to his father via his bank balance. All Sullivan's tape proved was that Abbot was prepared to indulge Sullivan's obsession with finding the bodies while it benefited him to do so. There was nothing on that tape that none of us hadn't already seen a dozen times over. The tape to you, on the other hand, will probably help to convict Boyd of the murder of Angela Hill, and as far as I can see, that's what it was intended for. Abbot probably showed Boyd the Sullivan tape and told him yours was an exact copy.'

We arrived at the car lot and crossed the muddy ground to where the two blackened shells sat. Foam still covered the ground around them. The owner of the lot watched us from the doorway of his Portakabin, but made no move to approach us. Beyond him, the boy who washed the cars sat in the open door of a recently cleaned Allegro, holding a battery-operated vacuum, the box of sprays and cloths at his feet.

'He told the investigating officer that it was just kids,' Smart said, indicating the owner.

'We're going to ask him for the paperwork on every car he's ever bought, sold, hired or wound back the mileometer on in the past five years,' Finch said.

I saw one of the men who had been going to attack me on the day of my visit to Roper. He stood beside the owner and watched as the three of us inspected the burned-out cars.

'It won't be of much use to the investigation,' I said.

'No, but some days I just feel vindictive,' Smart

said. He waved to the two men, neither of whom responded to the gesture.

We returned to the road, where Smart told us to wait while he walked back over the puddle-filled ground to the boy in the Allegro.

46

Back at Humber Street I had three calls waiting for me, all from Kelly McLean, all from a call box, and each time she called she told me what time it was and that she'd call again soon. On the second call she shouted for me to pick up the phone and then apologized in a whisper, telling me she didn't know who else to call. I heard the insuppressible fear in her voice. On each call there was a crying baby in the phone box with her.

I dialled the number, but no one answered.

I called the number I had noted on my visit to see her, but got only the unavailable tone.

Uncertain of the strength of the connection between Wallis and Boyd – or of the animosity that might now exist between the two men – I decided to go and see her while Boyd was still in hospital. Five hours had passed since the first of the arson attacks, and the first of her calls had come only an hour before my return.

As I hung up from ordering a cab, she rang again and I told her immediately that I was on my way to see her. I told her to go home and to wait for me there.

'Where else would I go?' she said. 'Even after all this.'

I asked her if she knew what had happened to Boyd and she said she did. I told her I'd been to see him, expecting her to ask me how badly injured he was. The baby she was still carrying drowned out most of what she said.

Outside, the cab arrived.

I called Smart and then Finch, but both their phones were engaged and neither of them allowed me to interrupt.

I went down to the cab.

I arrived at Kelly McLean's to find her house in darkness. It was a dark day. Even the lights on the small silver Christmas tree standing in her window were not switched on.

I knocked, and she immediately called for me to identify myself, and I waited while she unlocked and unhooked the door.

I knew as soon as I entered the house that she had not called me because of the attack on Boyd and her fear for what might now happen to Wallis. The phone which had stood on a table in the hallway was on the floor, broken, and the table lay beside it in pieces.

'Did they think Wallis was here?' I asked her before she said anything.

She shook her head. 'They told me what had happened to Boyd and that the same could just as easily happen here.'

'Did they tell you they were looking for Wallis?'

'Wallis?' She seemed confused.

'What time was all this?'

'Half past seven. I was still asleep. I thought it was him.'

'Wallis?' I said.

She bowed her head for a moment. 'No, Boyd,' she said, and I began to understand what she was telling me about herself and the two men and the pretence that she maintained with Wallis that he was the father of her daughter.

He's going to be a real father to her.

The child was Boyd's, not Wallis's. She was

401

involved with Boyd, the child was his, and Wallis didn't know.

'They were probably the same men who set fire to Boyd's house,' I said.

'They made that clear enough to me,' she said. 'One of them had a bottle of petrol and kept flicking his lighter on and off.'

'Were you alone?'

'Just me and Ellie Marie.' She indicated the baby asleep in her pram further along the hallway.

Then she opened the door into the room which had served as her unofficial nursery. Everything in it had been smashed to pieces. All of the brightly coloured toys which had filled the floor had been destroyed. Stuffing from the slashed furniture lay everywhere. The posters on the wall had been shredded, the mirror shattered, and even the electric fire kicked from its surround. She started to cry at the sight of it all.

'They knew Boyd was at home,' I said. 'There was no need for any of this. So what were they after here?'

'I couldn't call anyone until they'd gone and then I had to walk to the nearest box that was still working. I didn't know what to do. I went first to a friend. She called the police and the hospital.' She picked up one of the broken toys and then dropped it back into the wreckage at our feet.

'Is the rest of the house the same?'

She nodded and went on crying.

I left her and went through to the other room and then the kitchen. Every door was open, every drawer on the floor. She came to stand beside me.

'What were they looking for?' I asked her again. 'And if you lie to me again or say "Nothing" or that they were just there to scare Boyd off by scaring you, then I'm leaving now and I'll do nothing to help you.'

'Or him?'

'Neither of you is in much of a position to start making demands,' I said.

He'd killed Lindsey Perry and, probably accompanied

by one of the men from the car lot, he'd killed Angela Hill, and she knew nothing about either of them, not even their names.

'I presume Wallis knows nothing about you and Boyd,' I said. 'What's the arrangement – Boyd comes round here when he knows Wallis is on a shift?'

She nodded.

'It was Boyd in the green Polo, wasn't it? You were expecting him, and instead I showed up. That's why you were so anxious when it was time for me to leave.'

'We have a code,' she said. 'The half-drawn curtain means there's someone here.'

'You knew Boyd right back from when Roper took your photo, didn't you?' I said. 'The "For Your Eyes Only" referred to him, didn't it – Boyd – not Wallis?'

She nodded again. 'They kept saying "Where is it? Where is it?" But when I asked them what they were talking about they told me not to get clever. Then Ellie Marie started crying upstairs and they both laughed and said they wouldn't have to beat me up or burn the house down after all. One of them went up to her. I tried to stop him, but the other grabbed me round the neck and held me down. Everything was just one big joke to them.'

She came into the kitchen with me. I switched on the light, a bright, fluorescent strip, which revealed that here too everything had been scattered and smashed. We walked over broken crockery. I checked that the electric kettle still worked, filled it and plugged it in. She picked up two cups, both of which had lost their handles. I swept everything from the small table and stood two chairs at it.

'What happened after I'd gone?' I asked her.

'Boyd wanted me to try and find out how much you already knew about Roper. He wanted to know if you'd got anything that would go against Sullivan because of what Sullivan did to his father. He keeps saying that he'll be happy to go to prison himself if it means that Sullivan gets what he deserves at the same time.'

'He *is* likely to go to prison,' I said.

'What about Sullivan?'

I shook my head. Beside us, the kettle boiled. I started to make coffee, but she took over from me.

'What else did he want you to learn from me?'

'Just whatever you might have found out about a man called Abbot and what happened all that time ago when Roper was caught for killing those girls. He keeps telling me it could just as easily have been me.'

'So he's convinced his father was used and then cast aside by Sullivan.'

'Tell me about it. It's all he ever talks about. I get sick of hearing it.'

'Until he told you how much money he looked set to earn?'

'He said there'd be a fortune in it for us. He said he'd got his hands on something he could sell.'

'It never happened,' I said. 'He wasn't smart enough or quick enough.'

'No, but he thought he was.'

And she was desperate enough to allow herself to be convinced by him.

'What did he promise you?' I said.

'That we'd get out of this dump, for a start, that I could go to college, get the proper qualifications to open my own nursery, that he'd get a new job and that all this would be behind us. For ever. All he ever really wanted was to set things straight for his father.'

'Very noble of him. And you believed all this?'

She thought about it and then slowly shook her head. 'I suppose I thought that I'd put up with it all for so long – and all the stuff with Wallis – that I might as well hang on for a few more weeks to see if any of it actually came true.'

'Meaning the money?'

'That, and getting away from here.'

'And from Wallis?'

'Yeah, him too,' she said, her face half-turned from me. She looked in the fridge and found a carton of milk. The sugar bowl had been thrown against the window, leaving the glass cracked from top to bottom, and the sugar everywhere.

'How badly burned is he?' she said eventually.

I told her, knowing my answer might help her decide to tell me whatever else she knew.

'When I thought he was dead,' she said, and then faltered. 'While *they* were still here . . .'

'What – you didn't feel how you thought you ought to feel?'

She nodded. 'Why is it that all those people with nothing to start with end up getting it taken away from them, while those who've got too much to begin with just get more and more?'

'I don't know,' I said, unwilling to indulge this self-serving reasoning. 'Perhaps if Boyd had been an honest and decent man to begin with . . .' I said.

She looked at me. 'You think I'm like him, don't you?'

I didn't, and I told her I didn't.

'I only talked to you about that picture Roper had taken because he said you knew about it already.'

'He wanted to get me to open up, to lead me on with something he thought I might want,' I said. 'That's all. Most of the time he used Wallis to do it.'

'He used to laugh at Wallis behind his back, call him stupid, laugh at how pathetic he was.'

'Boyd was Abbot's way of keeping his own hands clean. Have you ever met Abbot?'

'Once,' she said. 'About a year ago. We went to a club on Holderness Road. Abbot was there. You could tell it wasn't his sort of place. There was Boyd and Wallis and a load of others. Abbot was paying for everything. It was Mister Abbot this, Mister Abbot that, all night.'

'The men who did this were probably there,' I said.

'If they were, I didn't recognize them. The one who went upstairs to Ellie Marie came down with the toy she always sleeps with. He poured some of the petrol out of the bottle onto it and set it alight. They kicked it about between them while it was still burning, and then it went out and they lost interest in it.'

'I suppose their meaning was clear enough by then. It probably convinced them that you didn't know what they were looking for or where it might have been hidden.'

Again she bowed her head at the remark and I knew not to force the point.

'You know Martin Roper was killed,' I said.

'Of course I do. It was in all the papers, especially the ones stupid people like me read.'

I ignored the sudden note of hostility in her voice.

'Boyd had nothing to do with that,' she said. 'It didn't even happen in Hull.'

'Did he tell you I'd been to see Roper?'

'No. Why should he? The man was a pervert.'

'Is that what you thought of him when he took your picture?'

'No, but nobody knew then what he'd been up to with all those girls before he killed them.'

'And I daresay Boyd has filled you in on all those particular details.'

'I know, OK?'

'You didn't call the police about what happened here,' I said.

'Boyd said—' She stopped abruptly.

I stood up. 'I think we're wasting each other's time,' I said. 'Go and see him in hospital. It might be the last chance you get for a while.'

'Will they protect him?'

'"They" being the police, in whom you have so much faith?'

'The men *you* know.'

'I doubt it. Boyd would have to be worth something to them for them to be interested in him as someone who might testify against Abbot, provided he lives that long. I personally have no desire to see him guarded and protected.' Her feelings for Boyd as the father of her child, and her uncertainty regarding what she might still salvage from her involvement with him, remained confused, and I needed to exploit this confusion before she understood for certain what was now likely to happen to her.

'He told me he was going to sue the papers to get the money that was owed to him,' she said.

'Perhaps he will,' I said. 'Perhaps he's worked out a way of doing that without implicating himself as a thief, murderer, kidnapper and blackmailer.'

There was nothing she could say to counter the remark. 'He'll come here,' she said absently.

'It would be a stupid thing to do,' I said. 'But I suppose he's desperate enough.'

'Why? Because they'd come back here looking for him?'

I said nothing, letting her work out for herself that Boyd would be better protected from Abbot were he to be charged and held for questioning once his arms and hands were sufficiently healed.

'Those pictures never meant that much to him,' she said.

'Then what did?'

She hesitated before answering me. 'He had another picture,' she said. 'He's had it for years. He told me that one day, after everything else had been sorted out, it would be the picture that would finally put Sullivan behind bars, where he belonged.'

'Doing that wouldn't automatically get his father off the hook,' I said.

'He never saw it like that. The two things were much the same as far as he was concerned.'

'Getting what sorted out?'

'I don't know. All this business with Abbot and Roper and his appeal, I suppose.'

Meaning that Boyd had intended waiting until the killing of Lindsey Perry and Angela Hill were no longer the focus of any inquiry before revealing what he might know about Sullivan.

'If you're going to show me, show me,' I said. It was by then fully dark outside and I saw the two of us and the room in which we sat in the cracked window.

She left me and returned a few minutes later with an envelope.

'He hid it behind a panel at the back of the bathroom cabinet,' she said. 'It belonged to his father.'

She gave it to me and I opened it.

'I always told him that he was making more of it than it warranted, that it showed the police in a bad light, and that they always looked after their own – it's what Sullivan and his father had always done – but he said I was wrong and that all he needed to do was wait until the time was right and then put it into the right hands and everything would be sorted.'

I slid the photograph from the envelope.

It was the same picture Sunny had shown me of Sullivan and Lloyd and their squad standing with their glasses and the bottles of champagne at their trophy table of long-lost evidence on the day Roper was convicted of the murder of Hayley Forbes.

I had hoped for something different – something which, for once, might have lived up to Boyd's own expectations – and I made no effort to disguise my disappointment at seeing the picture.

'He said it would only make sense to somebody who knew what they were looking at,' she said. 'Does it make sense to you?'

And then I looked more closely at the picture and I saw that circles had been drawn around the heads of a dozen of the jubilant men, and that these were connected in straight lines to other circles drawn around the various pieces of equipment and evidence arranged along the table.

She went on talking, but I barely heard her. 'He said that if the first appeal had gone ahead and failed like everybody knew it would, then he could have shown this to somebody then, and that Sullivan would already have been rotting in jail for years.'

There was no circle around Lloyd's head, no incriminating line, nothing left behind to sour his son's remembrance of him.

I counted the circled heads. Twelve. Like the disciples without Christ, each with its own thin, slipped halo.

'Will you be able to show it to somebody and do what Boyd wants you to do with it?' she said.

I looked more closely at Sullivan in the centre of the picture and saw the circle around his own head, tracing the unbroken line to its corresponding circle on the table. I traced it again to ensure that I hadn't made a mistake, and then I closed my eyes and tried hard to envisage everything I had seen in Sullivan's bungalow.

'Do you see what it is?' she said.

In the hallway, the baby finally woke up and started crying.

I returned the photo to its envelope, careful not to put my prints on it. I picked up a carrier bag from the floor and put the envelope in it.

'Will you make sure somebody looks after him?' she said. 'He's still her father.'

I told her I would. I told her she would have to tell Smart everything she had just told me. I told her it was unlikely that the two men would return, and I tried to sound convincing as I said it.

She picked up the crying child and held it into the hollow of her arm, stroking the back of its head and whispering to it.

I took a hundred pounds from my wallet and told her it was all I had. She asked me what it was for and I told her that I would get it back from the father of one of the missing girls. It was the second time I had given her James Bishop's money. I told her he was one of those people who had everything, and that everything he ever wanted he was given.

She took the money and held it against her daughter's head. She wanted to ask me if Boyd was responsible for the death of this other man's daughter, but the words were beyond her, and I left her before she found the courage to say them.

47

I showed the photograph to Smart and Finch and told them where it was from. A copy was made from the original and then this was sealed and taken away for analysis. Likewise the envelope, upon which Boyd, establishing the foundations for his revenge against Sullivan, had written down details of the time and place the picture had been taken.

A dozen further copies were made from the first.

We were at Queen's Gardens. Finch gave the picture to several detectives there and told them to identify each of the circled men and to find out which piece of evidence they had taken as their own particular trophies. He told them to tell no one else what they were doing. He faxed copies of the photograph to members of his team in Leeds and Sheffield.

The line from Sullivan's own circled, unsmiling face led directly to the computer on the table in front of him, and there was a strong possibility that this was one of Roper's own machines, from which information had been extracted and used to convict him.

I told them of the computer in Sullivan's bungalow, which he professed to keep only for his visiting grandchildren.

Smart speculated that Sullivan had probably been

411

urged by the other members of his team, Lloyd included, to take this major piece of evidence as his own trophy because, bearing in mind how the press had treated this technological focus of the investigation, it had been considered commensurate with Sullivan's role in catching and convicting Roper.

He phoned someone and said he needed a warrant to seize the machine and then to search Sullivan's home. He said we were on our way there now and that he wanted the warrant to be delivered to him at Sullivan's as soon as possible.

He then called the men who were still watching Sullivan to move closer to the bungalow and to ensure Sullivan saw them there. He told them to watch the phone in the window and to make a note if Sullivan answered it. He told one of the men to go up to the garden gate and determine whether or not the computer was still sitting where I had seen it. There was a delay of several minutes while this was done.

'It's still there,' Smart said eventually as we left the building and got into his car.

On our way to Spurn, Finch said, 'Lloyd must have done all the circling when he realized what was happening to him, and when Sullivan started putting a bit of distance between them.'

'Possibly even at his son's urging,' Smart said.

'It's likely that Abbot never even knew the picture existed. Boyd had only ever shown his copy to Kelly McLean, and Sunny's had been buried in his files for ever,' I said.

'And if it had been left amid the police evidence, Sullivan would have made sure it quietly disappeared,' Finch said. 'He held on to the computer because it was a trophy, that's all. He knows fuck-all about them.'

Although none of us said it, it was where we now all hoped Roper had hidden his evidence against Abbot and the others.

'And if that's true,' Smart said, 'we may finally get to

Roper's pointing finger because Boyd kept his own insurance – the photo – for the sole purpose of discrediting Sullivan and restoring his father's reputation.'

A two-man guard had been sent to the hospital and Boyd had been moved to a more secure room. His name had disappeared from the computer at reception.

'The polish we found on your letter-box and on the package delivered to Sullivan turns out not to have been used on gloves, but on the steering wheel,' Smart said. 'The boy at the car lot uses it on all the interiors. It makes plastic smell like leather, apparently. We found it out too late, of course, but it's one more nail in Boyd's coffin for when he starts to imagine he's clever enough and brave enough to try to make a deal leading us past him directly to Abbot.'

We arrived at the outskirts of the city and our speed increased. Smart called the watching men again to see if anything had happened at Sullivan's. Nothing had.

'Even if he knows we're coming, he won't know why. All he'll know is that Boyd has finally been flushed out, and perhaps that we know about Lindsey Perry. He'll be sitting there now thinking that all he has to do is deny all knowledge of what Lloyd and his son were up to. What could be more natural than one good old copper looking out for another one?' Smart closed his eyes, a look of satisfaction on his face. 'Oh, I'm going to enjoy this. I'm going to hold him by the balls, tight, and tell him which prison he's going to die in. And when I've told him that I'm going to work out for him just exactly how far it is from the grave of his wife, which he'll never again be able to visit.'

I exchanged a glance with Finch, who knew as well as I did that a secure conviction against Sullivan for murder was unlikely, and that Smart was likely to be thwarted on all charges other than those relating to perverting the course of justice. It was still enough to send Sullivan to prison for a good part of his remaining life, but any conviction remained uncertain, and everything Sullivan now did to assist in the capture of Smart's bigger prize would work to his advantage were he ever to face trial.

We arrived at the road leading to the bungalow and drove slowly along it. We passed the car of watching men and Smart exchanged words with them. The warrant would be there within the hour.

'We ought to wait for it,' Finch said.

But even as he said this, Smart got out of the car and told us to stay where we were.

Ahead of us, I saw Sullivan standing at his window and looking out at us, and I saw from his gaze that he knew as well as any of us that his five uneasy years of retirement were at an end.

Smart listened to none of our arguments and he approached the bungalow alone. He raised his hand to Sullivan, as though he were an old friend arriving to talk over old times. Sullivan made no gesture in response. Smart went up the garden path and rang the bell.

Finch called someone and told them what Smart was doing, but this caused no real concern.

'This isn't going to work out,' he said, more to himself than to me.

'How Smart wants it to work out, you mean?'

'He wants Sullivan just as much as Boyd wants him,' he said.

'Either way, he'll uncover the evidence he needs to convict Abbot and the others.'

'Will he?' he said.

I watched as Sullivan opened the door to Smart and then as he stood aside to let Smart enter. The light from the porch was the only light showing at the end of the road.

I wound down my window and heard the invisible sea. It remained a cold and empty part of the world, and I could still not completely rid myself of the notion that, for all its spartan beauty, something terrible had once happened there, and that the place still clung to its secrets. The noise of the tide against the shore persisted, like a slow and taunting handclap in the darkness.

48

After five minutes, Finch's phone rang. He answered and listened without speaking.

'They've located seven of the circled men and asked them in for questioning.'

'Have they found any of the stolen evidence?'

He smiled and shook his head. 'I imagine most of that went up in smoke the minute Roper's first appeal became a distant possibility. Two dead, and one living in Spain.'

'What's his name?'

'Adam Lynch.' The man John Maxwell had pointed out to me as Lloyd's partner. 'He was Abbot's inside man on the team. It was Lynch who first arrested Roper for hanging round schoolyards two years before the murders.'

'And who then, with Lloyd's blessing, put him into Sullivan's frame?'

'It's possible.'

'Will you get him back?'

He shrugged. 'He went there before all the new extradition laws and treaties were ratified. There are some changes on the way. We might have a better chance then.'

'Is he still working for Abbot?'

'To the best of our knowledge. He speaks Spanish. It's a big market.' He wound the window down to speak to a man who had approached us from the observation car.

'The warrant's been issued,' the man said. He asked how long Smart was likely to be and whether he and his partner were needed there.

'Stay,' Finch told him.

Shortly afterwards, two more patrol cars and six more men arrived.

Finch watched them come along the narrow road and then got out and waved them to a halt. He came back to me.

'Back-up,' he said. 'Not local.'

'What for?'

'Smart wants Sullivan to understand that this isn't yet another friendly little "let's-clear-up-that-old-mess" chat.'

'I imagine Sullivan already knows that better than anyone.'

'He does,' he said. 'This is for the benefit of everybody else involved. Four of the seven men we're talking to are still serving officers.'

'Who will say what – that they were only following Sullivan's orders?'

'We'll put our fingers in our ears when they say it.'

His phone rang again. This time the short message made him swear. I waited for him to tell me.

'One of *our* contacts – Abbot's old travel agent – just phoned in the news that Abbot is booked to fly to Bangkok in six days' time for his Christmas holidays. He did the same thing last year.'

'And this "travel agent" only just saw fit to tell you?'

'His information's been good in the past. Abbot and his associates do a lot of business overseas. Abbot booked the tickets three months ago. Apparently, he just called to confirm the dates and times.'

'Is he travelling alone?'

Finch nodded. 'Unlike in the past.'

'They all went together?'

'Art-lovers visit the Louvre, sun-lovers go to Greece.'

The men from the recently arrived cars left them to stretch their legs. Their fluorescent jackets and hatbands reflected the light from Sullivan's porch and made them look like puppets.

'I told Smart that someone else should take Sullivan in,' Finch said. 'Without Roper, he's back at the centre of all this again.'

'You think Smart's personal feelings might cause him to slip up?'

'Yes. No. He's too good for that. It's just been such a long and complicated case. I don't even think—' He stopped speaking at the reappearance of Smart and Sullivan in the doorway. Sullivan wore his coat, a scarf and a hat, and the two of them came out together. Sullivan turned to lock the door, but Smart stopped him. He beckoned the nearby officers to the bungalow.

Smart came to us. 'Wait here until the place is searched,' he told Finch. 'It's too late for the SOC squad, but I want this done properly.' He kept his eyes on Sullivan as he spoke.

'We've got seven of the others,' Finch told him.

'Any evidence?'

'Not yet.' Then he told Smart about the travel agent's news and Abbot's imminent departure for Bangkok.

The news briefly alarmed Smart, who turned back to watch Sullivan being led to one of the cars.

'What do you want me to do?' Finch asked him.

'I've told you what I want you to do,' Smart said angrily, and then signalled his apology.

'And Sullivan?' I said.

'He knows what's happening,' Smart said. 'And the instant he says anything – *anything* – to implicate Abbot in the proceedings, I want Abbot and the others brought in for questioning on the strength of it.'

'Before we have anything solid to hold them with?' Finch said. 'Before we even know for certain whether or not there's anything in the computer?' He was unable to mask his disbelief at what Smart had just suggested.

'It's in there,' Smart said, again angry at having his decision questioned. 'Alex and Rachel are on their way, probably already waiting for us.'

Another car arrived. These were the men who had come to remove the computer and to search the bungalow.

'Abbot won't come in voluntarily,' Finch said. 'You'll have to arrest him, and the minute you do that, the clock starts ticking.'

'We'll have everything we need before that happens.'

Finch shook his head.

'Are you still watching Abbot?' I said to Smart.

'Of course we are. Which is why I need to put him where he can see Sullivan talking to us before he decides to take his chances and tries to disappear.' He kept his eyes on Finch as he spoke.

The men about to search the bungalow walked past us in their white suits and hoods. Smart told them to secure the computer and where to take it. He left us, went to another car and was driven away. By now, most of Sullivan's neighbours were watching us from their windows.

'Alex and Rachel?' I said.

'Our computer people. Alexandra Carr and Rachel Evans. If there's anything there to find, they'll find it.'

'It's an old machine,' I said.

'It'll be an antique as far as they're concerned.'

There was a further rap on his window and one of the officers handed over the search warrant.

We waited there for a further hour, after which one of the men in white came out of the house and signalled to Finch that they were finished. Finch went to him, spoke briefly and then returned to the car.

'Not much,' he said. 'The computer, disks, manuals, a few old photographs, some of Sullivan's notebooks in a shoe-box at the bottom of his wardrobe.'

'He wanted you to see them.'

'They'll come back tomorrow and search the garden and the surrounding land,' he said. 'They won't find anything, but Smart wants them to go through all the motions.'

'Those roses were planted by Sullivan's wife,' I said.

'I'll be sure to mention that to Smart,' he said. He started the engine and we drove back into the city.

49

Sullivan's interview had already been under way for an hour when Finch asked the duty officer who else was sitting in with Sullivan and Smart. The man assured us that there were two others present, one of Smart's team who had come from Leeds, and one of their own officers. The interview was being both taped and filmed.

Elsewhere in the Tower Grange station, three of the seven other men were also being questioned, but so far little had been discovered or revealed.

Finch left me and returned twenty minutes later.

'They're all shouting that nobody understands the pressure they were under to get the job done and to catch the girls' killer. Sullivan kept a tight grip on everything. They act as though whoever drew those circles and connecting lines was playing a dirty, unfair joke on them.'

'You haven't told them it was Lloyd, one of them?'

'We'll save a few things for later. They'll know by now that we've brought Sullivan in. They all behave as though they all owe him some allegiance, some loyalty.'

'Perhaps they do,' I said.

Everywhere we went in the building, there were

421

men who looked at us with suspicion and contempt, and who went out of their way to make their feelings known to us. They made remarks as Finch passed them by, and whereas Smart might have responded to these taunts, Finch said nothing, well aware that his own rank did not protect him, and that, under different circumstances, he might feel exactly the same as they now did.

He pointed out to me the members of Smart's squad. There were others from National Crime and Child Protection, a team from Obscene Publications, and two men from Scotland Yard's Paedophile Unit.

At first the whole operation appeared in disarray, but it was quickly organized, and the two sets of men, the incomers and the locals, were separated and kept apart.

Finch took me to meet two women setting up their equipment in an empty room. An electrician was working at the power supply by the door.

'Alex Carr and Rachel Evans,' Finch said. 'Cagney and Lacey.' He asked them if they had everything they needed.

'We have our looks, our charm, our wit and intelligence, our sense of humour and our deep and abiding understanding of all those things you will never have even the most rudimentary grasp of, Birdy,' Alex Carr said.

' "Birdy"?' I said.

'Thank you for that,' Finch said to her.

She came to him and kissed him on the cheek.

'Where is it?' Rachel Evans asked him.

'On its way.'

'And Mr Rivers's part in all this?' Alex Carr said, smiling at me, but making her meaning clear.

Finch explained my involvement.

'Don't go too far away,' Rachel Evans told me. 'If these files are encoded, there are easier ways of getting to them than working our way through the *Longer Oxford*.'

'She's serious,' Finch said.

'Of course I am.' She smiled at him and I saw what a common bond of affection existed between the three of them, and I guessed how it had been forged.

Beside us, the first of four screens came to life.

'We have lift-off,' Rachel Evans said.

The screen went dark.

'Hull, we have a problem.'

The screen came back to life.

'So much excitement,' Alex said. 'I take it Smart's got his eye on the prize.'

Finch looked at his watch. 'He'll be out soon.' He explained to me that it was Smart's policy to interview a witness for no more than two hours at a stretch, knowing that only the first hour of that was likely to prove truly productive.

Alex Carr told me where they were staying in Hull and asked me what there was to do there. She had a two-year-old daughter and needed to do some Christmas shopping.

'Ignore her,' Finch told me. 'She won't have time for shopping.'

'I might,' Alex said. She put her arm round his shoulders. 'Go and make us some coffee,' she said to him.

Finch went and I was left alone with the two women and the electrician.

They began to ask me about the case and told me to start making lists of every name and every location and every date that might be either contained on a file somewhere or of some significance to the man who had created and then encoded that file. They knew almost nothing of Roper and the background to the case, and when I mentioned this, Alex told me that it was better for them to work that way.

'It's "signal" we want,' she said. 'All Finch and Smart do is create "noise".' She asked me if I understood.

'Probably,' I said.

423

The electrician told them that everything was ready. He laid out three connector boards for them and unravelled a skein of cables.

'Do it for us,' Rachel said to him. 'It plays havoc with our nails, all that rough stuff.'

The man began disentangling the cables and connecting the various pieces of equipment.

Finch returned with the drinks, followed by Smart, who greeted Alex and Rachel, both of whom said only 'Smart' in reply.

He asked Alex about her daughter and said he had a present for her to take home to her.

'Shit,' she said. 'And I have such bad thoughts about you, about how objectionable you are most of the time.'

'You should compare notes with Finch,' Smart told her.

She went to him and kissed him.

Rachel Evans approached him from the opposite side and brushed non-existent dust from his shoulder. 'You're a cold, self-serving and mistrustful bastard, Smart. But at least you're *our* cold, self-serving and mistrustful bastard.'

'Thank you,' Smart said, accepting the remark for the compliment it had been.

We were interrupted by the arrival of the computer. The man who brought it gave Smart half a dozen forms to sign.

As Finch had predicted, the age of the machine disappointed the two women. They carried it together to the empty table at which they had already placed their chairs. They spoke to each other in a language of which I understood almost nothing.

'Problem?' Smart asked them, his hand still signing his name.

'ISP?' Rachel asked him.

'I'll find out.'

The man collecting the forms examined them as Smart handed them back to him and then sealed each one in a separate envelope. Then he and Smart went through the ritual of writing their names over the sealed edges.

'Has it been dusted and searched for explosives?' Rachel said to Finch, who looked to Smart, who nodded once.

Alex came to stand beside her. Behind them, on the table, the computer started to flicker and click.

A second man entered, carrying a large sealed bag of disks and all the manuals they had gathered from Sullivan's.

'Shouldn't you boys be getting back to your rubber hoses and batons and leave the experts to get on with this?' Alex said. 'We'll need at least an hour to make sure it isn't going to self-destruct on us. And, remember, I'm using language now that at least two of you will understand. So if you don't do exactly what I tell you to do, we'll go back to our own special way of talking and make you all feel *this* big.' She measured out an inch between her forefinger and thumb. 'We'll need a constant supply of better coffee than this. And in three hours we'll need a decent meal, two vodka tonics and a bottle of chardonnay retailing at not less than eight quid bringing in to us.'

'They work on the understanding that a criminal who also believes himself to be a computer expert will always be a better computer expert than a criminal,' Finch said to me.

They were all avoiding mentioning what it was they were about to start looking for and what they hoped to find.

Smart told them he wanted to know about everything they came across. Nothing was to be lost or allowed to drift; everything was to be copied, and their own records of the search were to be scrupulously kept.

'Damn,' Rachel said. 'We'd hoped to go the sloppy, unprofessional route.'

We left them. Smart stopped a man in the corridor

and told him what the two women wanted. The man was aggrieved that he was being sent on a shopping errand, but took the money Smart gave him and walked ahead of us.

'We're in here,' Smart said at the far end of the corridor, and led Finch and myself into a small room in which there was only a table and a phone. 'I don't want any local interference in any of this.'

'Hard to avoid,' I said. I told him that John Maxwell had mentioned Adam Lynch to me during our late-night phone conversation six days earlier.

'There was a lot of time wasted watching him,' Smart said. 'The original investigating team took their eyes off Sullivan and Lloyd because they thought Lynch was the only one passing on information to Abbot. Abbot knew Lynch was exposed and it suited him to leave him out in the open. Forget Lynch; he's not going anywhere. All *he's* got to worry about is Abbot turning up on his doorstep to call in a few favours. The Spanish police know what's happening.'

'Are they co-operating?' I said.

'Sort of,' Finch said, and again the remark was intended to let me know that he did not share Smart's confidence in the way everything was beginning to unravel ahead of them.

'Has Sullivan implicated Abbot yet?' I said, hoping to relieve the sudden tension between the two men.

'Not yet. But he's close,' Smart said. 'The very fact that Abbot hasn't even been mentioned yet is suspicious in itself. It was never a secret at the time of Roper's arrest by Sullivan that Roper was connected to Abbot.'

'But you still want Sullivan to be the first to say it now?' I said.

'Coming from Sullivan, it would be enough for us to bring Abbot in and hold him.'

'And presumably you'd want Abbot to know it was Sullivan who directed you to him.'

'I think it's fair to assume that Abbot will make that

assumption whatever Sullivan does or doesn't tell us. In fact, I wouldn't be surprised if Abbot isn't sitting somewhere with his brief right now, waiting for our knock, and both of them ready to declare his innocence and outrage at the way he's being treated.'

'Is that the same brief who persuaded Roper to bear the weight of the blow aimed at Abbot in the first instance?'

'It is. Except the blow was never aimed at Abbot, remember. Sullivan made sure of that.'

'What's he told you so far?' Finch said.

'Mostly the same old story – that he was under pressure to secure a conviction, and that with the discovery of Hayley Forbes's body and all the evidence Abbot had made sure it contained, he knew he had enough to make it stick to Roper.'

'*Did* he have any idea what Lloyd and Boyd were up to with Lindsey Perry?' I said.

'He says he only found out about it afterwards.'

'After she'd gone missing?'

'He said Lloyd got drunk with him one night and told him what they'd done. He said his son had set it all up, and that Lindsey Perry would lead them directly to the men involved.'

'And Abbot realized what they were doing and threw Sullivan Hayley Forbes's body instead,' I said.

'Something like that.'

'And Sullivan kept quiet about what Lloyd had revealed to him?' Finch said.

'When he sobered up, Lloyd tried to convince him that Lindsey Perry had just gone off somewhere – she was unreliable, a dope-head; it's what she did.'

'And Sullivan believed him?'

'I doubt it,' Smart said. 'But I don't imagine he considered exposing Lloyd for too long – not once Roper was securely in the frame and everyone was patting Sullivan on the back.'

'And Lloyd didn't understand or believe how quickly and completely he himself was then going to be left out in the open once all the criticisms concerning the investigation and the girls still missing were voiced,' I said.

'Lloyd told Sullivan about the cancer and his prognosis. Perhaps Lloyd even offered himself up as a sacrifice in return for Sullivan pulling strings to get his son into the Prison Service after he'd failed to become a copper.'

'Perhaps. Or perhaps the three of them were already swimming against the tide and the weakest drowned first,' Finch said. He took off his jacket and stretched his arms. 'Is there anything apart from all this hearsay to connect Sullivan to Lindsey Perry?'

'Not yet,' Smart said. 'We'll know better where to start joining up more of the dots once we find out what Roper's left us.'

Figures passed back and forth across the glass of the door.

'They'll start looking for code-names to open the files,' Smart said. 'Whatever else he was, Roper wasn't stupid. It's why I wanted you wired when you went to see him.'

'You think he'll have said something then?'

'Angela Hill had just been killed. It was why he agreed to see you. As far as I read it, she was still his back-up – whether she knew it or not – and without her he only had the files hidden in his computer.'

'Which he always imagined would be filed away and held secure for ever, waiting for someone like you to turn up,' I said.

'Waiting for someone like me,' Smart said.

'Why did Sullivan hang onto it for so long? Why didn't he get rid of it?' Finch said.

'Because he had no idea what he'd been coerced into taking? Because he knew he'd been outsmarted by Abbot, and because the technology involved had played a part in that? All Sullivan wanted was the collar. The men we've already spoken to talk about taking tapes and pieces of equipment as though they had a God-given right to do it.' He looked at his watch. 'I'm going back down to him. As soon as I call you, get the teams watching Abbot and the others moving. They'll be expecting us. Abbot will know what's happening by now, and if he knows, they'll all know. When we move on him, he'll be ready and waiting. I don't want anyone working on the assumption that we've got the upper hand, because we haven't.'

He left us, pausing at the door.

'Leave Alex and Rachel alone,' he said. 'No inter-ruptions. And keep the locals away from them.' The door closed behind him.

'He wants them to come up with something he can wave in Abbot's face,' Finch said, but his voice was flat, unconvinced.

It had been a long day. My visit to see Boyd in hospital felt as though it had happened three days ago rather than that same morning. I told him I needed some air and that I was going out.

He indicated the phone. 'I'll wait for Smart's call.'

'You've seen it all before,' I said to him.

'True,' he said. 'And the trouble is, once you've seen it, there's no going back.'

I walked down the stairs, past reception and out into the car park.

I sat on the low wall of the neighbouring church of the Latter-day Saints. In the high lights, the inter-mittent rain looked like snow, but by the time it landed in the puddles at my feet, it was rain again.

50

There was something I needed to think about. Something that had first occurred to me while I was talking to Roper, and which I hadn't yet mentioned to either Smart or Finch. It was Smart insisting that Roper had told me more than I probably realized that made me reconsider.

I went back up to Finch, past the same averted faces and hostile looks. Some men stopped talking as I approached them, some talked louder so that I might hear them, and some changed the subject to include me.

Finch was sitting at the table where I'd left him. He showed me the pager which, when secretly pressed by Smart in the interview room, would tell Finch to call him there and interrupt his questioning. This allowed Smart to be called out of the room without Sullivan suspecting that he was acting on something that had just been revealed to him.

'He thinks Sullivan took the computer at Lloyd's urging because Boyd believed it contained something that implicated him and his father and how they tried to use Lindsey Perry,' he said.

'It would be another good reason for Roper insisting on including her in his confession,' I said.

'Smart thinks so.'

'And you?'

'I think everything's too tightly wrapped up in a five-year-old dead case, and with the crimes, foibles and weaknesses of dead men. We've got Boyd where we want him. *He's* the key to all this, not Sullivan.'

'Perhaps Sullivan imagines there to be something in the computer that implicates *him*,' I said.

'He'd have smashed it up long ago if he thought that.'

'And so you believe what – that he held onto it believing it contained something that might one day exonerate him and put Lloyd and his devious son in the dock?'

'It would be a better reason for hanging onto it all this time.'

'And so once again Lloyd and his son were working at cross-purposes with Sullivan when Lloyd later decided to tie each member of the squad to what they'd stolen,' I said.

He shrugged. 'If each of them was trying to get something on the other, it makes perfect sense.'

'And then Lloyd died.'

'It makes even more sense *because* Lloyd died,' he said. 'Boyd had lived in his father's shadow all those years. Everything his father told him to do, he did. When Lloyd died, Boyd didn't have the first idea what to do next. Everything was over by then, all the evidence gathered in and safely in police custody. Abbot and his associates were scattered in the wind and Roper was firmly at the centre of everyone's sights.'

'If that was why Sullivan kept the computer, it might mean he knew more, or knew earlier, about Lloyd and his son using Lindsey Perry to get to Roper.'

'Hopefully, he'll be telling Smart all about it right now.' He looked at his watch.

'But Sullivan still believes he's going to walk out of here at the end of it all, and that everything that was either covered up or allowed to blow away once will be covered up or be allowed to blow away again?' I said.

'It's why Smart wants him to implicate himself.'

I went to the door and looked down the corridor to where Alex Carr and Rachel Evans were still working on the computer. Although told to stay away, men from the station came and went from the locked door, trying its handle and calling in to the two women in an effort to intimidate them. I asked Finch if he couldn't keep the men away.

'They're used to it,' he said.

'Have you worked with them often?'

'Six or seven years. Rachel and me, well . . .'

'It shows,' I said.

'Only on my part.' He smiled at the distant, still-painful memory.

'Have they come up with anything yet?'

'They're not likely to. It takes time to secure and copy everything, to even find out if there's anything there, let alone what that something might be.'

I sat at the table opposite him. 'I've got something Smart ought to know,' I said eventually.

'Now?'

'Can you phone him?'

Smart would be angry at being interrupted and Finch was reluctant to do this.

'I take it this is something you should have told us earlier,' he said.

I took a deep breath. 'I think Roper believed that Sullivan was responsible for the death of his mother,' I said.

He closed his eyes for a moment. 'The caravan fire?'

'I think Roper believed it was Sullivan who turned on the gas tap and threw in the match.'

'Knowing the woman was asleep inside?'

'I don't know.'

'Did Roper say as much to you?'

'No.'

432

'Shit,' he said.

'Even if Roper was wrong, it might still be some-thing for Smart to use now,' I said. 'He could suggest to Sullivan that it was what Roper *had* said to me.'

'It isn't evidence. None of it would stand up. The inquest said Accidental Death.' But I could see that he was beginning to consider what I'd said.

'A lot was made of her being there illegally,' I said. 'Even the camp superintendent didn't know she was there.'

'And you think Sullivan might have thought that Roper had hidden something there that would impli-cate him and so he destroyed the caravan to get rid of it? They'd already searched the thing twice and found nothing.'

'And if Roper waited until the searches were over and then asked his mother to do it for him?'

'Why didn't Sullivan just break in and search it again? There must be dozens get broken into during the closed season.'

'Perhaps that was his intention. Perhaps he'd gone expecting to find it empty. Perhaps the last person he expected to find there was the mother of the man for whom he had just diverted the course of justice in order to prosecute him. He lived less than two miles away. He was officially bound for a happy retirement with his halo still intact, but none of this was properly over or cold by then. If something *had* shown up, then everything would have been turned on its head. Lloyd's death was timely in more ways than one. Sullivan could have walked to the caravan in con-siderably less than an hour and no one would have seen him. His own wife was in hospital when it happened.'

'Are you sure?'

'She died less than a month later.' I'd checked.

'Death and destruction all round, then.'

'It doesn't have to be true,' I said. 'It just has to be what Roper *believed* for it to be of some use to Smart now. Even if—'

We were interrupted by the pager.

'Tell him,' I said.

Finch rang Smart, and Smart said, 'Right, right. Now? Right,' to Finch's silence.

'You tell him,' Finch said to me.

Smart was with us five minutes later.

'He's mentioned Abbot,' he said immediately. 'Get everyone moving. Don't bring Abbot here; take him to Queen's Gardens. I want Josephs and Hill to stay with him. I want him isolated, brief or no brief, and I want him left alone until I get there. If he's thinking about anything, I want him to be thinking about Roper's killing. He knows there's nothing connecting him to that. He knows we haven't charged Boyd with anything yet, and he probably still thinks he can get to Boyd if he needs to. I want him to be completely unprepared for me.' His excitement was uncontainable.

'What did he say?' Finch asked him.

'He told us about Lloyd, his son, and Lindsey Perry.'

'And that's all?' Finch's disbelief was emphatic. 'Abbot will deny all knowledge and laugh in your face. He'll know you've got no proof to back anything up. His brief will see what you're doing straight away and tell him not to answer any more questions. You'll have had your chance, wasted it, and Abbot will walk away laughing at us.'

Even Smart seemed surprised by this assault. He considered everything Finch had suggested and said, 'By which time Alex and Rachel will have turned something up.'

'And they might not have,' Finch said. 'And even if they *do* come up with something afterwards which ties Abbot to the girls, any defence barrister worth his salt will point to the sequence of events to let the world know how desperate we were to have something to hold Abbot on.' The 'we' was his only concession to Smart.

'Tell him,' I said to Finch.

'Tell me what?' Smart said.

Finch told him everything I'd suggested before his arrival.

'But Roper said none of this for certain to you?' Smart said.

He destroyed us all, Mr Rivers, he destroyed us all.

'It would be something new to prod Sullivan with,' I said, knowing this would appeal to Smart, and, seeing what easy advantage I had taken, Finch turned away from us.

'How long have Alex and Rachel been on it?' Smart said to him.

'Two hours. The prelims will take at least four.'

'Midnight?'

'At the earliest.'

'I want to be able to move the minute they find anything encrypted,' Smart said.

'I've a feeling that might be easier than you're anticipating based on past cases,' I said.

'Oh?'

'If it's there, then Roper *wants* you – you, or whoever else turned up and started looking – to find it. It's why he put it there in the first place, remember? He was only ever hiding it from Sullivan and Abbot.'

Smart considered this.

'It occurred to me downstairs that Sullivan might have known about what Lloyd and his son were up to with Lindsey Perry *before* she was killed,' I said. 'What if she was still alive when Lloyd made his drunken confession and then only killed afterwards because Boyd told Abbot that his father had told Sullivan about her. How clean would Sullivan be then?'

'Which is why it makes more sense to go on pushing Sullivan than to bring Abbot in,' Finch said.

Smart closed his eyes and let out his breath. 'Let's go and see Alex and Rachel,' he said.

We followed him to the room at the end of the corridor. Two men stood at the door and then moved to one side as we approached.

'Go and play somewhere else,' Smart told them.

He knocked on the door and called in to Alex and Rachel.

Rachel unlocked the door and let us in.

'Anything?' Smart asked her.

She looked first to Finch before answering him. 'You know we need at least three hours to prep the thing.'

Alex sat behind her, studying the lines of letters and numbers which scrolled quickly up two of the screens in front of her.

'*You* might be ready to pop,' Alex said to Smart. 'But Rachel and me, we're women, we like a little more involvement, we prefer to take our time. You'll be the first to know when we're ready to make you happy. Besides which, another Cardiff would do none of us any favours, least of all you.'

Smart flinched at the name, turned and walked quickly back to the room at the far end of the corridor.

'Cardiff?' I said to Rachel.

'A case which fell apart because the defence was able to prove that we'd had the opportunity to add something to the files which were being used as evidence.'

'But you hadn't?' I said.

She looked at me for a second, closed her eyes for half that time, opened them and went on looking.

I apologized. 'But Smart had insisted on speed?'

'And like the young and foolish virgins we then were, we didn't stand up to him. We should have known better.'

From her seat at the monitors, Alex called for Rachel to return to her.

Rachel pushed Finch and me gently out of the room and then locked the door behind us.

'The Cardiff crack certainly got to Smart,' I said.

'It's the only error of judgement I've seen him make in eight years,' Finch said.

'Until now?' But by then we were too close to Smart for him to answer me.

Smart beckoned us in to him.

'I'm going to wait another hour,' he said. 'I'll see how Sullivan responds to some indirect remark about the death of Roper's mother, let him start to imagine that I might know more. I've just called the hospital. Boyd is jumpier than ever. Another push and he'll do everything he possibly can to implicate Sullivan.'

'Even if it means that you charge him with the abduction of Lindsey Perry?' Finch said.

'He'll claim he had no idea what Abbot was going to do to her.'

'Either that', Finch said, 'or he'll know how keen you are to charge Sullivan with being complicit in her murder and for perverting the course of justice so he'll know he has something to deal with.' He'd paused between the words 'how' and 'keen', leaving neither Smart nor myself in any doubt that his first choice had been 'desperate'.

'Boyd still killed Angela Hill,' I said. 'Whatever he thinks he has to deal with as far as his father and Sullivan are concerned, you can't let him work *that* into his negotiations.'

Neither Smart nor Finch answered me.

'We have to play this as we see best,' Smart said eventually.

'Don't worry,' Finch said. But even he was unable to look me in the eye as he said it.

'One hour,' Smart said, and he left us.

51

I went back outside and walked to the nearest bar. Football was showing on a large-screen TV, but few of the other drinkers paid it much attention, just a table of men sitting immediately beneath it. Christmas lights flickered all around the room. Merry Christmas was spelled out in half a dozen languages on the walls.

I called James Bishop and told him that Smart was questioning Sullivan about the incompetence, the manipulation and the omissions which may have led to his daughter's death. I'd expected him to show some enthusiasm for all this, but it was too late for enthusiasm, and other than make the usual polite remarks to signal that he was still listening to me, he said little.

I felt discouraged by this response, and told him that I was telling him all this because it was why he'd hired me in the first place. I also hoped that if Sullivan did manage to walk away from it all again through a deal with Smart, then there would be sufficient grounds now for Bishop to bring a new civil action against him.

I asked him if he was with his wife.

'She thinks we should leave, go somewhere else,' he said, and I knew then that he and his wife had finally been broken in half, and that in all likelihood she was sitting in the same room, as close to and as distant from him as she'd ever been. 'She's had the house valued. It's worth four times what we paid for it,' he said.

I heard her voice in the background.

'Even taking into account all the improvements we've made,' he said.

'Including the pool?' I said, intending the remark to both wound him and remind him of his fourteen-year-old daughter on the day she was filmed walking at the water's edge.

He understood this perfectly. 'Even the pool,' he said. He took a deep breath. 'You called at a bad time.'

'Alison Menzies?'

'That's part of it. What has Sullivan said?'

I told him about the retrieval of the computer. He was not convinced that it held Roper's secrets. I tried to persuade him otherwise, knowing that either way – that whatever the files did or didn't reveal – there had never been any possibility of a happy outcome for him. My optimism was forced and wasted.

He asked me to let him know if anything was found and I said I would. It was almost nine o'clock. It would be a long night ahead for everyone involved, but his would be the longest night of all.

Next I called Sunny.

Yvonne answered and said that Sunny had gone home to sleep for the first time in three days. She would be in the office all night, until his return. I told her about Sullivan and Roper's mother's death, but insisted that this wasn't yet news.

'Then don't tell me,' she said.

Her tone made me cautious. 'How's Sunny?'

'Like everybody else in this evil, pathetic, crappy little world – exhausted.' She said nothing for a moment. 'And does James Bishop know they'll soon be digging up his daughter's bones?'

'I just called him,' I said.

On the television above the bar, someone scored,

439

and the table of men rose as one, punched the air, cheered, danced and hugged each other.

'Who's winning?' Yvonne said.

'Nobody,' I said. I told her I'd call again in the morning.

She told me to wait, as though she wanted to say something more to me, but either the words would not come to her through her own exhaustion, or she finally considered the effort too much for her. 'Nothing,' she said. 'See you tomorrow.' And she hung up.

I waited where I sat for another forty minutes, until the match was over.

I walked back to the station and encountered Finch on the low wall outside the church.

'Have you seen Smart since—?'

'Since when? Since he last stopped playing his own little games with Sullivan?'

I sat beside him.

'I'm due back up in ten,' he said. 'I've had two calls relayed to me from the men watching two of the others.'

'Abbot's associates?'

'Behaving very strangely, by all accounts.'

'Do they know what's happening?'

'Of course they know what's happening. This is the Information Age, remember?'

'Can you do anything to keep them where they are?'

'I'll have to wait and see what Smart says.'

'For what it's worth,' I said, 'I don't think he had any option but to bring Sullivan in.'

'And when *he's* finished covering his own back again and been released in, oh, five or six hours' time?'

At first I didn't understand what he was telling me.

'You think Smart will release Sullivan just so that Abbot might try and get to him?' I said.

'The small fish eat the tiny fish, and then the big fish eat the small fish,' he said.

I told him he was wrong in believing Smart capable of doing what he'd just suggested.

'Then you're either very stupid or very forgiving for a man who's been used by Smart even before he met you,' he said.

'I knew what I was doing,' I said.

'Not as well as Smart knew what *he* was up to.'

'Does he want Sullivan to ask for police protection?'

'Probably. But only so he can refuse him it. You think Sullivan didn't run through all these unhappy alternatives on his own ride here? Anything he tells Smart now, he's had five years to consider.'

'So do you, too, wish he was back out there in the open water with Abbot swimming up behind him?'

'It's what the fucker deserves,' he said. 'All this crap about bent coppers getting it hard in prison. They'd send him to a fucking rest home. They look after their own. They always have done and they always will.'

' "They" and you not being a "we", then?'

His laughter was as cold and as dismissive as James Bishop's had been.

'Every one of those fuckers in there still thinks more of Sullivan than they do of you, me and Smart put together.'

'Not necessarily,' I said.

'Yes,' he said. 'Necessarily.'

He stood up from the wall and I followed him back inside.

Smart was waiting for us in the small room. He sat with his head in his hands and looked up at our arrival.

'Any progress on the caravan?' Finch said.

'He did it,' Smart said. 'He won't admit to anything. He won't even talk about it, but he did it, and he knows I know he did it. He's started conferring with his legal before answering me.'

'And?'

'And the minute he did that I told him he was free to go. I told him he'd been very helpful and wished him a long and happy retirement.'

'Which probably won't last until Christmas,' Finch said. 'Where is he now?'

'Still down there. Arguing with his brief and wondering what else I know.'

'There won't ever be anything to pin him to the caravan fire and Roper's mother,' I said.

'Who asked you?' Smart said without looking up at me.

Finch laughed at the remark.

'I feel as though I'm being used,' I said.

Finch laughed again, followed this time by Smart, who said, 'It's what you're good at, being used.'

'And presumably you did nothing to dispel Sullivan's fears about Abbot getting to him,' I said.

'Nothing whatsoever. Bit of a joke, really – here's me wanting Sullivan to rot in hell because of what he could have done, but didn't, and in the end we only get to nail him because of Boyd's determination to get revenge for his father and Roper determined to do the same for his mother. Christ, whichever way it falls, there's going to be somebody waiting to kick him.'

I told him I'd called James Bishop.

'The more the merrier,' he said, and then fell silent and held a hand over his mouth.

We were interrupted a moment later by Rachel Evans who came in without knocking and stood at our centre.

'We've just about completed the prelims,' she said. 'Everything's isolated and fire-walled and ready for us to go digging.'

'Anything unusual?' Smart asked her.

'Nothing so far. In fact there isn't much of *anything* so far.'

'But there are hidden files, something Roper stashed away?'

She shrugged. 'We haven't started looking. I meant in comparison to what we're used to finding, there isn't much. Not much capacity, not many add-ons, only one careful owner, nothing out of the ordinary.'

'Which is just how Roper would want it to appear. Where's Alex?'

'With a police courier. The sealed copies of the disks need to be sent off and deposited, you know that.'

'When will you start looking?'

'When we've had a break.' The two women had been working for almost four hours without a pause. 'You?'

'I don't think Sullivan had the first idea what he was sitting on,' Smart said. 'I want you to tell me about everything you find in terms *he* would understand. He'll have searched through all the files that are listed.'

'I doubt he'll have come across anything that attracted his attention,' she said. 'Anyway, I don't need to know any of this. Not yet. I'll let you know when we're ready to start. And all I'll need to know then is some idea of what we're looking for and how competent the user was who hid these things away.'

'Very,' Smart said.

'Good,' she said reassuringly.

The phone rang and Smart answered it.

'Sullivan's brief wants a word. I'd better go down and wipe everyone's brow.'

'Are you serious about letting him go?' I said.

'As serious as he is about staying,' he said.

As I waited with Finch for Smart to return, James Bishop called me back.

'I'm out of the house,' he said, and then paused, as though considering why he'd told me this. 'I told Patricia what had happened and she said I ought to call you back. She thinks that what happened to Nicola has no bearing on what's happening to us now. Neither of us believes that, of course, but it might be easier to think it's the truth. What's Sullivan said?'

'Roper believed Sullivan was responsible for his mother's death,' I told him again.

'I don't care about her,' Bishop said. 'I don't care about either of them. My daughter's dead and now they're both dead. Who do you think suffered the

443

most? Who do you think least *deserved* to die?' He was shouting and I tried to mask his voice from Finch. Men still came and went in the corridor outside.

'I don't think any of them *deserved* to die,' I said. 'Not like you mean.'

'You're wrong,' he said. '*He* deserved to die. And whether she deserved it or not, I won't pretend to be sorry for her. Just as I won't try and convince myself that, however awful and painful *his* death was, it was the tiniest fraction as painful or as undeserved as Nicola's was. I lied when I told you I wasn't in this for revenge. I've wanted it for five years, ever since I first heard his name and knew what he'd done. I even wished he'd got a daughter so that I might get my hands on her. You've gone very quiet, Mr Rivers.'

'You don't mean any of this,' I said, knowing I was wrong.

'Why? Because I'm an educated, decent, civilized man? You're wrong, Mr Rivers. I might be all of those things, but none of that prepared me for what happened to Nicola, none of it.'

I waited for him to finish speaking. 'The man I believe was ultimately responsible for your daughter's death was the man you fired for spreading malicious gossip about you and Alison Menzies,' I said, knowing even as I said it that it was the last thing in the world I should have told him.

At the table, Finch rose and drew the blade of his finger across his throat.

I heard James Bishop gasping for air.

'The man who subsequently turned up as a waiter at your home and who you then had thrown out,' I said.

Finch held out his hand, expecting me to give him the phone. *Shut up*, he mouthed.

'No,' Bishop said. 'You're lying . . . I don't . . . you can't . . .' The sentence stumbled and fell. 'Why are you saying this?' he said eventually.

'Because someone else is going to tell you the same thing sooner or later. It changes nothing.'

I waited for him to deny this, to say something, but nothing came as he searched for himself in the impossible story I had just told him.

'You're wrong,' he said quietly, several times, his voice slowly drying.

'I'll see you tomorrow,' I told him.

'You're wrong,' he said again, and I let the word hang before putting down my phone.

Finch looked at me across the desk.

'That was a clever move,' he said.

'I would have told him sooner or later,' I said.

'I'm just thinking that later might have been better than sooner. Later, as in after we'd actually found something on the computer, which to my mind is looking less and less likely; or later, as in after Sullivan had told us everything he knows; or later, as in after Boyd had decided to tell us his particular version of this drawn-out tale; or later, as in after Abbot and his evil companions had finally managed to get at each other's throats. All those kinds of later.'

'Will you tell Smart?' I said.

'No, you will.'

There was laughter in the corridor outside, where the men still gathered there had heard him shouting and were now passing their own remarks on us.

'Do you think Bishop will know about the arson attack, that Boyd's in hospital?' I said.

'How could he?' he said. 'Like everything else in this operation, it's one big secret.'

The men outside fell silent and Smart appeared at the door a moment later.

'Sullivan's brief has advised him to stick to why he was brought in here. So no more questions about the unrelated and unfounded matter of Roper's mother's death.'

'And?' Finch said.

'And Sullivan's rattled that I'm trying to connect him to it. He still keeps bleating on about how Roper's conviction for the death of Hayley Forbes was a fair one. His brief is the same one who held his hand through the first inquiry. All *he* can keep saying is how unfair it is that Sullivan has to go through all this again after being cleared the last time.'

'He sounds a lot less concerned about Abbot than Sullivan is,' I said.

'Who cares? I made a point of telling Sullivan that I still intended parading those five girls' corpses in front of him.'

'How did he respond to that?' Finch said.

' "Ashen" and "shaken" are good words,' Smart said. 'His brief said I was behaving outrageously, unprofessionally and intimidatingly, and that my completely unfounded allegations were preposterous. Presumably, Sullivan will now be telling him all about the computer and what he thought it might contain that would have incriminated Lloyd and his golden-haired son.'

There had been no further calls regarding the activity of Abbot or his associates.

'Has Sullivan gone?' Finch said.

'Presumably. I pushed the brief into a corner until – surprise, surprise – he said, "Either charge my client or release him." Then I gave him a long stare, became goodness and light itself, thanked them both for their co-operation, told Sullivan he was free to go, and left them.'

'And?'

'And I could hear Sullivan shouting down the corridor for me to go back to them and his brief telling him to shut up and calm down.'

52

An hour later, shortly before midnight, Alex Carr came to us and said that she and Rachel Evans were ready to start examining whatever lay on the computer.

'Any idea of how long?' Smart asked her.

She looked at him without answering.

'OK,' Smart said.

We followed her into the room at the end of the corridor. We passed four other rooms, in each of which waited a group of men.

'They want to see what we find on Sullivan and his old squad,' Smart said, making no effort to lower his voice. 'They probably think they're going to bury this like they buried practically everything else.' To Finch, he said, 'They know Sullivan's already gone. Some of them have probably gone with him.'

We arrived at the door and Alex knocked. Four raps.

'We have a secret knock,' she said to me.

Rachel opened the door and we went in.

Trays containing the remains of meals and half-empty cups and bottles of water covered what little space remained.

'This is Rachel's machine,' Alex said, indicating the computer at which their two chairs sat. 'And this is the control. Seal it,' she said to Smart.

She explained to me that the control machine would record every operation that was carried out on Roper's computer. An aluminium seal had already been fastened around the second machine. A tag protruded from the soft disk slot. Smart picked up the pliers beside it, held the two ends of the tag together and pressed. He read the numbers out and Alex typed these into Roper's computer, along with the time, date and the names of everyone present.

Rachel Evans sat beside Alex at the table and both of them waited for Smart to say, 'Let's start,' which he did.

They spent the next fifteen minutes listing the specifications of the installed hard- and software and then ran through all the files listed in the various directories.

'Nothing out of the ordinary or unusual,' Alex said. 'Nothing dodgy. Nothing anyone with a machine this age might not install for themselves. However . . .' She paused, opening the first of the listed files created by Roper.

The file-name appeared, but the screen remained blank.

'Can't you get into it?' Finch said.

'We're in,' Alex told him. 'There's nothing there. It's empty.'

'Deleted?'

'Not as far as we can tell. It's been opened and named and saved, but nothing's been put into it. It hasn't been encrypted, and there's nothing to stop anyone from opening it.'

'Are there any more like it?' Smart asked hesitantly.

'That's the bad news,' Rachel told him. 'As far as we can tell, they're all the same. They're all there and named and easy to open, but there's nothing in any of them. We've run all the programs we have to find if there once was anything there, but so far nothing.'

'So far?'

'We've tested all of them. It's like a brand-new diary,

448

all the days and dates, months and special occasions listed, but nothing personal, no day-to-day activities listed.'

'Which suggests what to you?' Finch said.

'Could be one of several things. The most likely alternative is that your man created a duplicate of something he already possessed. Say he believed somebody was going to come and steal what he already owned – all those bulging files. He makes a copy and they take that away instead, imagining it to be the original.'

'Or they find what we've found and stop looking,' Alex added.

'Would Sullivan have known enough about the things to realize what Roper had done and go on looking?' Finch said.

We all considered this unlikely.

'He'd look, find nothing, and then sigh a sigh of relief because Roper had apparently wiped everything clean,' Alex said.

'That was what Roper wanted him to think,' Smart said. 'Knowing that when someone who finally knew what they were doing looked at the directories, they would know exactly what had happened.'

'That the full files are still there?' Rachel said.

'What mattered is that Sullivan believed everything had been wiped,' Smart said. 'And via him or someone else on the team, both Boyd and Abbot got to know the same. I think Roper made this dummy copy of everything especially for us, to encourage us, to question why all the empty files were still there and to go on looking for what he'd hidden.'

Alex and Rachel exchanged a glance.

'We call this "Straws, open bracket, grasping at, close bracket",' Rachel said to me.

'And once Sullivan and the others believed that it was harmless, there was no reason to destroy it,' Finch said.

'And which leaves *us* with what?' Alex said to him.

449

'With whatever's still deep inside there that you're now going to tell us about,' Smart said.

Alex smiled. 'People always underestimate you, Smart,' she said.

'But not you two.'

'No, never us.'

'Two unnamed files,' Rachel said. She closed the directory listings and returned to an overview of the hard drive. 'Everything's been shuffled up into a nice neat space,' she said. 'Except for something here and something here.' She tapped a pencil at the two empty segments of screen, like missing books along a shelf.

'How do you know there's meant to be anything there?' Finch said.

'Because we're too clever not to know. And because our boy's telling us.'

'Our paedophile and murderer,' Smart said.

Alex dropped her eyes. 'Because our paedophile and murderer is telling us.'

'And there's no reference to either of these two files in any of the directories?' Smart said.

'Which is why, to people who know how to go about looking for these things, they stand out. He could just as easily have hidden them for ever.'

'So what makes you so certain there *is* something?' I said.

'Because someone's gone to too much trouble both to hide them and then to leave these invisible markers pointing directly at them,' Alex said.

'And all Sullivan saw was the nothing he was meant to see,' Smart said.

'Something like that.'

'And we get into these files how?' Smart said.

'"Access" is the word.'

'And I presume that's the first of our problems.'

'You presume right,' Alex said. She slid her chair to the control computer to ensure that everything was functioning as it should.

'Any ideas?' Finch said to me.

'The best way', Rachel said, 'is to return to some form of search mode and start bombarding it with possible key words. Just like in the films.'

'Do you think there's a hot-word to connect the two files?' Finch said.

'My my,' Rachel said. ' "Hot-word". Whatever next? To link the two files? There wouldn't really be much point. Remember Portsmouth? The hot-word there dumped almost three thousand separate user files in our laps.' She removed the diagram from the screen and initiated the program which would begin the search.

'It's now just little more than a process of elimination,' Alex said. 'We start with fifty million words and whittle them down to two. I'm hoping you three stooges know what those two words are.'

'Any restrictions?' Finch said.

'Seven letters or fewer, the usual.'

'Great.'

'There will be some logic to it all,' she said. 'It's just a question of working out how that logic proceeds. Let's start firing a few shots in the dark.'

'And the cut-off?' Smart said.

'Curiously, as far as we can tell, there isn't one,' Rachel said. She tapped the pencil again. 'The guess box on programs this old – and this is *old*, remember – usually contains its asterisks. Each guess, one less. Five wrong guesses and the box knows you're guessing and shuts down on you.'

'But just because there are no indicators, it doesn't mean that there might *not* be restrictions?' Smart said.

'Oh, restrictions always apply,' Alex said. 'But in this case, we doubt it. We opened our own test file, encoded it using the same program, and then tried to open it using false names. It hadn't closed after fifty-one attempts.' She turned to me. 'You suggested earlier that whoever put the files there wanted you to find them.'

'And this overgenerous opportunity to do that is another reason for believing there's something there in the first place?' Smart said.

'Trust me,' Alex said. 'We would have known soon enough if we were knocking at something non-existent.'

'Pick a name,' Rachel said. 'Any name.'

We waited for Smart to speak.

'Abbot,' he said.

Rachel typed it in and pressed Enter.

The screen flashed clear.

NOT FOUND.

A double asterisk flashed, awaiting further instructions.

'Shit,' Finch said.

'You might have to say that fifty million times,' Alex told him. 'So save your breath; we'll just imagine you saying it all night.'

If the name had appeared, Smart would have had the perfect reason for arresting Abbot.

We all looked hard at the empty screen.

'What's all this?' Finch said, running a finger across the tool-bar and stopping at a date.

'It's the computer's own automatic dating program,' Rachel said. 'We wondered about that. Whoever created the files left it operational.'

'Which again suggests that a file exists,' Smart said.

'And which has opened for no good or apparent reason.'

'Why would something non-existent have a date attached to it?'

'What is it?' Finch said, moving closer. '13.10.98.'

'Close to Roper's arrest for the murder of Hayley Forbes,' I said.

Smart opened his case and took out a file. 'Roper was arrested on the tenth, three days earlier. He never went back home after that.'

'Perhaps he knew they were coming for him,' Finch

said. 'He was busy making his empty copies of every-thing and got the dates wrong.'

'He knew exactly what was happening,' Smart said. 'And more to the point, he knew exactly what he was doing.' He turned to Alex. 'Start changing the date backwards,' he said.

She did this. Thirteen to twelve to eleven. Nothing. But as the second digit of eleven turned to a zero, the screen was suddenly filled with lines of writing.

It mattered to her. She even had my birth certificate changed.

'Well, Jesus, fuck and shit,' Rachel said. 'Welcome to the Geniuses' Club, Smart.'

The writing consisted of names and addresses, each followed by a succession of coded letters and numbers. The first name on the file was Ackland, the last, Atkinson. Thirty names stretched between them.

'Still no Abbot,' I said.

'Scroll them,' Smart told Alex.

The names and details ran into the hundreds.

'It's Roper's own directory,' Finch said. 'It's what attracted Abbot to him in the first place.'

A count revealed two hundred and eighty-five names.

'Now we're into the thing, try Abbot again,' Smart told Alex.

She opened a search box and typed in the name.

The file continued scrolling long past its final names – two sisters called Young – and after a few seconds of empty space, a further list appeared, at the top of which was Abbot's name, followed by confirmatory details.

Smart gave Rachel six other names.

All Abbot's known original associates were listed.

Smart rose from where he sat on the edge of the table and took out his phone.

'We still don't know what it's a list *of*,' Finch told him.

'Don't we?' Smart said. 'I don't care.' He went to the

door to make his call. At first, he whispered, but then grew exasperated and started shouting. 'You heard me. Every fucking one. Now. And don't listen to anything any of them has to tell you. If they start to squirm, stand back and watch them. Let me know. Anybody fucks up on this and they'll be fucking me – me, personally.'

'Charming,' Alex said.

'Old silver-tongued Smart,' Rachel said. They'd heard it all before.

It was ten past one in the morning.

The two women had pushed their chairs back from the screens and were now smoking.

I went closer to the table and scrolled back up the list until I found Nicola Bishop's name. There was no entry for James Bishop. I found Hayley Forbes, Lindsey Perry and Jennifer Wilson. There was no reference to Angela Hill.

'Are they all there?' Finch asked me.

'All except Angela Hill.' Roper's deletion of her name had been his final favour to her, a kind of love letter in reverse.

'Are they all dead?' Alex asked me. I nodded and she put her hand on my arm. 'I'm sorry,' she said.

Rachel Evans sat and watched us.

Smart came back to us. He looked at the names and let out his breath.

'We need to work out what all those coded letters mean,' he said.

He asked Rachel to make a dozen copies of the list, which she did. The control computer had its own printer and the copies were duplicated there and deposited into a sealed tray.

'The coding refers to various acts, specialities,' Alex told us. 'Preferences and specialities. You don't need too much imagination.'

' "ME 3"?' I said, reading from the file.

'The first word's "multiple",' she said.

Some of the codes revealed themselves to us; some didn't; it made little difference.

Rachel went back to the keyboard. 'That's the whole file,' she said.

'Most of the names will come to nothing,' Smart said. 'My guess is that they were all the girls and clients known to Roper before Abbot got his claws into him.'

'It's still more than we need,' Finch said.

I went back to each of the dead girls' names. I tried to remember the surname of the man Jennifer Wilson's mother was now living with, but couldn't. I said nothing to Smart. I searched for Claire Madison, but there was nothing.

Wallis was there, and Kelly McLean.

Boyd was there, his name appended to his real name, along with his father.

There was nothing on Sullivan.

There was nothing on Paul Hill, Angela Hill's father, and nothing on either Sunny or Yvonne.

Smart saw what I was doing. 'You're doing this because no one's watching you,' he said. 'And don't type "Hull Police" into the search box. *I* want to do that.'

Alex and Rachel stubbed out their cigarettes together.

The two printers fell silent.

'Nothing relating to Sullivan's wife or Roper's mother's death,' Finch said.

'Will all this be enough?' Alex said to Smart.

'It proves a lot of connections – ones we already knew about or suspected – but it doesn't really give us much else in terms of what those connections signify. The National boys will have a field day with the list.' He turned to me. 'A lot of the names will crop up on other files. Paedophiles, of necessity, tend to be well-organized and well-informed.'

'There's an entry for Roper himself,' I said.

'What did he have to lose?' Finch said.

Smart took the lists from the printer tray and went out with them, returning a few minutes later with a pot of fresh coffee.

'Nobody went home,' he said, meaning the men outside.

We drank the coffee while Smart went up and down through the names, alerting Finch to those he recognized from the operations in those other cities he was always visiting.

Beside each of the girls named by Roper in his confession was the same sequence of letters. Alex searched for this sequence elsewhere and found a further three occurrences. She read the new names to Smart, who checked a list of his own.

'All still missing,' he said eventually.

There were no other details, no dates, no places.

This brief interlude of success and its muted euphoria was punctured by Alex Carr, who said, 'That was easy wasn't it?' alerting us all, especially Smart, to how readily the file had revealed its contents to us.

We waited in silence as she copied the file onto several disks. Smart and Finch each took one of these. She stacked others in a low mound alongside the screen. She told me that the measure was a precaution, that in the past files had deleted themselves upon being entered and searched. It confirmed for us again that Roper was a willing participant in all that was happening.

'He wants it to happen,' Smart said.

'*That* easily?' she said.

'She's right,' Finch said. 'Roper anticipated being alive when we did all this, waiting for our call to beg him to help us, waiting for a deal to be made in his favour. He gave us all this to whet our appetites. We know it's genuine, and in normal circumstances it might have been all we needed. But these aren't normal circumstances. The investigation is going to be closed down soon, and we've already been forced into bringing Abbot and the others in. It isn't a healthy situation.'

'We had no choice,' Smart told him.

'I'm not saying we did. Just that the files were

intended to be in our hands and Roper still alive and looking over our shoulders as we searched them. We were lucky with the first one, that's all. He gave it to us.'

'Thanks,' Alex said to him.

He signalled his apology to her. 'Roper intended us to get our hands on all this, but it's still not what he really wanted to give to us. This isn't his bargaining tool, that's all I'm saying.'

'And you think all that's on the second file?' Smart said.

'And I'll bet ten pence there's no wrong date flashing away at us on that one,' Rachel said. She put her hand on Finch's shoulder.

'Only one way to find out,' Alex said, and she sat back at the screen and keyboard and opened the second hidden file.

This time, the screen showed nothing.

Alex continued working, and a few seconds later a box demanding a key word appeared at the centre of the empty space. She whispered something to Rachel.

'What?' Smart said.

'I'm not sure,' Alex told him. She indicated the top of the screen, where the misleading date had been shown on the first file. Eight asterisks showed. 'There's eight,' she said. 'Strange for a seven-letter key word.'

'Suggesting?' Smart said.

'Suggesting they may have nothing to do with the code-word as such.' She and Rachel conferred again.

'What?' Smart said again.

'Russian dolls,' Rachel said.

Smart and Finch said, 'Fuck,' together.

Rachel turned to me. 'It means that it's a single encrypted file with another inside it. Until you get to the first, you have no chance of reaching the second, and so on. Each of them has a separate key, and they're designed to open only in the sequence in which they were encrypted.'

'You've come across the same thing before?' I said.

'Last time, it took us two months to prise our way into the final file.'

Smart's phone rang. He looked at the caller number before answering.

'They've got Abbot at Queen's Gardens,' he said.

'What do you want to do?' Finch said, knowing that Smart would want to go and interview Abbot personally. 'We're just doubling up here. Go and see him.'

Smart looked at each of us. 'Anything I get from Abbot, I'll let you know immediately,' he said.

'And vice versa,' Finch said.

Smart gave him a wad of papers from his case. 'They're every name, date and place the investigation has thrown up in the past three years,' he said to me. 'We're hoping Roper decided to be predictable.'

53

Neither Alex nor Rachel seemed as concerned about the complexity of the task ahead of them as Smart had been, and I remarked on this to them.

'Perhaps we're not as intimidated by the technology as Smart is,' Rachel said.

'We've been using washing machines and heated rollers for decades, remember,' Alex added. 'Besides which, it's not so much *our* work now as *yours*. Yours and Finch's here.' She turned to Finch. 'How about it, Finch? Are you going to crack this during the long dark night of the soul while Smart's off playing Harvey Keitel? That must be worth a pat on the head from someone whose pats count. I hear they're not very happy with Smart now that Roper got killed.' It was clear she knew considerably more about the case than she had originally let on.

'Without this, he'll lose his grip on the thing,' Finch said, meaning Smart.

Rachel returned to her seat in front of the monitor. I could see that the two women operated a long-practised and mutually beneficial scheme of working. She started on the keyboard, and said, 'Good.'

' "Good" as in . . . ?' Finch said.

'Good as in, as before, no restrictions on our

guessing. We can run all fifty million code-words without being shut out.'

'Why *are* you so optimistic?' Finch asked her.

'Because we've got a series or a succession of clues to find,' Alex said. 'And series and successions, however complicated they might appear to the uninitiated, do at least suggest an order or a way of thinking.'

'And because we know that the key words were thought up and used by a single person, my guess is that everything will relate,' Rachel added. 'Everything will be personal. I assumed that's why you were here,' she said to me. 'I've never known Smart let an outsider sit in on anything like this before.'

'And because Roper isn't really trying to keep all this from *us* – just from the men who possess none of our capabilities. If he'd ever been serious about keeping it to himself, no one would ever get to what he'd hidden.'

'So you think we probably already know everything we need to know?' Finch said.

'I hope that's a big "probably" and not a small one,' she said. 'Everything you know, Finch, a dozen others know or can get their hands on.' She turned to me. 'And everything *you* know includes the stuff none of those other dozen will ever learn. *That's* why you're here.'

'And all the time I was with him, Roper knew Smart was pulling my strings,' I said.

'It's why he agreed to talk to you,' Finch said. 'Whatever you prefer to believe. He was confirming for himself that you were locked in tightly enough with Smart to provide us with what he wanted us to know when the time came.'

'He locked me in by agreeing to see me,' I said.

'Precisely.'

'But he still expected to be alive and about to benefit from a deal with Smart,' I reminded him.

To end this speculation and the unhappy course it might now take, Alex said, 'Right, let's get started,' and began typing.

The same empty screen and its open box reappeared.

The four of us sat and looked at it without speaking.

'The Chinese say that a journey of a thousand miles begins with a single step,' Rachel said.

'They also fed us all that monosodium glutamate for decades without telling us and invented crispy prawn balls,' Alex said. 'The opener will most likely be a name. Give me one of Smart's lists.'

Finch gave it to her and she typed in name after name after name.

For twenty minutes, nothing registered.

'Now I'm worried,' she said. 'Kids, mothers and fathers are usually our best bet.'

She resumed typing, Rachel reading the names to her.

'The first key word will be the hardest,' Rachel said to us, hoping to encourage us. 'Hopefully, whatever it reveals will suggest a way forward. Do I sound hopeful?'

Finch gave me another of the lists Smart had left with us, and when Rachel fell silent, I continued reading to Alex the names and places it contained.

It was after two in the morning.

Thirty minutes later, the names and places were exhausted. No response to any of the other names that had featured so prominently; no response to the places; no response, even, to the caravan site and every place I could think of associated with it.

In one of Smart's folders there were several photographs. I came across the picture of Roper as a boy standing with his mother outside her caravan. If ever a book was written about the case, it would be used for the jacket. Proud mother, a boy in shorts holding her hand, both of them squinting into the sun.

I wondered who had taken it. The shadow of the photographer stretched over the grass towards them.

'What is it?' Finch asked me, seeing how hard I was looking at the picture.

For the first time, I saw the vague outline of several others, children, at the caravan window, hoping perhaps to be included in the picture.

'It's got a name,' I said.

'What has?'

'The caravan.'

Both Alex and Rachel turned to face me.

I looked harder at the barely visible name-plate. 'Something "-view",' I said. 'Five or six letters and then "view".'

'Too many letters,' Alex said.

'Try "Sea-view",' Finch suggested.

Nothing.

We came up with half a dozen alternatives, none of which worked.

I took the picture back from Finch and looked at it again.

Only ever the two of us there, never anyone else.

'It's not their caravan,' I said. 'It must be one close by – the photographer's perhaps.' I showed Finch the other outlines in the window.

He took the photo from me. The caravan in the background also had a name-plate, but this was far too distant and indistinct to be read.

Rachel went to him, took the picture and held it to the light. 'We could wake up someone from the imaging team,' she suggested.

'It'd take hours,' Alex said. She took the photo and flattened it on the table in front of her. 'Go and find a good magnifying glass,' she told Finch, who left us. 'It's readable. There's always a point at which something will either come towards you or disappear completely. This one will come.'

Finch returned with a glass attached to a heavy stand.

Alex studied it. ' "M"-something. "M" something "A".'

Roper's mother's name was Mary.

' "Marina",' I said. It was their way of remembering

and of doubly disguising their lost daughter and sister, Gina. Their way of taking her with them to that place. And even Roper himself probably didn't understand all the implications of that. It was where she was conceived, and where, until the fire and the death of his mother, she would have lived happily and for ever beside them in that land of lost content.

Alex typed the name, and the instant the completed word filled the box, the box disappeared and the computer began to tick.

The screen remained blank for several seconds, and then four lines appeared running evenly spaced from left to right across it. Immediately afterwards, another four lines appeared, this time running from the top to the bottom of the screen, creating a series of squares.

The lines and the ticking stopped.

'Whatever it is, that's it,' Alex said.

The three of us looked hard at the lines, either trying to understand their meaning or wondering if they had any meaning at all.

After a minute of this, Alex said to Rachel, 'Software printout.' She tapped the screen where the cursor sat below the tool-bar. '*This* is what he likes to do,' she said.

'What?' I said.

'It's another pointer,' Rachel told me. 'Like the false date on the first file. We make a good guess and he throws us a fish.'

The printer came to life and a single sheet slid from it.

The two women studied this.

Into the waiting rectangle, Alex then typed 'OS' and immediately a reference number and a catalogue number appeared.

'It's a map,' Finch said. 'Grid lines. Which ones?'

Rachel showed him the printed sheet of everything that had been installed in the computer. 'OS CD rom. They're not that uncommon. People use them to plan journeys, plot routes.'

'When was it installed?' Finch asked her.

She ran her finger across the line of print. ' "13.10.98".'

'The same date,' Finch said. 'Roper wasn't going anywhere that he might need a map for. Run the serial number.'

Alex did this, and another box appeared, along with the notification that the map was the East Riding Landranger, No. 107.

'This is it,' Finch said, but still without any true understanding of what was almost within our grasp.

There was no record of what use Roper might already have made of the software.

'The point is, he left it listed on the directory,' Alex said. 'Even if he deleted the symbol from his homepage. And judging by all the unused crap he did leave on there, I'd say the deletion was another of his pointers.'

'Like the wrong date.'

'Exactly.'

Finch suggested trying the reference number to see if it brought up the features of the map corresponding to the grid lines.

Alex did this. But instead of the relatively small area contained within the grid lines appearing, the whole map materialized. It was easy to see by the number of grid lines on this that the area already denoted by Roper – four lines by four lines – was only a very small part of the whole.

Alex returned to this smaller, featureless area. We estimated this to be four miles square, sixteen square miles. We had no way yet of determining which part of the undrawn map it represented. Scrolling in any direction, the lines disappeared.

'He's been very clever,' she said. 'If what we're going to get is part of the larger map, then he's manipulated the working sequence of the disk to encode each part of its own sequence of superimpositions. Either that, or he's redrawn it completely – it's possible – using only the OS grid references for absolute location-finding, and then chosen his own symbols and features for what he wants to show us next.'

'What's the catalogue number for?' Finch said.

'Presumably for when someone wanted to order a map.'

'How does it work?'

'Let's see.' Alex resumed typing, bringing up the details for ordering. There was no indication that Roper had previously bought anything. She keyed in the catalogue number. 'Problem,' she said. '"Incorrect Code".'

'Try it again,' Finch told her.

She did. The same thing happened.

'It's another of his clues,' Rachel said. '*We* look at the picture while *he* studies the frame.'

'So if it's not the OS catalogue, what is it?' Alex said.

'And what if it isn't shorthand for the catalogue at all,' Finch said, looking at me as he spoke. 'What if it's just longhand for "cat"?'

The cat Roper gave to Angela Hill with its one blind eye and decreasing lives.

I made a quick calculation. 'Type in "Five",' I told Alex.

She did this. Nothing.

'Try Four.'

Still nothing.

'Try—'

'Let me guess,' she said.

At the word 'Three', a succession of letters and numbers appeared around the outside of the grid, followed by a series of black, blue, yellow and red uneven lines across the squares.

'The coast, roads and rivers,' Finch said.

In the rectangle in which the cursor still sat, the word 'Three' turned to 'Four' and then all the way back up to 'Nine', confirming and congratulating our guess.

After 'Nine', the letters disappeared completely, and

the instant this happened, the faint miaowing of a cat could be heard in the depths of the speakers.

Finch was more convinced than ever that, though she may not have known it, Angela Hill had been chosen by Roper as his fall-back option. In the event of his death, presumably, a letter would have been sent to her telling her everything we were now so laboriously discovering for ourselves. It was also his belief that either Boyd or his father had realized this at the time of the original investigation, but that with the conviction of Roper, the abandonment of his first appeal and the undoubted failure of his appeal now, they had not needed to act on this understanding.

My return to her after all those years had only confirmed what they had already guessed, and when Boyd told Abbot about his suspicions and about my visit, Abbot told Boyd to kill her, which he did. As an added bonus, Boyd was now acting on behalf of Abbot and thereby deflecting all interest away from his own true motive in killing Angela Hill.

'But how could Roper have possibly known the cat was still alive?' I asked Finch.

He considered this. 'He didn't need to. It didn't need to be. Either he would be, or Angela Hill certainly would be. It was all he needed. The cat was his gift to her, a permanent, living reminder of him. All he needed to flash up to anyone else was that something still connected them.'

'"Anyone else" being someone who had either spoken to Angela Hill, seen the cat, or heard about it from her.'

'How many other close friends do you think she had?'

'He thought he'd left her safely out of everything,' I said. 'By warning her off and then erasing her name from all his files. He must have known she was still alive, that nothing had happened to her.' Until I showed up.

It was no consolation, but I knew that either Boyd or

Abbot would have reached her eventually when they once again considered her a threat to them.

I looked up to see Finch watching me.

'Don't,' he said.

'I wonder what happened to the cat?' I said.

' "Zero",' he suggested.

I heard Angela Hill saying that she hadn't wanted to take the animal, but that it was a living thing, so what could she do?

Two days later, Boyd had killed her and filmed her death and the cat had gone, only to reappear upon my visit to the flat with Finch.

'He's going to show us where the bodies are,' Finch said eventually.

It was by then almost three o'clock. The men being questioned elsewhere would all be complaining about the uncivilized hour. Their lawyers would be insisting that their clients were being treated unfairly.

The men who had earlier congregated in the corridor were no longer there, but they could still occasionally be heard on the floors beneath us. Phones rang regularly through the night, and patrol cars came and went from the car park below.

I tried to imagine where Sullivan might now be, and all he might be considering. I wondered if he might attempt to visit Boyd in the hospital, just as he had visited me with the news of Angela Hill's death. I wondered about the true nature of the guilt or remorse he still felt. Survival of the fittest, he had insisted. But it was fitness defined only in terms of strength and greed, subterfuge and manipulation. He deserved to suffer now for everything he had done, or not done, or allowed to happen, and this time he would not be left in a position to choose the nature of his suffering or to mould it to his own self-serving needs.

Finch began to speculate on what the simple map already revealed to us. The holiday camp was some-where in its emptiness, along with Sullivan's bungalow, along with the slender spit of land curling into the sea and then back into the estuary. He compared it to one of the maps in Smart's file.

'They searched everywhere they could think to look,' he said. He held the map to the screen.

'Sullivan never wanted to find what he was supposed to be looking for,' I said. 'They only found Hayley Forbes because that was what Abbot intended. Sullivan was adamant all along that they were looking in the wrong place and that they ought to concentrate their efforts to the west of the city.'

'Which is why Hayley Forbes was left where she was.'

'And which allowed Sullivan to crow that he'd been right all along, and that all those allegations of wasted time and resources should not be laid at his door.'

'All of which was academic, because without Roper we were never going to find anything anyway.'

Martin Roper's body was still being held pending an inquiry into his death.

And Angela Hill still rested in the Spring Street morgue in the same state of uneasy, tainted grace.

Alex Carr leaned back in her chair and yawned. Rachel Evans stood behind her and massaged her shoulders. Their growing exhaustion was now apparent in everything they said and did.

We all considered the map.

'Roper wouldn't necessarily know precisely where the searches had taken place,' Finch said. 'He'd know they were looking, but he wouldn't know for certain *where*, not when they were in three or four places at once.'

'Or perhaps he realized that the heart had already gone out of the operation, that Sullivan had all he wanted and that the rest was only window-dressing for the watching public and press.'

'I think we're closer to the end than we think,' Rachel said, causing us to fall silent and turn to her. 'The map isn't going to show anything in any greater detail,' she said. 'We've established that this is as small as the scale gets.'

'Right,' Finch said, neither of us yet fully following her reasoning.

'We have GPS,' she said. 'Anything marked by a cross inside any one of those grid squares is going to be fairly easy to locate give or take a few metres.'

'*One* more level of detail would be good,' Alex said, meaning that even sixteen square miles was still too large an area to search thoroughly, especially if the bodies were buried.

'Perhaps,' Rachel said. 'But my guess is that if we've been clever enough to get this far, our encoder will want to make the rest as straightforward as possible for us. So far, the clues have all been based on what he knows *we* – via Rivers – will know about.'

'He knew we'd bring Angela Hill into the picture,' Finch said.

'Whether he did or not,' Rachel said, 'it was a risk he had to take. What I'm saying is that if we've come this far, and knowing what he wants to achieve by his revelations, then there's no real need for him to hide the rest from us.'

'We've proved our credentials?' I said.

'You remembered what he told you,' Rachel said to me. 'So far, everything's been encrypted largely to ensure that the right information has fallen into the right hands. No one else would even have got to first base.'

'Which leads you to think that I also possess the remaining clues?' I said.

We were interrupted by a call from Smart. Finch told him what we had so far found.

'He says "Well done",' Finch said flatly when Smart had hung up.

There was nothing yet from Abbot.

Rachel worked at the keyboard and superimposed the third waiting box over the centre of the map.

We were running out of guesses.

'*Think*,' Alex said. 'Think how he's been setting things out for us so far. One thing leads to another. The edge of the picture points to something at the centre; something out of focus points to something all too sharply *in* focus.'

'Something still connected to the OS?' Finch said.

'Everything he gives us, he gives us for a reason,' Alex said. 'Nothing's wasted. Nothing. Every single tiny little thing he's given us so far has led us forward in some way.'

'The sound of the cat,' Rachel said suddenly, typing in the word 'miaow'.

The screen responded by going briefly blank, its already sparse features disappearing completely. And then this same landscape re-appeared with yet another box. Except this time, the box was larger and contained the words 'Laid On In Reverse Numbers'.

'Does that mean we're not looking for a word this time?' Finch said.

Alex and Rachel looked suddenly concerned.

'What?' Finch said.

'With letters in sequence, there's usually a logic to it – those letters making a word or an acronym. With numbers, that same logic doesn't apply. Things get mathematical. The chances of us coming across the right sequence of numbers – if that's what he's asking us – is—'

'It isn't,' Finch said. 'It can't be. You said he'd started to ease up on us, and with good reason. He wouldn't suddenly make it this difficult. He's too close to telling us what he needs us to know.'

'He's right,' Alex said. 'If it is a number, then it's one that already means something – either to him or to us.'

'Or one that meant something five years ago,' Finch said. ' "Laid On In Reverse". Does that mean we have to find it and then reverse it?'

'Too simple,' Alex said.

'Something to do with the girls "Laid" in the ground? Something about the order in which they were killed? Or perhaps "Numbers" refers to the fact that Roper knows there were more girls killed and buried than we ever knew about and this is his way of making his evidence more credible and ensuring that no one involved escapes.'

Alex gestured him to silence. 'For the first time, we have the advantage of knowing what it is he is about to reveal to us. If Rachel is right and we're closer to the end of the sequence of encryptions than we think, then we have to use that understanding and start working backwards for a moment instead of forwards. He's got us to where he wants us. He knows that. And presumably we're at or reaching the point where Smart would have been promising him all kinds of deals if he'd been alive.'

'Numbers, dates, birthdays, court appearance dates, the dates the girls were reported missing, house numbers, anything,' Rachel said.

We ran through a long list of the more obvious of these, but nothing turned the key in the lock. The box remained immovable, hovering over the land beneath it.

After half an hour we were no further forward.

Rachel stopped typing and laid her head in her arms. 'Miaow,' she said.

And immediately she said this, Alex said, 'Cat.'

Finch and I looked at her.

'Cat,' she repeated. It was clear to us that she was thinking as she spoke. 'We thought "Cat" meant catalogue. It didn't. It meant "Cat".'

'And so "Laid On",' Rachel said, rubbing her eyes, '"In Reverse".'

'Is "No Dial". Number, dial.'

'The non-existent fucking telephone,' Finch said.

The two women looked at him and waited.

I searched my pockets for the piece of paper which contained the number Roper had stamped on the reverse of Kelly McLean's photo. I found it, unfolded it and laid it on the table.

'Less than a hundred fucking yards from where Roper's fucking mother died in her fucking caravan. Jesus fucking Christ.'

Alex picked up the piece of paper and typed the number into the waiting box.

The computer resumed whirring, its light blinking occasionally.

We all watched it closely, waiting for the box to disappear and for the screen to reveal something new to us.

We were all startled by the sudden loud dialling tone and then ringing from the speakers.

No one spoke.

After only ten seconds, the ringing stopped, and as we watched, the numbers in the box began to disappear, one by one, slowly, and in reverse order, after which the box itself disappeared.

We waited, but nothing happened on the empty map.

'He's dropped us?' Finch said, his voice a mixture of anger and disbelief.

'Perhaps you could try swearing again,' Rachel said. 'It worked last time.'

54

Alex sat with her head cocked, listening intently, and if she'd told me she could hear the electronic whispering of the connections still taking place in the machine, then I would have believed her.

She spoke to the computer, coaxing it into telling us what we wanted to know.

The whispering ended.

Nothing.

'He's finished,' Finch said. 'That's it – sixteen square miles.'

No one answered him.

After a moment, Rachel said, 'Everything's followed the same pattern as before. We've done what he wants, and he's done what we want. So why this?'

We all considered her words.

'There,' Alex said eventually, and pointed to where the cursor, after a five-minute delay, had just then started tracking back and forth across the screen, over that open and empty landscape, leaving nothing in its wake except its own swiftly gone ghost. We all watched as it went back and forth, making its predictable journey down the screen.

As it neared the bottom, Finch said, 'Can't you stop it?'

Alex tried, but the cursor continued moving.

In less than a minute it would have ended its all too efficient striding and completed its journey.

'It's only doing what *he's* told it to do,' she said. 'It isn't acting randomly. Wait.'

'What if there's nothing there?' Finch said. 'What if all this – Roper bringing us this far – and, let's face it, he hasn't exactly shown us anything we couldn't all already have guessed at – what if it's all one big scam, leverage. Perhaps what comes next he only ever intended to reveal to us after he'd been released.'

'Don't be ridiculous,' Alex told him, but her denial was forced.

'OK,' Finch said, his eyes still fixed on the moving cursor. 'Suppose Roper knew he'd achieve nothing by giving us everything up front. Suppose he planned on being somewhere we couldn't reach him before sending us the final pieces of information.'

'Like he is now, you mean?' Rachel said.

'Suppose he's led us to a dead-end. Suppose—' He stopped. 'Suppose he was going to get well away from here and then sell all this to *Abbot* and not to us. He wasn't stupid. He must have known that handing *everything* over to us wouldn't necessarily have given him what he wanted.' He stood breathing heavily, more convinced at the end of this short speech of what he was suggesting than he had been only seconds earlier at its beginning.

The cursor was now tracking back and forth across the bottom inch of the screen. It had neither slowed nor paused nor done anything other than tick towards its inevitable conclusion.

Rachel looked at Finch and then at me. I saw the growing doubt in her own eyes. Everything Finch had suggested made perfect sense. It was what any of us might have done in Roper's position, and knowing what he knew.

And as though reading my mind, Finch said, 'We don't even know for certain that he ever knew – not knew for certain – what happened to those others or where they were buried. All we ever did was make assumptions.'

'You're wrong,' I told him. Too much else, too much of what had already happened over the past twenty-seven days made too much sense for this damning information not to have been known by someone else – Roper – and for it not to be sought for now by the man – Abbot – it damned.

'Do *you* want to tell Smart that?' Rachel said to me.

At the machine, Alex raised her hand to silence us.

The cursor had stopped moving.

It stood now at the bottom right-hand corner of the screen.

'It's finished,' Finch said.

Alex shook her head. 'There are another four or five courses,' she said.

I guessed at three.

'No, it's finished,' Finch said again. 'Like us.'

Alex grew angry with him. 'It happened,' she said. 'And it happened for a *reason*.' She looked enquiringly at Rachel, who understood her and shrugged.

'Try it,' Rachel said.

Alex clicked the cursor and a box opened, but no beckoning asterisks appeared within it for any further password to be inserted.

'Curiouser and curiouser,' Alex said.

'How much more does he want from us?' Finch said, finally exasperated.

'He doesn't want anything,' Alex told him. She sat back from the screen.

Rachel drew closer to her.

'Meaning?' Finch said.

'Meaning this is it, we've arrived.'

A button appeared in the top right-hand corner of the waiting box.

'That's it,' Alex said. 'Drink me, eat me, press here.'

She clicked on the button and the screen changed immediately and dramatically. The landscape was enlarged. Names and buildings appeared, woodlands and copses, contours, rock outcrops, drains and field boundaries, pylon lines and farm tracks. And within seconds this filling-in was completed, and at the centre of all this, behind the vanished box, was an arrow pointing to a dot within a square along the track of a line of diamonds.

'Can you get any closer?' Finch said.

Alex tried to enlarge the map, but nothing changed.

On the control screen Rachel brought up the OS key.

'The diamonds denote a waymarked path and the square is just a building of some sort.'

'And the dot?' Finch said. 'Is that what the arrow's really pointing at?'

'Could be. Or it could mark a triangulation point. Whatever it is, it shouldn't be too difficult to find.'

The road between Patrington and Welwick ran nearby. The same road Roper and his mother would have followed from Hull to Easington each summer. The dotted red line of a public path followed this for half its length and then turned south across the fields.

'There are a lot of reference points,' I said. 'If there is something there, he's chosen it because it won't be too difficult to locate on the ground.' There were no other buildings close to the one indicated.

'They based the software on the latest surveys,' Alex said.

'Is that it, then?' Finch said. 'Does X finally mark the spot? Have we come all this way for that?'

'Are you *ever* truly happy?' Rachel asked him.

'Once,' he said, and he immediately signalled his apology to her.

We fell silent as the full realization of what we might now be looking at struck us all.

It was quarter to four on a December morning.

'Call Smart,' Alex told Finch, which he did.

He told him what we'd found. It might be a sharp enough blade to stick into Abbot to see what came out.

Smart asked to speak to Alex. He asked her for some

names off the map. He wanted copies faxed to him immediately.

Rachel made and sent these. Duplicates fed simultaneously from the control printer into its sealed tray.

When the printers had finished and Smart had hung up, Alex backtracked on the screen to retrieve the box and to hide what it had just revealed.

I checked the printed sheets to ensure they showed everything. They did.

'What now?' Rachel said. She watched Alex closely as she spoke.

'If we'd finished, he'd have told us,' Alex said absently.

'I was thinking the same,' Rachel said.

'He's always left us something to move on to. He wouldn't just drop us like this without waving goodbye.'

'Unless all he ever intended to do was to give us one of the bodies as a sign of good intent before revealing in person where the rest were,' Finch said.

'He wouldn't just drop us,' Alex said. 'I *know*.'

I agreed with her, but said nothing.

She went back to work at the keyboard, exploring everything the box might yet have to give to us, but it revealed nothing. She reduced it and enlarged it. Searched it with the cursor, tried to examine how it had come into being, but still nothing came of this.

'Try clicking onto some of the individual features on the map,' I suggested, uncertain what this might achieve, but aware that after revealing almost nothing to us in its early stages, the map was now overloaded with information. If the building indicated by the arrow still existed, then there were countless other points on the map which might just as easily be located and searched.

Alex asked me what I was hoping for and I told her.

She closed the box and enlarged the map to its original size. This wealth of information now existed there, too — as though, having distracted us for a moment, Roper was now performing his sleight of hand behind our backs.

'Does anyone want to say "Bingo" or "Eureka"?' Rachel said.

Alex printed copies of this new map. Again, the control printer duplicated everything.

The OS key had appeared with this larger map and we were able to confirm everything Rachel had already told us about the arrowed building and its surrounding landmarks.

'What made the cursor start wandering last time?' Alex wondered aloud.

'Nothing,' Rachel said. 'We didn't know the way ahead and so we left it alone in the top left-hand corner. Try it again?'

Alex returned the cursor to its previous starting point.

It stayed motionless where she had put it.

'Five minutes,' Rachel said.

'So you don't think that whatever lies at the first pointing arrow is all he wants to show us?' Finch said.

'He went to an awful lot of trouble for there not to be something more,' Alex said. 'Even if it's only a note saying "Ha ha".'

The cursor remained motionless. I could hear Finch counting beneath his breath.

'Be patient,' Alex told him. 'And look on the bright side. Our encoder is being methodical. If something was over, finished, then he'd have let us know. He had a lot riding on this, remember?'

We waited a further ten minutes and still the cursor didn't move.

'It's twice what we waited last time,' Rachel said.

'You think he's used a timer?' Alex asked her.

Rachel went to the control keyboard and started typing. 'It's there,' she announced triumphantly. 'And he's used it. No numbers. But he's definitely used it.'

We were again interrupted by Smart, who called Finch to ask him what else we'd discovered.

'Nothing,' Finch said, and Smart hung up immediately.

'Keep thinking while we wait,' Alex said. She stretched her arms and walked around the small room.

In the car park below, a patrol car arrived with its siren wailing. I looked down, perhaps expecting Smart to emerge from it, but only the driver and his partner climbed out. The two men stood together for a minute and then entered the building. There was already traffic on the road.

Twenty minutes had now passed since the cursor had been taken back to its hoped-for starting point.

'Do what we did before,' Alex said suddenly. 'Think *forward* – think about what we know we're looking for. It's a map, and maps only exist to show you where things are. That's their whole point. He wouldn't have left the map up there if he didn't have something more to show us on it.'

'Plus this larger map now has all its details,' I said. 'Before, there was next to nothing on it.'

'And we were only given all that detail because we found the first thing he wanted to show us. The purpose of all this previously withheld detail is to know exactly *where* he's pointing when he next decides to point.'

Finch held my arm, drew me to him and started to whisper.

'It's rude to whisper,' Alex said. 'Surely your mother told you that much.'

'I was about to say that if he is about to lead us to the missing girls, then I doubt they'll all be in one place.'

'Unless that first building is some kind of mausoleum,' Alex said, and the suggestion shocked us all into silence.

'It would make more sense to—' Finch began to say.

'To dispose of them all separately?' Alex said. 'Of course it would. Just as it would make more sense for them each to be revealed separately to us now. Write their names out for me.'

Finch did this, and Alex put the three names in front of Rachel.

'Is this the order in which they were killed?'

'The order they disappeared,' he said. 'We still don't know about the sequence of everything.'

Lindsey Perry. Jennifer Wilson. Nicola Bishop.

Rachel spoke next. 'And our belief – our assumption – is that they are buried, separately or together, somewhere within the area of this map and that the exact location or locations of these burials is what Roper now wants to reveal to us.'

'What search facilities does the OS software have?' Alex asked her.

Rachel chose a place name, went through Edit and Find and typed it into the box provided. A yellow rectangle appeared on the map highlighting the place. A second rectangle appeared, then a third, highlighting places which took their name from the first – a farm, a drain, a copse.

'He's reinstated the search facility,' Alex said. 'It wasn't there before. We had to come this far for him to give it back to us.'

'Meaning it's back there for a reason,' Finch said. 'That simple? What do we do now, type in "Murdered Girls"?'

'When you've apologized for that facetious and unthinking remark, I shall endeavour to find out if our encoder has made use of the same bog-standard facility to his own ends,' Alex said.

She waited.

'I'm sorry,' Finch said.

I remembered then that Alex had a young daughter.

'Did that sound heartfelt to you?' Alex asked Rachel.

'Punish him some more,' Rachel said.

Alex resumed work at the keyboard, and after only a few seconds she sat back from it, her finger raised and waiting. She looked uncertain about either what she had just done or what was being asked of her next.

'What is it?' Finch asked her.

I saw again the uncertainty in Alex's eyes, the way she looked only at Rachel.

'They're there,' she said quietly, her eyes fixed on the unchanging screen, her voice faltering.

A box appeared at the centre top of the screen, and in it sat the three girls' names.

'You just typed them in?' Finch said.

'I began to type in the first. They appeared because someone else put them there, and me starting to type the first name was a trigger.'

Rachel came back to the table and put her hands on Alex's shoulders.

'He's telling us they're definitely there?' Finch said.

No one answered him.

'I'll do it,' Rachel said to Alex, and Alex rose from her chair without answering.

'What?' Finch said.

'I've seen one too many bound and gagged, mutilated, bruised and naked teenage girls, dead or alive, for this month,' Alex said. 'Perhaps I ought to find another job.'

Finch put his arm round her shoulders. 'I'd miss you,' he said.

'What a recommendation.'

'You think he's going to show us pictures?' I said. It was the first time I had considered the possibility since the appearance of the map. It was what Finch, Alex and Rachel had anticipated all along.

'They usually do,' Alex said. She held Finch's hand for a moment and then took it from her shoulder.

'I don't think he will,' I said.

'He doesn't think Roper is as black as we paint him,' Finch told Alex.

'I hope he's right,' Alex said. She tapped Rachel on her arm and Rachel started work.

After the first two letters of Lindsey Perry's name the rest appeared of its own accord.

'It's what he's done,' Rachel said. 'He's added the three names in his confession to the key directory.'

'Check it before you try to locate them individually,' Alex told her.

'Why?' Finch said.

'Just in case he only gives us one chance. In finding the names, we might still simultaneously delete them.'

'Why, after everything else he's given us for keeps?'

'Because then we're left in possession of the information without any courtroom-strength proof of how we got it.'

'Proof leading straight back to Roper,' Finch said.

'They're there,' Rachel said. She highlighted the three names for us in the closely printed file.

'Print it first,' Alex told her.

The two printers came to life. Alex checked them.

'Print all the installation details,' Alex said. 'I want to know how he's done this for future reference.'

Rachel did this.

Finch grew impatient, considering their caution unwarranted. 'I want—' he said.

'I know what you want,' Alex told him. 'And *I* want to make sure that we hang onto everything so that nothing trips you up in court. Too many people, too many kids, were denied justice because of what happened in Cardiff.'

'That wasn't your fault,' Finch said.

'It was *all* our faults.'

He conceded this in silence.

After a minute, the printers fell silent.

Alex turned to me. 'I know there'll be no pictures,' she said. 'Neither the hardware nor the software's there. It's why I've been so cautious. Usually, it's *all* pictures. It's how and why these people work. There's probably nothing either Rachel or I haven't seen before now, but it never makes having to look at it all over again any easier, and the worst invariably comes when you least expect it.'

I was pleased Roper hadn't included pictures. I hoped I wasn't making more excuses for him.

'With modern programming, all the systems and

options available, you don't have to be clever, just able to read the instructions,' Alex said. 'Luckily for us, computers make people think they're clever just because they know how to use them. Understanding everything about how these things work is seldom an advantage.'

'I read somewhere that even anaesthetists don't really understand how their anaesthetics work on the brain,' I said.

'It's probably something they're better off not knowing.'

We talked because we were painfully close to what we wanted, what we had come looking for at the start of the night and what we had now found, and because none of us would now be able to bear our disappointment if our reach continued to outdistance our grasp. I imagined every single symbol and feature on the map disappearing one by one, the lost girls among them, undisclosed and unsought, and for ever afterwards undiscovered as their bones turned to artefacts and their bodies to the convenient dust of yet more old and uncaring history.

Finch moved closer to Rachel.

'How do you start searching?' he said.

'Press "Search",' she said, and slid the mouse to him.

He aligned the arrow to the word, hesitated a moment, and then pressed.

Lindsey Perry's name remained highlighted.

And despite what Alex had told me, I braced myself against her face appearing on the screen, and realized only then that I had forgotten what she looked like.

The two other names disappeared.

The box shrank until its black border fitted around Lindsey Perry alone.

The cursor began its new march across the screen, this time coming to a halt after only a few seconds.

Rachel enlarged what we were looking at and then removed the box. Leaving the four of us staring at the same flashing arrow, this time pointing to a place at the end of a track leading from a farm road between Weeton and the Humber estuary, a short distance from a disused sandpit, and directly beneath a line of pylons.

Again, the reference points were specific, absolute and unmistakable. A short distance from the point of the arrow stood the cross denoting the site of an unnamed antiquity.

We all looked at this without speaking.

Then Alex said, 'Print it,' and the two machines had started work before Rachel had finished at the keyboard.

After Lindsey Perry we turned to Jennifer Wilson, and the same flickering funeral march was repeated.

She lay half a mile from a farm called Northsetts at the boundary of a small orchard, and where a broad drain was bridged alongside the track between South End and Skeffling. A disused glasshouse stood close by. The road from Hull to Spurn passed within a mile of the buildings. Here, too, beyond the orchard, lay a cross denoting the site of an antiquity, and I wondered at the coincidence.

We followed the same procedure. The point on the map was as precisely and as clearly pinpointed as on the screen.

And from Jennifer Wilson we turned to Nicola Bishop.

Rachel brought up her name.

Finch left his place at the monitor and motioned for me to take it.

I sat with my hand on the mouse, the cursor positioned over Nicola Bishop's name, waited a few seconds, and then clicked it.

The cursor resumed its journey.

I left the table and Rachel took my place to complete the proceedings.

I waited until she had finished before looking back at the screen.

Nicola Bishop lay buried closer to the shore of the Humber than either of the other two, a few hundred yards from where the mud of the high-water mark ended and the reclaimed land of Sunk Island began. She lay at the otherwise undistinguished intersection of two farm tracks, close to a path which also served as the parish boundary, and where the road beyond Lockham ended at the broad bank called Easington Clays.

Again, there would be no difficulty in finding her. And again, beyond the boundary and across the first of many drains stood the site of an antiquity, in this case the ruins of a small private chapel.

Rachel printed copies of this final site.

I took one from the tray and told Finch I wanted it for James Bishop.

He objected to this, but I told him that nothing he said would stop me from taking the map.

Rachel printed up several more.

I didn't know what the map would achieve. Perhaps it might be the starting point of James Bishop's final understanding of what had happened to his daughter. Perhaps he would look at it, at her burial place, and all his sour and painful memories of her would start to come back to him clean and sharp again. Or perhaps it would jolt him to unstoppable tears with its finality, with its uncertain offer of some kind of resolution, of an ending, and he would press it to his face and soak it with those tears until the ink ran and the paper disintegrated with the force of his grief, and his daughter, though found, was once again lost to him.

I was distracted from these thoughts by Rachel Evans, who laid her palm on my forehead and then brushed it lightly down my face, as though I, and not he, was the one crying.

55

Finch called Smart with the news of what we'd found, and was then silent for several minutes as Smart outlined to him what he wanted everyone to do next. The small measure of pride Finch had allowed himself faded and died in this listing of orders.

When the one-sided conversation was over, he told Alex Carr that Smart wanted her to ensure that nothing of what had just been revealed to us was leaked to anyone else at the station.

'We know what to do,' she told him, and she and Rachel began their work of concealing and dismantling. They, too, were aware of Finch's disappointment.

'He wants everything kept quiet until he's sure of being able to hold Abbot for longer, or of charging him without him walking on bail.'

It was unthinkable to me that this might now happen, but Finch shared Smart's doubts.

'He wants the names, addresses and coded references faxed to this number.' He held out a pad and Rachel took it from him. 'He thinks *this* is where we'll find something to wipe the smile off Abbot's face.'

'Enough to convict him?' I said.

He clicked his lips. 'He wants to take a team to the first of the map references – the one not necessarily connected to the bodies. He thinks it's where we'll find the bulk of what Roper left us.'

The sense of anticlimax was palpable in everything that happened and was said in the room.

I began to consider my own options now that the ghosts were being released back into the machine.

'I let him think you'd already gone,' Finch said to me.

A new seal was placed round Alex's computer and it was taped into a bag. The same was done to Roper's old machine. All the disks and printed sheets were listed and bagged.

Finch tapped the folded map in my pocket and said, 'Show it to no one until we know what Smart wants us to do.'

It seemed unlikely to me that there was anything other than a single course of action open to any of us now.

A car drew into the car park below and the driver sounded his horn.

'That's for me,' Finch said. To Alex, he said, 'Everything has to be left here, but make sure we have a copy of everything.'

'How soon will Smart want to start digging?' I said. 'I want to be able to keep James Bishop informed.'

'I'll let you know,' he said.

We were all tired, and our exhaustion, finally overpowering after everything we had achieved through that long night, showed in all our actions.

I said my farewells to Alex Carr and Rachel Evans, both of whom would shortly return to their hotel and their unused rooms and unopened cases. They would leave Hull later in the morning.

When I told Rachel I hoped I'd see them both again, she said she hoped I wouldn't.

The driver below pressed his horn again.

Finch told Alex that he would contact her later,

that Smart would want to see them both before they left.

I followed him down the stairs a few minutes later. The same men who had made a point of watching my arrival made a point of watching me go.

In the room in which Finch and I had awaited the arrival of Alex and Rachel, someone had pinned a photo of Sullivan shaking hands with the Chief Constable to the wall and written on the whiteboard 'Sullivan Is Innocent'. I wondered what preparations *he* might now be making for the events ahead of him.

I knew that, in all likelihood, and against Smart's own judgement and condemnation of the man, Smart would now make a deal with Sullivan, and in return for not being prosecuted himself, Sullivan would ensure that every omission, contrivance and mal-practice of his old investigating team would be brought out into the open. When the bodies were found and uncovered, the light suddenly shining on Sullivan would be blinding and every last shadow would be finally dispelled.

I left the building and walked towards the city centre. The rain of the previous evening had turned briefly to snow and this lay on the ground in places.

The room at the end of the corridor had been warm and airless, and I felt the cold in the wet and early morning darkness. The dawn was two hours away, and even when it came it would herald only a few hours of lesser night before the darkness returned.

A few people gathered for early buses; a few cars passed back and forth.

I bought a paper and found a café.

I sat by the door, read the paper and considered how best to tell James Bishop about everything that had been revealed to us.

I called Sunny and told him where I was. He told me he was already at the agency and that he'd wait there for me. I heard the wariness, the suspicion in his voice.

When I arrived twenty minutes later, he showed me a list of all the publications that had contacted him upon Roper's death. The questioning of Sullivan had almost doubled the number. Whatever else he might have wanted keeping secret, Smart had always made certain that everything connected to Sullivan had always been public knowledge.

'Before Roper was killed, it was all turning into loose ends and unanswerable questions,' he said.

I heard that same wariness in his voice.

'What?' he said, seeing my lack of interest in his list.

'You *know* what,' I said.

He screwed the list into a ball and let it fall to the floor.

'When I was attacked and put in hospital, Finch called you – *you*. Why was that, do you think? And when I came to you with the news that Roper had agreed to see me, you already knew.'

'I knew because—'

'You knew because Smart had already told you.' I didn't want to hear him lie to me again. 'In fact, you've known almost everything, right from the start.'

'We were only making sure—'

'What? That I was exactly where I needed to be according to Smart's plans?'

'Smart called me and—'

'Smart called you and you called James Bishop,' I told him. '*You* were the one who told him about Roper being back here. Smart made sure Roper was brought back here immediately before his appeal so that all this could happen, and you jumped at what he offered you. What was it – an opportunity to get a lead on all those lucrative stories, or just the chance to get your own back on Sullivan for having you thrown out of his press conference all those years ago?'

'Roper wasn't killed here,' he said.

'No. But he was killed because of what happened here.'

'Smart called Bishop himself,' he said. 'He pretended

to be a reporter. Said he'd spoken to someone at the agency who'd given him the brush-off.'

'And the mention of the agency led Bishop to call you, covering Smart's tracks, and giving you the opportunity to unofficially confirm what you already knew – that Roper was back here. What did you think you were doing?'

'My job?'

I shook my head. 'No, you weren't. Whose bright idea was it for James Bishop to call me?'

'Smart asked me if I knew of anyone who could take care of Bishop's interests for them.'

'Someone to stand between Bishop and all that Smart hoped to uncover?'

'Something like that.'

'Someone whom Smart could use like he was using you and Bishop. How long before Wallis came into the picture?'

'I'd been buying stories off Wallis for the past year. He saw the opportunity to make a bit of money for himself before his tribunal, that's all. He didn't exactly need any prompting.'

'And he completed the chain. Wallis, you, Bishop, Smart and me. Which is all Smart ever wanted.'

'He knew what would happen once someone started stirring things up.'

'And he saw nothing wrong in manipulating a man who had lost his only daughter to get to Sullivan and Abbot?'

'He never went into the details of how it would all pan out.'

'He never does,' I said.

I saw his own lost daughter in his eyes, heard her unspoken name in the sudden faltering in his voice.

'Does Yvonne know about all this?' Yvonne had told me that Wallis had tipped Sunny off about Roper's return, but Sunny had learned everything from Smart, and this had been his lie to her. It was why, on that first visit, he had insisted on the two of us leaving the agency and talking outside. He had been waiting for me to turn up there for three days, ever since Bishop's first call.

He shook his head. 'Boyd and all that stuff about Sullivan shitting on *his* father was a sheer fluke,' he said. 'All that was meant to happen was that you were to contact Wallis because you were a friend of mine and I'd given you his number. And all he was meant to do was start making public everything there was to know about Roper.'

'You're kidding yourself,' I said. 'To start with, you and Wallis were Smart's smoke-screen, that's all.'

'Bishop would have heard about everything eventually,' he said.

'Except this way, Smart made sure everything was in place well before Bishop came knocking on my door.'

'I knew you'd do your best for him,' he said. 'Smart had already heard of you. He said he thought John Maxwell had been the brains of the operation.'

'John Maxwell would have tempered things,' I said. 'He would have held back where Sullivan, Lloyd and all the old squad were involved. That wasn't what Smart wanted. All Smart ever wanted was for me to either share or indulge his own self-serving indignation and push Sullivan into exposing himself.'

'I suppose so,' he said.

'You suppose so. And in the getting of all this, Angela Hill and Martin Roper got killed.'

'I felt bad about Angela Hill,' he said.

'You felt bad. *You* were the one who gave me the clipping – presumably pointed out to you by Smart – of her father's threats to Roper. You knew I'd go to him, and from him to her.'

'But not that this would happen.' He looked directly at me for the first time.

'You used me,' I said. 'And as a consequence of that, she was killed, and it's something I'll have on my conscience for the rest of my life.'

He considered this and then nodded once.

'I gave you the trophy photograph and pointed out the resemblance between Lloyd and Boyd that everyone had missed without Smart's knowledge,' he said eventually.

'Without his compliance or agreement, you mean? I hope it's enough to assuage your own conscience.'

I rose from my chair opposite him.

'What now?' he said.

'You mean Smart hasn't been keeping you informed of all the latest developments?'

He was about to speak when the door opened and Yvonne came in to us. She was surprised to see me there so early. She came to me and held me for a moment before taking off her coat and gloves. I told her I was just leaving. She looked to Sunny and sensed the tension between us.

'What's happened?' she said. She looked from him to me and held my gaze.

'We think we might have found the graves of the three missing girls,' I told her.

She covered her mouth with her hand.

I turned back to Sunny. 'I doubt Smart wants it made public,' I said.

He closed his eyes.

His own daughter's name was Isobel, and for each of the thirteen years before she was killed alongside her mother, I'd bought her a birthday present and a Christmas present, and once, after she'd had an argument with Sunny, I'd let her stay with me for three days, pretending to her that no one knew where she was, and every few hours I'd called Sunny and told him how she was.

I hoped there was some way forward for us.

I told Yvonne again that I had to go.

Sunny rose from his seat. 'I never believed it would come to this,' he said.

'You and James Bishop both,' I said.

Perhaps there was only ever a single course through

life for any of us, and perhaps, deep inside, we all knew that.

'Watch him,' I said to Yvonne as I went. She understood what I was asking her, and the instant I was out of the room, she closed the door behind me.

56

At midday, Finch called me to say that he, Smart and a dozen others were at the first of the sites Roper's files had revealed to us.

The pinpointed building was a long-abandoned Water Board store. The relevant authorities had been contacted, and someone had found a record of the building, which had been built in 1936 and abandoned in 1971. It was built on a block, six feet square, one side of which consisted of a pair of metal doors. It had once housed an inspection valve for the mains water supply between Patrington and Welwick. The valve had last been inspected in 1967, and had been removed from its concrete plinth the following year. The pipe beneath had been made good and the hole filled and sealed. The function of the valve had been supplanted by another, installed during renovation work at Patrington in 1987.

There was no further reference to the structure, known officially as a valve-housing, since the time it had become redundant. There was even some surprise that it remained standing, though it was not the Water Board's policy to demolish the structures, even though they no longer served any purpose.

The waymarked path and footpath were both in sight,

Finch said. There was no other building close. The metal doors to the housing had long since rusted shut. Finch spoke to someone and then came back to me.

'It looks like they've been welded,' he said.

'Would the Water Board have done that?'

Neither of us knew. He rang off.

Twenty minutes later he called back to say that Smart had ordered one of the concrete walls to be demolished, and that they could now see inside. Smart was already picking at the rubble. Someone called to Finch and he had to go.

When he called back, he said they'd found a galvanized steel box, which was now being photographed *in situ*. Smart had picked it up and shaken it, he said. It was full, but not heavy. Whoever had put the box there had pressed the fingers of both hands onto its lid and had then protected these beneath taped and weighted polythene. As far as they could tell, the structure remained watertight and otherwise undisturbed.

As he spoke, someone removed the steel box from its wrapping. A folded newspaper was found alongside the box and given to Smart.

'He's opening it,' Finch said to me.

I heard the voices of several other men.

'That's it,' Finch said.

'What is?'

He told me: on the front page of the paper, dated the seventh of October 1998, was the grinning schoolgirl face of Hayley Forbes, whose body had been discovered the previous day. Three days before Roper was arrested and charged with her murder.

It was Roper's way of making sure there would be no mistaking who'd put it there.

I asked him where he and Smart were going next.

'We'll need to know what's inside,' he said. 'Then we need to make sure Abbot is going nowhere. After which, we'll see if it's possible to get Boyd out of hospital and somewhere more secure.'

'What about the other sites?' I said.

'We can't do anything until we get the proper people here. Smart wants to check them against records of all the original searches.'

'He thinks Sullivan knew where they were even then?' I knew this was unlikely.

'He wants to make sure, to see how close they might have come, or how far away they stayed. It's just possible that Lloyd and Boyd had a hand in getting rid of Lindsey Perry to cover their own tracks. And if they did, then it's equally possible – especially in light of Lloyd's drunken confession – that Sullivan might have known about it.'

'And if he did, then Smart wants to make the connection and find some proof?'

'Something like that.'

It was already a blighted, falling tree, but its lesser roots and uppermost branches seemed never to stop growing.

'Let me know what you find,' I told him.

57

The sealed case contained nine films, all on video, five of them finished and labelled, and four cassettes of unedited footage awaiting completion. In addition, there was a cache of over three hundred photographs sealed in seven airtight bags. A further plastic envelope contained the directory already revealed by Roper, whose prints were again clearly visible on, and retrievable from, everything the steel case held.

Attached to the printed directory was a handwritten note explaining some of its more arcane symbols.

A further packet held a disk which Smart believed would contain all the cartographic information already revealed to us. It was the first of Roper's back-ups in case we had been unable to come that far through the encrypted files on his computer. It was how, even if I had seen neither Angela Hill nor Roper himself, the information would still have been revealed.

Everything that was found was catalogued and listed, and copies were sent immediately to the men working elsewhere.

The derelict structure was opened at one-fifty in the afternoon.

At four, Smart, Finch and almost two dozen others sat together in a projection room and watched the contents of the films. This audience was divided between Smart's own National Crime squad and local officers who had played no part in Sullivan's original investigation.

The new case against both Sullivan and Lloyd was to be made alongside that already being built against Abbot and his associates.

The viewing lasted until half past eight.

Of the finished films, none lasted longer than twenty minutes, and the unedited fragments lasted an hour and five minutes in total.

Everything Roper had once seen, the films showed, and others now saw.

Few of the photographs duplicated what was shown in the films, although it was clear that some of these had been included to reveal and confirm what several of the films successfully concealed.

Everything would be watched again, over and over, by these same men and by others, until every possible identification had been made. Again, no one who had been in any way involved in the original investigation would take part in this identification and collation work.

All the men Smart and his team were currently investigating were included in the films and the photographs, and it had clearly been Roper's express aim to both identify and incriminate them beyond all possibility of error or escape.

I met Finch later, in the bar I had visited on the night we searched the computer.

He told me that several of the men present had remarked on the period of time over which Roper must have compiled this evidence. Some expressed their doubts that it had all been done in the few days prior to his arrest, those three days of waiting when he must finally have known that Sullivan was coming for him.

Finch also told me that there had been several calls for the most explicitly brutal of the films to be interrupted while men left the room. Smart had refused to do this. There had been three women present at the viewing, and all of them had wept at what they saw. Some of the men, too, Finch told me, though their tears were less evident, even though badly concealed in the darkness.

I asked him if either he or Smart had cried.

'Of course not,' he said.

He said that there were separate films of Lindsey Perry, Hayley Forbes and Jennifer Wilson; and a series of photographs showing Nicola Bishop, topless, sitting with Abbot himself, who was naked. Nicola Bishop, he said, wore only a pair of short white socks and a pearl necklace, which someone had opened and arranged so that its loop lay around the curves of her small breasts. Abbot sat with his hand cupping her head, the other between his legs. His erection was clearly visible against her thigh.

I told him that if he was keeping the fact that Nicola Bishop *did* appear in any of the films from me, then I would find out and tell James Bishop. He assured me there was no film of her.

I asked him if he didn't find that strange.

'Perhaps it's strange in the same way that Angela Hill never appeared anywhere in his files or directories,' he said. 'The photographs are enough to keep Nicola Bishop included,' he said. 'Even if it's only because they contain some of the most explicit and incriminating shots of Abbot himself.'

There was a piece of film of the man called Lynch performing violently with both Lindsey Perry and Hayley Forbes, and another of Abbot sodomizing Lindsey Perry and Jennifer Wilson.

I asked him why he thought they'd allowed the films to be made.

'It's the kind of thing they did,' he said. 'It happened. Why worry about it?'

There was an eighteen-minute film of Hayley Forbes being abused by two men as one of them strangled her. This was followed by a minute of film showing only her bruised and naked corpse lying on a mattress. Her eyes were closed and the mark around her neck looked like a black band.

There were several girls in the films whom no one had yet identified, and one of these – a girl who looked no older than twelve or thirteen – was also shown being killed by strangulation. There was a film of three men masturbating over her face, her eyes and open mouth, when no one in the projection room could be certain whether or not she was already dead or still alive. The same vivid marks already showed on her neck.

It was obvious, Finch said, that many of the girls were either drunk or drugged during the making of the films.

Someone had suggested to Smart that I ought to be present at the viewing, but Smart had rejected the idea.

'He was doing you a big favour,' Finch told me.

'I can still imagine it all,' I said.

'I know. But that's *all* you can do, and it's infinitely preferable.'

'Try telling that to James Bishop,' I said.

'Or to the loving parents who never even cared enough to report that some of these girls were missing in the first place? Or who didn't care enough beyond filling in that one form and then leaving it at that? Don't fool yourself into believing that they're all like Bishop. Abbot certainly never made that mistake.'

Smart was supposed to be with him, but had been delayed following the viewing.

'What did *you* say when it was suggested that I might be present?' I asked him.

'Nothing. I didn't need to.'

'And if Smart had asked for your opinion?'

'I'd have told him to keep you as far away as possible from it all. It's over. Your hands are still reasonably clean.'

I wondered if he knew about Smart's calls to Sunny and Bishop, and then guessed that he did. He had never once raised the question of Bishop's mystery caller. It wasn't something with which I wanted to confront him now.

I asked him what was being done about the three grave sites Roper had revealed.

'Some of the locals are still insisting that they're further caches of more explicit films.'

'They're graves,' I said.

'I know. But whether they were directly involved or not, they were still the ones who stood around watching while all this was happening. They're the ones sniffing their own palms now to see if they've started to stink. They can't help themselves.'

The three sites had been sought, located and photographed. Nothing could be done for several days until the necessary teams could be assembled and the graves excavated. Smart was insisting that all three be uncovered simultaneously.

I asked him how long they would be able to keep the revelation of the sites out of the public domain, and he repeated the phrase and laughed.

'What is that, exactly – the *public domain*?'

I said nothing to encourage his angry speculation. We'd been in the bar less than an hour and he'd already drunk five large whiskies. He looked up at the dark screen above the tables and said he wished it was on. He said his mind was still filled with everything he'd seen.

I asked him what he thought would now happen to Sullivan.

'The solid ground just turned into very watery shit,' he said.

'So he'll be charged in relation to the original investigation whatever else comes to light?'

'Smart had run out of fingers when I left him.'

'He's convinced Sullivan knew what Lloyd and Boyd were up to.'

'Of course he fucking knew.'

Again, I doubted this, but said nothing.

A moment later, Smart came in, going to the bar before joining us. He looked from Finch to me.

'I would have had you in if I'd thought it would have served any useful purpose,' he said to me.

'I stopped serving a useful purpose once Sunny had handed over the trophy photograph and he and I had put two and two together where Lloyd and Boyd were concerned,' I told him.

He didn't answer me. Instead, he rose and went back to the bar to collect the drinks he'd ordered. Coming back to the table, he was smiling.

'You did it, then?' Finch said.

'Did what?' I said.

'He arranged for a few minutes of film to be copied and shown to Abbot over at Queen's Gardens.'

'Is that proper procedure?' I said.

'I *made* it proper procedure.'

I knew by the way Smart held my gaze that he knew I'd found out about the phone calls.

'I'll drink to that,' Finch said, emphasizing his growing drunkenness, and leavening the sudden tension between us.

'These things don't concern you,' Smart said to me.

'Obviously. But you'd appreciate it if I kept my mouth shut about the graves, right?'

'You'd do that anyway,' he said.

'Why would I? Because if you looked hard enough you might just find a piece of film that *did* include Nicola Bishop and that her father might yet get to see?'

He raised his glass to me and said nothing.

Finch watched us. 'He's lying,' he said to me. 'There's nothing with her in it except the photographs.'

Smart looked at him in disbelief.

'I know,' I said to Finch. 'I just wanted to clear a few things up.'

'Glad to have been of assistance,' Smart said, his glass still held between us.

'You help only yourself,' I told him.

'Meaning?' If Finch hadn't been sitting beside him, he wouldn't have spoken.

'Meaning I've just worked out something else about the file Boyd stole.'

'The file *I* gave you after—'

'The file you gave me after convincing Abbot that it contained something far more incriminating than it actually did. I always knew you'd given it me for a reason, but I never really worked out why. At the time I thought it was to flush out one of Sullivan's old team, someone who was still passing on information to Abbot.'

'Go on,' he said.

'That's why you booked it out – so that someone would know. And however word got to Abbot, you wanted him to think that there was something in the file that he couldn't afford *not* to find out about. That file was your way of getting Abbot to *do* something, not of flushing someone else out into the open. You already knew who everyone was. Why, otherwise, would Abbot risk sending Boyd to try and retrieve the file unless he believed there was something he dare not ignore in it? It's why you were angry about me not having picked up on Abbot's first phone call after I'd been to see Sullivan. If you'd known about that, then perhaps there would have been no need for the file.'

Smart considered all this without answering.

Finch looked at him, caught Smart's own sharp glance, and looked away.

'Like I said,' I said to Smart. 'You help only yourself.'

'You have my permission to bring Bishop to the exhumation,' he said.

'We were coming anyway,' I told him.

'No, you weren't,' he said, and finally drained his glass.

58

Two days later, Finch called me to say they would disinter the bodies the following day, the day before Christmas Eve. If they didn't do it then, he said, the task would have to wait until almost a week into the new year.

'By which time their whereabouts will have been public knowledge for a fortnight,' I said.

'There you go again,' he said.

He told me that an hour earlier a package had been received by the Assistant Chief Constable containing a disk pinpointing the location of the mains valve-housing between Patrington and Welwick. It had been sent by one of Roper's legal team, an accompanying note indicating that the disk was sent under instruction in the event of Roper's death while still in custody. Roper himself had specified a delay of five days, which had become a week in the Christmas post. It was the second of Roper's safeguards, the one ensuring the discovery of his final revelations.

The next day, the day before Christmas Eve, was cold and clear, and the winter sun rose into a sharp and empty sky at exactly the time the weather girl said it would rise, and later it would burn back into the earth at the time she said it would.

And in between, Smart and the three squads of experts and diggers would assemble and then exhume the bodies of the three missing girls.

Bishop came to me at eight, before the sun, and I was waiting for him.

We sat together by the window, in our coats, drinking tea and watching all the cars coming into the city, heliographing their presence on the raised flyover of the dual carriageway. Beyond, we could see the river, calm, and seemingly motionless, a solid bronze plane awaiting only the sun to die and to kill the illusion.

He wanted to know if Smart knew for certain where his daughter was buried, and I told him he did. Tests had been carried out at all three sites, and the results had suggested that there was something at each of them to be uncovered. He wanted me to convince him of everything that was about to happen.

'Will I be able to take her away with me?' he said, his eyes fixed on the river, and already knowing the answer.

'It's unlikely,' I said, meaning it was impossible.

'I'll still have to identify her for them,' he said.

'Probably.'

'Did they say when it would all be over?' He was talking just to say something, the way people sitting in hospital corridors talk just to say something – talking to convince himself of his involvement in what was about to happen, to convince himself that this was what he had always wanted to happen after every other possibility had been taken away from him. And talking to fill the silence which surrounded us in the empty building, a silence inviting all those other unasked and unanswerable questions.

Our breath clouded in the cold air and condensed on the dirty glass. A thick frost still coated the nearby roofs.

At nine, Smart and Finch arrived, parked beneath us and waited.

James Bishop and I went down to them. Smart got out of the car to shake Bishop's hand and express his condolences. He said he hoped the day's events would not prove too painful for him.

From behind the wheel, Finch watched me.

'If there's anything at all I can do,' Bishop said to Smart.

'Of course,' Smart told him. He held the door open for him, anxious to continue moving.

In the car, Smart told us that the three of us would be dropped close to where they believed Nicola's body to be buried, and that he would go on alone to visit the remaining two sites.

'I've put DS Finch in charge of recovering your daughter,' he told Bishop.

'I appreciate that,' Bishop said.

We negotiated the traffic out of the city centre.

The sun was fully risen by then and already showed in the glass of the taller buildings we passed.

Everyone tried not to speak.

Leaving the city, we all looked out over the level expanse of fields for the first signs of the distant estuary.

'I wonder why they brought them out here?' Bishop said as we rose slightly over a broad drain and saw the water for the first time.

None of us could answer him. And if we could guess at the answer, then we kept those guesses to ourselves.

Beyond the dead-end road south out of Easington, we followed a single-track lane towards the water until we reached a strip of barrier tape stretched taut ahead of us. Several other vehicles, cars and vans, marked and unmarked, were already there and they lined the roadside.

Finch stopped the car and we all got out.

Smart made several calls and then took Finch to one side and spoke to him.

Afterwards, he came to where I stood with James Bishop and told us that he would return to us before the work there was finished. Anything Bishop needed to know, he had only to ask Finch. He said he would appreciate both of us staying clear of the other men.

Finch stood behind him, stamping his feet and clapping his hands together.

There was day-old snow in the ploughed fields, and long shadows where the sun fell.

The snow in the lane and on the verge had already been trodden away.

Smart returned to the car, reversed for a short distance, and then turned and left us.

Finch told me he was going first to where Lindsey Perry was buried, less than a mile away, and then from there to the farm track between South End and Skeffling, beside the disused glasshouses and beyond the orchard to where they hoped to find Jennifer Wilson.

'He seems very certain of what he's going to find there,' Bishop said to Finch.

'He is,' Finch said. 'We are.'

Several men approached us and Finch went to them. Some wore overalls and waist-high rubber waders. Others stood in their uniforms and suits. The men in overalls carried spades, and as he approached them, Finch gestured for them to make these less conspicuous. He spoke to them and they looked to where I stood with James Bishop, none of them certain which of the two of us was the father of the girl they were about to uncover.

We walked past the tape towards the river. One of the men had given Finch a map. He showed it to me, outlining the intersecting farm tracks and the parish boundary.

We rose onto an old embankment and were able to look out over the river, at its widest there. It was brown now, not bronze, and it flowed in slow eddies where it came close to the shore. It was still fifty yards from us, and beneath us where we stood and watched. And where the land and the water met in their own lost boundary, stood another dozen men.

An inflatable canopy had already been erected above where Nicola Bishop lay buried, and seeing this so suddenly caused James Bishop to catch his breath and stop walking.

Finch told me again to stay with him while he went alone to the men who awaited him.

I looked to the left of where we stood on our vantage point and saw the small abandoned chapel someone had chosen as Nicola Bishop's headstone and marker. James Bishop saw where I was looking, and he, too, studied the structure.

'Is that how they know she's here?' he asked me.

I nodded.

Finch came back to us.

'They're ready to start digging,' he said, looking directly at James Bishop as he spoke, as though a single word from him was now needed to set everything in motion.

'Are there likely to be any complications?' I said in a low voice.

'It's the least certain of the sites because of where it is in relation to the river. It's a long way from the water now, but there's some concern that the site might have flooded in the past.'

'How much concern?'

He glanced quickly at James Bishop, who was still watching the men around the canopy. 'We can only start,' he said. 'And see what happens.'

A small mound of recently dug earth had already appeared. The diggers took it in turns in the confined space. Behind us, along the lane, other cars came and went.

I waited on the embankment with James Bishop for a further hour while the work continued. Finch walked back and forth across the site and then in circles around it. Other men wandered back and forth to the river.

It remained a bright day, but lights were erected and switched on, making the white and yellow of the plastic tent appear even more vivid against the surrounding expanse of land and water.

After saying nothing for half an hour, James Bishop told me that his wife was at home waiting to hear from him. He said he should have called her upon our arrival. I told him to call her now, which he did. He walked away from me along the raised bank to talk to her.

He finished talking and came back to me.

He was about to say something, when a call from below distracted us both.

Two diggers emerged from the canopy and then stood back from its entrance. The mound beside them now rose to their waists. Several others made their way to the opening. Finch stood close to the water, his phone already to his ear.

When he'd finished speaking, he joined the others at the canopy entrance. He looked up to where James Bishop and I still stood, but neither gestured nor called to us.

'Should we go down?' James Bishop asked me.

I told him to wait.

Several minutes later, having been inside the tent, Finch re-emerged and walked slowly towards us, his head down, as though searching for each step forward over the wet, uneven ground.

'They've not found anything,' James Bishop said to me.

But I knew by the way Finch was coming to us, by his reluctance to reach us, that he was wrong.

Finch stopped in front of us, and then diverted to one side so that he might come up to where we stood on the old bank.

'They've found something,' he said to James Bishop.

'Nicola?'

'It looks like a body wrapped in black plastic and sealed with tape.'

'And the other sites?' I said to him.

'Same thing. This is the last.'

'Can I see?' James Bishop asked him.

Finch looked first to me. 'I wouldn't advise it,' he said. 'We can't unwrap her here.'

'I'll come with you to wherever they take her,' I said to Bishop.

'Are you sure it's her?' Bishop said.

To me, Finch said, 'It's definitely Lindsey Perry and Jennifer Wilson at the other graves.'

'They're certain it's Nicola,' I said to James Bishop. I put my arm around his shoulder.

'I'm very sorry,' Finch said to him.

James Bishop thanked him.

Around us, the light changed and the sun lost some of its strength. There was still no cloud in the sky, but a low winter haze had formed across the distant fields.

Shortly after noon, Smart returned and came to us. He, too, told James Bishop that he was sorry for what they had found, and again James Bishop thanked him for this courtesy.

Smart left us and went with Finch back to the others.

We watched as a space was cleared, and as something was brought out of the tent and carried by two men to a waiting container. This was then picked up by another two men and carried towards the end of the lane and a waiting van.

Behind us, several of the cars moved closer to where we stood.

The men carrying the container in which Nicola Bishop's wrapped and bound corpse was contained came close to where we stood. They knew who we were by then.

Arriving at the lane's end, they paused, exchanged words, and then put the container on the ground.

James Bishop went to them. They spoke to him and then stood away from the container so that he might be alone with his daughter for a moment.

He stood beside the container, his head bowed, for only a few seconds. Then he thanked the two men for what they had done and came back to me.

'It's her,' he said, and then turned away from me to look back and forth along the expanse of the river.

Behind him, the two men picked up their load and continued walking towards the waiting van.

'I told her I was pleased that they'd found her at last, and how angry I was at what she'd done. I told her not to worry about that, though, that we'd get everything sorted out, and that – that—' He started sobbing, convulsively, loudly, causing everyone around us to turn and look at him, and he held his face in both his hands.

The van containing his daughter's body began its own slow journey along the narrow lane.

I waited beside him until his crying finally subsided and he fell silent. He took out a handkerchief and wiped his face.

'Thank you for not trying to console me,' he said. He looked down to where Smart and Finch still stood together. 'I want to go down now,' he said.

I followed him across the grass and the mud to his daughter's first grave. I left him as he went into the tent and stood alone there over the hole it covered.

I continued walking towards the river.

Neither Smart nor Finch spoke to me as I passed them.

Vessels came and went along the deeper channels of the far shore. Nothing of the land there was any longer visible, and every now and then the calm water ahead of me was broken by a succession of dying ripples and I tried to guess which ship might have caused these. I felt the salt air against my forehead and I imagined I could taste it on my lips.

Eventually, I left the water and walked back to where all the other watching, waiting men stood in a circle around James Bishop, and who silently thanked God that it was his daughter and not their own that they were all in their own way mourning.

59

The following day, Christmas Eve, the same sun rose again into the same bright and cloudless sky, and until the day warmed to a degree above freezing and the same low vapour rose off the land, it was possible to see for twenty miles in every direction from any one of the burial sites.

On that day, less than an hour after the sun had risen and was still low on the horizon and at its brightest, still bearing the orange glow of the atmosphere that coloured it, a man walking his dog close to where Sullivan lived, intent on walking to the entrance of the nature reserve, saw Sullivan standing alone and motionless on the estuary bank opposite his home.

At first Sullivan did not appear to hear the man as he greeted him, but then he turned at the sound of the barking dog to shield his eyes and talk to his neighbour. The conversation was brief – the glory of the coming day, the arrival of Christmas and all that this engendered for the empty space of the coming year – and the dog-walker remembered that all Sullivan said to prolong their short exchange was that the river looked unnaturally calm again. Sullivan pointed, the man said, to where it seeped thickly among the tumbled concrete blocks directly beneath him.

Sullivan was holding a plastic carrier, and the man imagined this to contain bread or other scraps for feeding to the terns and gulls it would quickly attract once scattered on the water. It was clear that Sullivan was in no mood for conversation and so the man left him.

A minute later – the man measured this by the distance he had walked with his ageing dog – he heard a gunshot, and when he turned back to where Sullivan had been standing, he was no longer there.

The man said gunshots in the fields bordering the nature reserve were not uncommon – unchecked foxes foraged back and forth across the open land, he said – but this one had seemed much closer, sharper somehow, a more 'contained' explosion than a shotgun might make. He looked more closely at where Sullivan had been standing, he said, and he saw there a small cloud of pale smoke, which remained intact in the still air as he retraced his steps towards it.

He saw that the door to Sullivan's bungalow was open and that several lights remained on inside. He could hear a radio or a television. Further along the coast road, a woman appeared. She, too, had heard the noise and had come out to investigate. The man remembered looking at his watch. It was eight fifty-five.

Only when he reached closer to where Sullivan had been standing and looked down over the concrete blocks at the water's edge, did he see Sullivan's body, only his legs above the waterline and splayed over the rocks, his chest, head and arms invisible beneath the silt-laden current. One of Sullivan's submerged arms rose and fell in this movement, and looked to the man as though Sullivan were motioning to him. He said the smell of the small cloud remained sharp in the air above where Sullivan lay. The empty carrier floated on the water. There was no sign of any weapon.

Realizing what he was seeing, the man then shouted for the woman – who remained in her doorway – to call the police.

He left Sullivan's body and returned to his own home.

Word of what had happened quickly spread in that isolated place, and by the time the first patrol car arrived thirty-five minutes later, fourteen people stood above the corpse looking down at it.

The tide had ebbed a little in that time, and Sullivan's head and arms were now revealed, as dark and as shiny and as moulded in the liquid mud as the blocks amid which he lay.

I learned of the death from John Maxwell, who called and told me about it less than an hour after it had been reported. I asked him how he'd heard of it and he said he wasn't going to tell me. Though the death did not surprise him, he said it was unnecessary, and I knew by his tone that he held me in some measure responsible for it.

He knew all there was to know about the three bodies that had been recovered, and he expressed his sympathy for James Bishop and for those among the others whose grief and sense of loss remained genuine.

The city was full of the discoveries. We talked for several minutes and then he hung up.

I sat with the news for a short while and then I called Finch.

He already knew.

Sullivan would have been Smart's key witness – against himself and against all those others who had wilfully confused the distinction between corruption and advantage, who had submitted and abandoned themselves to their greed, who had sacrificed others to satiate themselves, and whose debt to the dead girls and their families could never now be repaid.

He told me that twenty-one separate and proven charges had been drawn up against Abbot, and fourteen against Boyd.

Among them, the others involved were being held and questioned on a total of forty-seven charges.

I heard talk and music in the background as Finch told me all this and I realized that he had answered my call at home.

'Once every rotten little connection begins to unravel, they'll be at each other's throats, still climbing over each other to the top of the pile,' he said.

He told me that sixty-one individual girls had been identified from the films and photographs, and that nine separate forces were already checking on the names. So far, only fifteen of the girls had been found listed as missing.

'You and Smart must feel very satisfied,' I said.

'Which still leaves forty-six unaccounted for,' he said.

'What will happen to the new inquiry into Sullivan?' I asked him.

He considered this for a moment and then said, 'Fuck him. Let him rot in hell, where he deserves to be. Let him and Lloyd watch the flesh fall from each other's bones, link arms and do a little fucking dance together like the fucking heartless and savage bastards they are.'

I asked him to keep me informed on what happened to Abbot, Boyd and the others, but I knew that I would learn everything now from the television news and the newspapers.

I told him James Bishop had formally identified the remains of his daughter at the Spring Street mortuary at nine o'clock that morning. She had been buried still wearing the stud he had bought her after she had secretly had her navel pierced.

James Bishop had followed his daughter to the mortuary the previous day and had insisted on waiting with the body inside the container until it was finally taken away from him for the first of its examinations.

Someone had brought the stud out to him an hour later.

Finch said he had to go. 'Keep in touch,' he said.

I wished him Merry Christmas.

'That, too,' he said.

60

Nicola Bishop's body was released eighteen days later, on the eleventh of January, along with the bodies of Lindsey Perry and Jennifer Wilson.

James Bishop called me with the news. Her funeral was arranged for the eighteenth and he gave me the details so that I might attend.

I called the number I had for Jennifer Wilson's mother, and her boyfriend answered. I told him I'd called to express my sympathy and to ask if there was anything Jennifer's mother wanted or needed to know from me.

He repeated everything I said, mimicking me. Jennifer Wilson's mother tried to take the phone from him, but he refused to give it to her. He accused me of everything he could think of, and I listened to his venomous tirade without speaking, his closing accusation being that if I hadn't started interfering on someone else's behalf, then none of this would have happened. I'd taken away all their hope, he said, though I knew what a small part of this hope had been his own, and how he had cultivated it in Jennifer Wilson's mother to his own ends. I could imagine him in front of the television cameras. He said he was look- ing for a lawyer to sue the police. He said he didn't want anyone else to have to go through what Jennifer's mother had gone through those past five years.

I hung up on him, regretting the conflict I had caused in that claustrophobic household.

I called Claire Madison at the Marfleet Lane hostel.

'I heard,' she said, as though hoping this might be both the beginning and the end of our conversation.

I told her about all the other girls who had been identified and as yet unfound. I told her that nothing she might have done would have stopped them taking Lindsey Perry from her. But even I was growing tired of all my explanations, and she was neither prepared nor willing to be convinced.

'Boyd will be charged with her abduction, abuse and, possibly, her murder,' I said.

'Good,' was all she said.

I told her that, as yet, no one had come forward to claim Lindsey Perry's body, and that the police and social services elsewhere had been unsuccessful in tracing any of her distant living relatives.

'There are procedures,' she said. 'I imagine they'll run their course. Even a loose end is an end of sorts.'

It was an unnecessarily callous remark to make, but I understood why she'd made it and so I said nothing to refute it.

On the eighteenth, I went to the Kirk Ella cemetery, where Nicola Bishop was finally buried. A second memorial service was held before the ceremony at Saint Andrew's church, and knowing what was happening there, hundreds of onlookers stood around the churchyard and along the surrounding streets.

Nicola Bishop was laid to rest alongside three of her grandparents, four great-aunts and an uncle, James Bishop's brother, who had died of cerebral meningitis as a boy of fifteen.

James and Patricia Bishop stood together at the head of the grave, and both of them cried as the vicar said his words and as the earth was thrown in gentle handfuls over the coffin.

Almost two hundred people were present, including a dozen officers from both the Tower Grange and Queen's Gardens stations. Most, I imagined, had already attended Sullivan's funeral, and I avoided them.

I spoke to Alison Menzies, who stood as far from James Bishop and his wife as she could. I told her I hoped things worked out for them both, but she did not share my hope, and told me so.

' "In my end is my beginning",' she said. She asked me in a whisper if this was how I imagined everything would end, and I shook my head.

'Me neither,' she said.

James Bishop saw us standing together and briefly raised his face to us.

'We spent last night together in the Royal,' she said.

When the ceremony was over, and as people began to disperse, both James Bishop and his wife came to where we stood.

'We hope you can come back to the house,' Patricia Bishop said, looking only at me.

'Yes,' her husband said beside her.

Both Alison Menzies and I made our excuses.

Patricia Bishop immediately turned and walked away from us.

James Bishop shook my hand and thanked me again for all I'd done. He looked hard and with an almost unbearable affection at Alison Menzies beside me. And then he, too, turned and walked away from us to where his wife was waiting for him beside the cars.

Alison Menzies took a deep breath and turned to me, and in that instant, as though the simple act of turning her face had been enough to break the reverie of her own constrained affection, tears ran silently from her eyes into her mouth. She licked the first of these and then wiped away the rest with her gloved hand.

We parted soon afterwards.

Nine days later, I attended Lindsey Perry's burial.

The mourners numbered no more than a dozen. Claire Madison was not among them. No family had been found. The service was perfunctory and devoid of all its necessary reassurances. Only two senior police officers attended, neither of whom had known Sullivan when he was a serving officer. I knew from their glances at me that they knew who I was.

This time I threw my own handful of earth down onto the coffin.

The ceremony took place in the vast Eastern Cemetery on Preston Road, and when I asked the man officiating if a headstone would be provided for the grave, he assured me that one was already waiting to be placed.

I wondered how far away from her Lloyd lay buried.

There was no reception afterwards to celebrate the short, untethered and directionless life of Lindsey Perry, just a round of insincere remarks and farewells at the ornate cemetery entrance as everyone who had attended returned to their jobs and routines, their homes and their families.

I waited alone at the grave. A small mechanical digger stood beside a mound of sheeted earth. No one told me how Lindsey Perry had been identified. No one had come to her and told her that she was once loved, or even wanted, and that she would be missed now.

Earlier, learning how Nicola Bishop had been identified, I'd hoped that perhaps the musical jewellery box that had been Lindsey Perry's only treasured possession might have been found buried with her – even, perhaps, that she might have been finally claimed via this – and that the small, cheap box might have sprung open in the hands of the man who picked it out from beside her in her makeshift grave, and that its plastic ballerina might have danced for him as her mechanism turned and the long-silent lullaby once again encouraged her to spin.

A man climbed into the open cabin of the small digger, started its engine and flexed its small grab back and forth over the mounded soil beside Lindsey Perry's grave.

Hayley Forbes had been buried five years ago, two months after her body was discovered.

Only Angela Hill remained unburied, her body still awaiting the formality of the coroner's release.

The Eastern Cemetery stretched away from me on all sides. The clean December skies had turned to the cloud and cold rain of January. It was raining then, and there was already a skim of water at the bottom of Lindsey Perry's grave. I wished there was something I might say to her, but there was nothing, and so I left her there, never to return.

Jennifer Wilson's funeral had taken place four days earlier, and almost forty reporters and photographers had been notified of the ceremony and had congregated at the grave to capture, package and sell the outrage, grief, sadness and regret of both Jennifer Wilson's mother and the man who had never known her.

I saw a photo of the woman with her arms around her two younger daughters, all three of them standing as though they were leaning into a fierce and rising wind.

THE END

SIREN SONG
Robert Edric

Hull private investigator Leo Rivers is approached by
Alison Brooks, the mother of a girl who disappeared in
violent and mysterious circumstances. When the luxury
yacht her daughter Helen was last seen on was found
abandoned amid the treacherous marshlands of the
Humber Estuary, foul play was suspected. However, in the
absence of a body, nothing could be proven. The owner of
the yacht, ambitious businessman Simon Fowler, seems
unprepared to offer any sort of explanation as to what
Helen Brooks was doing on the boat.

A year later, investigating both the background to this
disappearance and Fowler, the man largely held to be
responsible, Rivers is drawn through a long, hot summer
into a world of human trafficking and governmental
corruption at every turn. In the stifling heat there are many
questions and very few people prepared to offer adequate
answers. Each unravelled piece of the mystery moves
Rivers further from the vanished girl and deeper into a web
of exploitation, greed, temptation, revenge and violence,
from which even he is unable to extricate himself without
unforeseen and tragic consequences. . .

'A CONJURER OF STYLES AND THEMES, A VERITABLE
STANLEY KUBRICK OF THE WORLD OF FICTION'
The Times

NOW AVAILABLE AS A DOUBLEDAY HARDBACK

0 385 605765

BLACK SWAN

PEACETIME
Robert Edric

'HAS A SERIOUSNESS AND A PSYCHOLOGICAL EDGE THAT
NINE OUT OF TEN NOVELISTS WOULD GIVE THEIR EYE
TEETH TO POSSESS'
D.J. Taylor, *Sunday Times*

Late summer 1946: the Wash on the Fenland coast. Into a
suspicious and isolated community comes James Mercer,
employed in the demolition of gun platforms. He befriends the
wife and daughter of Lynch, a soldier soon to be released from
military gaol. He also finds himself drawn to Mathias, a German
prisoner with no desire to return home, and Jacob, a Jewish
concentration camp survivor.

Lynch's return threatens violence; and in a place where nothing
has changed for decades, where peacetime feels no different to
wartime, Mercer finds himself powerless to prevent events
quickening to their violent and unexpected conclusion.

'A MARVEL OF PSYCHOLOGICAL INSIGHT AND SUBTLY
OBSERVED RELATIONS. ITS SPARE, UNADORNED PROSE HAS
POETIC RESONANCE'
Ian Thomson, *Guardian*

'EDRIC'S LANGUAGE HAS A MYTHIC, ALMOST BIBLICAL
QUALITY, WHERE EVERY WORD CARRIES DUE WEIGHT AND
YOU HAVE THE EERIE SENSE OF THINGS BEING LEFT OUT . . .
WHAT MAKES EDRIC'S WRITING PROFOUND IS HIS REFUSAL
TO BE TIDY OR DOGMATIC . . . HE IS A GREAT NOVELIST'
John de Falbe, *Spectator*

'*PEACETIME* GRADUALLY UNRAVELS THE CONTRADICTORY
HUMAN IMPULSES THAT BIND LIVES . . . A MORAL
DISSECTION OF LOYALTY, FORGIVENESS AND HATRED'
James Urquhart, *The Times*

'A NOVEL OF AMBITION AND SKILL, AT ONCE A HISTORICAL
MEDITATION, AN EVOCATION OF A DISINTEGRATING SOCIETY
AND, PERHAPS MOST STRIKINGLY, A FAMILY MELODRAMA'
Francis Gilbert, *New Statesman*

0 552 99971 7

BLACK SWAN

THE SWORD CABINET
Robert Edric

'A KALEIDOSCOPIC MEDITATION ON CELEBRITY,
MUNDANITY AND HORROR'
Mark Sanderson, *Time Out*

Robert Edric's brilliant novel recreates a faded world of
seaside entertainers, stuntmen and illusionists. Mitchell
King, failed impresario, ruined club-owner and embezzler,
searches for his lost mother, the former girl-assistant to
Morgan King, escapologist and chief suspect in an
unsolved case of serial killing dating back to 1950.

'SPECTACULAR . . . EDRIC DARTS BETWEEN
INTERLINKED STORIES, SPINNING THEM LIKE PLATES
ON STICKS'
Ruth Scurr, *The Times*

'GLORIOUSLY DISCOMFORTING AND MYSTERIOUS . . .
A PHILOSOPHICAL PUZZLE'
Alison Huntley, *Independent*

'EDRIC'S TECHNIQUE RESTS ON SUBTERFUGE AND
CONCEALMENT . . . A THOROUGHLY ARRESTING
PERFORMANCE'
D.J. Taylor, *Sunday Times*

'THE REWARDS COME FROM THE CLEAR AUSTERITY
OF THE PROSE, THE UTTERLY BELIEVABLE
CHARACTERS AND THE SATISFYING MIXTURE OF
REAL AND METAPHORICAL ILLUSION . . . IMPRESSIVE'
Natasha Cooper, *Sunday Express*

1 862 30066 6